Virg

Virgin Fiction

Rob Weisbach Books
William Morrow and Company, Inc.
New York

Excerpt from *Song of Solomon* reprinted by permission of International Creative Management, Inc. Copyright © 1997 by Alfred A. Knopf, Inc.

"Love Will Keep Us Together," words and music by Neil Sedaka and Howard Greenfield. Copyright © 1973, 1978, ENTCO MUSIC, international copyright secured. All rights reserved.

Published by Rob Weisbach Books
An Imprint of William Morrow and Company, Inc.
1350 Avenue of the Americas, New York, N.Y. 10019

Copyright © 1998 by Rob Weisbach Books

Library of Congress Cataloging-in-Publication Data

Virgin fiction : an anthology of unpublished writers.—1st ed.

    p.   cm.

    Contents: Trout Lake / by Alexander Ralph—C-clamp / by Amy Gebler—The middle way / by Paula R. Whyman—A note to my translator / by Ed Park—Wasn't that it? / by Todd Dorman—Live bait / by Lee Harrington—Memory of a dog / by Michael Nigro—Waiting for the John Cheever / by Amy Boaz—Beefeater / by Rebekah Rutkoff—Collecting the dead / by Kathleen Holt—Pillowcases / by David Rowell—Second skin / by Shamira Gratch—Pussy basketball / by Timothy Hazen—Buying beer / by Erin Garrett-Metz—Wes looks like Paul Newman and I don't / by Courtney Saunders—the end of the beltline / by Tony Carbone—Comprehension test / by Myla Goldberg—Given the scalpel, they dissect a kiss / by Robert A. Cucinotta—The comfort of paper trees / by Tamar Love—Aubergine / by Jeff St. John.

    ISBN 0-688-16081-6 (alk. paper)

    1. American fiction—20th century.

PS659.V57   1998

813' .0108054—dc21   98-2966
                                                CIP

Printed in the United States of America

First Edition

   2   3   4   5   6   7   8   9   10

BOOK DESIGN BY BERNARD KLEIN

www.williammorrow.com

Contents

Contents

Contents

Virgin Fiction

Trout Lake

Alexander Ralph

There were no trout in Trout Lake, but it was jam-packed with bass, only I hadn't caught a damn thing because Phil Pike was talking nonstop and scaring the fish. Phil didn't care jack for fishing, and His Royal Fatness was sprawled out on the raft, going on and on about the bomb shelter he was building in his parents' backyard. I'd broken my cardinal rule—spend as little time alone with Phil as possible—by inviting him to the raft. But I was after his sister Ruth, and since he was real tight with her, I thought he'd give me some info. I should've known better.

"World War III is going to make me the Casanova of Teaneck," Phil said. "When Khrushchev drops the big one, I'm only letting chicks into my bomb shelter."

"What makes you so sure the girls are going to put out?" I asked.

"Because I'm the only guy around."

"You should make them sign a contract: No entrance unless they schtup."

Phil thought my idea was all right and said he'd reserve a place for me in the shelter as his second-in-command. The image of spending my life in a darkened bunker with his sister sounded like paradise. But I didn't want to wait until the Russians bombed us, and so far Phil was keeping tight-lipped about Ruth. This was his last day at the lake, but all I'd gotten from him were mosquito bites. Lots of them. Bugs followed Phil around like he was the Pied Piper, and today it was even worse. He wore a T-shirt with primary colored horizontal stripes that, to an insect, must've made him look like the world's largest bull's-eye. I kept telling him to take off the damn shirt, but his titties embarrassed him and he wouldn't.

We'd only been out on the raft for an hour, but I was already sick of Phil. I was going to leave him the canoe and swim the two hundred feet back to the shore when he sang out, "Do you see what I see?" I followed his gaze, and saw Ruth swimming freestyle toward us. She cut through the water like a female Johnny Weismuller; you'd never have known her left leg was two inches longer than her right and she walked with a limp.

Phil cupped his hands around his mouth megaphone-style, and called out, "Harketh, Juliet approaches. What sayeth thou, Lord Noah?"

I shot him a look to say don't start. But Phil stood up like he was the Laurence Olivier of Trout Lake and the raft was his stage, and said, "Most fair maiden, do thee search for thy forlorn prince?"

Ruth was now treading water a few feet from the raft. If she'd heard Phil, she didn't act like it. She brushed the hair from her face and spit out whatever water she'd taken into her lungs. "Catch anything, Noah?" she asked.

"Only bug bites."

"Actually, Noah's after a very special fish," Phil said knowingly. "One of the pike variety, I believe." If I wasn't trying to appear like a mensch to Ruth, I would've kicked his ass right then. Phil was fifteen—two years older than me and Ruth—and had seventy pounds on me, but he was a pussy.

"Not many fish are bigger than you, Phil," Ruth said in the little-girl voice she used when she teased him. That was as rude as she got. It would've taken a harpoon to haul Phil's Jell-O ass from the water, but I kept my mouth shut. Ruth was real protective of her brother, and only she was allowed to make fun of him, which is kind of how my older brother treated me.

"Phil, are you scratching again?" Ruth asked, pointing at the bleeding scabs on his arms.

She climbed onto the raft, and I had a first-rate look at her chest. Her knockers were the big news at Trout

Lake this summer. My family had rented the same cabin from her and Phil's old man the last eight summers, and in all that time little else had changed. Each morning my dad climbed into his Continental to commute the twenty-eight miles to his furniture store in Easton; Mr. Leibner, a Nazi camp survivor, was in his canoe by 6:30 and skimming through the water to get to his favorite fishing hole; Leah Pike woke up at nine and started eating strawberries with powdered sugar and calling her friends. But this summer Ruth was no longer Alan's cute little sister. Now, she was a real dish.

"Well if it isn't the Grand Poohbah himself," she said, standing over her brother. "Just lounging around Noah's Ark, waiting for the bugs to feast on him." Because I fished on the raft every day, Ruth called it *Noah's Ark*. I liked her renaming it after me, and I carved the initials N.A. all over the raft.

Ruth shook the water from her blond corkscrew curls on her brother. "Where's your repellent?" Phil tapped on the tackle box he'd been using as his pillow. She took out the repellent and squeezed some onto her palm. "The doctor is in," she announced. "Arm." Phil held out his right arm. "Why do you do this to yourself? It's gross." She rolled his sleeve up to his shoulder and kneaded his doughy arms. Then Phil held up a leg and she rubbed the stuff up to his knee. Phil sighed and acted like he was put out by her fussing over him. But I knew he liked all the attention. Who wouldn't want to be touched by this sexy, limping girl, even if it was your sister? What I didn't get was how Ruth could stand him. If he were my brother, I would've avoided him as much as possible. But Ruth would hold his hand when they took walks and sometimes even feed him from her own plate. As if Phil needed any help stuffing his face.

Ruth put the repellent back in the tackle box, wiped her hands on her thigh, and dove into the lake. When she came up, she said, "Noah, eat with us tonight. Dad's bringing home lobsters." The light only cut an inch or two through the surface and it made her arms look yellow, like the edges around an old-time photo. The rest of her body was invisible in the dark water, but I knew her uneven legs were scissor-kicking to keep her afloat. She swam a few backstrokes, her cupped hands looking like she was waving to me with each stroke, before turning onto her stomach and curling into the water so her legs kicked up and followed her body under.

"If she wasn't my sister," Phil muttered, and shook his head wistfully.

"If you weren't related, she wouldn't let you wipe her ass," I said.

"Listen, amigo, I need two hands to count the girls I've been with. And, correct me if I'm wrong, but you're not even out of the dugout."

I'd made the mistake of telling Phil that I hadn't yet kissed a girl. My experience deficit embarrassed the hell out of me. But the idea of Phil getting steamy with some girl didn't provoke much jealousy in me. Most of what came out of his mouth were lies, but if he were telling the truth about his times with girls, they must've been total dogs.

"What's Ruth say about me?" I asked.

"Oh, I really don't know," he replied in a voice that made it clear he knew plenty.

I threw another cast and tried to strike an indifferent pose. But Phil was playing it cooler. He took the pack of Kents he'd lifted from his mother's dresser out of his tackle box, looked over his shoulder to see if the coast was clear, and lay down on the raft, his arm hanging over the side so the cigarette was concealed. A small cloud of smoke rose up and disappeared into the air when he lit the cigarette.

"C'mon, Phil spill the bag. What'd she say?"

"Ruth? Nothing specific. But I know she's got a thing for you."

This was good news, but I wanted some serious proof. "She didn't say anything?"

"My sister and me, we're tight." He crossed his fingers and held them up in case I'd missed his point. "She doesn't need to say a word for me to know what she's thinking."

"And what's she thinking?"

"She's confused. She thinks you're cute and all, but she's got Barry back home."

"Barry?"

"Going to be a freshman. Co-captain and quarterback of the JV football team."

"The quarterback?" Girls always went for the quarterback. In the Chip Hilton books I was reading this summer it didn't matter if a guy was the biggest bastard around, if he was the quarterback, there was a bird on his arm, usually the head cheerleader, or at least the class vice president who could've been a Junior Miss America in spite of her brains. Clair Bee never wrote a word about anything more than holding hands, but you knew a goody-goody like Chip Hilton could get laid just by snapping his fingers. And while I was athletic, I was small for my age and played receiver.

Phil took another drag. "She let him get to second base."

"She told you?"

"I watched."

"You're a perve." I shook my head to try and clear the

image of Ruth's breast in Barry's hands, toughened from thousands of snaps of pigskin, and watched over by Phil, who I was sure would've been beating off.

"She knew I was watching. She gets off on that stuff."

"Phil, you're so full of shit." The guy was a compulsive liar.

"Believe what you want. She may not look it, but she's hornier than a toad."

I saw Ruth climb out of the water and limp up the dock toward her cabin, tilting her head to shake the water from her ears.

"You should've heard her," Phil continued. "Moaning and rolling her head back and forth. 'Oh, Barry,' " he cooed in a high voice.

"Fucking perve." I bent down and hit him hard on the thigh, keeping one knuckle raised to increase the likelihood of a charley horse. He pretended that it didn't hurt, but I saw his cheek twitch with pain. And then he started up again.

" 'Barry, put my titties in your mouth. Oh, like that, Barry. I'm getting wet. Bite my red, ripe nipples. Oh, Barry.' "

"You're such a putz."

Phil was still hiding the cigarette below the raft, and his dark underarm hair peeked out of the sleeve of his mosquito magnet shirt. There was a tug on my line and

I started reeling it in. "Noah, touch me down there," Phil continued in his altar-boy voice. He rubbed a hand on his crotch. "Noah, stick your little willie inside me. Oh, Noah. You make me wet. Noah, Noah, Noah."

A small brown bass dangled from the line. I slipped the hook out of its mouth and weighed it in my hand.

"Too tiny to keep," Phil said.

I opened my penknife and pried out both of the fish's eyes. A rim of blood seeped from them and dribbled onto the outside of my hand. The fish shook wildly in my fist.

"You're messed up, mister," Phil said, pointing his finger at me as he spoke each word. I stared him down and hook-shot the fish into the lake. Then I tossed my fishing rod and tackle box into the canoe, stepping over the fish's eyes, which lay on the raft like forgotten buttons.

I dove into the water and submarined down. I was aiming for the bottom, twenty-five or forty feet. It was rumored a forest of children were frozen like statues on the bottom of Trout Lake. The mud was so thick and gluey that the merest touch trapped a heel or hand or toe forever, and the children died as their lungs exploded. My ears started ringing, and the pressure increased with each downward stroke. I kept going, counting the seconds underwater, trying to break my record. My eyes were open but I couldn't see any part of my body. The air in my lungs was thinning out, my ears were pounding. I swam down and down, and then I couldn't go any further. Forty-three seconds underwater, a new record. I needed air. I pushed up with all of my strength, and stroked like mad, torpedoing up. Light creaked into the water and then more light and light and I splashed through the surface and sucked in the air.

That evening I put on my best white button-down shirt and assumed my usual spot on the Pikes' porch, leaning against the banister by the steps. The Pikes had money but they took shitty care of their cabin; the banister was one of the few posts still attached to the railing that wrapped around the porch. The rest were rotting or had broken off or in half, and hung from the railings like stalactites.

If Ruth was crushed on me, she sure wasn't showing it. She was in the hammock reading a fat book called *Great Figures in World History*, her good foot swaying over half-filled boxes they were taking back to Teaneck. She'd already finished a couple of books like these this summer, titles like *A Short History of the World* and *The Lifetime of the Plague*. I didn't know how she got through them. They hardly had any pictures—just some maps about agricultural yields or infant mortality rates in the middle ages—and the words ran all the way to both edges of the page. I was glad she was reading though, because

I could watch her without having to talk. I never knew what the hell to say to her, and tonight I was real nervous and my words were coming out as a whisper.

Fortunately, the Pikes were busying themselves and I didn't have to make chitchat with any of them: Mrs. Pike was inside the cabin giggling into the phone; Mr. Pike had started spreading a two-week-old *Easton Express* on the plastic all-weather patio table—which he'd bought from my dad at cost—but was now hunched over the racing scores like a Talmudic scholar in a trance, crumpling the edges between his hairy knuckles; and Phil was teasing the lobsters with a stick he poked through the gaps in their crate.

"Ever play lobster hockey?" Phil asked me.

I looked at Ruth for an explanation. She put the book down and clapped her hands in excitement. "It's the bestest game in the world," she shrieked in her little-girl's voice.

"Rawzick, go under the porch and get the broom," Phil said. If Ruth and Mr. Pike weren't around I would've told him to stick the broom up his fat ass. Instead, I went and limboed my way under the porch. I saw why Phil didn't get the broom himself: the porch was only a few feet above the ground and he probably would've gotten himself stuck.

I returned to the porch as Phil bent down and turned

over the crate of lobsters. Out tumbled six of them, land-ing in a pile on top of one another. The lobsters righted themselves and moved across the porch, the thick blue rubber bands around both their claws causing them to waddle. They looked funny but you could tell they were pissed; their antennae were twitching fast and they made all these clicking noises. Phil stood watch over them, and whenever one moved close to the porch's edge, he'd nudge it back with his foot.

"Make sure none escape," he said. By habit I ignored Phil, but Ruth hopped off the hammock and stationed herself on a side of the porch. I didn't want to be the pisser so I moved to the other side, below a strip of fly-paper that hung from the gutter. The flypaper had been up since last summer, and hundreds of dead black bugs covered every spot of stickiness on it.

Ruth was serious about the lobsters. Whenever they came near her, she slammed her right heel, which was fitted with an extra few inches of rubber, hard on the porch and yelled, "Get back." Her show of force surprised me. Maybe Phil was telling the truth when he said she was a moaner.

Phil took the broom from me. It was the kind my dad had me use to clear leaves from the driveway, with a horizontal bar of tough brown bristles attached to a long, thin pole. He moved behind a lobster and started lining up to give it a heave. I tapped him on the shoulder and whispered, "What about your old man?" Mr. Pike was sitting at the table right in the middle of the porch.

"He doesn't care," Phil said, and looked at me like I was a retard. He stood behind the broom and spread his legs the way a sprinter does at the start of a race. Then he gave the lobster a push. It skidded across the porch, traveling no more than six feet before it rolled over a couple of times and stopped by the white table. The lobster looked pathetic: it was on its back, its claws moving uselessly in the air. Phil was pleased with himself and handed me the broom. I chose a smaller lobster whose back had less of a hump to it than the others. "That one's got luck written all over it," Ruth said, her elbow resting on Phil's shoulder. I gave it a heave and the lobster rocketed across the porch, somersaulting to a stop two feet past Phil's.

Ruth whistled her approval and said, "You're a natural, Noah." It was her turn but Phil grabbed the broom from me and went again. His lobster didn't pass my mark though, and he got sore and started cursing the lobsters like it was their fault. Then Ruth went and her lobster was going pretty far when it hit her old man's shoe. From all the years of being married to Mrs. Pike, Mr. Pike must've developed the ability to hear practically nothing, because it was only then that he looked up from the paper and told us to quit it. Man, my dad would've pounded my tuchas raw if he caught me doing that.

Still smarting from his defeat, Phil said, "It's about time for the death march," and went inside to check on the water. "Poor, poor, Phil, losty-wosty," Ruth sing-songed. She gathered up five of the lobsters and dropped them into the wooden crate. One of them was AWOL, and after hunting around, we found it amidst an over-turned box of Mrs. Pike's cosmetics. The lobster faced the inside of the box, as if it couldn't bear to meet its fate. Ruth reached in and pulled out the creature, holding it behind the claws, where they attached to the body. The lobster was a fighter, and it jerked about in her hand before letting loose a stream of piss.

"Ever put a lobster to beddie-bye?" Ruth asked me, holding it away from her so it didn't get her wet.

She held the lobster tightly in one hand and squatted over it, motioning with her other hand for me to join her. She spoke to me like I was her doll. "We take your li'l ol' hand like this," and she curled my fingers into a fist, pressing down on the nails so the knuckles stuck out like I was about to give a noogie. Then she lifted up the lobster's tail and rubbed my hand in tight circles on its back. "The creatures need our love, Noah. We must ad-minister to their happiness before they pass to the great lobster unknown."

I thought she was crazy. She'd just smacked a lobster across the porch with a broom. But she was holding my hand close to her and I could taste her breath and damned if I was going to say anything. She kept circling my knuckles on the lobster's back and they started to tingle with numbness.

"Is it working?" I asked.

"Patience, Noah." She stared at the lobster's back like she expected something magical to happen. And then, sure enough, the lobster went limp and curled over, its head resting on the porch. It looked like a diver in the middle of a flip.

"Where'd you learn this?" I asked.

"I'm the Queen of the Sea." She winked at me. "I know how to do all sorts of things."

Did this mean she was going to take me around the base paths? I felt light-headed. But then her awful mother appeared and Ruth let go of my hand, releasing the lobster from its spell, and it jumped out of its sleep.

Even without speaking Mrs. Pike gave the impression of noise. She started fanning her hand in front of her nose like someone had farted. "Dammit, Ike," she said, "you know I'm allergic to newspaper." Each summer, her list of allergies grew. Last summer they moved from a large house with a barn a half mile down the road into a cabin three doors from our own because of Mrs. Pike's hay fever.

Being near the water supposedly made her breathing easier.

"How are we supposed to eat lobsters then?" Mr. Pike protested without much protest.

"Are you trying to get me sick, Ike? Is that what you're after?"

"Just be quiet and look at the lake, Leah," Mr. Pike said. He hadn't looked up once from the paper. "Nature's beautiful if you stop yapping long enough to look at it."

"I don't see why it's called Trout Lake when there ain't a single damn trout in it." Mrs. Pike took a drag on her Kent, which had burned down to the filter and a cone of ash.

Phil came onto the porch and picked up the crate of lobsters. He pulled one out and held it up to his face. "Maybe I'll put you in tail first," he said to the creature. "Would you like to die like that?"

"Stop fooling around," Mr. Pike said as Phil headed toward the kitchen.

"Noah, dear, go tell your mother we have lobsters."

"She's in bed with a headache, Mrs. Pike," I replied in my most polite voice. My mom said the Pikes were the type of Jews who gave the rest of us a bad name, and she avoided them as much as possible. As soon as she saw Mr. Pike haul the crate of lobsters from the trunk of his Cadillac, she told me to cover for her.

"Woman sickness," Mrs. Pike said and winked at me. "Women never feel well, Noah, remember that." I looked at Ruth. Phil had told me she'd been bleeding for over a year. It made me queasy to think about it. "It's a big cry we didn't get to see your brother this summer." Mrs. Pike adored my brother—hell, everyone did—and I knew she was keeping an eye on him for her daughter. I was damn glad that he was working as a camp counselor in the Poconos. Otherwise he'd have been all over Ruth.

Phil returned with a black metal pot and Mrs. Pike fished out a lobster onto each of our plates. I was seated between them, and directly across from Ruth. All of them, including Ruth, wasted no time ripping into their lobsters. They sounded like an elementary-school orchestra: the pliers cracked out a rhythm on the lobster's claws, and then the woodwinds came in as they slurped up the juice. Ruth's face was practically on top of the table and she was chowing down like a Viking. This was the first time I saw she actually was a Pike. I'd always thought she had to have been adopted. With her blond curls and prim button of a nose, she could've stepped right off the May-flower.

I didn't know what the hell to do with the lobster in front of me. It was smaller than its kin, and I knew it was the one that had led me to lobster hockey victory. I tried to imitate the Pikes, but even using the pliers, I couldn't cleanly break open the claw.

"Look, Ruth, isn't Noah cute?" Mrs. Pike said. "He doesn't have the foggiest idea of how to eat the creature." Ruth smiled at me; her warmth was almost enough to erase my embarrassment. Phil kicked my leg and started humming "Do you see what I see?"

"Here, Noah," Mrs. Pike said, picking up my lobster and snapping off its tail. "Break it just like the girls' hearts." She held the tail-less lobster up to my face. It wasn't a pretty sight: whatever appetite I still had vanished when Mrs. Pike dug a long pink nail into the creature and fished out some meat. "Voilà," she said, holding her finger out like she expected me to eat from it. Finally, she dropped the meat into my hand and returned the lobster to my plate. I puttered over it, moving my jaws so they'd think I was eating. When Phil finished his lobster, I slid mine in front of him. I knew he'd eat it with no questions asked.

Once the Pikes were done, Mrs. Pike asked me to hose down the table. Ruth said she'd show me where they kept the hose and I followed her down the steps and around the side of the porch. I slowed down so we could walk side by side in the narrow alley between the cabins, and our arms brushed against one another. The black hose wasn't on its stand, but lay in a tangled clump on the grass.

"Here's the hose, Noah," Ruth said overly loud. Then she whispered, "Just nod if it's okay." She pressed a folded square of lavender stationery into my hand. I unfolded it, and perfume wafted up like the spray from an orange when it's first separated.

The words NOAH'S ARK AT MIDNIGHT were written in her compact, all-capitals script. I was stunned and nodded several times; I didn't want there to be any confusion. I moved toward her but she put a hand on my chest and mouthed the word, *Tonight.* I swear I popped a hard-on right then and there. She walked toward the porch and, without looking back at me, waved her hand over her shoulder.

I read the sheet of paper again. The letters remained unchanged. I refolded it along the creases and put it in my pocket. I couldn't believe my luck.

As I finished hosing off the table, I heard my dad's Continental pull up the gravel drive and stop in front of our cabin. The car door opened and closed, and I heard his footsteps moving behind the car to make sure the trunk was under the canvas awning, safe from bird shit and sap. At the start of the summer I'd helped him measure and cut the canvas, and he'd hoisted me onto his shoulders and into the branches of an oak where I'd knotted the sheet.

I went to my cabin and chatted my folks up about the sun and being tired, and made sure to yawn lots between bites of meatloaf before escaping to my room. Then I climbed out the window and up the drainpipe onto the tarred roof. From here there wasn't much of a view of the Pikes' cabin, just a corner of their porch. But if I had X-ray vision, I would've seen Ruth helping her mom pack; taping up the Parcheesi and Monopoly sets so no pieces were lost, zipping closed Mrs. Pike's zebra-skin hatboxes and stacking them in the shape of a wedding cake, twisting a curl around her finger as she counted and recounted the number of suitcases, sighing to herself as she stole glances at the clock whose hands were stuck at twenty past ten.

Their screen door creaked open and I hoped it was Ruth coming outside to give me a sign that all was well. But it was only Mr. Pike, the end of his lit cigar glowing in the dark, coming over to talk my father into a game of horseshoes. I put my watch in my pocket and passed the time listening to the sound of metal grazing metal and the solid thud of horseshoes landing on the dirt, to Mr. Pike's too-loud voice repeating his lucky words—"Good as gold, sweeter than silver"—before each one of his tosses, and my dad saying, "Darn't," when he was unhappy with his own throw.

Their match ended, handshakes were exchanged, and they returned to their own cabins. It was a quarter of midnight and I was nervous as I'd ever been. I could feel my pulse twitching through my thigh. The light was still on at the Pikes', and I worried Ruth wouldn't be able to sneak out. Finally, their light turned off and I shimmied down the drainpipe and walked barefoot to the lake. A sliver of moon was tucked behind clouds, illuminating them like a halo. I heard no human noise, no bark of a parent onto me sneaking out, but the night was filled with thousands of crickets tuning up.

The stench of the lake hit me as I got close. It hadn't rained all summer and this bubbly green algae that looked like barf had spread around the sides of the lake. The algae stank like the boys' locker room. I lowered myself into the still water as silently as possible and pushed off one of the slimy poles that held up the dock, breaststroking toward the Ark. Halfway there, I saw Ruth's outline silhouetted in the darkness. Each time I came up for a breath, she took on more features, her arms wrapped around her pulled-up knees, a hand combing through her hair.

"Hi, Noah," she said when I reached the raft. Her voice was calm.

I lifted myself out of the water, loosening the elastic of my Hanes, which had tightened around my crotch beneath my cutoffs. Wet tighty-whities were a big problem; they kept bunching around your privates and it looked like you were playing with yourself when you adjusted them.

"You took the canoe?" I said, noticing its outline on the far side of the raft.

"You're shivering." She tapped on the raft and I sat down next to her.

"The air. It's cold." I cursed myself for saying something so obvious. But my teeth were chattering like those wind-up, palm-size kinds that my dentist seemed to find funny and kept on the tables in his waiting room. She put the ratty towel we left on the raft all summer around my shoulders and started drying me off. Her body heat warmed me and my shivering slowed and soon I couldn't tell the sound of my own breathing from hers. The light of fireflies flickered on and off around the edges of the lake. It was so quiet I imagined that the Russians had dropped the hydrogen bomb on the White House and Ruth and I were the only ones left in the country. Her gross parents and pig of a brother were burnt to ashes; my family was wiped out, no longer alive to tell me how I'd done everything wrong. It was just me and Ruth and the Ark.

I put my arm around her shoulder and she leaned her face forward for me to kiss. We kissed and her tongue exploded in my mouth. I was on first base. I looked at her, trying to collect as much earnestness and desire into my eyes as possible. And then I stole second. I had a handful of her left tit before she lowered my hand. Did feeling her up on the outside of her dress count as second base? Was there a time requirement of more than five seconds?

"Not now, Noah," she said. This wasn't how it was supposed to be. There was an unwritten rule that once you'd gotten to a certain base, you couldn't go backwards. Ruth wasn't a complete virgin, yet here she was reforming on me.

"You go back to Teaneck tomorrow," I pleaded. I was already way hot for her.

"For girls, you can't rush," she said, and put her hand right on my thigh. "You haven't been with a girl before, have you?"

"What are you talking about? Damn right I have."

"Phil said you hadn't."

"That bastard. He told you that?" I was such a fool for thinking that Phil would keep his trap shut. "Your brother lies and lies."

"No, he doesn't."

She started rubbing her hand up and down the length

of my thing. "I want to do something nice for you," she said. There was no embarrassment in her fingers; she'd definitely done this before. The friction of her hand and the denim were feeling good—too good—and I knew I was going to come.

She undid my top button with her free hand and that was it: I came right then. It only felt good for a moment though, and I was ashamed, so I didn't make any noise. I slid my lower half away from her before she could reach inside my cutoffs and find out I'd already lost it. Then I grabbed her tits real quick. She squirmed but I had one in each hand and held on.

"Quit it, Noah. That hurts." She hit at my hands and I let go.

"You let Barry touch them," I protested.

"That's different." Her back was to me, her knees pulled up to her chin. She didn't seem surprised that I knew about her quarterback boyfriend.

"I'm going to touch you, Ruth." I inched closer.

"Don't, Noah."

"So I can't touch you?" She shook her head. I stroked her back and gave her neck a little squeeze. "I'll be gentle," I said, and rubbed her stomach like a little kid does when he's hungry. I put my hand on her tit and circled around her nipple. Her face had no expression and gazed at some invisible horizon like a department-store mannequin. I smiled, trying to coax some sign from her. She gave me a sign all right: she elbowed me hard in the chest. "Leave me alone," she said coolly, and shuffled away from me. "You killed the mood."

"C'mon, Ruthie." She acted like I was air and stared into her knees. "Don't be like this." I was getting pissed. "Ruth."

"I was wrong about you, Noah. You're not any good with girls." She whispered these words but they stung me like I'd been whipped.

"You fucking cripple."

I stood up and kicked her in the hip. I meant it just to be a nudge, but she let out a yelp, like a dog whose tail's been stepped on. I was surprised by her noise, and then I wanted to hear her in more pain. I moved back a little so I could really get my leg into it, and kicked her again. She didn't cry out this time, but she curled up on her side and started whimpering, stifling sobs and snot. I leaned over, my hands on my knees, catching my breath. Trying to hurt someone could make you really winded. Then out of the darkness I heard Phil saying my name. I couldn't believe my eyes but Fatty had a knee on the raft and was pulling himself out of the canoe. My mind was working in slow motion.... *If he was in the canoe and the canoe was tied to the raft, then he's been here the whole time.* I felt like I was watching a movie and suddenly saw myself appear on the screen.

"Phil, what are you doing?"

"Leave her alone, Rawzick." His voice was much lower than usual and he stood straight up, his chest puffed out.

"Both of you are f-f-fucking sick," I stammered, moving away from Ruth to the other end of the raft. Phil came forward, trying to corner me. I saw he was set on kicking my ass.

"You got it all wrong, Rawzick. Ruthie was trying to do you a favor, but you'd fuck up a wet dream."

"How many times has he stuck it inside you, Ruth?" I said loudly.

"Shut your mouth." I could hear Phil sweating, his voice winded from panic or exertion. Ruth had stopped her sniveling and the only sign of life in her was that she'd sat upright.

"You don't know anything, Noah," she said.

I gobbed up a loogie and spit in her direction. It must've hit her because she whined and slapped at her face.

Phil was almost close enough to land a punch. Ruth crab-walked toward me, kicking in wild circles like she was pedaling a bike. Her cripple foot got me good in the knee. I dove into the lake and swam furiously. Finally I tilted my head out of the water and listened for sounds of a canoe or Ruth's splashing. It was silent. I looked back at the raft and saw their shadows overlapping. Alone in the cold water, they looked like two trees that had grown too close to one another, the branches becoming so inter-twined that you couldn't tell them apart.

C-Clamp

Amy Gebler

If anything, Hillary is optimistic. She believes that if you behave as if everything will work out, it will, and she has tried to get me to believe her a number of times. "It's an imaging theory," she explained to me once while we were in high school. She was trying out for the tennis team and our parents were trying to encourage me to try out with her. They'd decided that year that team sports would be good for me. But while Hillary could rally back and forth, I was stuck on the practice wall, missing even my own shots.

"Picture yourself making a connection," she'd call over to me, her short white skirt flapping as she ran to the net.

"It's sort of like praying, right?" I asked.

"No, it's nothing like praying. Don't hope. See yourself hitting the ball."

But I saw myself missing every shot at the tryouts, and

I did miss all of them but one, while Hillary skipped junior varsity and pictured herself right onto the varsity team.

My sister has always been confident that things turn out in the end, or that everything happens for a reason, and when they don't, she waits patiently for the tables to turn, because for her, they always have. She believes the good guy won't die, she doesn't even want him to, and she thrives on upbeat self-improvement books with titles like *Change Your Life in 20 Days* or *Get the Mad out of You.* Among packs of adoring friends, she floated painlessly and uneventfully through high school and college, and then immediately landed a somewhat lucrative position as a sales rep for a computer consulting firm, serving as a perfect prop to our parents' endless mantra, "See what you can do when you put some effort into something?" So when Hillary and her boyfriend, Tom, announced their engagement on the first warm weekend of May, we all imagined that the planning of the first wedding of our family, the planning of Hillary's wedding, would take over our lives. Together, the four of them planned a June wedding for the following year and almost immediately our mother began talking china patterns.

You can only imagine my mother's distress six months later when the only thing that has been decided about the wedding is the deposit on a banquet hall in a hotel on the beach. All of the other plans have been put aside for months, and whenever our mother asks why Hillary is waiting until the last minute to plan her wedding, Hillary answers without looking at her, and says, "It'll work out."

Hillary sits on the couch with a bridal magazine on her lap and as she turns the pages, she throws a tennis ball to her dog, a one-year-old husky named Alexis who is not allowed in the house. My brother, Ellis, and I are home for the weekend and he has gone shopping with our parents to buy groceries for dinner.

"Do you think they'll smell her?" Hillary asks, and I shrug. Our mother has a way of noticing these things and quite frankly, I hope she comes back soon so that the dog will be put out. Alexis is too big and badly trained to be inside. Hillary says she took her to puppy kindergarten, but whatever either one of them learned there remains a mystery. When Alexis climbs up to lick his face, Tom absent-mindedly swats at her, pushing her away, and her wagging tail sweeps everything off the coffee table in a single motion. Tom is watching the football game, so Hillary jumps up to grab some towels, and Alexis turns to me and jumps up on my lap, crumpling the glossy pages of another one of Hillary's bridal magazines. She stares at me with her clear blue husky eyes, and with her mouth full of grubby tennis ball, she drools onto a picture of a short-sleeved, tulle-skirted Mon Amie gown I was just about to point out to Hillary.

"She's so smart," Hillary says, looking at Alexis after shaking her head at the dress I've just shown her. "Uh-uh, Kate. Way too plain. Here, watch what she can do." My sister picks up a plastic mouse that squeaks and then, taking the ball from the dog's mouth, she throws both toys into the kitchen. "Alexis, get mousie," she says, and Alexis plods after the toys, her nails clip-clipping on the kitchen tile. "Mousie," Hillary calls after her in a high singsong voice, but the dog picks up the tennis ball and cheerfully brings it back to my sister.

Tom grunts and rolls his eyes at the scene before returning his attention to the football game. He is wearing his Steve Young jersey and is concentrating on the television. For Tom, everything has to do with the Forty-Niners. When they lose, he is of course personally offended, and he doesn't usually talk during Forty-Niner games unless he's swearing about the other team or hooting about a touchdown. Once, though, he tried to explain the game to me, drawing field diagrams in my parents' new summer-wheat-colored carpet with his finger. He was a surprisingly patient teacher and I was beginning to really understand the game when my mother walked into the room and asked, "What are you doing to my new carpet?" with a disgusted look on her face.

"Let's try again," Hillary says, holding Alexis's muzzle in her lap. "Mousie," she says firmly, and this time she throws only the mouse and hides the tennis ball behind her.

"Maybe she doesn't want to get the mouse because it's a cat toy," I say. "It's cats who chase mice."

"This is not a cat toy," she says, sounding offended, and looks after Alexis, who is searching the kitchen for her tennis ball. "Mousie, Alexis. Get Mousie," Hillary calls. The dog looks up and then at the mouse and finally, in a motion that seems resigned, grabs the mouse and brings it back to Hillary.

"Oh, good puppy," she croons, "you're such a smart dog, yes you are. See," she says to me, "Alexis understands English."

The time Hillary spends on her dog drives our mother insane, because she feels strongly that Hillary could make much better use of her time talking to caterers and researching photo opportunities so that she can advise the photographer. Since this is the first wedding in the family, my mother wants to make this occasion an event. She is very good at this sort of thing. Growing up, even dinner-time at our house was something of an affair. She always made meals that strategically combined the four food groups, and desserts were chosen for their ability to be served in the crystal goblets my parents received as wedding presents. And, no matter what the meal or who was eating it, the table was always set with a white linen cloth. I actually hadn't noticed the absurdity of this tablecloth habit, though, until once, at a Passover seder, my cousin brought her two-year-old son, Sam. Right about the point in the seder when you're supposed to eat the Hillel sandwich, Sam dipped his matzo into a nearby dish of hot-pink horseradish and started spreading it on the cloth in front of him. My cousin was embarrassed and offered to pay for the cleaning bill, but my mother just clenched her teeth, smiled, and said, "Now don't be silly."

"I guess white tablecloths weren't such a good idea," I said later as we were rinsing the stain in cold water.

"Don't be silly," my mother said again, with the same frustration she'd shown to my cousin. "Without a certain amount of ceremony, there's no significance to any ritual. And, my grandmother always set her table with a white cloth."

When we hear the garage door open, Hillary jumps up to get the dog out.

"Quick, grab the toys," she says to me as she opens the sliding glass door to the backyard patio and ushers Alexis out. Then she throws herself on the couch next to me just as our parents and our younger brother walk in the door with grocery bags. Ellis has just finished college and has his own apartment across town, but he always makes sure his visits home include a trip to the grocery store with our mother. He pushes the cart and walks down the aisle behind her, throwing items into the basket that he'd rather not buy himself. Mostly he chooses the more expensive items, like spices and toiletries. My mother never notices until they are at home, unpacking the bags. This time he pulls out a clear plastic toothbrush, the new kind with the rippled bristles.

"I got one for you, too," he says, handing me one with a green sparkled handle.

"Honestly, Ellis, I wish you'd told me you threw those in. Did you at least get one for Hillary, too?" our mother says and then pauses to sniff the air. "Do you smell dog in here? Did you let that dog in here, Hillary?"

Hillary shakes her head and gives my mother this look to imply she's losing it. And then she says in an innocent voice, "That's okay, I don't need a toothbrush."

My mother frowns for a second and then shrugs. "I've got the cutest idea for centerpieces," she begins.

*　　*　　*

For my birthday, my parents sent me a card that said *For a Very Special Daughter* in pink calligraphy on the front and when I opened it, a single plane ticket home fluttered out. Inside the card was blank, except for where my mother signed, *Love, Mom & Dad.* I was actually disappointed when I opened the card and found the ticket instead of the usual fifty-dollar check. My boyfriend, Tanner, and I had planned on using the birthday money to buy a VCR. But when I called home to ask what the ticket was about, my mother said she just wanted the family to get together to talk about the wedding during the holiday. She said she wanted to make the wedding a family affair.

"And I knew you'd never be able to afford the ticket on your own, sweetie," she'd said. "Oh, and wait until you see Hillary's ring. It's an emerald cut."

"What about Tanner?" I asked. "Isn't he invited? He's practically part of the family." Tanner was sitting on the couch with a book in his lap, pretending not to listen to my conversation. We'd been together for six years, lived together for three, and usually my mother invited him before she invited me.

" 'Practically part of the family' are the key words here, Kate. Until you're married or engaged, we have no reason to always invite Tanner to family occasions. We don't have to award all of your boyfriends paid vacations."

"Who said this would be a vacation?" I shot out before I wished I hadn't.

"You just let me know what you decide," my mother said in a falsely cheerful voice. I knew she'd tell my father every word of this conversation and the entire trip would be colored with this idea that I'm jealous of Hillary's engagement.

After dinner and the pink Jell-O salad my mother serves for dessert, she gives Ellis and me money to go to the store to pick up the newest edition of *Bridal Vogue* magazine.

"Hillary's already got a whole stack of magazines," Ellis says as she hands him a ten-dollar bill.

"This is a new one," my mother tells him. "Besides, it can't hurt to get another one. It never hurts to be informed."

Ellis drives us in my father's convertible. It's clean and smells like leather, and I'm always afraid to drive it. The top is down and the dimming sky has that shininess of a new night. Everything seems very clean in these suburbs where I grew up. Even car headlights and the lit windows of neighborhood condos seem especially bright. And when we get to the supermarket, the neon lettering above the Safeway is half burnt out and the red lights only spell SAFE against the darkness.

Inside the store, Ellis grabs a pack of cigarettes and a six-pack of beer and when I add the two bridal magazines I've found, the total comes to fifteen dollars and he leaves it to me to pay the difference. The cashier looks at the magazines and then at us and when she asks, "When's the big day?" Ellis grabs my hand and smiles.

"August," he says.

"Oh, that's wonderful," the cashier says, looking at me. "I hope you'll be happy. These days lots of kids get married too early. You know, almost sixty percent of marriages in California end in divorce."

"Is that so?" Ellis says sounding interested. "Well, we'll be happy. We've been together forever." The cashier beams at us. She thinks she's seen love.

"What was that for?" I ask when we get to the car.

"I don't know," he says. "Just for fun." We pull out of the parking lot and into the streets where all of the houses are painted in pastel shades and look alike. "I'm glad you came home. I didn't think you would."

"Why wouldn't I?" I ask, my voice sounding sharper than I'd meant for it to. "Mom and Dad sent me a ticket."

"I don't know. Maybe because of Tanner, or because he didn't come. Or because everything is changing." Ellis is quiet for a minute as he turns onto our street. "I just didn't think you'd come home."

*　　*　　*

When we get home, my father and Tom are watching television in the living room. My father nods at me without saying anything and Tom is tapping his feet anxiously. I can tell he wants to go home; he has nothing left to do since both the game and dinner are over and my father is falling asleep in his chair. Hillary and my mother are in the kitchen looking through magazines and when she sees me, my mother points to a seat.

"You might as well look with us. You can help pick out bridesmaid dresses," she says. Hillary has ripped out pages of both wedding and bridesmaid dresses that she is considering. The wedding dresses she likes have full, beaded skirts and puffed sleeves and the bridesmaid dresses she's chosen for her friends and myself are in a color called Deepest Sea Blue. They have three fat bows that sit at the back of the waist.

"Are you trying to make everyone else look awful so that you look better?" I ask, and Hillary smiles in a way that makes me know she's considered this, but my mother gets upset.

"For God's sake, Kate, act your age. This is an important day for Hillary," she says to me as if I've forgotten.

They've already picked the colors—the previously mentioned Deepest Sea Blue and a Sea Foam Green, and now my mother wants to talk about flowers.

"You could do something with seaweeds and algae to go with the ocean color theme," I try, and my mother glares at me and then begins to talk endlessly about how original it would be to have a bouquet of calla lilies, but also how risky.

"How could you know it'll go over well when everyone knows roses are perfectly beautiful?" She asks this to herself, though, because my opinion is no longer appreciated and Hillary isn't listening. She is staring at the photograph of a milk pitcher that has always hung above the kitchen table. Hillary is so completely oblivious to our discussion that my mother and I both sit uncomfortably and watch her for a minute or two to figure out what to do. When Tom comes into the kitchen to say that he's taking Alexis home to feed her, he doesn't look surprised to see Hillary staring off into space, but she turns around when she hears his voice.

"Oh," Hillary says, shaking her head a little as if she'd awakened from a trance. "No, don't take her back yet," she tells him. "I'll just feed her some leftovers. But if you want to go home, I'll get a ride home from Kate."

When our parents go upstairs to bed, I think Hillary will tell me what is wrong with her. I think we'll have a long sisterly talk about why she is so visibly unexcited about getting married, and I imagine the sort of stock conversation about not being sure he is the *right* one. But instead, she grabs a magazine and stands up.

"Let's go outside," she says. "I want a smoke."

It's almost winter, but outside there is a warm Santa Ana wind and the shiny pages of the magazine sparkle and rustle in the light breeze. With one hand, Hillary quietly earmarks the page corners of dresses she likes and in the other hand she holds her cigarette. She doesn't notice the tip growing long and I watch her, waiting for the ashes to fall into her lap. The truth is that Hillary and I never have sisterly talks. When we were younger, Ellis and I stood together against Hillary's perfection. We suffered our teachers' disappointment after having Hillary first. And we were the ones to make forts out of the bunk beds while Hillary sat alone in the other room listening to records. If the Ferris wheel at the carnival was only a two-seater, it was a given that Hillary would go with our dad. I have no idea what's going on with her, and I've never known from which direction to approach her. There was a point in our relationship growing up that consisted of me copying everything she did, from the Shaun Cassidy red satin jacket that she never wore after I got one, too, to trying out for the cheerleading squad even though it interfered with band practice. I copied her even though I knew better, even though I thought she was an idiot, and every copycat act struck quickly and left me reeling in shame. I hated the way she giggled when she talked to boys behind the high school gym and the way she rested her hand on her hip when she wore her short cheer skirt and a perfected bored expression on Friday game days. Sometimes when she'd go out on the weekend, I'd go into the closet that we shared and try on her cheerleading uniform, posing and practicing my own bored look in front of the mirror.

"You don't want to be like her," Ellis kept telling me during that time. He'd sit on my bed and watch me practice the cheers I'd seen Hillary do at football games. "Why do you want to be like her?"

"I don't want to be like her." I knew that I didn't want to be her, but I did want to try her on, to understand what it'd be like to be blond, popular Hillary. "You don't understand," I told Ellis.

"Well, you look stupid," he said. He'd been practicing his violin and when he spoke, he waved the bow at me. But the way his T-shirt was too small and how his skinny arms cradled the instrument on his lap suddenly made me furious. "Get out," I told him, and when he didn't move, I gave him a shove and yelled, "Get out!"

"What's going on here? How come you always have to shriek?" My father filled the doorway. And then he noticed my outfit. "What the hell are you doing in that?

That uniform is not a toy, young lady, and it's not yours." He was furious. And Hillary was his angel, though at this moment I imagined her drunk and on some couch in a dark room, making out with a football player. He was probably talking her into doing it with him and she would say, "Yes, yes, oh baby," the way she did to the bathroom mirror.

"Take that uniform off this instant and you can sit in here until you understand what it means to respect other people's privacy." My father shook his head at me with disgust before heading back downstairs.

"Ellis," I said slowly after my father left the room, "get out of here, please." He looked hurt, but didn't move. I sighed and then changed into my pajamas in front of him. The wool uniform had left red splotches on my skin and they burned as I carefully hung the outfit up on Hillary's side of the closet. Ellis watched me without saying anything and when I climbed into my bed, he climbed in with me and curled his body around mine while I tried not to cry.

"They're all beginning to look the same," Hillary says about the dresses, and she slams the magazine shut and lights another cigarette. "Maybe chain-smoking will help me lose weight before this whole thing goes down." She inhales and then breathes out a silvery veil of smoke.

"Wouldn't Mom like be happy if I lost some weight before the wedding?" Alexis is sitting expectantly at Hillary's feet and she rubs the dog behind her ears before leaning over to croon good-dog sweet nothings to her. "What about you?" Hillary asks suddenly. "Are you and Tanner ever going to get married?"

"No, we never talk about it," I lie. "We're not ready yet." Tanner talks about getting married, though. He says he's ready, and that he can't imagine being with anyone else. I'm not sure how to tell if I'm ready for marriage, and then sometimes I'm convinced that everyone is just making a big deal out of nothing. I mean, living together is practically like being married, isn't it? But there are times when I wake up in the middle of the night and I'm shocked to find Tanner in bed with me even though we've been together now for so long.

"Want to hear something?" Hillary asks after a long silence, and then without waiting for me to respond she says, "I was pregnant."

"Was?" I suck in my breath.

"We'd already decided to get married before it happened," she says quickly. "That's not why we're getting married. Though, believe me, I wasn't looking forward to everyone counting the months between the wedding and the premature birth."

"Nobody does that anymore," I say, but we both know

our parents would do this. They'd lie in bed at night and count the months in their heads over and over as if they were sure the miscalculation was their own.

"Tom wanted it. He was crushed when I lost it," she says looking at the sky. "He was mad at me even though he knew it wasn't my fault." There are only a few stars out and one of them turns out to be an airplane. "But he's okay now, I think. Don't you think he's okay?"

"Sure," I say slowly, unsure whether or not she's asking how I feel about Tom or how he feels about the miscarriage.

"I feel like I wished it away," Hillary says. "I'm going to be punished for this." She puts out her cigarette and I notice she has started biting her nails.

"Don't be silly," I tell her. "This happens all the time."

"Maybe, but usually you're upset, not relieved."

"I would be relieved," I tell her.

"You wouldn't really," she says. "You're too sensitive. You wouldn't be relieved."

Hillary looks like she is about to cry, and when she notices me staring at her, she turns away and I raise my voice. "Jesus, Hillary. Don't do this."

And then she looks me square in the face and says in a challenging voice, "Don't do what?"

When I don't answer she stands up and says in a frighteningly cheerful voice, "Well, it's getting late. I guess I'd better be heading home."

We go inside where Ellis is sitting on the couch, watching reruns of *Lassie* in the blue light of the television.

"Oh," Hillary says, sitting down and pulling Alexis to her. "I love this episode."

I haven't watched the show since I was about eight years old, but I sit down with them. The mother is trapped in a shed and she is begging Lassie to help her. "C-clamp," the mother says to Lassie as the collie cocks her head thoughtfully to the side. "I need a C-clamp," she says, making a C with her thumb and forefinger and showing it to the dog. "C-clamp, girl. Go get it for me." Lassie runs off and returns with the clamp. I have no idea what the clamp is supposed to be used for, but somehow it gets the mother out of the shed. She is saved by Lassie and they all live happily ever after.

"That's such a good show," Hillary says. "Lassie is just so dependable." She makes a C out of her own hand and shows it to Alexis. "C-clamp, girl," she says. "Can you get it for me? Do you understand?" When Hillary notices Ellis and me staring at her, she blushes and laughs nervously. "I think I'll just walk home," she says. No one walks at night in the plastic-looking tract-home developments of southern California, despite the fact that there is very little crime in this neighborhood. "I'll be safe," she says. "I have Alexis with me."

We let her go and when I go up to my room, I see that my bed is unmade even though I just arrived home this morning. Some of Ellis's clothes are on the floor and when he walks in the room behind me, he says, "I slept here last night. I could hear Dad snoring from my room." He begins to collect his things and looks at me. "I'll go sleep in the other room to give you some privacy."

"That's okay," I say. "I'll just sleep in Hillary's old bed and you can stay in my bed."

But Ellis is already shaking his head and gathering his things. "No, it's better this way. I've got to sleep in my own room."

Through the thin walls, I hear Ellis getting ready for bed. I imagine him throwing his clothes on the floor and climbing into bed and then switching off the lamp that sits on the small oak bedside table. I don't fall asleep right away and lie in bed for what seems like hours as I hear him cough a few times, and then there is silence as I listen to the dark house sleep. Once when Tanner was going through a bout of insomnia, he came up with this theory that there is only so much sleep possible per household. In his frantic exhaustion, he blamed me for sucking up all the sleep in our little apartment. At the time I'd laughed. "Here I go," I teased, "I'm sucking up all the sleep and you'd better grab some before it's all gone." Naturally, Tanner's sense of humor leaves much to be desired in the middle of the night, and in a huff, he'd gathered up his pillow and the extra blanket off the foot of the bed and slept soundly on the couch. And when I woke up in the middle of that night, I felt relieved to have the whole bed to myself until I remembered he was mad at me.

When I do finally fall asleep in the tiny bed of my parents' house, I dream. I dream I'm pregnant but there is a problem. I keep feeling my stomach to see if it's growing larger, but it stays flat and I'm having difficulty swallowing. The baby is lodged in my throat and there is a bulge on my neck as if I had an Adam's apple. It keeps growing until even speaking is painful and the doctor tells me, "It's you or the baby." I can't decide. Tanner tells me to act like a mother and save my child. I can feel the baby move and I throw up. I worry that I will vomit up the baby and that when I look into the toilet, I will see a perfectly formed infant the size and color of my pinkie. They are waiting for a decision—everyone is waiting for me to decide, and I wake up shouting.

Ellis is next to me when I open my eyes. My shouting did not wake him and he murmurs something that makes him smile in his sleep. There is not much room on the twin bed and he throws his arm around my waist as an anchor to keep himself from falling off, and I feel safe. I know in the morning, before the sun comes up, he will have to go back to his own room so that we can wake up in our own beds. And tomorrow night, the same thing will probably happen again—night after night until I go home to Tanner. We will go to sleep in our own beds and wake up in our own rooms, and everyone will believe everything is fine. But what happens in the middle is always so unclear. The middle of the night is undepend-able. Outside in a neighbor's yard, a dog barks and I think I hear Hillary crooning to Alexis. "C-clamp," she says to the dog. "Help me, girl."

The Middle Way

Paula R. Whyman

Nil leans forward, hands resting on her knees. Her toe traces abstract pictures in the dust. She sits in a molded plastic chair in front of a simple two-story house with a corrugated tin roof. She has been in this position so long, she could have traced a scene from the *Ramakian*. The air presses heavily against her cheek.

When Nil arrived with her mother, Phanvadee, other girls around Nil's age were gathered outside, but they floated like seeds at the edges of her awareness. Now they have dispersed by prearranged signal from the house-mother, Maylao. Nil straightens in her chair as Maylao examines her. As always, Nil wears an impossibly clean white cotton blouse, short-sleeved with rounded collar, and a brown skirt.

Maylao leans close and finds that Nil smells like soap

and ginger. And something else. She smells like a child. To Maylao, this is the best, and saddest, smell of all.

Large puffy clouds hang in the blue overhead, trapped and inert in the heat.

Phanvadee knows to begin with an unrealistic number. "We were hoping for sixty-thousand baht," she says. That would be twice one year's income for the family. She fingers a sleeve on her yellow housedress and nods firmly to herself.

Maylao crosses and uncrosses her arms and waves dismissively. "She's not pretty," she responds. The gauntness of Nil's face, an awkward, youthful boniness, makes her eyes seem too prominent, bulging like black marbles from her skull.

"Not yet." Phanvadee brushes imaginary dust from Nil's immaculate blouse, then smiles and urges Nil to imitate her. Nil smiles back. Her teeth are small and regular, her lips thin but well-shaped. "Her brothers are handsome young men," Phanvadee says.

"So bring me her brothers," Maylao laughs. "Who needs this one?"

"Sixty-thousand is a good price. She'll be loyal and obedient to you," Phanvadee insists.

"And at a lower price her obedience is not guaranteed?" Maylao's face twists into a leer, which she quickly converts into a grim smile. "Obedience isn't a problem with my girls," she continues. "They have incentives to be so." Maylao likes this game. It's better than being the spider who traps the fly, because she gets to be the mantis who preys on both.

She bends over the girl, and Nil's toe freezes in the dirt. Maylao's skin is sallow and uneven, bloated as though some force presses it out from the inside. "How old is she?" Maylao asks.

"Eleven," says Phanvadee, with a sharp glance at Nil. She knows that the younger her daughter, the more Maylao will pay, because Maylao's clients desire innocence and the safety they believe accompanies it.

Nil blinks. She's been twelve for a while now, but her body won't give her away. Her narrow frame is all angles, her hips straight like a boy's, her breasts barely anthills in the open plain stretching from collarbone to belly.

"She's small. Perhaps she won't eat much," says Maylao. Maylao produces a pineapple, slices off the top, and begins digging out the flesh with a small, sharp knife. The sweet fragrance permeates the air, momentarily displacing all other smells.

"She'll want no more than what she's given." Phanvadee doesn't look at Nil when she speaks. She sees quite clearly that this is what she must do. This is Nil's destiny. Although Nil will be fulfilling men's desires, contributing to the stuntedness of their souls, her soul will be clean, and the result of her work will be the improvement of the family's status. Phanvadee knows that her sacrifice of Nil will bring enough money for Nil's brothers to finish school, and they, in turn, will bring favor to the family. "She's a good worker," Phanvadee adds.

Maylao squints at her and wipes the perspiration from under one eye. The knife in her hand catches the sun. When she was younger, she learned, along with everyone else, about Buddha's three pillars of practice: morality, concentration, and wisdom. Two out of three, I'm doing okay—better than most, she thinks, laughing to herself. Maylao doesn't see herself as a corrupting influence. If people around her stray from the path, they've made this choice themselves. She's there simply to benefit from their oscillations.

"Why give her up?" Maylao finally asks, eating successive chunks of pineapple from the flat side of the knife. Drops of juice cling to her chin.

"It's a decision I have not made lightly. The family requires money for other things." Phanvadee absently massages the tendons in the back of her hand. She has anticipated Maylao's questions, and designed her answers to convey need but not desperation. "And her father isn't well."

"Yes, yes. Other things," says Maylao. "Always." She looks at Nil and licks the juice from her fingers.

Nil thinks about the last time she saw her father. He left with the Royal Army to harvest teakwood in the north, just after she turned seven.

Maylao tosses the empty pineapple shell to waiting strays. They fight over it, snarling. She pours herself into her own molded plastic chair and fans her neck with her palm. "I'll give you thirty-thousand baht," she says.

"That's too little. Nil's my only daughter. You must see how I can't accept that," Phanvadee answers.

"For what should I pay more than this? Such a small girl. What if she becomes ill? She could be a sickly child," Maylao says, gesturing vaguely toward Nil.

"Never sick. Look at her color," Phanvadee lifts Nil's chin to display the flush in her cheeks. "Look," and Phanvadee takes Nil's hand, showing Maylao the hardness of her fingernails. "Forty-five thousand," Phanvadee insists, waiting.

Maylao blinks slowly and raises her chin. Her head remains still while her eyes move over Phanvadee and, disregarding Nil altogether, fix on the tower of some distant *wat*.

Nil's hands appear folded in her lap. Unseen, her fingernails dig into her palm until it hurts, one of the tactics she uses when she needs to distract herself.

Maylao exhales, breaking the stillness. "Forty thousand baht," she says.

"You are most kind." Eyes cast downward, Phanvadee smiles and smoothes her dress.

"When she's worked off your debt, she can return to you." Maylao sees the momentary crease appear and disappear in Phanvadee's forehead. Is she concerned for the girl, or for herself? Maylao wonders. "Don't worry. We take good care of ours," she tells her.

Nil stares at her hands in her lap, the short half-moon fingernails and smooth skin. She imagines returning to her best-loved place, crouching in the cool green of the rice field in the early growing season and letting the muddy water run between her toes. The only sounds would be the swinging of tall reeds and the quiet chanting of grasshoppers. She digs her toes down into the ground, but gathers only dust.

In the latter part of the dry season, the light is yellow and searing hot, yet filtered through papery fingers of occasional clouds. It creates crisply defined shadows— even in the shade, one must squint at it. It's a light from which nothing can hide.

Nil waits.

Each day she awakens expecting it to be her turn. Each day she awakens with a pervasive feeling of dread.

Nil becomes closest with Rae, fourteen, who met a

woman while out walking two months before. The woman gave her a banana to eat, and Rae fell asleep. She awoke on a bare mattress at Maylao's house. Her mother has found her, but is afraid to try to take her back. Unlike Nil, Rae has softly curved hips that have helped her become one of Maylao's best workers.

The chief of police bought Rae's virginity. He is short and round, and Rae says he was not unkind. He held onto her shoulders and looked into her eyes, calling her "my child, my child," as he rocked inside her. Even so, Rae says it hurt, scraping, scraping like when they cut her and took her appendix out, but nothing like that. In the morning, Rae scrubbed her bedsheets in a tub while Maylao looked on approvingly. In the evening, Rae's price went down.

Two weeks have gone by that way, Nil waiting, tossing a ball in the street with the girls who aren't too tired to play. Maylao berates Nil to grow prettier or she'll have to drop the price: Nil's virginity for 12,500 baht.

Slowly, travelers begin to move through the village, as they normally do during this season, although they're more notable for their otherness than their numbers. Germans, Swedes, and Americans; Japanese, Taiwanese, and South Koreans. Nil wonders at the occasional new faces. The *farangs*, especially, fascinate her. She's never seen them so close up before. So much hair, like animals, such sickly skin. And wide round eyes, as if they could see what she could not, as if something frightening were always before them.

Nil thinks she's not angry with her mother. She doesn't believe in choices. She's here, at Maylao's, because she must be here for her family. Before, it was her job to help tend the rice fields. At the start of the growing season, she would step carefully around the tender shoots that grew in swampy canals, pulling the weeds that would otherwise soak up the precious water. If it weren't for their meticulous care of these fields for others, Nil's family might starve.

After the rice harvest, Nil sold produce, grown by land-owning farmers, at the market with Phanvadee. She would peel the spiked skin off of rambutans and offer the fruit to critical shoppers. She had always liked the smells of the market, the fresh chiles, pungent orchids, and rich fruits, the garlicky sauces boiling in cauldrons, and even the meat, turning rancid in the afternoon sun. But Nil disliked the market's noise, its constant urgency and motion. She preferred the quieter corner of town where she lived, at the end of a dirt road. It didn't occur to her to be bothered by the heat in her family's crooked wooden shack, and she had grown used to sweeping the dust and chasing the mice from the linoleum floor every day. From her home, Nil could see the glittering tower of Wat Thani, painted in gold leaf. It made Nil happy to think that the Buddha was watching over her.

Nil's trip to Maylao's is her first to another village. Does the Buddha watch, does he notice her now that she's gone from home? she wonders.

Nil's brothers have been working in the fields, but now, with this money, the money from Maylao, they can go on to learn trades. Now her oldest brother has bought a motorscooter, and takes his girlfriend around town in style. This is the only time the girl can touch him in public, while they ride together. It's a common sight, a young girl riding sidesaddle on the back of a motorscooter. She clings to the driver's shoulder with one hand and with the other hangs onto her purse. Her feet dangle casually just above the street, barely retaining thong sandals as her boyfriend weaves carelessly among the *songtheaws* and *samlors*. Nil imagines her brother with his girlfriend. This girl has never worked at a place like Maylao's. If she had, wouldn't everyone know it? If she had, would her brother still ride through the village with her where everyone could see? Or would he get all his touching in private? Nil wonders if she'll ever cling to a boy's shoulder on the back of his motorbike.

To Nil, her mother's debt is her own debt as well. If Nil's father came back, perhaps she wouldn't need to work for Maylao. But her father will not come back.

In front of Maylao's house, Nil perches atop a Formica table, a makeshift bar for the customers, and sips a guava-flavored yogurt drink from a paper carton. There's no one else around, but it's approaching dusk, so soon they'll arrive, the *farangs* with their glinty eyes and liquor breath, with their twisted tongues and heat-reddened faces, and the locals, too, mostly the locals. She worries about her first time, but she knows it has to come quickly so she can begin to make back the loan. She has listened quietly to the stories the other girls tell about their customers: this one's fat stomach, that one's sharp nails, the other's slobbering lips. Rae told of a tall German who tied her hands and took her from behind, and a Japanese man who tried to choke her when he couldn't reach climax.

Sometimes Nil looks at the men and imagines herself with different ones, how they would be. She shuts her eyes and listens to their strange voices as they haggle with Maylao. She opens her eyes and looks at their unfamiliar faces to see which ones she thinks are kind. It's hard for her to imagine being with anyone besides a Thai man. She finds it strange that she can imagine being with anyone at all.

A Thai man, she's certain, would allow her to undress

herself in the dark and cover herself with the sheet. The man she imagines would have smooth brown skin like hers and would be wiry and strong, not heavy on top of her. He would smell like fruit or sandalwood, and she wouldn't bleed too much when they were done. Maybe his Royal Army boots would wait outside her door. And yet, she knows this is impossible. She knows she'll be lucky if this man whose face she can't see even looks at her face or asks her name. She knows she'll be lucky if he smells clean and if he uses a condom.

Daydreaming, Nil tips her drink and spills some on her bare foot. Almost immediately one of the self-sufficient dogs that always lurks outside the house falls upon her toes to slurp up the sticky sweetness. She pulls her foot away, and the dog growls at her, its pointy ears laid back, then barks, front feet beating the dirt to the rhythm of its own voice. Shaking, Nil draws her knees up and squats in the middle of the tabletop, beyond the dog's reach. She looks at its efficient, short coat, which is brown like the dirt and covered with battle scars.

I'll have a coat like that, too, Nil thinks, if I stay here long. How long? she wonders.

Darkness bleeds through the light of dusk until the sky is black. During this season, there's no relief from the heat, not even at night. The air is close and oppressive, carrying the insistent hum of mosquitoes. The effect can be hypnotic.

Maylao smacks a mosquito that has grown fat on her punctured forearm, and her own blood smears across her skin. She watches appreciatively as Nil applies the makeup she's been taught to wear. Nil's lips are a deep plum to match the dark circles of rouge on her cheeks and powder on her eyelids. The strap of her sundress slides off of her shoulder. She looks like a child playing dress-up in her mother's clothes. But on this night, it's a look that charms.

His name is Kurt. He's short, compact, and muscular, with precisely combed blond hair. It's his first trip to Thailand, and he's heard about the beautiful soft-skinned girls with winking eyes and how gentle they are, how happy they are to wait on American men.

Back home, his girlfriend left him a while ago, due to an irreconcilable difference: Kurt wanted to be alone, and she did not. He doesn't believe that he's a selfish man; he just likes things to be a certain way. When they argued, she would turn away from him, and just seeing the stiffness of her back would fill Kurt with poison, make him want to lash out.

So now he's here, looking for a girl whose own ideas are his ideas only, at least for an hour. He's traveled from Bangkok, not wanting the hard sell of Patpong clubs. He has come alone, having heard about the untarnished girls in the village.

Kurt sits at the Formica table and drinks a bottle of beer that Maylao gave him, on the house. Maylao has made this small investment because she thinks she can sell Kurt on one of the rarer commodities. She thinks this *farang,* eager for a certain kind of experience, will buy himself a virgin.

Kurt considers Nil, who smiles widely and eagerly, yet shyly, just as Maylao has taught her. He considers the clean young girl, the freshness and promise of her open face. He considers Maylao's demand for $500. He offers $250. He pays $300.

The day before Phanvadee brought Nil to Maylao, she brought her to their village *wat* to worship. The jade Buddha that stands in the *bot* at Wat Thani is said to be the largest of its kind in Thailand. Nil and Phanvadee removed their shoes and entered the sanctuary, dropping coins in bronze buckets along the way, each donation a separate prayer. They settled onto the floor with their legs folded underneath them, their toes pointing behind them. Incense softened the air. The Buddha image, ensconced in its shrine of gold leaf, orchids, and patterned bits of porcelain, stood silently.

Phanvadee prayed that she would be guided wisely in

all her decisions, that the family would make more money, and that the Buddha would protect Nil and keep her on the right path, the Middle Way, during the difficult times to come. A monk in terra-cotta robes conferred a blessing on Nil at Phanvadee's request, a blessing acknowledging the family's need for good health and greater income. In return, Phanvadee donated money to the *wat*. Nil caught the solemnity of her mother's mood, but thought Phanvadee's private burden, as always, was the disappearance of Nil's father.

That afternoon, Phanvadee told Nil to go for a walk, to walk as far and as long as she wanted, because she was getting older, and soon she wouldn't have time for such things. She needed Nil to leave just then, in order to banish the last bits of her own regret about what she had planned. Regret was not practical.

Phanvadee could not know whether Nil understood what was going to happen, but she did know all along that her daughter would do what she asked of her when she was ready to ask. The boys would be trained; they would honor and support their mother in her old age. Nil would not be able to offer her any material comfort; she might look after a husband (One hopes, thought Phanvadee), or work in a menial job. Nil would understand that this was the practical way.

In the rain forest, Nil climbed a narrow path that she had known for years, although she had never been there without her brothers. Damp air clung to the back of her neck as she climbed. A giant earthworm, maybe ten inches long, crossed her path, and she stopped to poke it with a stick. It turned and wriggled under her inspection. Finally, she used the stick to toss it into the undergrowth beside the trail. When she reached the top and pulled herself up over the rocks, she gazed down on the forest canopy, then edged over to the mouth of the cave and waited. The sky was empty except for raptors coasting on an unseen current over the trees. The smell from within the cave was acrid and sulfurous and familiar and comforting. Her effort was quickly rewarded. It was dinnertime, and the beating of wings began with a few blind hunters, like the first tentative raindrops before a storm. Then the mass exodus from the cave was under way, and wave after wave swept out into the failing light. A wide shadow passed across the sky, then broke like shattered glass as the bats scattered after their prey. Nil flicked a green beetle off her knee. It tumbled onto a lower rock, then in a squeal and a flap of wings it was dinner. She wondered if it was worse to be the bat who could hear but never see what it ate or where it lived or who was near, or to be the beetle who knew these things all along, who could see its enemies.

Nil descended the trail in a darkness punctured only by the light of the waning moon.

Nil does not speak. The blood hammers inside her ears as she precedes Kurt into the house, past closed doors, into her room. She finds that Maylao has set orchids on the sheets and in bowls filled with water. The sweet smell turns her stomach. An electric fan, an uncommon luxury reserved only for special transactions, rotates back and forth, displacing and rearranging the dense air.

Kurt sits on the bed. As she has been taught, Nil bends down on her knees before him, unties his shoes, and slips them off his feet. Kurt looks at the shiny black of her hair. He leans forward, closer, to absorb her smell. Her shoulder blades jut out against the low back of her dress, and her spine ripples underneath her skin as she rubs his feet and ankles.

How thin and small she is. He can't help noticing.

Nil wonders if she's doing it right. "Start with the feet," Maylao had said. "*Farangs* have sensitive feet." A Thai man would never let Nil touch his feet. The feet are the lowest part, closest to the earth, unclean. While in a temple, one's feet must point away from the Buddha. Kurt's feet feel damp and callused in her hands.

"Talk to him," Maylao had said. "So he'll think you

care about what he wants. But not too much. If you talk too much he won't like it."

Before she arrived at Maylao's, Nil had begun to learn basic English in school. Maylao taught her phrases that were important to her work.

"Like this?" Nil asks, looking up at Kurt and smiling.

"That's enough," he says, and he draws her to her feet, stares into her brown eyes. He admires her skin, her youth, and thinks she could be twenty years younger than he is. The question forms in his head, but he doesn't pursue it. He begins to unbutton the front of her sundress, then changes his mind and slides the straps over her shoulders so it falls to the floor all at once.

Sometime, this has happened before, he thinks. The urge to penetrate her overwhelms him. Wait, he tells himself. It'll be that much better.

Nil stands in her underwear, a lacy black bra almost laughably padded, and matching panties. She knows what to expect from talking with Rae and the others. But knowing is different from experiencing. She knows this is her cue to begin undressing Kurt, but she can't move. The electric fan rotates toward her, and she shivers as it passes. She clenches her teeth to keep them from clacking.

Kurt pulls his T-shirt over his head. His chest is solid, but his stomach is round from beer. He has no thoughts of waiting for Nil to act. He's lost in a reverie, a recollection of some teenage misadventure that Nil's presence has somehow called to mind.

Nil looks at Kurt's chest, at the fine yellow hairs that cover it. She reaches out, with a child's curiosity, and runs her fingers over them. They're soft like the fuzz on a caterpillar. She realizes this is the closest she's ever been to a man. She giggles nervously and begins to draw her hand back.

Kurt mistakes Nil's curiosity for ardor and, grasping her hand to his chest, he pulls her toward him until she's seated on his knee. He guides her hand over his chest and across his belly. With his free arm, he reaches behind her to unfasten her bra, then runs his hand up and down the unbroken line of her back.

She felt the same as this one, Kurt thinks, like she wasn't finished growing. But her hair was shiny blond like mine, like feathers. When I was on top of her, her breath rattled like a wild bird in a cage.

Nil's skin turns clammy in response to Kurt's touch, in a show of revulsion. She thought she'd be able to block it all out, that her mind would take her elsewhere, but her mind can't seem to place her anywhere but on this white man's knee. Her shoulders slump. She's trapped. Why hadn't she known it would be this way?

The *farang* smells like milk, Nil thinks, and wrinkles her nose. The other girls had said he would. A cat could come and drink him. But there are no cats, only dogs who could tear up his limbs with their teeth. And then she chastises herself for thinking bad thoughts.

She perches awkwardly on Kurt's leg waiting, as always, to find out what will happen next. Against her hand, she feels his breathing quicken, his skin grow warm. She wants to run. What would happen if she just ran until she had to stop running? Would they follow her? Would her mother have to give the money back?

And then she's naked on her back on the narrow mattress with Kurt on his side next to her, nuzzling her neck, chewing her nipples. He's like one of them, Nil thinks. Like the dogs in the market, fighting over scraps.

Kurt pushes her hand down past his waist. His pants are unbuttoned, and she can feel how ready he is. Nil squeezes her eyes shut so she can't see what she's touching. She's unable to move, unable to do any of the things Maylao has told her she should do when it came time.

Kurt doesn't seem to mind. He removes his pants and his shorts and tosses them onto the stained linoleum floor. Straddling Nil, he rubs himself against her skin. He kisses her neck, then glides in and out between her breasts and over her lips. Part of him thinks, She's so tiny I might as well be here alone, rutting against empty sheets. But the other part thinks, She couldn't be softer if she were just born.

Finally, Kurt pushes his way inside Nil, not without some effort. She spreads her legs awkwardly when she sees it is time, but he must hold her knees apart. And it does hurt her; every motion seems to tear something, to dig at her insides. She smiles so he won't know that it hurts, and presses her fingernails into her palm.

Kurt's head is bowed toward his chest, his eyes shut, and he doesn't look at Nil's face as he moves back and forth above her. He says nothing, but exhales heavily and deeply through his nose with each forward thrust. All at once, he's overwhelmed by Nil's tightness. He sees blackness as he releases inside her.

Nil thinks of her mother. The edge of the sheet twists in her hand.

Kurt begins to dress just as Maylao knocks on the door to signal that his time is up.

Alone, Nil curls up on her side and closes her eyes. In her dream, she squats to her waist in the rice field's cool, swampy water, and she's clean.

In the triangle of sheet where her legs had spread open, there are two patches of blood. Rich red, it engulfs the white cotton, spreading and expanding, and will be hard to get out.

*   *   *

When the rains come the sky turns to gauze, and the drops fall straight down, hard and heavy, leaving their footprints in the dirt. At its height, the monsoon season can transform the streets into seas of hip-deep water. When the monsoons pass, breezes and hot sun eventually turn the roads back to dust, as if the rain had never touched them.

Nil boards a bus for the two-hour trip back to her village and back to Phanvadee. In a canvas bag slung over her shoulder, she carries an assortment of leftover makeup, a change purse containing the baht she was able to save without Maylao's knowledge—tips for good work—and a twenty-four-ounce bottle of beer. She sips the beer periodically while she waits for the trip to begin. When she first tried beer at Maylao's she found it bitter, but she grew to like the way the bubbles felt going down her throat. And the way the alcohol helped her to become separate, separate from herself, so that she could stand in the corner of her room and watch while a customer manipulated her body.

Her family's debt is finally repaid, along with some extra, but Nil has just turned fourteen and looks even younger, so she could have brought in good money for Maylao for at least two more years. Some girls choose to stay with Maylao when they no longer need to because they have no place else to go, and because she doesn't beat them. But Nil has never considered staying. She has a place to go.

When I'm home, Nil thinks, things will be different. Things will be like before.

She feels an urgency in her bladder, and since the bus is not yet full, she decides she has time to respond to it. After disembarking, she walks behind the wooden shack that serves as the station, lifts up her skirt, and squats in the dirt road. It burns. It's been burning now for a couple of weeks, but she's sure it's just fatigue from her late nights. One of the girls told her that eating raw garlic would banish the pain. Maybe she'll try that when she gets home.

From her mother's periodic letters, Nil has been able to keep up with family events. Her oldest brother, Choopong, has married—the girl on the motorscooter of course. Nil laughs to herself to think of her brother a family man. Most of the local men at Maylao's place were family men, too.

Nil's other brother, Narong, has become a monk, just recently ordained. Phanvadee wrote reverently about Narong's decision to stay beyond the three months that most young Thai men spend as novices before they move on to other work. His choice would bring great merit to the family. Nil wonders what she will bring to the family.

Although Maylao didn't allow Nil to write back, Maylao herself sent occasional notes to Phanvadee on the status of Nil's debt, and in that way Phanvadee knew that Nil received her bits of news. Nil wonders what she would have told her mother if she had been permitted to communicate with her.

"Dear Mother," Nil imagines herself writing, "Last month my friend Rae tried to escape. She ran off in the early morning darkness, but Maylao and the police chief caught her. Maylao chained Rae to her bed for two weeks, freeing her only for customers. I brought her meals. Maylao escorted her to the bathroom and shower. The lady who sold Rae got a lot of money from Maylao, so it may still be a while before Rae's allowed to go home."

Perhaps, Nil thinks, she could have told Phanvadee about how she spent her time. "Dear Mother, usually I have six or seven customers each day, although in the early part of the dry season there have been more, and in the rainy season far fewer. Most of my customers have families; they have wives who are prettier than me. If I could go to school, I might even be in a class with their children.

"I've met some *farangs*, and they don't seem too bad, although some have rough skin and scratchy faces, and I don't like their smell. Mostly, there have been men from this village and other villages nearby. The local men usually treat me well, but they don't like to use condoms, because they say it feels better when their skin touches mine. I sometimes worry about getting pregnant or sick, but if I insist, then they might leave, and I won't make the money. Maylao says never to insist on anything except payment in advance.

"One of the girls became pregnant during the dry season, and she couldn't work for a while because it made her sick. She prayed for Buddha to help her go back to work. We all prayed with her. One night she began to bleed, and the child trickled out in her blood and was no more. In thanks, we made food donations to the monks who wander the village each morning collecting their daily meals."

No, Nil supposes it was just as well that she'd been unable to write to Phanvadee. It would have been useless and inappropriate to relay any of her experiences to her mother. Nil would only have written that she prayed daily for more money and a good life for the family, and that she hoped to come home soon.

On the television at the front of the bus, a Thai soap opera plays. Nil gathers that a man became drunk and cheated on his girlfriend with another woman, then his girlfriend found out. Now he begs her to take him back, and she throws flowerpots at his head. The man is shown drinking heavily, but he never kisses a woman on screen.

The girlfriend should be happy, Nil laughs to herself. Only on TV does he cheat with another woman. In real life, he sees someone like me. The television show continues throughout her journey, with the volume turned to its maximum level so it can be heard over the plangent rumbling of the engine.

The bus passes rice fields, still flooded with the remnants of the monsoons, and fruit trees beginning to bud. Gaunt water buffalo graze by the roadside. Nil falls asleep and will sleep for the rest of the trip. At Maylao's she couldn't sleep unless there was no work, except for a few hours in the early morning. If she wasn't with a customer, Maylao wanted her outside, waiting. She has not slept this deeply in a long time.

"I think you cannot stay here," Phanvadee says, pouring hot jasmine tea. "Yesterday morning, at Wat Thani, I spoke with a fortune teller. He told me that a hell-being could bring disease and bad luck to my house, that I must do all I can to prevent it." She sits across from Nil at a small wooden table in her kitchen. "I have never had such a poor reading, especially since Narong entered the *Sangha*."

Phanvadee is genuinely frightened. The fortune teller described a hideously disfigured and unwholesome creature who would disrupt her sleep and make her ill. After hearing this prediction, Phanvadee donated money to the *wat* and prayed. But even without the bad fortune, she knows that it would be unacceptable for Nil to stay with her, so this new circumstance simply makes it easier for Phanvadee to do what she would have done anyway. "I don't believe you're this creature the fortune teller speaks of, but the hell-being can hide and take on different forms. Where you have been, you might be vulnerable to its tricks. You might bring it to my house unknowingly," she explains.

Nil can't speak. She's beyond surprise and almost beyond caring. Placidly, she wonders what difference it makes where her body is anyway.

"Go to your brother, to Narong," Phanvadee tells her. "He can help you."

That night, Nil sleeps in an empty market stall. When the sun disappears, clouds cover the stars, and she's hemmed in by the darkness. She worries about the stray dogs that scratch for food nearby, listens to their yelps and growls. She'll have to awaken and leave her place before the sun comes out, before the merchants and farmers arrive.

The next morning, she wanders the rows of stalls, fatigued and disoriented. She buys fresh garlic, a papaya, and a new bottle of beer.

Nil makes her way to Wat Thani, following its tall, gold *chedi* to the center of the village. When she arrives, the marching band from the local school, which is located on the grounds of the *wat*, is practicing noisily in the square outside the temple. Trumpets and drumbeats echo throughout the complex, playing a fractured version of the Thai national anthem. The children laugh at their unintentionally syncopated rhythms. This was Nil's school. In another time, she could have been marching with the others. Maybe she would have played a drum. Nil likes the idea of the drum because its sound is one of strength and power. If she had one she'd beat it to keep time with the throbbing of the blood in her veins.

The sanctuary is dizzyingly fragrant with orchids and incense. She would like to curl up among the flowers and lose herself there, but the Buddha's raised palm, meant to relieve Nil of all fear, seems instead to warn her away. She folds her legs underneath herself on the cool, hard floor.

A family gathered around the shrine is taking part in a merit-giving ceremony, in this case because someone has died. Three monks wearing saffron-colored robes are seated on a raised platform near the Buddha. Nil's brother, Narong, is one of them. Together, the laypeople are led by the monks in reciting the Five Precepts. Nil sits away from the others, but mouths the Precepts along with them:

"I will not take the lives of others. I will not steal. I won't engage in sexual misconduct. I won't lie. I won't drink alcohol or take drugs," she whispers mechanically.

A young woman makes Narong an offering of rice and vegetables, but he may not touch the bowl while she holds it, so she places it on a handkerchief at his feet. Other family members of the dead offer food, money, and later, candles and incense sticks to the monks. Small symbolic dishes of the same food the monks eat are placed at the feet of the Buddha image, which is draped in thick Thai silk.

After they've eaten, the monks bless the dead and the family of the dead, and then bless all who are present. No one seems to notice Nil, failing even to offer a nod in her direction. Nil wonders if the dead person is someone she knows.

Nil has seen ceremonies like this many times at Wat Thani, some for the dead, but others to celebrate a new home or a birthday, to bring the celebrants luck in this life and the next. She wonders if, when she dies, such a ceremony might be performed for her benefit.

At first, she doesn't recognize Narong. His head has been shaved, and he wears a bright orange robe draped over one arm and under the other. He chants along with the other monks and, in a voice without inflection, recites words from the Buddha's teachings.

"All living things will come to an end, like water in a dried-up stream," Nil hears Narong say. And then, "Protect one's mind from bad thoughts, otherwise one's mind will turn to enjoyment of bad ideas." He still doesn't look at Nil or acknowledge her in any way, although she imagines this last admonition was recited for her benefit. She wonders if she was wrong to come here.

When the ceremony is finished, Narong finally approaches her. His gait is quick but his demeanor solemn. He has known this moment would come, and he confronts his sister with mixed emotions. What can he possibly say that could help her? He's wrestled with the problem for days, praying and asking the Buddha for inspiration. He's acutely aware that had she not helped secure the loan from Maylao, he might not have been able to choose his ascetic way of life. His brother, Choopong, has a high-paying job in a textile mill outside of town, but Narong makes no money and has few possessions. He can help his family escape their poverty only spiritually.

"Let's talk outside." He tips his head toward the door. They leave the sanctuary and walk across the courtyard, stopping at the edge of a pool filled with lotus flowers. All around them stand angry, colorful porcelain creatures with big white teeth, warning evil spirits away from the temple.

Nil fights an urge to run away. The smooth brown skin of Narong's exposed shoulder is like a reminder. She does not want to see any more bare skin, not even her brother's, not even a monk's. She's not sure what she expected.

"Mother told me you were coming," Narong says, looking her over uncritically but noting her soiled dress and reddened eyes, her jagged and blackened fingernails. "I know you can't stay with her. I have a friend with a rooming house; you can stay there for a while, then you must get your own place."

It's the first kindness anyone has offered Nil in more than two years, and she impulsively reaches out to take Narong's hand. He steps back, flushing. How could she?

"I'm sorry," Nil says, dropping her eyes. She's forgotten, because he's her brother, that a monk may not touch a woman. She's forgotten because she's grown accustomed to touching men.

"Mother told me about the sage's prediction. You smell like drink," Narong says. He knows he shouldn't judge, so he says it like a fact rather than an accusation.

"What can I do?" Nil asks.

"You must not speak of it, any of it. I'll give you my blessing. Have you continued to follow the teachings of the Buddha? Have you tried to adhere to the Middle Way?"

"Of course. I prayed every day, for more money and a good life for the family, and that I might come home sooner. I offered food to the monks. None of this is my fault," Nil insists.

"There is no fault. It's fated. In your heart, you are good," Narong reassures her, and he believes this to be true.

"I can't be mad at Mother. She needed the money. It's only a body, not my soul," Nil says, as though she's still trying to convince herself.

Narong isn't willing to address the details or to designate blame. There are too many shades of gray. Phanvadee prays and gives money to the *wat;* she's a good Buddhist. "You can't choose your position in this life; it's the result of what came before. But you can help influence the next one. Your body, as you know, is of no consequence. It is temporary," he says.

Nil wipes perspiration from her forehead. The sun beats down on them, but Narong is cool and dry.

On Narong's advice, Nil rents a room from his friend, and takes a job selling silk sarongs in the market. "I have much experience selling things," she tells the man who hires her. "I'm obedient and reliable, and I come from a good family. My brother is in the *Sangha*."

The man will pay her seventy-five baht per week. At Maylao's, she made more than that in a day, but of course, it wasn't hers to keep. She agrees to start the next morning at dawn.

Nil folds and stacks and straightens the sarongs at her table in the market and waits for customers to come to her. Older women walk slowly by her table at a distance, eyeing the goods and plotting bargains together, but only a few of them stop. One woman touches the cloth as she passes, and closes her eyes in judgment.

"Fair quality," she says.

Nil unfolds the sarong and holds it up for her to see better. "Would you like to buy?" Nil asks, prepared to negotiate.

The woman narrows her eyes. "I know you," she says. "You're Phanvadee's girl. I don't see you in the *wat* with your mother?"

"I go after work, and she goes early," Nil says quietly, and drops the cloth back onto the table.

"I haven't heard her speak of you. Your brothers are doing well, though," she says.

Why is this woman bothering her? So nosy. "Yes, ma'am, they bring us great merit."

"Merit, you'll surely need," the woman says. "I hear

you were in Khorat, visiting family. You were gone for a long time. I have a cousin in Khorat. Ananda. Do you know him?"

Yes, at Maylao's, she knew him. "I don't think so. I'll tell my mother you sent your wishes," Nil says, trying to turn away.

"So, you're selling sarongs now. Were you selling sarongs in Khorat, too?" the woman asks. "There have been whispers about you during the past two years," she continues, "and now you're back, the whispers turn to roars." She glances down at the fabric on the table, then back at Nil's face. "I'm sorry. I don't need any of these sarongs. They're not the quality I want."

"I don't know what you mean," Nil tries to counter, but the woman has already slipped away, and Nil feels the redness of her face and the wetness on her cheeks. She sees the woman gathering with others among the stalls, pointing and whispering. "But my body doesn't matter," Nil protests to herself. "It's only my soul that counts."

Nil sells only one sarong that day, and the next day she sells none. The man who hired her warns her that she needs to do better, or he might have to let her go. That evening, after the market shuts down for the night, she wanders the dirt streets of her village and drinks beer from a bottle. Instead of going to her rented room, she turns down the street toward Phanvadee's house. At the end of the road, at the border of the rice field she has worked with her mother and brothers, she stands outside the house, but doesn't knock on the door, doesn't go in.

On an impulse, Nil leaves the road and wades into the rice field. The growing season is just beginning, so Nil's feet sink in the muddy water, disturbing the new grasses, and mosquitoes buzz in her ears. Stopping in the deepest, swampiest area she can find, she squats and splashes water on her face. Her half-empty beer bottle, carelessly dropped, is sucked partway into the mud. Here, in her best-loved place, she stretches her legs in front of her and lays flat on her back in the cool water. The musty, green smell of the young shoots and the feel of the mud and water closing around the edges of her body fill her senses, and she is calm, at least for now. She turns herself to face Wat Thani's spire. It's still visible in the growing darkness.

A Note to My Translator

Ed Park

Dear M.,

Thank you for your letter. We are doing well here, relaxing as best we can, but a few of your queries anent the ongoing translation of *Mexican Fruitcake* (as you insist on rendering the title) disturb me profoundly, to put it mildly. Time prevents me from undertaking my own englishing of the thing, and since you had been recommended by a (once-) trusted friend, I agreed to have you do the deed. I understand that "French" is an obscure and obsolete tongue, but we must have something like standards, yes? To go along with some of your suggestions (not to mention your outright, brazen, unnoted blunders) would be akin to an automobile manufacturer issuing cars with only one deflated wheel and no brakes to speak of. To wit:

page one: The novel begins with a hailing of the muse and a quick history of man's moral awakening, mastery of his surroundings, and subsequent fall from grace. In my version. In *your* version, a man named Mr. Henry enters a flat in London and discovers that his wife is taking stomach medication. You go on to say that it is raining outside and that an oblong (?) Quaker youth is on a "hickey spree." I respectfully suggest you put aside whatever hallucinogens you might be keeping on your nightstand and concentrate on the text I have provided you with.

page two: Why "knickers"? Wherefore "fugitive uranium"? Why not call a spade a spade—or, as the case may be, a rubbery bathtub ornament a rubbery bathtub ornament?

page seven: Who is Solomon Eveready? What is he doing in my book?

page eight: You asked, in your letter, what sort of chess pieces I had in mind when I wrote this scene. Were they carved of wood, you asked, or ivory, or were they simply molded from plastic? I cannot answer this question for you, since there are no chess sets (and hence no chess pieces) in the meticulously researched milieu of my novel—that milieu being the incredibly serious, hands-pressed-in-a-gesture-of-prayer inner world of a man who sits alone and dundrearied off the western coast of Madagascar.

To add insult to injury, you muse that the novel might be strengthened if you—you, my *translator!*—"quietly added some minor details," such as "half a page or so" (kindly submitted for my inspection) in which you identify the chess pieces one by one, explaining how the tall one that bears the likeness of General Grant is the king of the "Union" side, how the eight men with bugles are pawns, etc. Even if I were to do the unthinkable and allow you to mention a chess set resting on my delicate "open-leafed end table" (or, as you have it, "dog"), why in God's name would you make it a Civil War chess set? And why are the pieces arranged in such a way that, when viewed sideways, the word "GOLF-NUT" is spelled?

page eight, a little lower down: The doctrine of transubstantiation has nothing to do with pinball.

page nine: Solomon Eveready reappears, this time smoking cut-grade reefer and imitating a trout. Explain this to me. Explain also the presence of scuba gear that "reeks of melon."

page ten: Only ten pages into my novel and already all seems lost. I no longer recognize characters, points of plot, dialogue. I frankly have no idea what the words before me mean. Here you present a heated argument between two nuns (and are they truly *robot* nuns?), both of whom speak some weird amalgam of Cantonese and the International Morse Code. Can you help me? Please?

*   *   *

So ends my criticism of the first chapter of your version of my novel. I have neglected, for brevity's sake, to note all the boners that litter every page of your rendition— solecisms that would be hilarious were not the matter at hand of such obvious importance. I am an unknown commodity in America; this is the book that will either build my stateside reputation or consign me evermore to the coldest remainder bin at the local Price Club. The minute I receive your letter indicating that you were pulling my leg, as they say, I will laugh and benignly destroy *my* letter to my American publisher, in which I go into excruciating detail about my proficiency in the deadly Brazilian martial art known as *capoeira*, and the stylish havoc I have been known to wreak.

Until then,
I am,
Hans de Krap

Wasn't That It?

Todd Dorman

Peace was all there was in that place. There were trees that whispered to each other about peace in the afternoon and all through the night, and there was clean air to whisper it with, and hardly even a blue jay to clatter things up. There was peace available at all times. All you had to do was let it happen.

And the opportunity was enforced. On the one or two occasions I tried to find a cheap substitute with a razor or a piece of rope, huge Mexican nurses appeared without speaking and held me down until I heard the wind outside or remembered my name.

Frank was never happy with me after I tried that. When he came to visit me back in the Hall I felt just like a prophet—one who had seriously fucked things up, the way some of them did, and who then had to give an account to the One True God. Not that I thought Frank was the One True God. The point is that he could get just about as pissed. He would show up out of the blue and let the door bang shut, and sit right down on the white bed without saying a word. I'd be standing in the corner with my arms crossed over my chest. There'd be a smell in the room like lightning had struck the earth.

"Here we are again, man," Frank would say. He'd point out the window at the trees. "Don't you like it out there? Don't you at least want to stay out of *here*?"

I wouldn't say anything. Frank would pat the mattress beside him. I'd go over and sit down, and then Frank would look me over.

God, those looks! Sometimes they made me feel like my balls would collapse. Frank was my brother. He knew everything I'd pissed away: marriage, fatherhood, career. He knew all the times I'd tried to piss away my own life, too. All that potential, it weighed ten thousand pounds and hit you on the small of the back—*wham!*—or right behind the knees. It hit you when Frank looked at you with his weird brown eyes, so sad and loving and unbelievably angry at the same time, like Christ's. Frank knew everything I'd done and he still kept showing up: that's what gave him such power over me.

"You broke the rules, man," Frank would say.

"I guess I did," I'd say. "I'm sorry, Frank."

Frank would wait for me to say something else. But I wouldn't say anything else. I wouldn't do anything except sit there and look at the floor. I had an idea that maybe I was supposed to be saying or doing something else, but I didn't know what it was.

After a while Frank would tell me he was going out for a walk to let me think about things. He'd get up and tap on the little square window in the door and the orderly would let him out. But when he came back I'd just be sitting in the same place I always sat.

You have a lot of time to think in those blank rooms, sitting there looking out the sealed Plexiglas windows. At night you stare at the walls till you feel you know the guy who painted them. Or your mind just turns white. One of the things I thought was: If this is peace then maybe I need something else entirely. I'd had plenty of peace. I'd had enough peace to last a lifetime. I was sick to death of peace.

I was sick of doctors, too. There were armies of doctors in that place.

"Why did you try to take your life?" they'd ask me. "What is it about yourself you dislike so much?"

As if anyone could answer those questions!

When they released me back to my cabin for what turned out to be the last time it was spring, and the woods had begun to dry out. The air was still and warm. It felt good to just sit in my own cabin and look out the window. I took an occasional walk out to the electric fences.

It occurred to me that I might visit with some of the weirdos in the common area—or maybe I had that thought after Frank let it slip that the common area was coed. I could hardly believe my ears when he said that. I hadn't seen any women around, but Frank said they lived in a different part of the Forest.

"What part, Frank?" I said. "Over by the gingerbread house?"

I'd only expected to see other men up there—men who had washed up like I had, on a tide of wealthy relatives. But if women had washed up too . . . I hadn't known a woman in my whole life who wasn't light-years ahead of me, in terms of evolution. I thought maybe I'd find a new wife up there, one who could understand and save me.

Frank spotted the wheels turning in my head right away.

"I wouldn't count on anything, man," he warned. "You probably want to lay off for a little while."

"Of course," I said. "Obviously I'm going to be laying off for a little while."

Frank looked at me a moment. "Shit," he said.

"What?" I asked. "What is it, Frank?"

But he would close his mouth, and that would be it.

Frank had a stern and beautiful mouth. He had a beautiful face, too. His face made women do crazy things, but he sure hadn't taken advantage of it the way I would have done. That's why he had it and I didn't, maybe. It was an honest face. When we were kids I was able to learn important things just by looking at it.

The women's cabins were off limits, which meant that technically I wasn't supposed to follow them home, the way I sometimes used to do, and ask if I could come into their lives. Instead I was supposed to go to this place called the living room, which is what they called the common area. But I didn't mind so much. There was only one place for you to go, so you didn't have to wonder what else was going on. You didn't have to worry about different bars or parties or parts of town. It was all right there for you: no decisions.

The living room was about a four-minute walk from my cabin. It turned out to be a ski-lodge type of place, with oak furniture, a fireplace, a pool table, pinball machines, video games, and a big television set. It was like a regular resort except for the weirdos and the fact that there were three-hundred-pound nurses standing in the corners. The nurses didn't say anything, though. After a while you forgot about them.

There were maybe fifteen people around the first time I went in. With a couple of exceptions it wasn't as bad as

I expected. There was a range of people in there. First there were people who seemed to have it pretty much together. Then there were people who took a minute to nail down—maybe they twitched, or spat on the floor once in a while.

And then there were the cartoon characters. For example, there was a woman in pink cutoffs who couldn't stop dancing. Her muscle tone was something to behold. She was almost always in there. I wondered how she slept—drugs, I guess. There was a guy who talked only in numbers. He inflected everything with a lot of emotion, though, so he wasn't a bad person to talk to. He reminded me of an acting class. He said his name was Ninety-eight, but I heard other people call him Mick. There was a chubby little woman who swayed back and forth with her mouth open like she was singing in a choir, only no sound came out.

Over by the pinball machines there was an actual dwarf. He was just sitting around, staring into the woods with a kind of medicated expression. When he saw me he came right over. He looked up at me with a spacey grin and told me his name was Roadhouse. He asked me to play pinball.

I thought, what the hell, pinball. I followed Roadhouse as he waddled over to the pinball machines on his short little legs. I watched him pull out a milk crate from under the *Indiana Jones and the Last Crusade* machine. He set the milk crate upside down on the ground. He stepped up on top of it so that his shoulders were just higher than the rim of the machine. He hit the two-player button.

"Lemme tell you what I'm doing in here," Roadhouse said, pulling back the plunger.

"Oh, that's okay," I said. "You don't have to do that."

Roadhouse didn't seem to hear me. He tapped at the flipper buttons. "See, I got this thing," he slurred, "where I just gotta *punch* someone. If I'm not doped up, I mean. I really gotta *tag* 'em. Right there"—he reached over and tapped my thigh without taking his eyes off the game. "I can't hold off unless I'm on this stuff pretty good. Just really gotta *tag* 'em. I don't know why."

He held the ball on one of the flippers, considering. "Nobody can tell me why."

Roadhouse confided to me that learning to punch people in the thigh had actually been a big step for him. He used to punch people in the groin, he said. He'd learned the thigh punch over in the high security wing of Evergreen Hall. He said they were working now to transfer his punches to a fake thigh that he would be able to carry around with him. This dwarf Roadhouse pretty much split his time between the Hall and the Forest, because he hadn't completely switched to the fake thigh and he couldn't stand being doped up all the time. No doctor could tell him why he punched, and no doctor could tell him how to stop.

The drugs didn't affect Roadhouse's pinball game, though. I found that out right off. Roadhouse slaughtered me. After we'd played two balls I started wondering how he'd play if he wasn't on medication.

When Roadhouse had won his second bonus he stopped and looked up at me. "So what's your deal, man?"

"My what?"

"Your deal," he said. "What are you in for?"

"Oh," I said. "I have no idea."

Roadhouse just nodded. "Okay," he said, and left it alone. That made me like him, I have to admit. He seemed like a good guy to me.

I kept looking around for the women. There were some there, but none I thought I'd be interested in. The dancer had a great body, although I was pretty sure she'd be too much for me to handle even if I could learn how to dance. There were a couple of quiet women over near the TV, but they didn't look like they wanted to talk to anybody. They weren't pretty, either. There was this tall sort of manly woman in a white shirt who seemed fine, but she gave off the dried-up air of a schoolteacher. I hoped there'd be others later on. But I wasn't having such a bad time just being in there, just being around some people. I hadn't been in a crowd in a long time. You could tell some of the others liked it too. You could tell some of them practically lived in there.

I thought I'd play a little more pinball with Roadhouse. He was a dwarf, yes, but what the hell—he was a great player. And he was game: Roadhouse would play as long as you would. He killed me twelve games straight.

By game thirteen it was getting dark out. I hadn't taken any medication or eaten anything all afternoon. I told Roadhouse I had to go. Roadhouse said okay and shook my hand with his tough little mitt. It felt like a little kid's hand except it was all rough and muscled; that freaked me out a little.

On the way out I saw a woman who must have come in while we were playing. She was a beautiful dark-haired woman with a large and beautiful head. She was playing pool. She had to wear a neck brace and move around the table very slowly. Her game took forever because she moved so slow. It kind of added to her beauty in a way, though, like she was drifting around under water.

I forgot about leaving. I sort of sauntered over to her, trying to drift like she was doing. When I got over there I said something like, "Jeez, you have kind of a big head, don't you?"

She looked at me. She slowly, sadly, gigantically nodded.

I was in one of my states, and blinded by love on top

of everything. I kept repeating my observation every few minutes because it seemed new, and in this way I drove her from me.

But conversations often went on like that up there. You'd be talking to someone and Roadhouse would come and sneak a punch to your thigh, or a deformity would catch your attention, or you'd fall in love, or lose track of yourself, or maybe all four at once. You could end up making someone hate you when all you wanted from them was love, and for them to tell you things would be all right. In that sense it was a lot like any other place, I guess.

Frank had to stop coming in regularly because of work. He told me there was nothing he could do about it. At first I missed him when he didn't come but then it was okay. He'd been asking a lot of questions. He wanted to hear what was going on—who I was spending time with and all that. I told him about Roadhouse and everybody else. I knew he'd be hearing reports from the staff or whatever, but I figured it wouldn't hurt to hear my side of things.

He always listened carefully, without moving, so that I felt I should go on talking. One time I even told him I was liking it okay there at Evergreen.

Frank didn't seem surprised. "That's good," he said. "Don't like it too much, though."

"Oh no. I won't like it too much."

He looked at me. "You won't be in here forever," he said.

"Sure, Frank," I said, wondering where else I could possibly ever be. "I know that."

Frank looked at me in a way that made me want to ooze into the couch. Finally he shrugged. He got up to go and said he'd see me later.

"All right, Frank," I said. "Don't be a stranger!"

That was just something our mom used to say to her friends, I think, but it caused Frank to stare at me with what seemed like a fanatical expression—from what I could glean by my peripheral vision, at least.

"I won't," he said quietly. "Okay, Zeke. Okay. See you later."

I just kept my eyes on the TV. For some reason I had to do that in order to keep from screaming.

And then there turned out to be this other woman, a woman named Linda, who didn't come around so much. She had a low, fragile voice and red hair. It took a few tries to get her to talk.

I actually got her to giggle first. I was just trying to

make her feel comfortable. I said my name, and told her I didn't know what I was doing there at Evergreen. She thought that was funny. Linda had a giggle like an ascending scale. It jumped way up high and then dropped down on the other side of whatever she was laughing at.

She giggled and told me *she* was at Evergreen because she sometimes screamed obscenely at nobody in particular.

"Oh," I said. I nodded in what I hoped was an encouraging way.

Linda smiled nervously at me. She reached out and deftly tweaked my nose.

"It's just that I get mad, that's all. I get really really pissed. You know?"

"Sure," I said. "Everybody gets mad."

Linda giggled. She told me she'd been dumped at Evergreen by her husband, her first love, her high school sweetheart. He was in Mexico with another man now, she said.

"Another *man*," I said. "That's no good."

"Nope." She tweaked my nose again. "You're bastards, you men. Shmuck-fucks."

"Not all of us," I said.

"Most of you," Linda corrected me. "A large percentage."

Linda didn't seem to have many friends at Evergreen. She knew Roadhouse, though not well because she didn't like pinball. She told me that people there didn't like her. They'd endured a lot of anger just for being what they were, most of them; they didn't need any more.

But I wanted Linda to marry me even more than the woman with the gigantic head. When she lost her mind her eyes were shot through with light. I couldn't help imagining what it would be like to have her all to myself when she was like that—the sweet torture of it, all that attention and rage directed into one place, like an orgasm through a wounded penis.

You couldn't predict when it would happen, though. Linda couldn't predict it herself.

"It's more like a dream," she told me once. "Like one of those dreams you have where you're in charge, you know what I mean?"

"Sure," I said—though I hadn't had any dreams like that, as far as I could remember.

The first time I saw her go at it was a night shortly after we met. She was in the living room gesturing obscenely and thrusting her hips. Everyone else was standing or sitting rigidly and trying not to pay attention. No one was talking. The nurses had stepped a little ways out of the corners. No one was moving but Linda, and she was really going for it. Her hair was in her face. She was wearing a long blue flowered cotton skirt that whipped around her legs.

"*Pig* penis!" she was yelling.

She swiveled her hips roundly, in a rough approximation of that animal's sexual thrust. "Piggy piggy penis!"

"Horse penis!" she yelled. Spit flew from her mouth. "You're a goddamn *bull* penis!"

Then she stopped. She seemed to change her mind, to realize she was going in the wrong direction completely.

"*Chicken* penis," she said softly. That seemed to be more the idea she was after. She tossed her red hair from her face and went on.

"You're a chicken penis," she said. She made tiny masturbatory pinching motions. "Chicken penis! *Chicken penis! Chick*-en! *Pe*-nis! *CHICKEN PENIS!*" At this crescendo she tore off her shirt, grabbed her large freckled breasts, and rounded off with a *"FUCK YOU, CHICKEN PENIS!"* that rang shrilly off the flagstone fireplace.

The room was silent except for the occasional bells and pings from the pinball machines. Linda looked around. No one looked back except me. I smiled back in a kind of drunken way, but I don't think she noticed. She just picked up her T-shirt and pulled it on over her head. She muttered an apology and shuffled meekly toward the door.

I followed her out of the room with my heart pounding. I couldn't help it. Or probably I could have helped it but

I didn't want to. She was walking pretty fast into the woods. I thought about calling to her, but then I just started walking.

There was no moon. Trees slipped past in the dark. I saw her heading toward a group of cabins about thirty yards ahead. She went inside one of them. The lights went on, and then they went off. It was almost pitch dark. I glanced back toward the lit windows of the living room to make sure I knew where I was.

When I turned toward the cabins again I bumped into a nurse's huge white chest. I took a step back and looked up at his face.

Crickets seemed to fade in around us. I began to sweat.

"Hi," I said.

The nurse didn't say anything. He stood there breathing. You could see the white breath flowing out of his dark nostrils. His white uniform and the whites of his eyes caught the light of the living room, but his skin caught none of it.

"I was just taking a walk," I explained.

The nurse folded his big arms.

"I guess I'll go back then," I said. "So. Okay. Good night."

And I jogged back up the path.

*　　*　　*

I didn't see Linda for a few days after that. Then one morning I found her sitting on a stool by the old Asteroids machine. She waved me over.

"You followed me the other night," she said.

"Sort of," I admitted.

She gave me a critical look and tapped idly at one of the Fire buttons. "What are you, anyway? A lurker? A deviant? A rapist?"

That held me up for a second. "What if I am?" I said. I eyed her in a way I thought would seem dangerous. "Maybe I am."

Linda shook her head sadly. The skin around her eyes looked tired and worn thin. "You poor baby," she said to me. "You poor child."

"What," I said.

She touched my arm. "I'm very sorry."

"For what?" I said. I didn't mind her touching me, but she didn't seem to be in a position to be giving me that particular brand of sympathy.

"For whatever happened."

"I'm not a rapist," I informed her.

She rolled her eyes. "I *know* that."

"I mean, I wasn't even trying to be one."

"Of course you weren't." She spoke so tenderly, we might have been in one of those rooms in hospitals where they incubate the newborn babies. "Of course you weren't."

"What I *used* to do," I told her, "was follow women, sometimes. Just to try to get to know them, you know." I paused and wiped my hands on my jeans. "That's *one* of the things I used to do," I added, as if that might clarify things. "But I only did it if I really wanted to get to know the person."

"I see," Linda said.

"I never followed anyone I hadn't talked to first," I explained.

This was all more or less true, by the way. That's how I'd operated. Sometimes things worked out, too. Sometimes they didn't, but it's surprising what some people will convince themselves of to avoid being alone.

"Yes, well, please don't do it to me," Linda was saying. "I don't want anyone following *me* around."

But her whole body seemed to loosen up right then, to soften, as though I'd said something that had transformed all her muscle tissue into goose down. I wondered what it was. I hoped, for once, that I might be able to say it again.

I kept Roadhouse up to date on the Linda situation. Roadhouse was more fun to update than Frank, who listened with a sad expression until I didn't want to say another word to him ever again. I couldn't bear to tell Frank what was going on because I knew it made him unhappy to hear about it.

Roadhouse listened, but he was a pessimist. He didn't have much hope for Linda and me. He'd been around for a while, and as far as he could remember no romance had ever worked out between anybody in the whole place. Even all the doctors were divorced, Roadhouse said.

I asked Roadhouse if he'd ever fallen for someone at Evergreen.

"Sure," he said. He stood straight on his milk crate and whacked the side of the Indiana Jones. "You know, a couple of flings."

"Oh," I said.

"Nothing even started to pan out."

"I see."

"You think I'm full of shit," Roadhouse observed. His glazed eyes followed the pinball.

"No I don't," I said.

"Sure you do. You think I'm up to here with it." He whacked my chest with the back of his hand while the ball was popping around the Temple of Quadruple Points.

"No," I said. "Hey, listen—"

"I've had my share," Roadhouse said simply. And he just kept playing. He didn't seem to care if I swallowed this claim or not. It was just out there for me to take if I wanted to, like a weather forecast or a communion wafer.

So I took it, I guess. I believed him.

Frank was still trying to change his work schedule. I wasn't too concerned about that, though. I liked to see him in a certain way, but his visits weren't much fun for either of us. Frank didn't ask many questions about Linda or even watch me too closely. He seemed to be waiting for something. I had no idea what it was, and he didn't tell me. I didn't know whether it was something to do with Linda or something else. But sometimes I would begin to tell him about this or that—maybe a pinball game, or a hawk I'd seen in the woods, or something Linda had said—and he'd turn to me with a look in his eyes full of hope and like he was glad to see me, and I'd want more than anything to tell him whatever it was he wanted to hear. But I'd have to tell him whatever little thing it was I was telling him, and his eyes would fade back, and both of us would be disappointed.

I didn't know what he was after, but I was getting sick of wondering. I wasn't doing anything wrong or even against the rules. Things seemed pretty good, over all. I had things to do. It seemed like a good time in life. It was more like I was waiting to see what would happen next.

One of the first things that happened next was Frank told me my wife and daughters said hello. It was the first I'd heard from them in about two years, I guess. They were all living with another man now.

Frank looked at me to see what I would do. I could feel him watching. I could see his lean, sad face out of the corner of my eye. I could hear him breathing through his nose.

I just kept looking out at the trees. I thought for a moment. Then I nodded.

"Tell them I said hello back, then," I said.

Frank didn't say anything. I didn't say anything either. It seemed as though I was supposed to be saying something else, but I didn't know what it was.

Finally Frank said okay. He nodded like I had just made a decision. He got up to go. He said good-bye and hugged me and went out and got in his truck and drove away, and then something was over but I didn't know what it was. Frank had told me hello from these people. I had said hello back. Wasn't that it? There had to be something else for Frank to react the way he had. I sat in my cabin and wondered what it was.

Then at the Fourth of July barbecue Linda told me her husband was coming back. We were eating hot dogs and drawing unbroken potato chips out of red, white, and blue bags, and the living room walls were decorated with paper fireworks. We were all drinking cream soda. And Linda was telling me how this guy, her husband, would be back for her in September.

I just chewed my hot dog and told Linda it didn't matter to me; I had returned to the concept of time popular with dogs and children.

Linda sighed and touched my hair. "Poor baby," she said.

"Shit," I said. "Have a hot dog."

"I don't want a hot dog."

"Okay, then."

She tweaked my nose. "I want to go for a *walk*."

"All right." I set my hot dog down in a little pool of sunlight on the windowsill and offered her my arm.

You could go for coed walks if you didn't go near any cabins and you didn't mind nurses following you at barely discreet distances. As soon as we started out a huge guy with a red bandanna on his head fell in line about ten yards behind us. Linda giggled and waved at him like a little girl. The nurse didn't wave, but he dropped back ten more yards. We walked through the woods, talking and looking at the trees, and before we knew it we were down on the lawn by the fence. We were done talking, but that was okay. And then Linda stopped walking and started mumbling. I could tell by her eyes that she was falling into herself.

I looked around. Our nurse was at the edge of the woods, just out of sight. He was probably watching. What the hell, I thought: let him watch.

Linda was talking under her breath. "Limpcock!" she murmured. "Soggystick!"

I moved in front of her. She didn't seem to recognize me. But her eyes flickered and flamed up.

"Flaccid-dick!" she spat, into my face. "F-Flopping Peter!"

I moaned and dropped to my knees. Linda's head disappeared into the sun.

"You're boneless!" she shouted down at me.

"Yes," I said. "Oh, yes."

"Jellydick!"

"Oh. Oh, *wow*!"

"YOU!" she yelled. "You *cowardly*!"

"Yes!"

"De-FLATED!"

"Oh, yes!"

"N! N! N—NUB!"

"Oh," I murmured. "Oh."

Afterwards Linda sighed and stared down at me. She shook her head and closed her eyes, then opened them.

Her face was transformed from an accusing mass of anger into a radiant smile.

"Hello," she said brightly.

I cleared my throat. I was kneeling on the grass with my pants all sticky.

"Hi," I said.

"That was *wonderful*," she said. She touched my shoulder softly.

I stood up, blinking. "It was?"

"You bet. Uh huh. Wow." She glanced down at my pants. "I guess it wasn't bad for you either. Or"—Linda giggled—"was it *scary*?"

"No," I said. "Not scary."

"*I* didn't know you wanted this," Linda said.

I shrugged, blushing. I felt twelve years old.

"Well I must say—you were *terrific*."

"Thanks. You were too. Where do you get all those words, anyway?"

Linda giggled and made a little curtsy. Then she frowned at me. "Are you okay?" she asked. "You don't look okay."

"Sure. I'm okay."

I felt like throwing up. People I thought I'd left behind came, completely uninvited, into my head.

"Maybe—some shade," I said. An ex-girlfriend, someone who I happened to know was dead, drifted through my brain in a lavender cocktail dress.

"Okay," Linda said. She took my arm and led me slowly toward the shade.

That happened a few more times throughout the summer. Once or twice the nurses stopped us, but they couldn't always tell what we were doing in time.

Whenever Linda started up I couldn't help going along with her. Afterwards I always felt like I'd been submerged in a latrine. But Linda was always talky afterwards. She took to asking me questions. Most of them I couldn't answer: what was I doing there, how had I lost my money, what had happened to all these people I'd known. Sometimes she reminded me her husband was coming back. His name was Tom, she said.

"Tom," I repeated. I couldn't seem to remember ever hearing that word before.

She asked me what I was expecting to happen with us. I took it as a metaphysical question. I assumed we would just live together there on the grass, not changing at all, telling each other the same terrible things over and over. But that never seemed like the right thing to say.

Instead I said, "I guess that'll be it."

Linda giggled a sad little minor scale. She reached up through the sunlight to stroke my hair.

Frank's visits grew shorter during the summer, I guess because there was less to say. He must have known what was going on, but he didn't ask.

We watched a lot of TV together. Sometimes I could feel him watching me while I watched TV, and that made me uncomfortable. But I knew that all I would have to do was keep looking at the screen, and then eventually he would leave. That almost always worked.

When fall came Linda's husband drove up and broke my heart from the cabin of his big white BMW. Linda leaned in through the window and gave him a kiss on the cheek. She looked all nervous and churned up inside. I guess I couldn't blame her; all that time she'd been talking to him and now here he was. He got out and she gave him a big bosomy hug. I knew exactly how he felt, too, because I had been inside that hug myself.

He was wearing a navy blazer and jeans and a white shirt that looked like it had been ironed seconds before. His cheekbones were lean and hateful. I watched him take her in his arms and begin explaining, I suppose, how he'd been crazy to ever leave her for the guy he'd run off to Mexico with.

I knew things would go badly for them. But there wasn't anything I could do about a man like that. I steered clear until they drove away, and then I went into the living room.

Roadhouse was in there. He grabbed his milk crate and started a game and asked me if I'd really been expecting things to pan out.

I looked down at him. Here was my only friend in the world besides my brother, a dwarf with a punching disorder, standing at a pinball machine on an upside-down milk crate so he could see over the glass. He was killing me, too. And he was asking if I had expected things to work out between me and Linda, the woman with the rich husband, the woman who'd gotten me off by calling me all manner of cocksucker, and whom I'd come to know outdoors and in public spaces so as to avoid the cameras and big Mexican nurses that watched us while we slept.

"No," I lied. "Not really."

Instead of going back to my cabin that night I went out to the lawn by the fences. It was a cold September night. There was a full moon that lit up everything like in a dream. When I looked behind me I could see two nurses standing at the edge of the woods in their bright white clothes with their arms crossed.

I let out a big sigh and lay down on the grass. The dew was already there. It soaked right through to my underwear, fresh and cold. I looked at the moon. I could see the face in the moon, and I could also see the rabbit in the moon. I could switch back and forth from face to rabbit whenever I wanted. I've always been able to do that, ever since Frank first showed me the rabbit when I was a kid.

I lay on my back, switching from face to rabbit to face to rabbit for a long time. The moon moved slowly across the sky, obscured occasionally by the mist of my breath.

But eventually I felt slow heavy footsteps in the ground, and then the two nurses were looming over me. One of them blocked the moon. His head was a circle of blue-white light.

I closed my eyes. But when I opened them the nurses were still there.

They motioned for me to stand up. When I didn't move they slid their big hands under my back and lifted me into a sitting position. They waited a moment to see if I would stand. Then they put a hand under my arms and lifted me to my feet. They stood me up, experimentally, and seemed to decide between them that they'd have to carry me. So they carried me, back into the quiet paradisiacal dark of the woods, back to my cabin, back home, with my feet skimming the underbrush every few yards.

Frank was waiting for me there. He had some sandwiches and ginger ale ready. He was glad to see me, I could tell.

He took me inside and we sat in front of the TV, eating sandwiches and sipping glasses of ginger ale. There was a college basketball game on. We watched with the sound off and the crickets singing through the windows. Frank asked me how I was doing.

"Fine," I told him.

He nodded. I could tell he was happy with me for not having taken any drastic measures. The truth was, I'd thought about trying to end it all right in front of a camera. But I hadn't done it. I don't know why I hadn't done it. I just hadn't. That's just how it was and God knows why.

"You knew her husband was coming back?" Frank asked.

"Yeah," I said. He hadn't asked about Linda in a long time. I knew he was just wondering, though. Frank wasn't the kind of guy to rub anything in your face.

"Yeah, yeah, yeah," I said.

We watched the players dribble up and down the court. We watched them pass, shoot, miss, and score. The ball went back and forth. The players kept it up. The crickets kept doing their stuff, too. Frank and I sat there. Nobody was quitting.

After a little while Frank patted me on the shoulder a couple of times. He gave my shoulder a little squeeze.

"Listen, man, I'm sorry," he said.

"Oh—forget it," I said. "You can't tell with women, I guess."

Frank laughed. He had a deep, throaty laugh like a pirate. It made the couch cushions vibrate.

It seemed as though we were sitting there for hours and hours, drinking ginger ale. The game was on cable. There weren't any commercials. My stomach was getting all knotted up from the ginger ale and thinking about Linda lying under the trees with the sun on her.

Suddenly a tear splashed off my nose and right into my glass of ginger ale. We both saw it go in. Frank and I looked at each other.

"Hey," Frank said. "Nice shot."

"Two points," I said.

"Two points," Frank agreed. He was watching to make sure I was all right.

I cleared my throat and stared at the screen, and I was all right. Okay, I thought. I am doing fine. And then just like that I wasn't all right. I dropped my ginger ale onto the carpet and it stayed right there. I ducked my head between my knees. I didn't know what was happening. I'd had other relationships that hadn't worked out—all of them, in fact, if you want to get technical—but none of them had hit me like this. I thought I might cough up my heart.

Frank laid his hand on my shoulder and left it there

while I let everything drain out. In the background the crickets went on. Every once in a while Frank gave my shoulder a squeeze. "All right," he said. "Okay."

His voice sounded like it was coming over a radio. But I was glad he was there, that's for sure. His hand stayed right there on my shoulder. It was getting warm where his hand was. I started sweating. I kept leaking sweat and snot and salt water onto the carpet. Frank kept talking behind me. The more he talked the more the distance between us seemed to close.

I started sweating all over. The drops were huge. I felt like I was sweating blood. It felt good in a way. But it also hurt like everything that had ever given me pleasure. I felt like I was being joined to myself, like I was finally being born.

"All right," Frank was saying, behind me. "Now we're getting somewhere. All right, now. Good."

Live Bait

Lee Harrington

So the fifth time Janet didn't seem to recognize—or, according to Dr. Lunig, *chose not to recognize*—that her husband, Fred, was going to have an affair, she decided to change her tactics. No more vaguely hoping *he* might change, no more asking *him* deliberate questions about where *he* had been. No siree. From now on, Janet told herself, she'd go after the women instead. Now, *going after* didn't mean anything vicious or vile, like running a *Master Wanted for Spankings* ad under the suspect's name, or dropping a sand crab down her shirt at the company harbor cruise. No, her plan was to befriend the next woman, to bond with her so completely that she wouldn't dare sleep with Freddy—or even think about it—out of respect and honor and love. For the sake of friendship, in other words. But the problem was, Janet wasn't certain if beautiful women were capable of making friends. These women were conditioned to be rivals, to mistrust and out-dress one another, to compete for the prize of all prizes: a man.

But Freddy's sixth target, instinct told Janet, was going to be this new intern named Annie, who was by far the prettiest of the budding marine biologists the aquarium would hire that term. Not prettier than Janet—a former Miss Atlantic and once a hair model for Vidal Sassoon—but younger. Which to Janet, at thirty-seven, was pretty enough.

Both Janet and Freddy worked at the New England Aquarium, where he ran the summer whale watches and she headed the publicity department downstairs. Every six months they hauled in a new school of what Janet called floating interns, because they were placed wherever they happened to be needed, like the seal pool or the biolu-minescence room, and because two or three of them every season seemed to float into Freddy's arms. Janet should know; she had been a floating intern herself, seven years back, when Freddy's smile seemed to contain all the se-crets of the universe and his promises carried weight.

Now, his promises couldn't outweigh a dead guppy. Dead things. They float.

Janet found out about the infidelities in the worst kind of way—from someone else. She would have preferred the drama and adrenaline of catching him midact, with his white butt hairily exposed and his face slowly mutating, as if in some high-tech horror film, from a look of ecstasy to one of surprise, then horror, then *I can explain.* But no. She had to get the news from Bob Herring—yes, that was his name—the director of personnel at the New England Aquarium. Bob had called Janet into his airless office four weeks ago and said that what he had to tell her was going to be painful, but he wanted her to know he was telling her this as a friend, not an employer. Janet, of coarse, expected the ax, or worse, some humiliating scenario straight out of a daytime commercial in which one coworker tells the other about her genital odor, the shrimp marinara sauce on her chin, or the flecks of dandruff in her long blond hair. So she smoothed her linen skirt down and checked her stockings for runs.

"Freddy's been having an affair with Heather," Bob Herring said, closing the door to his office. "And Ingrid before that. And Patty, too. And that little redhead, what was her name, the one who gave lectures two years ago at the stingray pool?"

"Cordelia." Janet tapped her Cross pen into her palm, first the side of it, then the point. Sure, she'd had her suspicions, but if you don't look straight at something you can't necessarily see it. "I think," Janet said. "I think Freddy and I are going to need to take the rest of the day off. Unless you have any more names to add to the list. Family emergency, we'll call it. Just this once."

Bob Herring nodded with all the poise and concise sympathy of a trained human-resources manager, but in his eyes Janet saw a trace of love, flickering its tails among the shadows like a bioluminescent fish. But maybe not.

Back at their apartment, Freddy turned white when Janet confronted him with the list of interns. Soon he was crying with great heaving sobs as he said—between gasps for breath—he was actually relieved that she now knew, had wanted her to know, but didn't know how to tell her. "I know it was wrong not to tell you," he said, covering his face with his hands like an anguished Thinker. "But I couldn't. They meant nothing to me. Nothing. But I was afraid that telling you would hurt you even more." He pulled Janet onto the sofa, into his lap, and nuzzled his face between her neck and shoulder as he promised to be honest from here on in, to never hurt her again, to love her like she deserved to be loved. "You are the most important person in my life," he said. "Don't you believe that?"

Janet shrugged his mouth away. She thought she could feel the slight wet irritant of his lips moving along her neck but not really, as if she were no longer resting inside her skin but elsewhere: deep, deep inside herself perhaps, where there were no lies and no failures and no promises to keep, no sights or sounds or smells even, just a nice zone of nothingness where . . . where *other women* couldn't go. "Was it trust?" she said from this place, not looking at Freddy. "Or was it stupidity that led me to believe in you all these years?"

Freddy shifted his legs beneath her and repositioned her onto his thighs.

"Because if it's stupidity, then I am the biggest idiot on this planet and I might as well toss my Harvard diplomas into the ocean and start selling French fries on the pier. But if it's trust, than I have been noble and I have been moral. Even in the face of your lies." She poked her fingernail into his kneecap. "I have kept my dignity. I have persevered." Then she knotted her arms across her chest and felt herself cocking one eyebrow, as if part of her questioned what she had just said.

"Of course you have," Freddy said, squeezing her importantly. "You're a bazillion times more noble than me. I admit it. I'm a jerk. But give me one more chance, Janny, please. I'll prove to you that trust is the greatest thing two people can share."

Janet never gave a verbal acquiescence. No, she simply smiled at him in a way that said maybe, just maybe, she would let him sleep with her that night, so he touched her, and took off her clothes, and pleasured her for the better part of four hours. To Freddy, Janet assumed, this act was a triumph, a clear sign of reconciliation and the strength of marital bliss. But to Janet this was simply four hours of pleasure, four points gained by someone who now had about negative seventy-five.

When Annie, that new intern, showed up for her first day's assignment with her blond hair woven into a nonchalant braid and her green eyes open wide to the possibilities of life, it was Freddy who suggested she work on the whale-watch cruise. "I heard she's been studying the migrating patterns of whales for three years now," Freddy explained to Janet as they stood beside the central viewing tank, a four-story cylinder of water and fish. "And she's actually *seen* a blue whale. That in itself is great publicity, we both know that."

Janet studied the viewing tank's contents. Hundreds of species of marine life all swam in the same clockwise direction, day in and day out. Every creature, from the cowfish to the great grinning shark, propelled itself with the same dumb determination, as if they were making progress, as if they would really get somewhere if they kept on swimming. "I think Annie should work in the gift shop, myself," Janet said. "We could double our retail sales."

"Well." Freddy stretched his arms over his head. "We'll see what Bob says."

*   *   *

But Janet got to Bob first. She explained her gift-shop theory to him in his office, while he ate a McChicken sandwich at his desk.

"Of course, Janet. I see your point about sales revenues." Bob closed his McContainer with a synthetic squeak and wiped some mayonnaise from his chin. "But I'm also making a professional decision here. She *is* the best candidate for the whale-watch post."

"But Bob, considering Fred's behavior, don't you think that would be like ladling a bucket of chum out for a shark?" Janet looked over her shoulder and shut the office door. For once, the smell of French fries overpowered the smell of fish.

As Janet advanced, Bob removed his glasses and fogged them with his breath. He wiped them nervously on the tail of his shirt. Janet took Bob's arm and led him to the file cabinet, where Annie's assignment papers lay waiting, faceup. "The last thing Fred needs is temptation," she said. She pursed her lips.

"Well," Bob put his glasses back on, looking more clearly into Janet's eyes. "I suppose even the coat-check attendants should know their marine life."

And so, with the beautiful Annie safely partitioned behind T-shirts and shark-tooth rings, Janet was able to concentrate on writing press releases and coordinating radio spots while Freddy went out on two four-hour cruises a day. Work got so busy that Janet couldn't imagine how people their age had time to form new friendships, what with mortgages to juggle and fashions to follow and thousands of whales to save. There were newspapers that demanded reading, and magazines, and books. And all those sources suggested that Janet read other books, and see movies, and the play that the movie was based on, etc., etc. It had no end. Life seemed to get smaller after thirty, and tighter, so that no room was left for unfamiliar people, who would bring with them stories and baggage and pressing demands for time. Take her new life with Freddy, for instance. At night, when he arrived at home all warmed and salty with his hair tousled by the wind, Freddy would strip off his clothes and cook Janet dinner. He'd make elaborate lobster dishes or scampied shrimp, and later, after the plates were dried and the leftovers wrapped in foil, he'd drizzle her body with the extra butter he kept warm on the stove. The trails he drizzled were long and endless. Yes, Freddy seemed to be navigating their marriage back toward fidelity and trust. By the time the local schoolchildren were released for the summer and the sun had begun to shine its toxic rays well beyond eight, Janet realized with relief that she might not need to go after Annie after all. The fish weren't biting, it seemed.

But then Freddy started coming home with little trinkets for Janet—shrimp key chains and little water pistols shaped like squid—that undoubtedly came from the Aquarium gift shop. Janet knew that with an employee discount these trinkets would have cost Freddy about fifty cents but, more important, they allowed him the priceless opportunity of flirting with the clerk. "You were right to put that Annie in the gift shop," Freddy said as he tacked a poster of coupling crabs to the bathroom wall. "She's read every book we have in the library, and she knows all the Latin terms by heart. That's a Stanford degree for you."

Janet studied the way the female crab seemed to be trying to scuttle away. "Harvard can still squash Stanford in a football game."

"Darling." Freddy waltzed Janet into the bedroom. "Harvard never plays Stanford. They're not even in the same league."

The next morning, Janet browsed nonchalantly through the gift shop, waiting for Annie's two customers to leave. Once they made their purchase, she told herself, she'd invite Annie to lunch. She picked up a calendar of sea predators and studied the cover, on which a large shark made its openmouthed way toward a pike. January, February, March, each subsequent month featured large scary creatures bloodily devouring small helpless ones. Janet pondered the gender issue. Women aren't trained to be hunters, she told herself. Women, by nature, have always been the prey. She watched Annie, who looked passive and decorative in a pretty pink blouse. The only seek-and-destroy skills Janet felt she had been bestowed with were bargain shopping and finding the ripest melon at the grocery store.

"Look, Henry," the woman at the counter said to her patient husband. "These octopus earrings are only two dollars. Or is it octopi?"

"Actually, they're squid," Annie said. "And if you buy two they're only one-fifty apiece."

Janet felt her heart pound. Annie could say no. Annie could say she's busy and doesn't have time for friends. Especially older friends. It's a woman's prerogative to reject, of course, but Janet had never been on the receiving end before. She almost pitied Freddy for having to subject himself to such rejection all the time, but as she walked toward the cash register she found it reeked of Freddy's arrogant cologne.

Janet sneezed violently and said hello. "How's everything going for you? Are you enjoying your job?"

"It's okay." Annie handed Janet a package of starfish-patterned tissues. "I'd much prefer to be out on the whale-watch boats, but the customers are nice."

Janet studied Annie's face for a trace of accusation, but

saw only kindness and boredom, the calm, ironic rebellion of her generation. *X,* they called it, *Generation X,* as if they were part of some mysterious, top-secret club.

"Are you?" Annie said. "Enjoying your job?"

Janet let out a startled laugh. "Oh, I don't know. After seven years you don't ask yourself that. You just go through the motions on autopilot and concentrate on getting through the day."

"I think that's kind of sad." Annie stretched her arms out and yawned, as if bored by her beauty and bored, especially, by those people who were struck by it.

"Why do you think that's sad?" Sad was a dying parent, a puppy without a home. Sad was an unfaithful husband.

"I don't know. It's sad because you're unfulfilled. You're settling for less."

It occurred to Janet that Annie might have heard something about her and Freddy. Unkind gossip. About his— reputation. She looked at her watch casually and drew a breath. "Listen, it's almost lunchtime. Would you like to join me at Au Bon Pain?"

Annie smiled. "Hey, that's really nice of you. But I can't today. I already have plans. How about drinks after work though? Tonight or tomorrow?"

Janet agreed to meet on the following evening so as not to appear too keen. As she left the gift shop and turned to wave a second good-bye through the glass, Janet felt a strange elation sweep through her, a new bounce to her step, a bright conviction that said she could be sought after, she was well liked. She thought at that moment she understood why primal hunters said a prayer after their kill, danced to drumbeats, drank bison's blood. They, the hunters, had taken a risk and triumphed. Janet saw her reflection in the viewing tank and stopped in her tracks. She was walking exactly like Freddy did when he was about to score.

That night, Freddy came home with a pair of squid earrings and a how-to guide for maintaining your own home pond.

"But we don't have a pond," Janet said as he fixed them drinks. "We live in a high-rise, remember?"

Freddy pirouetted across the living room and handed Janet a martini without spilling a drop. "I know," he said. "But I felt this urge to learn about new species. All species. I feel so—alive!"

Janet fished an olive out of her glass and chewed its tender green flesh. "Careful," she said. "I bite."

The next evening, Janet left work early to meet Annie at some Spanish restaurant by six. At her apartment, she changed her outfit twice, sprayed much too much cologne between her breasts, and applied her mascara one tedious lash at a time. Janet realized, with a giddy laugh, that this was how it felt to fall in love, only a certain risk was missing, perhaps the risk of someday being left behind. Her face in the mirror laughed back.

At the restaurant, Janet sipped her first sangria as Annie was led to the table by an ancient, scuffling waiter with a spotless white apron and no front teeth. People set their forks down and stared at Annie, at her gauzy slightly transparent blouse, at her flawless shining face, but she remained totally oblivious to their glances, just as she remained oblivious to the fact that the hem of her Indian-print skirt grazed the dusty floor. "I'm not late, am I?" Annie lowered an enormous backpack onto a chair. The waiter set the menus down, bowed, and scuffled away. "Because your husband, that chatterbox, kept talking and talking when I was trying to close up the store. I finally asked him to join us, just to get out of there."

"Here?" Janet polished her sangria off and crunched on the ice.

"He said he might drop by later, but he wanted to take a shower first." Annie shrugged. "You know, to wash off that smell of fish."

Janet knew. She signaled to the waiter to take their order and bring more drinks.

"He's funny, Freddy."

"Yes."

"He seems pretty smart, too."

"That he is."

"So why doesn't he wear a ring?" Annie said.

Janet gazed at her own diamond and the white-gold wedding band. "Freddy says rings are boring."

"Boring! How can a ring be boring? God, I'm so tired of that word. Everyone I know is bored. With their jobs, with their lives. Are you bored?"

To be bored, Janet assumed, required some element of consistency. But Freddy never seemed to give her that. "No. Boring maybe. But not bored."

Annie lit a clove cigarette, blew the smoke above her head. "There's no such thing as a boring person." She looked at Annie as if she believed this, as if Annie, despite what Freddy said, was the most interesting person in the world. "You're just not being asked the right questions."

Janet swirled the ice in her sangria, listened to the smooth, promising way it tinkled against the glass. "Okay, then, ask me a question."

Annie laughed, stubbed out her cigarette and leaned forward, her elbows on the table. "All right then. Freddy. Is he good in bed?"

This question made Janet knock her drink over, and their *hombre* shuffled over patiently, like a nice old nanny who never made you finish your peas. Janet knew she could tell the truth, and give herself at least one enviable quality in this young girl's eyes. Or she could start a rumor about Freddy that would ruin his chances for good. "Actually, no," Janet said. "He's lousy." She reached into the sangria jug and pulled out a lemon, wedging it into her mouth. "Horrible. The worst." She chewed the rind, hoping the sour citrus would keep her from laughing.

"That surprises me," Annie said. The *hombre* sponged off the table before setting down a fresh new jug. "He carries himself like such a stud, you know? I kind of figured he at least had a big dick."

Janet dabbed at the corners of her mouth with a napkin. "Puny," she said. "Diminutive. Smallest thing you've ever seen. You couldn't even use that thing for a fishing lure."

Somewhere, perhaps at home in the shower, Freddy was busily soaping himself off, oblivious to the betrayal that was now taking place. Janet thought she should feel guilty at the moment and waited for a wave of compassion or remorse. But nothing happened, no lightning struck.

"Well, shucks," Annie said. "We'd better get good and drunk then."

Four or five pitchers later, Janet and Annie were laughing so hard their fellow diners began to sneer at them and finally the patient *hombre* had to ask them to leave. Outside, it was raining, a hard, pummeling rain that within seconds had drenched their clothing and their hair. A cab came out of nowhere and splashed them with a layer of muddy water as it screeched to a stop. The girls found this hysterical, and they laughed all the way to Janet's apartment, up the elevator, through her front door. Inside, Janet fumbled through the kitchen for a wine opener, while Annie insisted stubbornly that they take a shower, because they could get hepatitis or something from that acid rain. "I'm serious," she said with a slur. "Totally, totally serious. We could get wicked sick." And Janet believed her, because she realized these Generation X-ers knew some things.

And so they took their clothes off, and giggled their way into the bathroom, and Janet, turning the water on, felt they were about to undergo some sacred initiation rite. She wanted to tell Annie that her motives weren't pure, that she had only sought the poor girl out to get even with Freddy, that she now knew she was wrong, but she realized this wouldn't matter. Not after they had washed away all this mud. So she closed her eyes and let the water beat onto her shoulders, her scalp, her naked breasts, and the sensation was so hypnotizing that she didn't hear Freddy come into the bathroom. "Oh, my," he said, swishing open the shower curtain. "What have we here?"

Annie gasped and tried to cover herself with the shower curtain, but Janet faced Freddy, hands on her hips, straight on. She saw herself and Annie as Freddy must have seen them—two wet slippery women, number one and number six, waiting to be reeled in and scaled. But he was wrong, so wrong, and from that point on Janet knew she had nothing to fear. She stepped toward him through the steam.

Memory of a Dog

Michael Nigro

Christ-on-a-bun! It's 4:09 A.M.

Waking up in this house is like purchasing an instant lottery ticket; I scratch away sleep's gray matter to reveal my unfortunate luck: Linda's manicured fingers snatching my glass eye off the nightstand. She exits to the living room, to tonight's boyfriend. I know what she's thinking: if I don't have my eye I won't leave her. Keep thinking, Linda.

But I'm not getting up, dealing with her nonsense. Not now. I'll look for my eye tomorrow—the last time, I found it in the fishbowl. For a full week I had to wear my black patch and she never—not once—asked why. Did I ever wear that spongy oval-shaped shit over my face? Not if I can help it, she's always known that. I was waiting for my Pop-Tarts to warm when I noticed my eye staring at me through this murky water, patrolled by three goldfish with pituitary problems.

The day after I plucked my eye out of that fishbowl, I asked her—in my vintage smart-assed way—if she was feeding the fish fertilizer. Linda took me seriously and asked, "Why, Stephen? Should I?" "No," I said in pure disgust, and left it at that, left her alone in the kitchen to make her feel stupid.

I've heard that goldfish are supposed to grow only in proportion to their environment—like breaking the bones of a young girl's feet and then wrapping them up so they remain small. That's an idea the fucking Chinese came up with, I think. I should have done this with my dog, wrapped his shaved body up after the accident, so he would've remained the small, cute mutt I named after my father. Dad gave me Bobby on a weekend visit, when he and Linda still used the word *separation*, when I still called Linda "Mom." But Bobby grew up all deformed. One of his front legs is now shorter than the other three and he also has this lurpy hunch, the consequence of which is the more appropriate and fucked-up name I came up with: Bobby Moose. I mean, my dog looks, stands, and walks like a moose.

Here's some advice if you find yourself going through a windshield: one, cover your eyes, and two, no matter the malaise you may feel for the planet at the moment, do not stick out your tongue. I lost my right eye—the eye that was always getting in the way, is what I tell people, ha-ha, ho-ho—and Bobby Moose had his tongue butter-flied. Much like my depth perception, his bark has never been the same; he must have swallowed glass, damaging his barking chords. That's what I think. Bobby Moose's tongue stayed intact—unlike my eye—but the suture left his little pink lapper looking like a shy vagina.

At the time of the accident, ten years ago, I was twelve, Bobby Moose was a pup, Claire, my sister, was nearly two, and Linda was our driver.

Bobby Moose still squeaks. I, on the other hand, have cut my talking in half—and half of that half, I bet, con-sists of the barbed comments I once kept to myself. I can be rude and crawl right up someone's nose. It makes me nervous when I'm in one of those moods because I can't fight worth a shit. As soon as I'm threatened, I cower; I concede without attempting to strike back. Funny thing happens, though, when the nonsense begins flying out of my mouth—for some reason my ass reaches a dew point and begins sweating. I think I have an extra gland in my ass, or something, because a light felting of sweat forms with the slightest indication that I'm about to get the crap kicked out of me.

I'm getting better at judging how far I can push a

person before they clock me, though. Most don't. The truth of the matter is, people want to avoid confrontation. So when I ask Mr. Zip-a-Dee Doo-Dah in, say, a food court, "What makes you think people want to listen to *you* whistle?" he'll apologize—to me—then stop. Or in a bar, when I'm being consistently ignored by the bartender, I'll "accidentally" knock a few glasses onto the floor. "Sorry. Didn't see those there," I'll say, "But I will take a Rolling Rock." Or gum chewers, where you can hear the cracking and smacking all the way in the back of the bus: "You chew your gum like a cow. You're disgusting."

It's 4:17 A.M. Maybe I should try and read myself back to sleep. I've turned *Madame Bovary* into a comedy by blotting out the B on the book jacket so it looks like *Madame Ovary*. Ha-ha, ho-ho. Not that funny. Juvenile, really.

Linda and the boyfriend are quiet now . . . so perhaps I can sink into sleep. . . .

Dreaming: me, on my banana-seat bicycle, and I'm attempting, like I had done during all of eighth grade, to pedal to school no-handed. Down the driveway, through traffic, slingshotting up a handicapped curb and across a dewy outfield, then onto the baseball diamond, over second base, pretending to punch the shortstop in the head, plow through third base and continue—not to home plate, but straight, where twenty feet later my front tire meets a big lip of asphalt—screaming, "Shit!"—and it's successfully negotiated, so I swivel my hips left, and then the palms of my hands are on my bony knees, and I piston myself along a narrow path—narrowed by a licorice-lacquered chain-link fence on one side and the Ravine of Holy-Shit on the other—then off a curb, this one rather unfriendly to the handicapped, through an intersection, and I can see the school. . . .

But . . .

I'm awake, again.

I have never made it all the way to school no-handed. Something has always stopped me: bump, breaks, balance, a fall down the Ravine of Holy-Shit—that happened once. Even in this dream I don't make it. I'm barely comprehending that what wakes me up for a second time is the combination of laughter—Linda's sour, the boyfriend's burlap—and the musky smell of marijuana. It's 4:27 A.M.

The squeaking of Bobby Moose pulls me out of bed. I pop my head into the hallway and see this naked man leaning over, holding Bobby Moose's snout and exhaling his lung load of doobage into my dog's face. Bobby Moose snaps harmlessly at the man and breaks away. The naked man gives chase.

Maybe it's the initial shock of genitals, or perhaps it's

not within my ken, but I don't seem able to recognize a person whom I am accustomed to seeing clothed—naked. It takes me a moment to realize the man lumbering his lipo down the hall, chasing Bobby Moose, is not simply the new boyfriend but also my boss, Chaz. His skin, the color of uncooked bratwurst, makes me contemplate becoming a vegetarian.

They're coming toward me down the hall, and neither appears capable of applying the laws of friction to his gait. They're both stoned; Bobby Moose's legs are going two times faster than his actual pace, claws clattering frantically on the waxy layer of polish, and Chaz's uncoordinated obesity flabbers him straight into the doorjamb of the bathroom, wherein Linda is throwing up.

Chaz looks up and curls his lip like Elvis when he sees me—but the lip-curl blooms disgust and shock rather than a tough and sexy Elvis visage. Chaz is more alarmed, I think, at seeing my face without an eye than by my actual physical presence—which leads me to believe that he knew all along that Linda was my Mom, that I was here in the house the whole time.

Chaz's Elvis expression is nearly identical to the confused grimace that overtook his face when I applied to work at his video store. My interview, I'll never forget, went like this: Chaz thrust a video box with a picture of two taut-muscled male bodies on the cover, one with his fist shoved up the other's ass, and says, "Does this offend you?"

"Only without lubrication," I said dryly and, I thought, without reaction. Sex interests me in that it can be anonymous. Immediately after I jerk off, sometimes I'll say out loud, "Thanks. Now get the hell out of here!"—and point to the door. Actually, I've never done that, but I think that should be in a movie.

Linda flushes the toilet. I don't have much to say to her, as usual, but what comes out sounds so banal and polite that I fear that I have turned British in my sleep: "Having fun?"

Chaz rubs his tattooed shoulder with his bloated sausagelike fingers. Either he has forgotten he's naked or he doesn't care.

"Put a Kleenex over that, will you," I say.

I've heard people say that if you enter a slaughterhouse, see all the hanging flesh and slosh around in the slurry of intestines and bladders, you'll never eat meat again. But it's too hard to be a vegetarian, too much to consider.

This could be me in twenty-five years, but without the moronic tattoo. I read the inking on his arm—New Hampshire's state slogan: LIVE FREE OR DIE. But this is Bexley, Ohio, the Home of the Tomato, and it seems so far away from everything.

Linda stumbles into the hallway looking a bit too much

like the painting *Liberty Leading the People*—except here the people have forgotten to show up and gravity now has her breast. She realigns the lapels of her robe, head lolling to the side. A coagulated freckle of cocaine punctuates the black hole of a nostril. She's paranoid but happy. She used to be beautiful. She used to cook us dinner. Sometimes I look at her now and lose my appetite.

Bobby Moose is scratching at the front door like a retard. He's completely baked.

"Linda, where is it?" Jesus, I'm so calm with her. I'm always so calm with her. "Where's my eye?" I say.

She's so drunk she can hardly blink.

I think Linda has acquired the memory of a dog. Have you ever seen a dog puke? They puke, take two steps away, but suddenly the olfactory senses flair, their wet noses take in samplings of the atmosphere: *Hmmm, what's that smell... something behind me...* And you watch the dog turn around and, really, it's as if the dog is surprised, it's as if they've stumbled upon it: *Hey! Food!* And they start lapping up their find.

Linda blacks out on plenty of nights but, no matter how trashed she gets, she has yet to forget why she wanted the memory of a dog in the first place: the accident, the brown station wagon, the distance of seventy-six yards from point of impact to Claire's baby seat. Her binges ebb and flow. Lately, a tsunami. She always makes it to work at the hair salon the next morning, however. She can cut hair blind. She says she gets satisfaction out of making people feel better about their appearance.

Two weeks ago, after a similar episode of coming home late, stumbling, slathering but (thankfully, I thought then) alone, she passed out on the couch. The next afternoon, I went into the salon for a haircut. She's the only person who knows how to cut my hair: the fault line of one hundred sixty-five stitches over my head has created a rather disastrous pattern as to how my hair grows in. I entered the salon, sat in the chair and she, as always, called me "sir" while misting my mop. She ran her fingers through it and said, "What would you like done today?"

"I'm feeling adventurous today. Surprise me," I said.

That was our routine when she cut my hair.

But tonight. I grab a towel from the hallway closet. "Here, fat man," I say. "You disgust me." Chaz skirts himself and I say thank you, as if it's a threat.

Linda grabs his arm. It could be anyone's arm. It could have been a railing, a doorknob, anything for support. I've seen her fall down plenty of times, hard and ugly, too.

The older she gets the more impersonal the relationships become, at least that's what I think, at least that's the way it is between us. And it seems that this attitude, more and more, has become my nature. I hate it.

Like last weekend with my dad's family in Cleveland.

I said perhaps ten words to him. When I arrived, my seven-year-old stepsister (Claire would have been twelve) was standing knock-kneed on the driveway holding a basketball as if she were pregnant. When I asked what she was doing, staying still as a sculpture, Anne said, "Turtle head."

I looked around. "Turtle head?"

"I'm waiting for it to go back in so I don't have to stop playing," she said.

I told her that she had, in fact, stopped playing and that I still didn't see a turtle. Anywhere.

She looked at me as if I were an adult. I'm not.

"I have to poo," Anne said. "I don't want to go inside. I want to keep playing. So I'm waiting for my turtle head to go back up."

"You're going to have to go sometime," I said, laughing just a tad. "When you gotta go, you gotta go." Ha-ha, he-he.

Her face turned sleepy and she said, "I'll go when I wanna go. It's a free country, you stupid-face."

Yeah, what did I know.

I sat on the back porch staring at the groomed yard, waiting for my dad to drive up. Eventually the echoing concussion began of an overinflated ball rhythmically encountering the fresh blacktop. She continued to play. When Dad drove up she mounted her bicycle. He didn't see me right away, so I watched him heave a long canvas bag filled with baseball bats from the trunk of a BMW. The back of his shirt said COACH with the number 1 beneath.

Anne now jerkily pedaled and yelled, "Look, Dad! No hands! Dad, no hands!" I kept thinking how strange it was for me to call him Dad, but if not Dad, then what?

He stuck out his hand to shake mine. It wasn't completely cold, we shook as if we'd just solidified a business deal. I said, "Hey, Coach," and thought, then, that a high five would have been more fitting.

Before he said a word, the crash of Anne's bicycle snapped our attention. The bicycle was on its side, the back wheel silently spinning, and she was scampering past us to the back door. When I turned, Coach was heading to the garage. Right then, I felt it was already time for me to leave, but Susan, my stepmother, was including me in on the dinner plans. She prepared lemon-pepper chicken with capers, asparagus drenched with garlic and butter, and potatoes whipped with sour cream, and, for the first time in I don't how long, I drank milk. Skim milk, but milk just the same.

"You want a beer?" Coach asked.

"Uh, no," I said, "Maybe later."

Anne poked at her food for about five seconds, stood

up and said, "Stephen's a stupid-face," and then ran out-side, jumped on her bike and pedaled down the driveway, giggling madly at God knows what.

Susan looked at me with these sad eyes. Even before she spoke, it dawned on me that she was apologizing to me for my glass eye, my scar tissue, my stupid-face. I didn't even realize that that's what Anne meant. Susan said, "Anne's at that age where she doesn't know how to act in front of people she's not familiar with."

I shrugged, took a bite of chicken and said, "This needs salt." And I ended up ruining my boneless breast of chicken with enough salt to have killed a half dozen gar-den slugs.

After dinner I nabbed a Bass Ale and said, "I'm going to check out this neighborhood of yours." The filthy arms of humidity wrapped around me as soon as I stepped out of the air-conditioned kitchen. I really missed air condi-tioning. Christ, I thought, it's a nice thing to have. Why haven't I missed it sooner?

Anne pedaled up the driveway and swerved around me. "Stupid-face. Stupid-face," she began singing in some fucked-up, made-up nursery-rhyme cadence. "Stephen's a stupid-face. Stuuu-ee-uuu-pid-face."

I continued walking down the driveway and took a belch-inducing chug from my beer. She came up behind me and stopped, at what she must have assumed to be a safe distance. "Stuuu-ee-uuu-pid-face, Stuuu-ee-uuu-pid-face," she sang again.

I whipped the bottle onto the lawn, turned around and made the most perfect grab for her neck. Clutched, lifted up and began squeezing. My hand seemed to be custom made for her neck. "Say it again, you little shit!" I said. "Go ahead!" And I tightened my grip; I could feel the wiry tendons in her neck tighten and quiver, and she began pulling at my wrist with her tiny hands. Her eyes squeezed shut and she started making these comic-sounding noises—half gurgling, half wheezing, half belching. Her face was turning stop-sign red.

Her neck felt so good in my hand. On her tiptoes, she struggled to follow the direction I was taking her: I pulled her from straddling the bike, onto the lawn—which was maybe two feet, yanking her by her neck. I felt as if I could have popped her head off, easy. Even with just one hand I felt it was possible. And her face started looking puffy, like it was going to explode. Yes, I thought, I could pop her head off; if I applied more pressure, her flesh would start oozing between my fingers like raw hamburger.

But, instead, I eased her to the ground—still choking her, but gently collapsing her body to the grass. Then I released my grip.

She opened her eyes and started coughing. My adrenaline was this screaming hot sauce pumping through me. My skin felt taut. I needed to walk, so I started down the driveway. I wanted to take a shower, get the world's humid funk off of me.

"That didn't even hurt!" Anne screamed, her voice shuddering as she tried not to cry. I walked down the driveway and heard her yell again, "It didn't even hurt!"

I kept walking and I wandered around until I was certain no one at the house would be awake. It was just before 2 A.M. when I returned. I went down to the basement and fell asleep watching bands on MTV walking together in perfect synchronization. Pure pap.

The next morning, Saturday, when I heard the back door slam—Coach was leaving to hit grounders to his prepubescent infield—and with Susan and Anne still asleep, I grabbed my gear and hoofed to the Greyhound station. I made it just before the bus backed out. The doors closed and we began moving. I stood looking for an empty row, feeling like one of those guys that people pray will not sit next to them—maybe I am?

Third row back, staring out the window, was an Ohio State sorority girl. Greek letters curving over her tits. She was stunning, too, blond and tanned like she just got back from Florida. When I sat, I realized that my crotch was all discombobulated, and the discomfort worsened because

I was getting a hard-on. Serious rearranging was in order. I raised myself a few inches off the seat, tugged right above the knees of my jeans, then pretended to look for something in my pockets. Maybe I should be an actor, I thought, but is she buying this act? Then, just above a whisper, I said, "Oh, where is it?" My rearranging was completed and by jingo if I wasn't fully erect by then, yet my package was comfortably positioned, so I could sit back down.

"Do you need a pen?" she asked.

I don't know why I said yes. Maybe I was still acting. Maybe it was her perfume, not flowery, but clean-smelling, what I would imagine ice to smell like if ice had an odor.

"I could tell," she said.

From her purse, she pulled out a pen that skewered a tiny troll with lime-green hair. It was one of those naked but genderless thingamajigs that six-year-olds and secretaries with big asses have.

She said, "Well, if you don't mind using this..."

I said, "No, not at all."

It was quite possible that I was going to have a hard-on for the next three hours.

I balanced *Madame Ovary* on my leg. She laughed when she saw it. She was an English major, and said she hated reading. "My adviser told me I had to choose a major, that I needed to have direction," she said. "So I've been having to read all this crap."

"You didn't like this book?" I asked.

"Never finished it," she said. "Too slow moving."

As the bus pulled onto the highway, she told me she was really hungover. I said, "I wish I was drunk right now." She giggled, closed her eyes, and slept for the rest of our journey south. I read the same paragraph over and over, never comprehending it either, because I couldn't stop glancing over at her. She looked like a porcelain doll, but tanned. I could see partially up her nose, clean nostril, raw, pinkish, sexy.

At the end of the trip I took it upon myself to wake her up. Touching her shoulder made my rectum pucker. This made me think of a camera's shutter taking a picture. But, Jesus, what's wrong with me? Who thinks of capturing the waking image of someone with the puckering aperture of your ass? She stretched out of slumber and told me she could sleep just about anywhere on the planet. I told her I was enormously jealous of that, and held out the troll pen, trying to return it to her. She told me to keep it.

I still have the troll with the lime-green hair, somewhere, but I also have this fantasy snapshot of her in my memory, but she's waking up next to me in my bed, not on a bus.

It's 4:57 A.M. Linda's crying. I'm looking for my eye (under the couch, on top of the opened long-neck beer bottles, in the now-empty fishbowl). I shove a few items in my backpack, put a patch over my wrinkled socket and take all of Linda's cash from her cowhide purse—about two hundred dollars of tips, in mostly ones and fives.

"I'm leaving. I'm gone," I say. I grab Bobby Moose by the collar and yank him up so we can exit, and he's looking at me like movement is the last thing he wants to be doing. "Too bad, ya pothead," I say, "We're fucking out of here."

It's 5:03 A.M. I slam the door behind me and Bobby Moose.

I don't care how we'll get someplace, but we will get someplace. New York, perhaps. Or, I'm thinking, maybe San Francisco. How about L.A., the City of Angels—that would be good, no? Yes, that would be a change.

Bobby Moose is walking stalker-slow behind me. "Why did I bring you along?" I say. He lifts his head and whimpers, as if he's explaining to me that he's got the munchies.

"Get up here, you stupid fucking dog!" I scream at him and slap my thigh so hard my hand feels like it's full of bees.

Bobby Moose starts coughing. He's actually hacking like a human being. I'm waiting for one of his lungs to fly out of his mouth and hit me in the back of my head. We make it to the Ravine of Holy-Shit. He's glassy-eyed and sluggish and I'm gonna let him rest. He's had a hard night. I watch him lower his misshapen body to the ground, but it's optically confusing to me, he's moving so slowly it looks as if he's sinking in quicksand. But I know he's not. He's simply had it. I'll give him ten minutes rest. Then we'll move on.

I lean against the licorice-lacquered fence, sit and stare through the boundary of my world with my one good eye. Bobby Moose falls asleep. I'm amazed he can sleep on the wet grass. Just like that beautiful girl on the bus, he too can sleep just about anywhere on the planet. But what about me?

5:39 A.M. I watch Bobby Moose jerk as if a small volt of electricity shoots through him, but he stays asleep, and I wonder if he's dreaming. I decide to watch the sun scratch its way through the dirty nickel sky for a few minutes before I turn back for home, where I'm sure I'll find my mom asleep on the bathroom floor. When she sees daylight, however, she will not realize her prize, the usual: to have been eased and gently collapsed to her mattress so she can wake up in her own bed.

Waiting for the
John Cheever

Amy Boaz

"The shape of desire never changes," Roger says to me, by way of consolation. He sits Indian style on the bed, under the hood of the cheap spread, smoking. The room is cold from the jet of air conditioning that cannot be adjusted, and we smell of the same tuna-fish sandwich. Sex doesn't relax the man so much as sharpen his nose— zigzagged from a Dublin bar brawl in college—sink the caves beneath his collarbone, stiffen his instep, which cracks when he gets up to go to the bathroom. I hug the pillow over my bare chest to soften his bony jabs.

We have paid for three hours at the Hotel Liberty, though we can scarcely use two. It is our lunchtime. Outside our room the river courses inexorably along Eleventh Avenue, where the heavy trucks strike the potholes, rattling the walls; closer still, the Hispanic maids yammer to each other across the corridor. Roger has been weighing the consequences of his wife's latest pregnancy for a half hour now. He will have to find a better-paying job. He will have to endure months of her postpartum aerobics classes. He will even lose me. Out of self-preserving habit, he considers all the aftereffects of this ill-timed detonation, all but the joy of a new birth.

He has not convinced me, because I start to cry. He turns and asks quietly, "What should I do?"

His face bears childhood scars of faulty parental supervision and dagger lines of accumulated grief. I like to imagine he has battled widely in the world like an angel, and that someday he will need to take me with him.

"There's nothing you can do now," I tell him, the corners of my mouth turned down tragically. I mean of course, "You've done it now, you brute," but I can't say it, he will extract from himself a worse punishment, and who am I to reproach him for being reckless? For two years I've come to this place to let his words order my life as the sure current of the river adjacent to the highway draws the barges solemnly toward their loading docks. First I came in fear, terrified that someone we know would see us, that our absence would be noted, and I couldn't stand to watch the disappointment on his face if I held back; then I came with shameless delectation. Today I feel keenly the passage of time, and it will not be kind to us.

Roger is still at it, his legs folded under him. He lights a fresh cigarette. I see from the numbers on the television set that there won't be time for another round.

Omar wanted to name our daughter Elizabeth, because it sounds stately and permanent; I chose Miranda for its fierceness. I am relieved to see how well the name fits this spirited, exuberant child. She has reached the age of toddlerhood and pushes me away as a matter of course, determined to do for herself. The only pink she owns are the playsuits my mother has sent; I dress her in blue and red, pants she can run in and T-shirts that are instantly stained. On outings or at our neighborhood park I am asked whether she is a boy or a girl, a question that secretly delights me.

Nonetheless, her beauty is disturbing. My father, when he visits with my mother on their way from gambling in Las Vegas, insists on Miranda's beauty. He praises her eyes, which are large dark pools; her smile, the winning effect of which she is already becoming aware; and her lengthening limbs. He is measuring her beauty in terms of her future success in the workplace. My mother (I was not her favorite daughter) confides with a look full of foreshadows, "But she looks just like you." The baby-sitter sings out, "Pretty girl, pretty girl," how many times a day?

And strangers at the playground direct at her their aggressive compliments.

I don't want her to know she is beautiful. I wish her to be spared being that thing of public scrutiny that will bend her to its illusory expectations. My Miranda is a warrior baby who will have to please no one.

A man I work with stands over me where I am seated in my editorial office and fixes me with urgently attentive blue eyes. He stands and I sit and between us, where I lower my gaze, is the unsmooth front of his trousers. Frank works in a different department in another city and visits our offices rarely; he has an accent that is not of this part of the country. In the next moment he brings down the dictionary to look up the use of the word *combust* in a story I have written and I see that his hands are shaking.

Frank takes me to lunch. We both have young children and we discuss most comfortably baby-sitting and cooking. I tell him that instead of moving to Chicago some years ago, which seemed to me the shining American destination, the city of Bellow and Sandburg, I got married, moved to the suburbs, and now, with a baby, am stuck. That's the word I use, *stuck*. He introduces the subject of television shows I never watch. As we rise to go, Frank kisses me on the cheek, slips his arm around my waist and keeps it there until we have to release our holds to catch the door.

Every day Omar meets me on the 5:14. He could stay many hours longer at his job for the amount of work still to be done, but Miranda must be retrieved from the baby-sitter's and it is important to my husband to be regarded as doing the right thing in the upbringing of our daughter. He carries rolls of drawings he will spend the evening hunched over in the basement. The sweat drips down his face from the exertion of running to jump on before the last bell. I would rather not kiss him; he never insists. He is ashen from having had no lunch, and once in his seat he stares straight ahead. It is best to ask generally about his day, since with increasing detail of his frustration I grow snappish and hostile. He is an architect whose success depends on the cooperation of crooked construction managers. I resent that my husband is not in a position of power. We sit in silence with the newspaper, or dozing.

He has a handsome head, my husband. An oblong face, with heavy brows, a shapely Slavic nose (his mother's side) and sensual mouth, cheeks shadowed perennially by whisker growth, luxuriant nose hair, and tufted ears. His hair is dark and thick, curly like Miranda's, though cut too short. He has his hair cut pending my parents' visit from Las Vegas; he enjoys hearing my father say he looks thinner.

From his breast pocket he takes out a bag of nuts, holding it by his thumb and forefinger, and dangles it before me. I am not tempted by his offer, or I take the lion's share, then stare out at the racing scenery with sticky fingers and a ruined appetite for dinner. Out of the corner of my eye, I can see him masticate: with the first bite his jaw cracks with a ghastly greediness that I feel at the pit of my stomach. He removes from the small plastic sack one nut at a time, chewing ponderously, keeping his mouth busy with the barest morsel, so that his mouth is never empty. He is most content this way, without having to speak. From time to time, as we near our port, skirting the river, with each stop of the train gaining, I glance at him against my will—I can't help but see what I don't want to see, a kind of awful confirmation—he's moving his lips in silent, impotent debate, shrugging, flicking his fingers emphatically, working his cheeks to dislodge sharp particles from the canyon below his molars. I glare without wanting to see and it is terrible.

I wanted to come to Roger like a whore, for whom nothing is secret or forbidden. I hated suffering moments of sudden modesty, when I had to turn away or hide; I conceded to his lingering regard of my backside after two years. Our diligence at trying positions that had never occurred to us with our spouses could yield revelatory pleasures. Of lean, lathlike frames, we clattered and racked when we loved like two skeletons wrestling. In the beginning we savored novelty; we spread the fleshtoned gadgets across the bed and tried them all once, resolved to do what people do who trespass in the illicit. The sensory-enhancing objects made us laugh, mostly, while prying us open to each other's inquiring eyes, fingers, mouths. I enjoyed watching his grinning face. "Tell me," I would hiss softly in his ear, "tell me what you want." He had the porn channel playing and the radio on to keep out the racket of the hotel's maintenance workers—or was it to keep up our courage? In time we forgot to turn the noise on, giving way to a silent, concentrated drilling. The most intense pleasure is the selfish surety of pleasing the other.

I notice the man on the train platform because everything about him violates the sumptuary laws. He is tall and good-looking in a southwestern manner, tanned and too casual for our crowd; in the winter, he wears a bright, authentic ski jacket rather than a dark wool coat, and his hat is pulled down for warmth rather than fashion. Perhaps I first notice the way he walks: unhurried, unobservant, like a kid strolling with a candy in his mouth. Or I first notice his wife. Our town is small, and there aren't many places you can remain unnoticed: market, video store, library, train platform. We have all scrutinized one another amply while waiting for the John Cheever, Eleanor Roosevelt, Nelson Rockefeller. I recognize the men with their shiny foreheads and shoulders stooped from stepping onto the train, the women desexed in flats and working hairdos. This wife, in contrast, is tight and organized. She is not beautiful, though her legs, bared in the summer under short swingy skirts, are really knockout.

Once—it is on a train ride home, a later train than I usually take, perhaps I missed the previous train though I can't imagine I would, since I leave work at the same hour every day, without fail, tearing through Grand Central and recklessly knocking aside fragilely laden travelers, running for that train as if the whole structure of my marriage, indeed my life, hinged on it, I would not have missed that train, but where is Omar? Ah, he is here—I see this man, standing up several rows away. We are nearing our station. He stretches, hitches up his jeans, adjusts the long-strapped bags over his shoulders. Without my glasses I can pretty well see that he is looking at me, sprawled on my seat, too tired to collect my limbs. I don't bother to wake up Omar; he'll come to when the train stops.

The man and I establish that we have met before, at the playground with his young daughter. I don't remind him that we've seen each other at the market, video store, library, on the train platform. Omar emerges with his rolls of drawings, blear-witted and pale, always polite. I offer David a ride—he's a photographer, hence the hard boxes and cylinders hanging from his person. He sits in the passenger seat and I feel an adolescent charge at showing off my practiced maneuvering of the village hills in our European car (a wedding present from my parents). He seems large in the seat next to me, his knees grazing the glove compartment, and I am talking too fast; he doesn't fasten his seat belt. Spiraling up Mount Hope, I spot Omar in the rearview mirror, his head thrown back and his knuckles white over the hand strap.

Later that night, Omar realizes that he has forgotten his wallet while at the A & P buying ice cream. He is lucky to run into David, who pays for it.

They've changed conductors on my train departing Grand Central. Formerly it was the tall fellow with the handlebar mustache who courteously but firmly refused to let slide the expiration of my commuter pass. I envied the way he indulged in amiable banter with the other passengers. I dreamed of him as a Confederate soldier coming at me with his cap lowered over his eyes and his big key chains clanging at his hips. I told Omar about my dream, as the young man made his gentle thank-yous down our aisle, and Omar flushed to the points of his ears.

The new conductor keeps me from nodding off to sleep in the feebly air-conditioned car. He is older than our soldier boy, beefy, in tight trousers and suspenders and cheap, thin-soled city shoes that make a union-hall clacket as he passes, twice, thrice, five times during the course of a ride. I lean in to inhale his manly wake. He never smiles save for the pull of contempt at the corner of his mouth when he's pretending he doesn't see me. And then a ripple of bestial satisfaction riles his molded chest and he struts like a pugilist, yanking at doors and pushing in keys with more violence than necessary. I like the way he says *Yonkers*, through the nose.

Our moment of intercourse arrives. He stands over me to take my ticket and I make him wait, make him rake me with his ferocious presence. I stick the pen I'm holding in my mouth and fumble deep in my bag, all the while watching his inscrutable poker face. His eyes narrow. I give him what he's after, my wrists limp, and he snarls, without a thank-you, moving away with a slackening of his jaw. We emerge from the Bronx underground into the dazzling river light. The passengers relax their necks, so that their heads spring gently back; their legs slide easily under the seats in front of them. Most of us are asleep in a moment. I'm satisfied, licking the tips of my fingers like a cat.

The river accompanies us, free of traffic now at sunset except for a single poky tugboat; the water gleams like quicksilver under the cottony frame of the Palisades. With each stop our car grows quieter; the groaning from some passenger several rows behind me has ceased. My town comes round next. I exit slowly, finding my legs, swaying with loose-hinged hips. I watch for my conductor where he sits alone in the fore cabin, staring impassively down the tracks.

Wednesday night is Omar's computer class. I remember because Wednesday is also diaper-service pickup, while Thursday is payday for the sitter, Friday is recycling. Monday I was meeting Roger at the Hotel Liberty. And Tuesday is trash collection.

Vera, the baby-sitter, has freshly showered and put on makeup when I arrive to pick up Miranda. She is a young woman who was brought up in our village and still lives in the neighborhood of Uniontown; she races motorcycles on the weekend. I don't like her boyfriends and I don't like her perfume, which clings to my daughter's neck where I bury my face. The smell irritates me. It puts me in mind of hurried sex in the beds of rusty hauling trucks.

Miranda has a wild look about her this night and I

sense there is going to be trouble. She doesn't want to be held; she wants to race across the grass, in pursuit of the cat, the ball, the toy car. She wants to get as far from me as she can. Just shy of two, she is already possessed of the willful, duplicitous nature that will sway her in life from now on. She needs me to define the borders of her small world, to keep her from tripping out of bounds, but otherwise my role has become largely functionary. The achievements we two shared so intimately during her earliest weeks of life are now entrusted to a larger audience of admirers—Vera, Omar, her grandparents. Her eyes still search for mine but they stop short defiantly before falling in.

She's waving to me now with rocks in her hands, pilfered from the neighbor's garden. Mrs. Totoro, the mother of the four children under the age of five next door, is shouting at one of them and pretends not to see Miranda's theft. I won't be able to complain the next time the neighbor's dog pees on my grass. The light sinks earlier into the trees and the houses are taking on the cold, stony look of fall; it's getting late. Dinner still has to be conjured and a bath for Miranda negotiated; there are picture books to be read and a warm bottle of milk prepared before bedtime. The two hours we spend alone together are the longest of the day.

I see her heading out into the street, where she knows

she's not supposed to go. She's waving her fists, glancing back, daring me. I'm already running, before I even tell my legs to go. The rage begins to churn in my gut. Mrs. Totoro, her heavy breasts swinging in her thin dress, snaps at another of her brood, the middle one who is fair and peevish, who wanders the neighborhood yards without listening. I shout Miranda's name, alerting the neighbor on the other side as he emerges from his garage dragging a lawn sprinkler attached to a hose. He raises his arm briefly. He is not accustomed to seeing me wearing work clothes, or anything for that matter, through the curtainless window of my bathroom. I don't care if he sees me: what do I think I'm hiding? I'm going to hit her here or inside; I can already feel the sting on my palm where it smacks her hand, her bottom, the tender curve of her shoulder. It's her cry I need to hear. I grab her arm and pull her out of the street. Her mouth widens like an empty cupboard when I strike; her eyes fasten on mine with blank misery. Then she wails, lifting her arms to me, and that is enough.

Norman reminds me of boys I was attracted to in college, with poor eyesight, hair thinning, a wrestler's build. I meet him at a professional function and can't shake him; since we live in neighboring suburbs, he imagines we have something in common. He is anxious to take me to lunch, and to a fashionable restaurant I have always wanted to sample; at the last minute he cannot get reservations. When he arrives late, deeply tanned in an expertly tailored, corporate-blue suit, the kind my father wore, the kind I always wanted Omar to wear, I am tight with an unnamable but familiar resentment.

Still, I answer his questions, which are intended to convey his interest in me. Norman speaks with difficulty, removing his glasses that have fogged up from his steaming dish of skate; at moments he seems close to tears. He needs to speak, and this, of course, is why we have come here, to allow him to talk about the affair his wife is having with a man she met on the train. Norman must take the same train every morning with this man, identified by his wife in a rash moment of confession; the indignity is beginning to wear away the outlines of Norman's being. He tells me he followed the other man to his office once and knocked him down, which I think very good, since it showed some old-fashioned virility. However, Norman cleared the assault with his lawyer first. His wife wants him to leave but Norman, wisely, won't budge. I urge him to kick her out by all means.

Understandably, Norman wants to know what is wrong with him. He has been a steady provider for his family, though his wife, who also works, has made it known that he could be doing more. He loves his kids and takes them to Columbia football games. He is bewildered by the destructive behavior of his wife. He asks me, "I sleep with the woman every night of my life, how can I have not known what was going on?"

How? How? How? Norman quells the spasm in his head. He gobbles the last of the tartin aux pommes we are supposed to share, distracted without his glasses, his eyes darting in their sockets like frantic schools of fish. He is forty-three—they are all forty-three, and bewildered. He wants to kiss my cheek, measure my waist with his hands, pretend like we're out on a date, feel the possibility of an erection. I oblige—when have I not obliged? This could be Omar, after all. In five, ten years, Omar will be broken by defeat and I shall be accused of murder.

Sometimes when I get off the train at my town I don't remember what I'm supposed to do next. It is dusk and my fellow passengers and neighbors, grim and uncombed, move with the last of their urban force to get up the hill and out of the parking lot; they will slow down once they are clear of one another. Have I left Omar asleep on the train, racing northward? I don't remember what we are having for dinner or where my car is. I spy David's wife, Gena, getting into her van with the single-mindedness that marks all of her movements; I note with some surprise that she is pregnant with their second child. Soon there will be no one left in the parking lot and I will have to move out of view of the taxi drivers left without a fare.

Just up the hill is a bar, Sheri's, where I head because I must go somewhere and suddenly I have to pee. If I've been drinking, it's a mystery. As I move I am grateful to be wearing my driving shoes, which I don't recall having changed into. The hill is steep and the sidewalk broken up like the erratic collision of tectonic plates. The pressure on my bladder becomes unbearable and I squat in the bushes behind the dry cleaner's. My thigh muscles shake and can't support me; I have to put my hand down in the muck to steady myself. If Omar were to see me he would turn away quickly, ringing his hands in that particularly futile fashion, glancing up and down the empty block; I remember his disapproving face.

My bag grows too heavy to carry and I abandon it in the bushes. There's nothing in it I need, maybe shoes, a book, my glasses. Someone will find it and return it to me just as Pete the stationmaster returned my Scottish umbrella that I once left at the train station. It has begun to rain, tracing my cheeks like molten tears; I am quite warm, sweating now from the climb. Walking backward up the hill I watch the river glide under me like a quiet extension of myself; I sniff Sheri's harbor smell of meat frying and stale beer. The place is brightly illuminated, and through the tall glass windows I can see clusters of animated diners hunched over their tables, ripping apart roasted chickens. I watch my neighbors at the bar in a pantomime of hilarity, among them Mr. Totoro, who raises to his mustache a heady mug of beer. There seems no reason to stop now, and the effort to puncture this insulated scene too great; I continue to climb—my town clings to the boulders rising from the river in crazy undulations—and turn onto Main Street.

The shops have closed except the pizza parlor. I expect a neighbor to pass me, David in his new Bronco with the ski rack attached to the back; Mr. Totoro returning from Sheri's. Presently I reach Broadway, slightly soaked but warm enough if I keep moving my arms. I hear a motorcycle pull up behind me. The driver is encased in black leather and elaborate headgear like an extraterrestrial bug. The helmet is unsnapped and deftly removed and Vera emerges, brilliantly made up. We discuss Miranda's day: she has been a good girl, no accidents. Vera revs her motor. I sense she is in a hurry so I wave her cheerfully on. I feel colder now, though the rain has stopped. Past the gas station, I smile at the high school student manning the pumps. If I turn left here I could find my way to my house, stepping quietly to keep from disturbing the loose dogs. Yet the highway is just up a way, and when I get there surely I'll run into someone, Pete who was so kind to return my tartan umbrella, or Omar with the luggage, to indicate what will happen next.

"It wasn't meant to be," Roger says with a smile he cannot conceal. His wife has had a miscarriage and he's hung-over, I suspect, because we're back at the Liberty, in rooms we enjoyed some months before. We are acquainted with most of the cells on the second floor, with their various configurations of bed, ceiling mirror, chair, and bathroom. The concierge has recognized us and favored us with river views, though this afternoon the windows remain shut-tered.

Roger doesn't want to eat the sandwich I've brought. He wants to drink the beer he's brought, and smoke. The small room has withstood a cataclysm and smoke rises in a lid to the institution ceiling. Everything we will take from this place to the next, our clothes, our hair, our skin, will reek of the sulfurous fumes of our affair—tobacco, beer, sex. I have lost Roger's smell in this pernicious caul-dron, and I stink of it too.

"Let's cherish what remains," he says simply. "Please, baby."

He has put on his shorts and crouches at the edge of the bed. He is trying to remember what brought him here, each step since he left his home that morning, the cause and effect that, once established, will allow him to get dressed again and return. I must help him, must encourage him, otherwise we will certainly start to weep. But I am choking in this room and am very hungry; as hard as I regard Roger he won't meet my eye.

My silence has frightened him and he looks like a guilty man. His memory, I am afraid, will serve him too late. I've extracted my arm from the snarl of bedcovers; I reach for the window to crack the blind. The river light warms my upper lip, and if I squint, I can make out the native baby in the canoe being rocked gently downstream.

Beefeater

Rebekah Rutkoff

He refers to himself in the third person: "Well, any documentary that Harry Neel works on . . ." He walks with an irregular gait, unsmoothly, with lots of vertical motion. He seems older than he is, unless he's older than I think he is. And he's sort of appealing looking, despite his unattractiveness. He's bald with a white bob, and has surprisingly fine skin for someone whose features are neither delicate nor bold, but kind of crooked and deteriorating.

It was Thursday, and lunchtime. I was feeling enervated by guilt. I had worked at home the previous day, supposedly mining seven books for 1920s-related excerpts for a television series on the decade; I got through three. I spent the better part of the day preparing for the next installment of my ongoing project: taking pictures of phallic symbols. I decided to go to the café in the health spa in the Forty-fifth Street housing complex and bring my work—maybe I could finish the other four books over lunch if I sped-read, an activity usually made possible by eating. I put on my coat and stuck my head in Harry's editing room, no longer taken aback by the gross, high-pitched, and unmodulated quality of my workplace voice: "Can I get you anything? I'm going out." A second later Harry was picking his coat off the coat tree to the left of my desk. He'd come with me, if I didn't mind.

On the way to the elevator, I carried on a rapid and gentle conversation in my head, urging myself to remember the Serenity Prayer. It seemed I was always losing control of my lunch hours at this job, unable to turn down invitations to get Thai or Vietnamese food when a yogurt, peeled carrots, and two mini pitas were waiting patiently for me in the little refrigerator on the right side of my desk. I had spent many an afternoon tallying up the lunchtime calories I had wasted, little columns of numbers dotting the corners of my legal pads and folders. However, the morning after I saw seven autobiographical video shorts by young women at Lincoln Center, three of which featured the number columns in eating disorder montages, I got to work fifteen minutes early and added a decimal point and a cents column to all the numbers so that it looked like I was adding up money.

Harry was thrilled with the café. One of the soup specials was borscht. He loved borscht. He loved it so much that he didn't actually include it in his order, assuming that the waitress would gather from his enthusiasm when she announced the specials that he indeed wanted a cup. He didn't remember that he had wanted the borscht, despite my having eaten a cup in front of him, until he was nearly finished with his hamburger, though. Then he pointed out to the waitress that she had forgotten part of his order.

Harry wanted to bond. He had already asked me seven times where I went to college, so we were ready to cover new ground. "I get the feeling that you're underutilized at work," he said. I brightened. At least someone noticed. "I can tell by your body language," he continued. "You sort of slump around." The paranoia was back. I started to feel anxious as I anticipated the time and energy I'd have to invest in feigning the good posture that might deactivate his awareness of my body.

"So the work doesn't move your soul, huh?" he pressed. In the space of the next nine minutes, we covered my intellectual life, Harry supportively rejecting what had suddenly become my hobbies (what I had once considered my pulsating subjectivity). Photography: What did I take pictures of? Things in Prospect Park. Like water fountains. (Water fountains?) And film: What did I mean by experimental documentary? I could only answer in the form of a *Jeopardy!* question: "What is not Ken Burns?"

Harry leaned in. "Did you ever consider . . ." He paused, providing him the time to screw up his courage, me the delusive opportunity to make a mental note: Work lunches are good. They lead to things. ". . . modeling?" I looked up. "I mean, I don't know anything about the industry, wouldn't know who to tell you to talk to."

"That's a great idea," I said appreciatively. Pleased to be able to simultaneously flaunt my expertise about a realm of aesthetics Harry hadn't yet mastered and discredit his male gaze by further objectifying myself, I offered the following: "You know, there are really stringent rules for modeling—you have to be so tall, so thin. . . ."

He felt for me, adding that it was my face he was talking about; he thought it was great—"from an audience perspective." I wondered what appreciating a woman's face from the opposite of an audience perspective would be, and was beginning to formulate a theory of the dichotomy between social approval and self-love when Harry swallowed the last bit of his hamburger, having first swiped it through the dregs of his cole slaw dressing, and said, as if the drenched beef had triggered a memory, "You know, at my last job, Keith Hernandez's fiancée was the office manager. I remember when she walked into my office on the first day, to introduce herself—she was very friendly . . . I couldn't believe it . . ." He reenacted the moment, eyes and mouth wide with debilitated gratification.

"She was a model," he explained. He struggled to capture her beauty, frustrated by his inability to describe what she offered. So he moved on to her body: "It was perfect!"

I enthusiastically reveled in the rare and satisfying presence of an ideal female form with Harry, my shoulders seeming to broaden and my neck thickening as I prepared to speak, metamorphosizing from Harry's lovely lunch companion into Keith Hernandez's fiancée's ugly foil: "I know what you mean . . . when you see someone who is a model, you immediately know . . ." Harry nodded absentmindedly, dividing up the bill in his head, and announcing the amounts we both owed.

As we stood up to leave, redressing ourselves for the permanent wind that inhabited Hell's Kitchen, I felt sort of hot and unbalanced, and decided I'd make a lunch date for the next day with Jerry, the field producer who had just been accepted to the Media Studies Ph.D. program at Columbia, to hash out Harry's disturbing behavior. I knew he'd sympathize: he invoked race, class, and gender on the half hour, and I once saw him nod sympathetically at one of our screenings when an interview subject described the harsh judgment she faced for wearing pants in the twenties.

About forty-five minutes later, I was back at work, as ensconced in my chores as I could possibly be, screening tapes on Eugene Debs and squeezing in personal calls when I felt particularly brave. I heard the key in the front door and abruptly hung up on a friend, a habit I keep reminding myself to break in the "Goals" section of my Day Runner. It was just Jerry, and I pressed Pause on the Beta machine and caught his eye as he walked by the screening room so that he'd stop.

"Heyyyy," he said with raised eyebrows and semi-clenched teeth, letting me know he was anxious to settle in at his desk with the alimentary contents of the plastic bag whose handles had twisted around his chubby fore-finger, creating a striking discrepancy between the white of his lower finger and the blood-rushed red of its pinched tip. "Listen," he went on, before I had the opportunity to ask him about lunch the following day. I was surprised that he would initiate conversation when there was food to be eaten—probably something good, too. Jerry was suffering through a familiar stage of delusional dieting—one in which the term *healthy foods* was broadly construed and great surprise greeted the failure to shed pounds when cream-based soups and burritos were readily consumed.

"I finally got a chance to look at your article," he said,

referring to the piece I had written for possible submission to a second-rate scholarly journal. He strongly recommended that I hold off on submitting my research on the feminist implications of Freud's "On Narcissism" based on his reading of the first two pages. "The thing you have to remember is that we're working within a patriarchal structure. We have to negotiate within those bounds— there is no utopia outside it," he said. He stood there, smiling sensitively. My eyes rested on his red finger, half expecting it to burst out of the confines of the plastic bag handles in which it was wrapped and produce a proud arc of semen. I smiled back.

I returned to Eugene Debs for a minute, and then calmly pushed my chair back and got up. I gathered the keys from my desk and slowly walked to the bathroom. I was comforted by the scent of oranges, a sign that the Orange Woman had recently peeled and eaten her daily orange in one of the stalls. I had never actually seen her, but I was simultaneously repulsed by her ability to eat in the bathroom and disgusted by the oppressive workplace that frowned, either implicitly or explicitly, on the presence of orange fumes. At this moment in time, the orange fumes were just what I needed, mixing sickeningly with the cherry disinfectant smell to help me throw up. The borscht came up easily, providing a watery pink color field to catch the smooth tubes of bread that were somewhat more hesitant to reemerge, but greeted the world impressively intact.

I looked down into the bowl, delighted. Next time I'd bring my camera. Then I'd be able to better explain my photo series to Harry.

Collecting the Dead

Kathleen Holt

By lunchtime on Monday, I have two strokes, five heart failures, one breast cancer, one lung cancer, eleven old ages, two diabetes, and even a helicopter crash. The photocopied newspaper article says the helicopter guy was recently married, a freelance writer in his late twenties who was interviewing the pilot for an aviation magazine. The pilot died too, but I don't make a note of him because he has no affiliation with my client, in this case, a local state university. They only get noted if they come up in the database and the pilot guy didn't, but I'm sure he was a decent and worthy person, and some other research company is probably cataloging him. My job is to look for the relevant dead.

"Got a helicopter crash," I say loudly to anyone who will listen. I spin my chair around to face the center of the office and find the others either occupied on the phone or not at their desks. I can hear Bob, the founder and owner of Taylor & Taylor Research, Inc., rustling around at his desk in the corner. Because he's the boss, he gets to be near the office's only two windows and has his own cubicle walls, which serve to block most of the natural light from the room. He even has a rubber tree. The four of us have desks that face the other three walls, no cubicles, no windows, no plants.

When no one comments on my find, Bob says, "Yeah?" politely but uninterestedly. I hear another rustle and figure he's turned back to the sports section or the crossword that he spends most of his time doing. Also, because he's the boss, he gets to keep his hands clean of actually looking for dead people; when he's in the office at all, he does what he calls "administrative stuff."

He and his wife started the company several years ago when they learned that organizations often needed someone to find information for them. Not detective work but "research." In this case, T&T's five-member staff will find dead people and their families at a very competitive rate. Our biggest account is the aforementioned state university, but we also have clients in other fields like financial-investment services and insurance companies. I'd like to claim ignorance in knowing what our clients do with the information, but I am fairly certain it involves making money off freshly grieving survivors. His wife left him a couple years back, couldn't stand being in the death business anymore, but they're only separated. He won't give her a divorce, and he keeps both Taylors in the name because it sounds better than just "Bob Taylor Research, Inc."

To be polite, but also to annoy him, I keep talking to Bob. "Yeah, the guy was only in his twenties. Newly married. Just writing a story about the pilot. Just doing his job," I say. "Bummer, huh?"

"Bummer," Bob says from his fortress.

"Well, you wouldn't catch me in a helicopter. No way." I rock my chair back and forth so it makes a high-pitched squeak that echoes off the bare walls.

Bob is still shifting and rustling about in his cubicle when Maxine walks in from her break, and I tell her the news about the helicopter guy. She is the other younger person besides me and the newest; she started about three weeks ago replacing the ex-long-timer. In the real world, I can't stand brash, loud women like Maxine, but in this business office, there is something about her dyed-red hair, noisy jewelry, and singsong voice that is very welcome.

"Michael, no! Really? A helicopter crash, really?" She skitters over to my desk enthusiastically. "Where? Let me see." I hand her the photocopied newspaper article. "Wow, there's a picture of him," she says, squinting. "He was young. And cute."

Maxine is always commenting on the physical qualities of our dead people and it makes me a little uncomfortable. I mean, they are dead, which is definitely their overriding condition, beyond cute, beyond young. If I was looking at Bob's mug on an obit, he would be dead to me, not big and fat. Seems like you should have at least a little respect.

Looking for the dead and collecting information about their survivors is not something anyone can do. In fact, when I started three months ago, I didn't think I'd last a day. The woman who trained me, a mother of three in her forties who'd just begun working again after years of staying home raising her kids, had been doing it for eleven months and was considered a long-timer. "You just can't think of these people as people," she told me. "It's much easier if you think of them in some other way, like by the way they died." She doesn't work here anymore. I was sitting at the desk beside her on the day she left. I noticed she had stopped sifting through her newspaper clippings, was just sitting there staring at them. Then she stood and picked up her bag, saying, "I'm going to grab a smoke," but she never came back, not even for her last paycheck.

My girlfriend, Luisa, thinks I'm nuts to do this. "Michael," she tells me at least once a week at breakfast, "what you do, it's not normal."

"Yes," I say, nodding. "It's not."

She said it again this morning before I left for work. She sat across from me and sighed, occasionally spoon-feeding her three-year-old son, Samuel, whenever he stopped feeding himself. Samuel is not a morning kid and has a tendency to fall asleep in his oatmeal, but this morning he was mostly awake and regarding me sullenly, as if I were responsible for the early hour. I stuck my tongue out at him and crossed my eyes, but he was not amused. The morning paper was spread across the table between us. From the way Luisa kept shaking her head, I knew she was reading headlines about car accidents, child abuse, domestic violence—all that sorry stuff. At one point, she glanced over at me accusingly and I had to show her my section so she could see I was reading the funnies, not the obituaries. Scanning the obits in my free time is a habit I've picked up since taking this job—"a dirty stinking habit," as Luisa would say scoldingly. She hates what I do but is good at not holding it against me; she always gives me an open-mouthed, coffee-flavored kiss at the door before I leave.

Most of the dead we collect for our university client fall in two general categories: "cause of death unreported" and "all others." The breakdown is about fifty-fifty. For some reason, people are very secretive about the causes of their loved ones' deaths, as if they are ashamed. The university doesn't care about the cause, doesn't care if there's none listed. They just want the names of the survivors. But we keep records anyway. We collect the dead, catalog them, sort them, and record them, just in case we can sell off parts of our research to another client: easy money since the work is already done. For example, a nonprofit cancer organization might want to buy a list of the cancer dead, probably so they can call the surviving families and encourage them to donate money for cancer research, hospices, support programs, stuff like that.

The "all others" are literally all others. The most common ones are illnesses and diseases: all kinds of cancer, heart failures, strokes. And then there's age-related causes. These are the saddest in a way, even though you know these folks probably died peacefully, just went to bed and didn't wake up. But there was no great battle, nothing to blame except the human duration of their lives. Nothing felled them, no disease or accident or murder. They just died.

Another way we find out about dead people is through the notes survivors send to the university that are photocopied, stamped RECEIVED, and sent on to us in large manilla envelopes. Those are the worst to get because they're usually emotional, handwritten letters. You have to learn to skim those quickly, look for the cause of death, make note of the survivors and places of residence, and move on. You cannot get wrapped up in the words because then you won't ever forget them: "My brother was taken by death . . ." "My grandmother, who we all called 'Cookie,' died after a long battle with . . ." "It is my sad duty to inform you of the untimely passing of my wife . . ." "I woke one fine summer morning to find my husband of forty-seven years had passed away in the night. I am so sorry." "Signed, a heartbroken father." You just have to move on.

The others want to go out to lunch together, but I have other plans and reluctantly decline. Their offer seems so much more attractive than the prospect of having lunch with a couple of former colleagues from school. They are back in town after spending the summer backpacking through Europe and are now working on their masters' degrees in geology. Even though I'm not with them in the program as originally planned, they want to see me on a regular basis, to make sure we keep in touch. I dropped out last spring, two weeks into the last term of my senior year, and Chris and Barbara, the couple I am meeting for lunch, took it harder than my parents. They all wanted an explanation but I couldn't give one to them then, and I'm not sure I'd be any more able to explain it today, even though I've had months to figure it out.

I am meeting them at the McKenzie, an off-campus dive near the science buildings, where we'd eaten most of our meals over the past couple of years. By the time I get there, they are already at a corner table downstairs, deciding from a shared menu. I realize how much they've begun to look alike and wonder when that started happening. We all met in one of the core classes, Structural Geology, I think, when the three of us were assigned to the same discussion group. Over the next couple of months, both Chris and I fell in love with Barbara, and she fell for both of us, which put her in the unenviable position of having to choose. By the end of junior year she'd chosen Chris, and I limped away to spend the summer licking my wounds. But by the next autumn, when I found them saving me a seat in a geophysics class, everything had reached some sort of equilibrium and we never looked back.

I embrace Barbara and shake Chris's hand—we've always been pretty manly around each other, have never lapsed into the comfortable genderless affection some men do, the kind that includes an occasional hug. They tease me about how grown-up I look with my short hair and clean-shaven face, and I endure their taunts without commenting on the "twinness" I noticed in them earlier. We order and I smirk when Barbara orders a veggie burger like Chris; she had once been a ravenous carnivore like me, and we'd laugh maliciously when Chris would moan, "How can you eat something that's been murdered?"

"So your girlfriend couldn't join us?" Barbara asks, munching on french fries, her large round glasses bobbing up and down as she chews. She absently pushes them to the bridge of her freckled nose, a ritual that would drive me to contact lenses if I were her, but one that has become an endearing physical quirk. "What's her name again?"

"Luisa," I say, reaching for a fry.

"That's right." She turns and looks knowingly at Chris, who nods back at her. "Is she Hispanic?"

"Yes," I say, squirming. They are not racist but WASP-ish, and can be fairly judgmental. Moreover, they are scientists and approach life with the intention of categorizing it: Is it igneous, sedimentary, or metamorphic? Test it, measure it, weigh it, break it apart, test it more. Reduce it to its basic elements (mineral? chemical?), name it, tag it, put it away for future reference.

"And you said she has a kid?" Chris says.

"Yeah. Samuel. He's three."

"Where's his dad?" he asks.

"He died in a car accident," I say, shrugging, then I change the subject. "So are you guys getting married or what?"

They laugh and tell me about their five-year plan: finish grad school, move wherever one of them gets a teaching position, get married, do research, get tenure, have kids, et cetera. I remember the list, once knew it well since it was my list, too. I nod at all the appropriate places and feel no pang of loss. For this, I'm surprised and grateful.

"So the short answer is, 'Yes. Some day soon,' " Barbara says laughing. "What about you and Luisa?"

"Well, seeing as we've only been going out for a few months," I say stiffly, although I'm trying to be a sport, "that seems a little further down the road, if at all. Who knows? Maybe so, maybe not."

Chris is shaking his head and staring at me with a surprised look on his face. "You have changed so much," he says. "You used to have everything mapped out. To a tee."

I feel the urge to blurt out, You're right, I was such a person, but it's all different for me now. I want to tell how it all started changing, slowly at first, then building up, layer upon layer. Don't you remember, I want to say, that first introductory class with Dr. Beal, how the first thing he said to us was, "If the earth had been born at 12:01 this morning, went about its development and creation duties, the human race would not even appear on the scene until 11:59 P.M." Then how he turned to a four-foot-tall chart permanently posted on the lecture-room wall, the chart that highlighted the geological time scale, ranging from Archean to Cenozoic, from primordial goulash to the World Wide Web. How he pointed to Quaternary, a thin sliver at the top of the chart that not even the students in the first row could make out from their seats. How we all leaned forward, straining to see. "There we are," he said. "All of human civilization a thin line on this chart, a blip in the scheme of things. Don't forget this." That, I want to say, is where it all started to end for me. But I just smile and finish my soup.

Why did I leave? It's got to be more than some stupid lecture, right? And of course it was. I have been lucky so far. Luisa is undemanding; she wants to know but won't ask. We met after the fact and she considers my history something that involves her only if I want it to. My parents are far across the continent; on the phone, I talk quickly and sound confident, as if I have all the plans and reasons in the world.

But I do want to explain, to say something brief and

final and true. Something to end the wondering looks. Something whole and satisfying. The truth is hard to say. But let me try.

The rocks got too big. Does that sound dumb? I was initially attracted to the substance of geology, the visible mass of rock and void of faults, the explainable pressure of gases and rush of magma. The making of mountains and crevasses, of prairies and ice caps. How plate tectonics made sense: a puzzle. Of course. You just put the pieces together. But then I started getting hung up on the time thing. Geological time. Not the suddenness of landslides or the fluidity of a desert. I mean the timeless weathered wound of eroding granite, the painful ache of a slowly widening river. The changes to the landscape that one human, not even the one very observant human I was studying to be, wouldn't see run its course in his comparatively short life, just a speck in the time line of geology. The rocks were too big, too old, too permanent. They saw too much and I, we, will never see enough. All of it began to seem pointless, useless, unfair.

That was when I began walking through the day expecting my life to end at any moment, because really, the way I had it figured, any moment was as much a possibility as anything else. On the way to school, I sometimes expected to get hit while crossing a street and I'd run like a madman to get across, even if the nearest car was blocks away. Whenever I had a stomachache, I'd suspect botulism or *E. coli* and crawl into the student health center, only to be sent away with a bottle of antacids. And when traveling into the mountains on field expeditions, I'd stare hard at each car heading toward us in the opposite lane, wondering, "Is this the one that will hit us head-on? Is this when I die?"

You see how it all got to be too much, got to be too crazy. That was no way to live, don't you think? So that's why I did it. That's why I walked away.

Back at work that afternoon, I receive lots of attention for my dead helicopter guy from Bonnie and Steve, who've been clued in by Maxine. They've both been here a few months longer than me, but neither has had a helicopter crash. "That tops the woman washed out of her car during the spring floods, for sure," Bonnie says appreciatively. "And the guy hit by a bus," Steve adds. As accidents go, a helicopter crash is pretty interesting. Only a particularly gruesome murder could have topped it, but we rarely get the details of those. If we only get the obituary and don't find the actual article about the murder, the obit will always say something vague, like "Family did not disclose cause of death," or worse, "So-and-so died"—that's it. No indication at all. Those about make me crazy.

Maxine makes me a copy of the helicopter guy's newspaper article—"a keepsake," she says—and I fold it up and put it in my wallet. I should ham it up and bask in the day's find, but lunch with Chris and Barbara has left me quiet. I spend the afternoon organizing the day's reports from my out-of-state correspondents, men and women I talk to on the phone but have never met, who read their local papers, clip relevant obits, and send them to me. "Need more SASEs," writes one correspondent in Missoula, Montana. "This old lady might have gone to your school 'cause it says she was born near there," writes another from Bangor, Maine. I sort the clippings, skim the obits, and check the names against my database, making note of how much I owe each correspondent in finder's fees (a sliding-scale commission that rewards quantity and productivity) until it is time to leave. No gruesome murders today.

I think the problem is, I was raised godless. Godless, Christless, Allahless, Buddhaless. Churchless, synagogueless, mosqueless. Rabbiless, priestless, nunless. Religionless. For a long time, I thought the term scriptures simply referred to cursive writing. My parents are academics; they believe in science and books and man, not God.

Luisa is Catholic. She never goes to Mass, has had a child out of wedlock, and never misses her birth-control pill. But she is sheltered in the familiarity of faith. She knows *how* to believe. She says that when her boyfriend before me, Samuel's father, died in a car accident, the hospital called her and told her to come in. She asked, "How is he, how is he, how is he," again and again, but the voice would only tell her to come to the emergency room. She says she prayed as she drove and when she got there and was told he was dead, that he'd had a blood-alcohol level of .14 and had careened into a telephone pole, a peace settled over her and she was calm. I tell her the peace she felt was denial, shock, even relief because the man had been an abusive, philandering asshole. She says no, it was God. My mouth fills with envy.

I want to say that finding God, any god, will save me from this slipping and shifting I feel inside. I want to say I believe that. But I don't. I know not doing a thing won't help either, but then again, maybe the rumblings will stop on their own. Sometimes a tremor is not indicative of an earthquake; sometimes it's the most the earth will move for years to come.

I pull up in front of Luisa's house and get out of the car. I still have my old apartment from when I was a student but only sleep there when Luisa's family comes around. They live in the next town over and come and visit her at least a couple times a month. I walk up the cracked sidewalk, stepping over an unrolled garden hose and an assortment of Samuel's toy trucks. Samuel's faded blue wading pool is half filled with thick greenish-brown rainwater and a thin layer of the season's first leaves; our Indian summer is drawing to an end. I climb over the unfolded lawn chair Luisa has jammed between the railings of the front steps—a quick-fix blockade she uses to keep Samuel from running into the street after he's escaped from the house.

The mess of her yard and house are endearing to me. It's her way of rebelling against the structure of the rest of her life, of the necessary reliability required of a good mother and daughter and sister and aunt and granddaughter. She hates her work as a shelver at the public library because it's too rigid and ordered, and has come to hate books because she thinks they're too needy and urgent and ever-there—"They just keep coming," she says grouchily. "I can see why post office folks go loco."

We met in the library, my second home after I dropped out—how I loved the undemanding presence of high knowledge shelved next to fluffy pulp, book after book, all around me, as I weaned myself from academia. I approached her in the stacks one day, innocently inquiring about why everything by and about riparian ecologists was gone. She was crouched down, struggling with some large, unwieldy books on the bottom shelf. Without looking up at me, she snapped, "I'm sure you're the *only* one in the world who wants them." She stood, looked me in the eye and said, "They're probably checked out. This *is* a library." And then her face softened, almost imperceptibly, but it did. It must've been my disheveled earnestness or the recently struck-by-catastrophe smell I gave off. "Well, I shouldn't do this. 'Only qualified librarians should help patrons in book acquisition,'" she said sarcastically. "Let's go find those weird ecologists of yours." Of course, I fell in love with her. I searched her out each day in those tall shelves, thinking up information I'd claim to need, categories that would make her scowl or snicker or laugh—"Statistics on lobotomies in upper-income Americans? You're a mental case! Go ask a librarian, you nut, I'm not messing with that stuff"—until I charmed some kindness and, soon after, some affection out of her. Our courtship made no sense at all, and it was perfect in all its imperfect, irrational, inexplicable ways.

As I open the front door, I hear her raised voice telling Samuel, no, he cannot watch his nature show if he won't eat his meat loaf. She looks up at me as I walk into the kitchen and smiles weakly. Samuel looks at me and continues to pout, his lower lip drooping lower and lower as I watch. "This kid," she says exasperatedly, "he'll eat his beans, he'll eat his potatoes, but he won't touch his meat loaf."

"Looks like you got a vegetarian on your hands," I say,

stooping to kiss Luisa and patting Samuel's head. I grab one of the tiny, precut chunks of meat loaf off his plate with my fingers and eat it. "Yum, yum," I say, "you don't know what you're missing." He almost laughs at me but remembers he's pouting and quickly looks away so he can better concentrate on his anger.

As I'm making myself a plate, I tell Luisa about the helicopter guy but she says nothing. When I look at her, she is staring at me, her dark eyes thin slits and her mouth a straight and humorless line. She watches me as I sit down at the table. Then she also looks away and pouts. I eat my dinner ignored and in silence.

Eventually, she gets up, takes Samuel's plate from the table and drops it in the sink, telling him to go ahead and starve, just don't come crying to her. Triumphant, he springs from the table and I hear the TV go on in the next room. A man with a deep monotonous voice is talking about lemmings.

"It's those damn nature shows," she mumbles as she scrapes the food from his plate into the trash. "He watches the little critters running around on TV and thinks I'm personally killing and cooking up the same ones in the kitchen. Of course he won't eat meat." She turns on the water and begins filling the sink with soap. "You know there's a difference," she shouts toward the door to the living room, "between livestock and wildlife. We're not eating squirrels and woodchucks here."

I clear the table and take the dishes to her. She smiles and thanks me. I roll up my sleeves to help her rinse and she thanks me again. We quietly stand there doing the dishes, the occasional rush of water from the faucet drowning out the talk of lemmings in the background. After I rinse them off, I place the dishes in the rack on the counter carefully, making a solid structure of the random plates and bowls and forks and cups.

"My mother and grandmother are coming later this week," she says after a while. "You have to sleep at your place but you can hang out with us. In fact, you should. You should meet them."

"Okay," I say cautiously. I've avoided meeting them for months, and Luisa has let me off the hook until now. I'm not sure how they'll feel about me, my white skin, fair hair, white ways. Luisa has told me several times that she is white also; her father was biracial. And that Samuel's father was biracial. Neither of those men are in the picture anymore, both dead and gone. I feel this will only make me more cursed in their eyes. White men are unlucky in death, they probably think. White, godless men, especially.

"Besides," she continues, passing me a glass, "it's el Dia

de los Muertos, the Day of the Dead celebration down at the university. You should come and make peace with the dead while you're still alive."

I'm so startled I almost drop the glass, but I recover. Luisa tosses her dark hair off her shoulders and laughs at me, her white teeth brilliant against her brown skin. "Day of the Dead," I repeat drily. "Sounds like a lot of fun."

"It's not what it sounds like," she reassures me. "It's a celebration. We eat and drink and dance and sing and visit with our dead. They come back and hang out with the living. It's a very nondiscriminatory party. Even living white boys like you can come."

Back at work the next day, my coworkers get a kick out of me taking Friday off so I can go to Day of the Dead with Luisa's family. "But every day is Day of the Dead around here," Bob says cleverly. "Yeah," says Maxine, in rare cooperation with Bob. "You could even say it's like Weeks and Weeks of the Dead." Assorted laughter and similar puns follow.

I'm late getting to Luisa's that morning because I can't decide what to wear. What is appropriate dress for a party for the dead? "Think 'Fun and Games with Dead Folks,'" Luisa says unhelpfully. Not formal funeral clothes. Not casual party clothes. Something in between. I end up wearing jeans and a black turtleneck.

When I get to Luisa's house, I see that in honor of the day, she's cleaned up the front yard, emptied the pool, and put away the folding chair. I'm nervous as I knock at the front door. I expect her mother and grandmother to be mysterious old Hispanic women, short and round and shrouded in black. Women who never smile and who cross themselves often, rolling their eyes skyward and mumbling prayers in Spanish. Luisa lets me in and leads me into the kitchen where Samuel has fallen asleep at the table and is flanked by two women who are smoking Camels. One of them is patting his back gently. I can't tell which is the mother of the other.

One of them jumps up to greet me, fumbling as she plucks her cigarette from her mouth and balances it on the edge of the plate Luisa has put out as a makeshift ashtray. She is plump in a motherly way and her dark eyes sparkle. "You must be Michael," she says, hugging me. "He's handsome!" she says in a mock whisper to Luisa before smiling back at me.

"Yeah, Ma," she replies, looking at me fondly. "I do okay sometimes."

The woman at the table snorts and says, "*Sometimes* is right, but I wouldn't start getting cocky if I were you." She smiles at me and says, "Sit down, boy. You're so tall my neck hurts just looking up at you."

As I sit, Luisa touches my elbow and says, "This is my

Grandma Izzie and my mom, Connie." Grandma Izzie offers me a cigarette but I decline. Samuel's still asleep across the table from me, a thin line of drool running from his open mouth, down his plump cheek. On the table before me, there is a plate of baked goods. Some of them are decorated as skulls.

Grandma Izzie and Connie take turns telling me about how they were up all night working on costumes for the local elementary school. The fifth-graders, one of whom is Luisa's niece, are doing a holiday play next month and the women have agreed to make a few of the costumes.

"They're doing this nondenominational thing," explains Connie. She takes one of the skull-decorated pastries and breaks it in pieces, eating as she talks. "Or I guess, a multidenominational thing. Not simple things like sugarplum fairy tutus or elf costumes. They're doing this 'Everybody of every religion sits down together to have a Thanksgiving-Hanukkah-Christmas meal and learns about each other' skit."

"We have to make a cardinal's miter, of all things," Grandma Izzie says irritably.

"Not just that, but a nun's habit and a priest's robe," Connie says. "We're doing the Catholic stuff 'cause we're experts, I guess."

"We got fooled," Grandma Izzie complains good-naturedly. She stubs out her cigarette and lights another.

"They said, 'It will just be three costumes.' But the three hardest."

"Too bad we didn't get the Buddhist stuff, eh?" says Connie. "Just get some long cloth and wrap it around and around the kids like sarongs." We all laugh and Connie winks at me. "You're not Buddhist, are you, Michael?"

"No, I'm not," I say shrugging. "Actually, I'm not anything. I mean, any religion."

"That's better, probably," Connie says, pinching my arm. "Then you don't get stuck making costumes."

Luisa pulls a chair up beside me. "We're going to the university later for the procession to the cemetery and to look at the altars," she says. She pulls the plate of pastries toward us and asks, "*Hojaldra?* It's just sweet bread." I choose a plain, undecorated roll. "But we just set up our altar here in the living room since our dead are all in different places."

"Will you bring your dead to our altar?" Connie asks.

"I have no dead," I say helplessly.

"You work all day with the dead and you have no dead," she says laughing.

"But that's my job," I explain. "I don't know any of them." No one says a thing. They're all looking at me, waiting. "See, all my close friends and immediate family are alive. I don't have any dead to visit, or whatever you do."

They keep looking at me, concerned and sympathetic. It's like they're the ones who are lucky because they have dead, because they know about sorrow and grief and mourning and life. After a while, Luisa says, "What about that helicopter guy?"

"Yes, there's him," I reply slowly. I look at Connie and Grandma Izzie and say, "He was about my age, a reporter." I reach into my wallet, unfold the photocopy Maxine made me, and skim it quickly. "His name was Gabe Meyers," I continue, saying his name for the first time. I hand the article to Luisa to look at. "He was interviewing a helicopter pilot when they crashed north of here, in the Cascades. Mechanical problems. Took search and rescue a week to get to the bodies. They died on impact. He had a wife. Her name was Sarah." No one asks why I'm carrying this piece of paper with me, which is fine because I have no good reason. They just pass it around, look at the picture, read the article.

"Put him on the altar," Grandma Izzie says, handing the folded paper back to me. Luisa gets up and smiles at me, and I follow her to the living room.

She's cleared the coffee table of its usual mess of magazines and Samuel's toys, has pushed it up against the large console TV, and draped both pieces of furniture with a printed, salmon-colored cloth. Photos of men and women and children, about ten or fifteen different people, are propped on the covered table in frames, some ornate, some plain. There are handwritten letters, documents, other mementos beside the photos, and another plate of pastries. A few candles are set up in holders but are unlit. There is a vase of marigolds and some oranges, as well as a bottle of tequila and three glasses of water. The whole setup reminds me of dioramas I made in middle school.

"This is Big Sam." Luisa touches one of the larger photos. "Samuel's father." He is young in the photo, a big, burly man, dark-skinned with a mustache. "And this is my papa and grandpa." She gestures toward two other photos of handsome dark men, both dressed in military uniforms.

"Did they die in wars?" I ask.

"No. My papa died in a car accident when I was little. My grandpa died of lung cancer not too long ago." She continues through the rest of the photos, telling me about lost aunts and uncles and great-grandparents, and even a younger sister. "Amalia died before she learned to walk, soon after my father left us. She just never woke up from a nap one day. My mom thinks she couldn't bear the thought of being raised without a father, so she went away."

"That's too bad," I say, reaching for her hand and squeezing it. "It's so unfair."

"Michael," she says, smiling and squeezing my hand in return, "unfair implies a broken promise, right? We weren't promised anything."

I don't know what to say. I'm thinking, that's what's so unfair. We should have been promised something, not immortality or earthly riches, but time enough for a good life, time enough to be complete. Maybe I don't deserve such a promise, but certainly Luisa and her family of faithful do. Yet, when I look into her eyes, I see no grief there, no marked pain that requires my embrace or kind words. The grief has settled into her, become a part of her, and she has made a space for it. Around me, on this altar, in this house of three women and one sleeping nature-loving child, there is the presence of the dead and the acceptance of the living. I feel lost in their grace.

"Here," she says, handing me a safety pin. "Pin Gabe on the cloth so he doesn't get lost."

I clumsily smooth out the photocopied article and pierce it with the pin. I then stick the pin through the cloth and back out, securing it. It dangles forlornly against the TV beside the picture of Big Sam. Luisa stoops down beside me and smooths it out more, until it hangs flat and steady.

As I crouch there awkwardly, Luisa slides an ottoman over for me to sit on. She kisses me lightly on the top of my head and leaves the room. I want to follow her, but I know I'm expected to stay and do something. I look at the altar, the pictures of Luisa's dead, read the death certificates and love letters. I try to avoid Gabe Meyers, his wide smile and long hair. It is longer than mine used to be, leonine, young hair. Long soft curls that his mother brushed out of his eyes when she saw him, that his wife caressed between her fingers before she told him she loved him. I bet he sometimes wore a backwards baseball cap to keep it out of his eyes, just like I used to when I peered over specimens in the lab. What team do you like, I want to ask him, looking at his picture for a clue. I'm a Cubs fan myself.

He was young like me when his life ended. Had been middle-aged in his teens but didn't know it. If someone had told him, "You will die before you're thirty," would it have mattered? Would he have lived differently, carefully, cautiously? Maybe he would have meted out his life into portions, spread his experiences thin, hoping a little would go a long way. Or maybe he would have gone for broke, lived like he was going to live anyway, regardless of sum totals, regardless of bottom lines. As if there were no standard for what a human life weighs at death, as if there were no such scale of measure.

But his family probably feels pretty ripped off, especially his wife who thought she'd have a whole lifetime with him, thought they'd grow old together. Maybe they are measuring the value and weight of Gabe Meyers's life and are finding it lacking, are wishing for more of him, are regretting things unspoken and craving a second chance. They have to go through that litany of grief and mourning, turning alternately to each other and then into themselves, a constant shifting to find comfort. In this way, Gabe got off easy. But maybe they're religious people and are finding a quicker way to acceptance than I can imagine. Maybe Gabe was a religious man and maybe his god was there for him at the end. Maybe that made some difference.

How did he feel being up there? With his own life in his own hands, so aware, so in tune, seeing the puzzle of the land, of all that matters and doesn't matter, and, maybe, understanding how it all fit together. He'd have seen everything up there, the geology of the Pacific Northwest, the same geology I'd studied from the safety of my lab in such detail, until the minutiae began to grow larger than life, out of proportion, and unbearably present. But he'd seen the large scale, the grand scheme.

He would've seen the rolling Western Cascade Range formed by the headlong crash of the Farallon and North American plates, how the North American had floated as the Farallon plunged, how the lava had bubbled up into the wound of contact creating the formidable stitch of mountains, hills, volcanoes, all flanked by rainy lowlands and arid plateaus on either side. He'd have seen evidence of old lava flows, dark basalt now mostly covered by conifers and high-altitude deciduous trees. In the distance, he'd have seen the glaciers of the Three Sisters in the High Cascade Range, with their millions of cubic feet of snow and ice. He'd have seen the rivers, tributaries, streams that run steadfast and sure through the forests, into the valley, clearing paths as they go.

You probably didn't know any of this, Gabe, any of this history of the earth, of life and time immeasurable. Maybe the weather that day was just right and the land was unspeakably beautiful, and that was all you needed to know about the sky around you and the land below you. Maybe nothing else mattered. But I can't help but wonder (it must be the latent scientist in me, still wondering, still testing, still trying to categorize): Beyond science, beyond geology and topography, was there something you wondered about that day? Was there something more you would have wished for? It could be anything—some fragment of knowledge, some question answered, some puzzle solved. Was there anything more you felt you needed out of life, something to make it all make more sense?

Or was it all, in the end, more than you could've ever asked for? Even better, Gabe, tell me: For all you knew and didn't know, for all that made perfect sense and for all that eluded you, was your life as much as you'd hoped for? In the end, was it enough?

Pillowcases

David Rowell

One Friday evening my mother came downstairs with three pillowcases in her hand and said, "I have a new game." My mother, whose love for inventing games was surpassed only by playing them, called out the impromptu instructions to me and my father with an eager, childlike excitement. The game, such as it was, involved putting a pillowcase over your head and then going about your normal routine—whatever that was—without bumping into something. You started with one hundred points, she explained, and every time you bumped into something you lost a point. What constituted as actually bumping into something was unclear to me, and the issue of whether you had to report on yourself was not raised, but these were the kinds of technicalities that my parents could not bother with before they began. They threw themselves into their games like varsity linebackers.

"I don't think I'll play," I said. I still had a burn mark on my hand from the stovetop game my father had invented a couple of weeks before. Too, I had missed a birthday party held at a bowling alley the previous Saturday because my mother had hidden herself in a sleeping bag in the attic, and I had decided then I didn't want anything more to do with their games.

"Well, then you can watch us," my mother said. I sat in the easy chair and pretended to read my Spider-man comic book. They giggled as they worked the pillowcases over their heads.

"I can't see a thing," my father said, decidedly pleased.

"Me neither," said my mother. "Okay, then. Let's begin."

My father got off to a less-than-graceful start. Groping his way around the hallway, he tripped on the stairs. He smashed into the desk when the phone rang. Twice he stubbed his toe. My mother, on the other hand, maneuvered around effortlessly, only occasionally reaching out with her slender hands to orient herself before she pulled something down from a shelf or reached into a drawer. She waltzed in and out of rooms. She even fried eggs for me, though it was close to eleven o'clock at night.

"You sure are missing out," she said, and hummed a muffled tune as she set a place for me at the table.

"Watching is not so bad," I said. From the kitchen I could see my father as his long fingers nervously probed the miniature bust of Beethoven, as if just touching it might get his confidence back.

When I announced I was going to bed, my mother floated up after me. Before I reached the top, we heard the coat rack crash down on my father.

"Seventy-two!" he yelled. "Damn!"

Other friends' parents had backyard barbecues, played Bingo or Monopoly or croquet, and asked questions like, "So how do you boys plan to stay out of trouble this summer?" without expecting an answer. At my friends' houses I stayed quiet and never touched anything so that I might stay invisible, blend in. Sometimes I'd stay until dinnertime, desperate for something as routine as pot roast or chicken, before one of the parents would think to say to me, Well, I'm sure they're looking for you at home.

My parents were so taken with their new game that they continued it through the weekend. At breakfast, my father's pillowcase was disheveled and twisted. He sat stiffly as my mother flitted around us and served a delicious meal of pancakes and bacon, crispy the way I liked. They ate with their lacy sheets rolled up loosely over their noses, drank their coffee as the steam dampened the thin edges. My father was impossibly behind, but he was not ready to give up. Now he moved in slow, almost robotic gestures.

"Just getting the old sense of surroundings," he said as he cautiously backed himself out of the kitchen.

My mother, who, as far as I knew, had yet to drop a point, went out of her way to look for things to do around the house. She resewed some loose buttons on one of her sweaters and dusted the bookshelves. She stepped outside to sweep the patio.

"Hey, son," my father called when the screen door slammed shut behind her. He stood in a tentative pose behind the reading lamp in the den. "How about checking on your mother for me? Just to see that she's on the up-and-up, if you know what I mean." I had the feeling, then, that he winked at me.

From the kitchen window I watched my mother work the broom around the wrought-iron chairs. I looked to see if the neighbors were out in the yard or eyeing her from their windows, studying her hooded figure as she vigorously swept the wood planks of our deck until they were free of debris. I was afraid the Timmons's dog, Brutus, might start to bark, but a piece of rope had his attention. So many things raced through my mind: I could have easily slipped enough money from my mother's purse and bought a bus ticket to somewhere; I could have taken pictures and tried to sell them to a detective magazine

(accompanying headline: KIDNAPPER TREATS HOSTAGES LIKE GUESTS!)

My father had tucked himself safely into the comfort of the reading desk. I tiptoed over to him to see how close I could get. His fingers glided over various bills marked with "Last Notice" on them. On a notepad my mother had written "Buy candles. Lanterns?"

"I think I hear someone," my father said in a singsong voice. "You can't see me, so I'm even harder to resist. Am I right? Come on over here, you masked beauty, and get a little cotton lip lock." The white pillow case bunched up around his mouth, the faint outline of lips pushing through.

Just then my mother came barreling in from the porch. "The McCoys' cat left another dead mouse on our porch."

My father reshifted his position, propped his hand thoughtfully under his chin, and shook his head in dismay.

On the fourth Sunday of every month, my Uncle Claude and Aunt May came for a visit, though in the last year or so their visits had become less regular and shorter. When they arrived that Sunday, I went out to greet them and described the game in progress. I sensed that they didn't quite understand until we stepped through the living room.

"Claude, I'd come over there and shake your hand if I

could find you," my father said cheerfully. At that moment the sound of his shin knocked against the end table and rang out like a wood block.

My aunt's shoulders arched into bony spikes. She and Uncle Claude stood frozen by the grandfather clock, considering my father, his hands fixed to his narrow hips. They turned to each other, forgetting, I thought, that I could see them perfectly well. Aunt May pursed her lips, maybe unsure what she was going to say, but Uncle Claude shook his head once quickly to cut her off. She then surveyed the room—I wasn't sure for what—before she looked at me and put her lacquered nails on the back of my neck.

"William, did you choose not to play?" she asked. At that moment the word *choose* drifted in front of me like a raft, and I understood that she wanted me to reach for it. Her eyes were wide, searching.

"I didn't want to," I said. "I'm tired of games."

"What can I get everyone to drink?" my mother asked, strolling gallantly into the room. In her bright summer dress and striped pillowcase, she looked almost elegant.

Outpatients. That was how my parents explained their arrangement to me, though it did not explain why they both had their own rooms at the hospital. I tried to make them think that it all made sense to me. The way they talked about it, it was as if outpatients were a new and affluent community group.

During my visits, it seemed that their enthusiasm for games had given way to conversation. They asked me questions rapid-fire, sometimes not waiting long enough for me to answer before they thought of more questions. As they spoke feverishly about the passing of their days—discussing the other residents they had gotten to know, describing at length the movies they had seen on movie night—I had the feeling that each was trying to outdo the other, though I didn't know how, exactly. I couldn't tell what their scoring method was.

They grinned like beauty pageant contestants when I ate with them in the spacious cafeteria, which was sunny and attended by pleasant, heavyset black women in sea-green uniforms. They introduced me to everyone they knew. Most of the people had slightly haunted and confused expressions, which did not resemble how my parents looked at all. If a dance had been held, they would have been the king and queen of it.

Uncle Claude and Aunt May drove me over for my visits. Sometimes they came in with me, and other times they waited for me in the parking lot or went into town to run an errand. I got the feeling that the smell of the place bothered Uncle Claude—his face puckered up when we stepped inside. The sharp, antiseptic smell didn't bother me. In fact, everything there was a little hazy to me: the reception desk, with its crudely cut crepe-paper messages, such as WELCOME SPRING! or SMILES ARE GREAT MEDICINE; the long hallway like an obstacle course with its abandoned buckets on the floor; the courtyard spilling over with ragged, sinuous ivy. The only thing about the facilities that really left an impression on me was the blinding whiteness of my parents' rooms, the radiant shine of their stiff, coarse sheets, the fresh ivory paint of the wooden chairs. And their pillowcases, which always appeared not fully on the pillows, as if they had been frantically thrown on at the very last second.

Second Skin

Shamira Gratch

> *Without wiping away the tears, taking a deep breath, or even bending
> his knees—he leaped. As fleet and bright as a lodestar he wheeled
> toward Guitar and it did not matter which one of them would give up
> his ghost in the killing arms of his brother. For he knew what Shalimar
> knew: If you surrendered to the air you could ride it.*
>
> —*Toni Morrison*, Song of Solomon

The children call him "Tumors," because he is fat, but
his name is Juan Carlos Marisco. His flesh seems stuffed
with lumpy pearls and bulbous cauliflowers. "I will strike
oil in your belly button, *mi hijo*," his mama would coo,
and Juan Carlos would swat his fists at her tickles. Everyone in their neighborhood of Fifteenth and Mission had
thought Senora Marisco was carrying triplets in her ket-
tledrum belly. After nine months of sitting in the front
of the bus and sucking on green mangos from Ziploc bags
there was just baby Juan Carlos, like a beach ball that
could scream and suckle. Senora Marisco believes that the

branches of the family tree buckled with the weight of ghosts and converged in Juan Carlos's mass. She reads his copious flesh as an omen of something profound, like a birthmark portending miracles. There are just her and him now, so she tries to give him the weight of family and memory with an heirloom of names and protective pounds.

Senora Marisco sews in order to keep a pot of beans on the stove, but the money never seems to be enough to fill the voracious landlord man. Sometimes the landlord man unlocks their door. His fingers are sticky with peppermint schnapps and his slippers scuff against the linoleum. "Senora Marisco?" He stubs his toe on the coffee table and curses. "Senora Marisco? Three months now and only you pay for one. There is something you must give me, Senora? Senora?" Juan Carlos wants to giggle because the landlord man draws his mama's name out through his nose, squeaky like bad brakes, but Senora Marisco clasps her hand over Juan Carlos's mouth. Usually the landlord man flops onto the couch. Sometimes he weeps and his sobs shift into snoring. Once he punched a hole in the bathroom door and passed out in the bathtub. Always Juan Carlos and Senora Marisco wait under the dusty wool overcoats until the landlord man stumbles out or can be drug by his stinky feet.

Senora Marisco sews frothy wedding gowns, quincinera

dresses, bat mitzvah suits, and red velvet curtains with gold tassels for the theater and the funeral parlor. Juan Carlos likes to nest under the card table while her sewing machine hums on top. He watches her bare foot press the black pedal. The midnight threads and gold ribbons ripple. Scraps of blue denim and mermaid-green silk sift to the floor like snowflakes from his mama's heaven scissors. When he is old enough, Juan Carlos is allowed pieces of fabric that are too small for knee patches or bed quilts. He gathers up his rainbow crumbs and stitches them awkwardly onto his old socks. He is enthralled with the glint of his jumbo silver needle. To him the device is a magic wand: he can prick his skin and make red blood weep, or he can make all the holes in the world disappear.

Juan Carlos's mother sews all of his clothes because stores do not carry circus-tent sizes for boys. She buys yards and yards of the cheapest fabric. She spreads newspapers out on the kitchen floor and lays his naked body down to trace his outline. His flesh drips in folds, conical breasts sag into the depths of his armpits. His body reminds her of the ocean waves, except pink and caramel. Then she cuts out this gigantic paper doll as a clothes pattern. The newspaper ghost frightens Juan Carlos. It is Scotch-taped together like an inky Frankenstein and his mother grapples with it, wrestling wrinkles out of the arms and sticking the crunchy skin with straight pins. The

final product is always clownish. Juan Carlos pops his head
out from the billowing collar of a shirt patterned with
mustard-yellow roses, and his mother hoists the elastic
waistband of baggy, target-red sweatpants over his barrely
butt. Senora Marisco's flair with ruffles is flattering to a
flat-chested young lady in her prom dress. However, the
same effects in Juan Carlos's ensembles trigger quivers of
sharpened pencils as he trudges to the front of the class
for show and tell.

Juan Carlos wiggles most of his baby teeth out and the
tooth fairy nestles silver dollars under his pillows. He
learns how to tie his shoes and say excuse me when he
needs the toilet. But time isn't melting away his baby fat.
Juan Carlos seems only to expand. Children sometimes
point at him and mothers slap their fingers away for the
rudeness or maybe because they suspect his obesity is con-
tagious. Their eyes linger on the fat of his male breasts,
soft and round as curled-up cats. Juan Carlos sees himself
through their eyes. He is a bulbous head overflowing into
the slope of his shoulders; he is a pillar of chins and
creases. His jowls dangle and his earlobes swell like shiny
red Christmas ornaments. His arms and fingers are squat
and snugged tightly against the curves of his torso. His
legs are stumpy and the flesh hangs in elephant ears off
his thighs. As he gets older the men don't try to hoist
him up and guess his weight. The women don't pinch his

cheeks or pat the "piggy tail" that they chide is sprouting from his tailbone. Now his paunchy body inspires people with the desire to playfully punch his stomach. "Can't feel a thing in there with all that padding, can you, boy?" the men outside the salsa bars slur and jab. Juan Carlos's lips tremble, he is no longer a roly-poly baby. His immense body makes him look old for nine years. The neighborhood gangs interpret Juan Carlos's mass for bullish force. He is often left snorting up his blood on the sidewalk, hugging his fat ribs, gangster rap booming and whining like a mean lullaby in his ears. The howl of a car alarm. The chatter of women at La Tienda as they squabble over gnarled yucca and plantains dappled black against yellow. Juan Carlos rocks back and forth inside his cement cradle. The sun strips brightly and rubs against his face lovingly.

Senora Marisco tries to soothe him. She smooths lush honey creams onto bruises, steaks for black eyes, and a cinnamon stinging salve into gashes he slinks home with. To Juan Carlos, his body feels like a vat of spiced quicksand.

Senora Marisco whisks him to doctors like a freak-show tour. "Hormonal imbalance, digestive tract slip knots, gut jam, and thyroid lethargy," pronounce the ringleader doctors. Doctors thump his stumpy legs and wrap his sausage arms with velcro bicycle pumps that read his blood. He is water-distended and bee-stung ballooned all of the time.

His mother makes him drink mud-bitter teas that she collects from the glass jars of *curanderas*. The neighborhood *abuelas* slip "remedies" from their purses and press them into her hands after church. *"Vaya con dios, mi hija, con dios."* The remedies are envelopes stuffed with prayer cards and dried weeds that stink like compost and pine needles. The herbs come with instructions to steep in rum for two weeks or boil until sludge. Invariably these potions make Juan Carlos gag, kick his mother in the shins, and sob until his face puffs like a bursted peach. Occasionally they cause him to spew a half-digested lunch of pizza and chocolate milk onto the dinner table.

Juan Carlos's mother lights red candles by his bedside. She makes him squat and mumble prayers to the Virgin. Juan Carlos doesn't like this; his legs always fall asleep and the pincushion flesh tickles. He stifles the giggles by gnawing his lip. His mother prays urgently; her words swish like the whisper of scissors against the coarse night fabric.

"Whatcha gonna be for Halloween, Tumors? The Pillsbury Doughboy?" Newspapers and leaves catch in the wire fence, wind chatters. There is only one week before Halloween. Teachers have stapled black-and-orange construction paper witches and pumpkins to bulletin boards. Today in Juan Carlos's class, the children conjured ghosts from white Kleenexes stuffed with cotton balls and rubber-banded at the neck. Juan Carlos inked his ghost's face with pointy teeth and red rimmed eyeballs. He is going to hang his ghost in the window when he gets home. "I'm gonna be a pirate and stab you, lardball." The two boys who have cornered Juan Carlos at the edge of the playground begin to prod Juan Carlos's belly. Juan Carlos knew he should not have wandered this far from the recess monitor. He had wanted to make a newspaper hat and drifted toward the fence where all the trash tangled.

"I'm a pirate, gonna eat you, eat you."

The boys begin to circle Juan Carlos. They joust with mock swords and duel his bloated tummy.

"Awn Gourd!" one boy shrieks in a cartoon French accent. "Thar she blows, mate! Release the torpedoes!" The two boys charge toward Juan Carlos, their fists windmilling and their shoulders hunched forward as if storming a castle. Juan Carlos stands dead still; his eyes glaze black and fix into space. He clutches a newspaper in his left hand. The autumn wind claws his cheeks and ears red-raw. Newspapers rattle hollow gray bones.

"Juan Carlos Marisco! Clean yourself up, young man. Get in line." Grass stains swathe Juan Carlos's knees and chunks of leaves bush from his bedraggled hair. "Everyone in this line has missed the last recess bell. You are all late to class and will receive a tardy. Go straight to Principal Maclatchey's office to get your after-school detention slips." The children groan and whimper like caged monkeys.

"Wipe up your face, young man!" Juan Carlos sniffles; he fishes in his coat pocket for a tissue. His fingers throb from being stomped on and his nipples burn from a riddling of pinches. He blows his nose and notices blood seeping through his Kleenex. He watches the shocking redness spread into the bleached white tissue. The crimson seeps across black eyes and a vampire grin, down to the rubber-banded neck. The thin flesh of his Halloween ghost shrivels as it sops up the humors of his bloody nose. He stuffs it back in his pocket and rubs his nose into his coat sleeve.

The children gather after school in the library where detention time is served. Juan Carlos settles himself in the back corner and bends his head over math homework. A few spitballs hop like wadded fleas into his hair. Some mysterious burps and wind are broken to the chuckles of the children and the admonishing stare of the detention supervisor. Juan Carlos raps his fingers backwards and forwards to calculate the solutions to arithmetic problems. A note steals onto Juan Carlos's desk like a little white mouse. It is folded into a triangle. On the outside of the note the author has drawn a skull and crossbones with the words: "Top secret reed at your own risk." Juan Carlos carefully brushes the note into his lap and unfolds it in hushed solemnity.

TO WHO IT MAY CONCERNS:

This is a true story that a very smart person who would no told to me:

There was a little boy like us who lived in a very dark plase called Yugoslaveea. Once upon a time it was Halloween and this little boy loved Halloween. Becuz he loved candy. He loved those really good red licorishes alot. So this boy dreamed Halloween all the time even when he was supposed to be noing his spelling words and praying to God. He was not very scary for Halloween, he was just a dum white sheet ghost. But he got alot of candy becuz he went to all the houses in Yugoslaveea. He ated all his candy so quick and grew fat like a balloon. He was scary now, he had to roll like a big ball. But the scary thing is the boy blew up! Guts and blood and eyeballs everywhere! He got so fat from his candy that he exploded. No one nos how come. Some peoples say he got so fat his bones all broke or maybe he bust his skin or he suffocated in his sleep, cuz his lungs broke under all his fat. To this today in Yugoslaveea peoples tell kids about the fat boy who bust cuz he ate all his candy in one night. In memories of this dead boy they carve scary faces from fat pumpkins and lite candles inside. This is where we got the idea to make jak-o-lanterns too. But in Yugoslaveea they smash the jak-o-lanterns to rememory the boy who exploded from his candy. I think this is a good idea and we should bust jak-o-lanterns too. I swear to God this is true and only the truth may I go to hell. Pass it on.

Juan Carlos glances around him. His heart quakes. He does not refold the note, instead he crumples it into his pocket.

It is as if he has learned a new word and now hears it everywhere. He begins to feel the pressure of his weight on his bones and feels his skin pull to near bursting. He feels the terraces of his fat-laden body pulling on his joints. He feels the anvils of flesh crushing his lungs. He suddenly wonders if the blossoms of carbuncles that riddle his skin aren't pressure leaks. Red oozy holes are always erupting on his shins, calves, and arms, on the hump of his back and the wattles of his jaw. Maybe he is trying to burst out of his own body. He supposes that as he ages and expands, his frail skin is becoming threadbare and he is spilling himself out of these pimples. He shivers involuntarily, uncomfortable in his body and hyperaware of every gurgle in his gut and itch on his neck. He begins to feel nauseous.

When Juan Carlos gets home his mother slops greasy pinto beans into a dish and presses her lips until they are bloodless white.

"Where have you been, *hijo*?"

"Detention. I'm not hungry."

"Again? Another fight? What is that on your face, another cut? *Dios mío.* Poor baby."

Senora Marisco drops the ladle into the pot and wraps her flabby wings around Juan Carlos. He squirms and slides through the halo of his mother's arms. He waddles to the front window and digs his bloody Kleenex ghost from his pocket. The balled up note tumbles to the floor. Juan Carlos stoops to pick up the note, and then tightens his fist around it. He opens the window and chucks the paper into the splash of late afternoon. He pinches the ghost's head and looks around for a way to hang it. He settles for tying the curtain cord around the neck of the scabby ghost and letting it dangle and knock in the wind. The car-crash red of blood that he accidentally smeared onto the ghost has faded to a dull brick color. He kisses his mother's cheek and buries himself in his bed.

But Juan Carlos does not sleep. He becomes flustered to sleeplessness trying to arrange his body in the least stressful way for his skeleton. He lies on his side, but realizes this might smash him lengthwise. Resting flat on his stomach poses the danger of sudden destruction from a different direction. He spends the night wrestling with his sheets and biting his tear-sodden pillow to muffle his moans of agony. The next day, standing in line for chocolate milk, he frets over the pressure his eggshell skeleton must withstand while upright. Might the colossal watermelons of his flesh implode into a puddle of gristle on the floor at any second? He imagines himself smashed into a lake of blood and tendons, as if one of those cartoon grand pianos plummeted from a skyscraper onto his body. Juan Carlos panics. He lifts each foot with exaggerated accuracy, hoping that he will not somehow trigger the collapse of his body. He pulls each breath in through his nose gingerly so as not to exert too much pressure on his overtaxed lungs.

Juan Carlos squirms in his fold-out chair. He can't squeeze his mass into the child-size desk chairs that line the room. Instead, he always sits with the guinea pig cage and goldfish bowl at the back of the room on a fold-out chair. The teacher stacks a phone book and a bible on his chair so he is elevated enough to peer over the table's edge at the distant blackboard. He spends a lot of his time slipping nibbles of soggy sandwich lettuce to the guinea pig and cookie crumbs to the goldfish. Today Juan Carlos cannot sit still and is fidgeting around trying to find the least harmful position to hold his body in. He accidentally slides off his perch in an effort to adjust his weight and topples over. The phone book and bible smack the floor and his chair snaps shut with a gavel clap. Juan Carlos thumps onto the floor, causing the guinea pig cage to rattle and the goldfish bowl to shake. The guinea pig squeaks with alarm.

"Juan Carlos, quit clowning around and get back in your seat!"

Everyone turns around with glee to watch red-faced Juan Carlos unfold his chair and restack his booster seat. He moves deliberately, feeling each of his body parts for possible ruptures. He glances at his arms and feels his sides for skin that might have split at the seams during his fall. He stares into the fishbowl to avoid the side-snuck glances and snickers of his classmates. The goldfish hovers in the water. It flicks its tail and flows through the clear space. His golden scales shine like sun rind. The filter motor purrs and the bubbles zigzag lackadaisically. A sprig of green sea fern is suspended near a plastic shipwreck. Juan Carlos becomes entranced with the goldfish's sleek body and effortless movement. Weightlessness. He sprinkles some shrimp flakes into the water. The goldfish's body undulates and tugs, the goldfish snatches up the treats as they sift down toward the blue-green gravel. The glass warps the goldfish's movements, refracting slick golden curves into a thousand shards. Juan Carlos swirls his finger into the bowl. The water is cool and smells like cat food and the ocean.

"Juan Carlos! Juan Carlos, get your hand out of the fishbowl! Would you care to join the class? We are discussing our Halloween costumes and why we chose them. Lisa is going to be a princess because princesses are pretty. Thomas is going to be a vampire because his older brother was a vampire last year. What are you going to be?"

"A fish."

Juan Carlos learned to sew from years of mimicking Senora Marisco: feed machine, pluck pins, cut and tuck. Stare at stitches zooming along. Press pedal gently, whir faster and motor goes high, shift gears and the needle jumps in its footprints, crazy bobbin spins and whirls drunk. He likes to sew fast so the machine gets hot and his fingertips can feel the needle breathing. Occasionally he helps his mother sew prom dresses for the boutique on Valencia Street, all lacy webs and greasy ribbons. He likes to imagine little limbs squeezed inside teethy zippers, sucking in tummies and sticking out breasts to get a dance. Juan Carlos knows he can sew the most beautiful fish costume in the world. Juan Carlos rushes home from school and sorts through his mother's remnants for pieces of fabric to incorporate in his fish suit. Instead of watching after-school cartoons he stitches bits of blue denim, chocolate corduroy and black mesh together, crazy quilt fashion. The next day he groans and gropes his stomach. "Mama, *me duele el estomago*, I can't go to school today."

Juan Carlos's stomachache doesn't hinder the creation of his fish suit. Juan Carlos sews late into the night. He hears the brushes of the street cleaner churning the gutters, and the shrill slurs of the stumblers dumped from the bars at 2 A.M. as they try to find each other's beds. He hears the silence of four A.M.

"Mi hijo." His mother awakens confused in the night, her voice brittle like autumn straw. *"Qué paso,* why do you not come to bed?" The light of the sewing machine illuminates Juan Carlos's face as he crouches over the sewing. His fingers dwarf the needle and bits of fabric like ridiculous stuffed turkeys.

"Go to sleep, Ma. I'm busy." Sometimes Juan Carlos's nest of foam pads and wool blankets go untouched all night. The sewing machine sings him into a trance, the needle marches up and down. The stitches begin to parade like ants in front of Juan Carlos's eyes, scattering across the fabric. He starts from these spells suddenly and notices that he has been sewing without thread.

During the day Juan Carlos floats with the goldfish. He notes how the gills puff in and out and the tail flutters. He studies the silver and black discs of the fish's eyes. He imagines the water enveloping his own skin, soft as a widemouthed kiss. The bonds of gravity broken, he would bob carelessly as the water held him. He wouldn't have to fear for his tired bones and flimsy lungs inside the water's beckoning buoyancy. He wouldn't be able to hear the snide jokes and mean words. The water would fill his ears with diamonds and let him drift away.

"But Mama, Halloween is tomorrow and I have to finish my costume." Tears smear Juan Carlos's face. His hands wring the half-finished fish suit. Threads fray from the edges like the frizzy locks of a lunatic. A tinfoil gill droops lopsidedly. Juan Carlos's body has a new sagginess to it; his skin bags. He seems to have lost weight in his fever to finish his fish suit.

"Baby, please. Listen to me. You can be a nice hobo or something simple like a mummy. Whoever heard of being a fish for Halloween? I can't let you stay home from school to sew like a crazy person."

"No! I have to be a fish, you don't understand. It's not just for Halloween; it's, it's, I have to be a fish." Senora Marisco grips Juan Carlos's shuddering shoulders. She can hear his asthmatic sobs like wind through a fine-toothed metal comb. "Okay, *mi hijo, mi pescado.* I will help you."

Juan Carlos skips home from school that day with a fire under his feet that spreads up to a ruddy flare in his cheeks. The autumn sun casts the streets and buildings in a pale filminess. Buses lurch like spasmodic dinosaurs. Mamas haul toddlers and bulging bags of groceries by spidery hands. The old men with smoky faces and faded windbreakers seem to have forgotten why they stepped out. Young men spit on car chrome until it shines like a jackpot. Gangster rap drones. Juan Carlos leaps up the two flights of stairs and smashes through his door.

"*Buenos días, mi hijo,* what a noise you make!"

"Mama, mama, did you finish it?"

"Finish what, my dear? Letting out the waistline of Mr. Parker's suits?"

"No, no, my fish, my fish!"

"Your fish, oh yes. I bought some lovely fish today, fresh orange roughy from Australia, I think. Only four seventy-nine a pound at the Safeway."

"No, Mama, my fish costume."

"Oh, that." Senora Marisco lets a smile seep into the fans of her crow's-feet. "Yes, I think there is something for you in the bathroom."

Juan Carlos rushes past his mother into the bathroom. His fish suit dangles from the shower curtain rod. He slips it off the hanger. He steps into the fish's body. It is wide at his hips and belly, and then narrow at the ankles where his feet come out. His arms fit snugly into the silver triangles of his side fins. There is a hidden zipper slit up the side. The hood pulls up and over his face so two tinfoil-coated tennis balls protrude on the sides of his head like fish eyes. The mouth is a black velvet circle with eye slits cut out for Juan Carlos to peer through secretly. These small eyeholes frame the world in shadowy tunnels. Inside of the fish suit Juan Carlos feels swaddled as if in a sleeping bag. He steps out of the cramped bathroom to behold himself in the full-length mirror. He is a sparkling king enraptured by his coronation. His scaly skin is a hodgepodge of forest-green velour, lilac terry cloth, gold lamé, rose chintz, and a thousand other jewels of color and texture. His fish mouth is frozen open as if surprised. His mother hands him a pair of swimming flippers for his feet.

"Can you see out the eye holes in the mouth? I don't want you to fall."

"Yes, Mama." Juan Carlos whispers, gulping down lumps of salt water that flood into his throat and chest.

That night Juan Carlos sports his fish suit at the dinner table. Senora Marisco serves batter-fried orange roughy with a heap of creamy mashed potatoes and special Halloween Ho-Ho's for dessert. He has to leave the fish head off to find his mouth with his fork. He kisses his mother good night and slithers into his bed, arranging the fish skin around his body so it won't wrinkle too much while he sleeps.

The next morning Juan Carlos wiggles out of bed and smooths his fish skin around him. October thirty-first. He buckles flippers onto his feet; gobbles his usual stack of buttered toast and guzzles a mug of hot chocolate. He waddles into the gloss of morning. He waits at the bus stop, slapping his flippered foot against the pavement. The briefcase commuters stare; the early morning joggers turn their heads as they huff. Juan Carlos feels invisible and superstar beautiful in their eyes. It is as if he has acquired an alias in a distant city. His skin protects him and renders him newly gorgeous. He rises onto the bus and settles in the front. The eyes that used to peck the dimples of his celluloid now smooth over the glint of silver gills and dazzle of velvet and cotton scales. He feels a pull between hunted and desired. Juan Carlos exits the bus and swishes toward school. The playground is seething with plastic witches and greasepaint werewolves. Juan Carlos glides through the children like quiet sunlight. One of his classmates recognizes Juan Carlos's bulk as the glittering fish. Through his eye portals, Juan Carlos observes the stunted Draculas, race-car drivers, cowboys, and princesses swarm closer. He sees them as if through cobwebs; their limbs move stickily and their eyes seem pried open. Slowly they swim toward him, clouds of pink lace, green faces, and plastic guns. He fans his shiny fins up and down, and thumps his flippers against the hard-packed dirt with excitement. The words of the children are muffled by the thick padding of his fish head. He hears blurred rumbles and bright squeals. He can tell from their expressions they are wanting him. Admiring him at last, they point at him and laugh. Red lips flap, thousands of eyes flash, fingers caress his skin. He smiles inside his darkness. He feels the tug of their little claws, he feels the slow bullets of gravity. Limbs jumble in a crazy dance. He is at the center of this whirling crowd of teeth and tongues. He is hot inside his fish suit, sweating. His skin burns and he tastes salt. His dark hair clings in sticky ringlets to his forehead. The shiny lining of his fish suit adheres to his wet skin. Juan Carlos topples over inside the frenzy of hands and feet. The children howl and descend upon him. Like lovers, like vultures, they swoop. He feels a release, as if his body was a cloud and a fat-lipped wind tore him into a thousand wisps. When his seams begin to unravel and his skin sheds in patches, he is already hovering above the crowd. He sees the children's hungry hands snagging bits of indigo wool and picking at gray houndstooth. He sees a body crumpled in a pile among their feet. Something is leaking from the holes. It is another body, melting into the dirt. He floats between the violet air molecules and spreads himself out comfortably across the morning sky. Finally he swims, he flies, and gravity is only a nimble dance partner. Scraps of burgundy corduroy tumble like exotic birds across black dirt and catch in the wire fence. A bell hums and small bodies dart. They kick a cloud of mud up from the bottom, until Juan Carlos sees only a swirl of dust obscuring everything below him.

Pussy Basketball

Timothy Hazen

On the morning of Kevin Beaman's funeral, a white ball arcs along the break of a green and runs into the cup with the determination of water down a chute. Josh pumps his fist while his boss walks off toward the cart, leaving the yellow flagstick lying behind. Once a month, at the suggestion of an overpaid industrial psychologist, the two of them golf at the boss's club, and even though Josh is in every way a better golfer—longer off the tee, crisper irons, better touch around the green—it is the first time he has allowed himself to win. He picks up his ball and replants the forgotten flag, terra incognita having been claimed.

"I don't goddamn believe it," his boss is saying. He slams the putter into his bag and digs out his wallet from one of the bag's zippered pouches. "Don't get me wrong, it was a hell of a putt. But god*damn*, you could set your shag bag down and not make it again." Nothing beats taking a sore loser's money, Josh thinks, slipping a little vinyl booty over his own putter's blade, except maybe taking it from one you work for. The man's puffy, sunburned hands are shaking, and his breath comes in polytonal whistles, a reaction Josh has seen before, in conference rooms, when the overhead won't work.

"Lucky for me I only had to make it once," Josh says.

"Lucky for you," his boss says, handing him one of those new hundreds with the big Ben Franklin. Driving up the cart path to the clubhouse, they pass an old black man perched atop a gang mower purling in low idle. Ticking sprinklers send up rainbows, a bank of blue and white flowers whizzes by. The wind in the speeding cart is cool, and Josh puts his feet up, savoring the other man's silence, relishing his defeated embarrassment. Thinking, *How long, fat man? Two years before your bloated salary catches up with your ineffectiveness? Two years before I'm the one calling for meetings? Before I'm the one driving the cart?*

In the men's grill the boss mutters something about his wife and leaves half a beer. Josh drinks two and, even though he has to be in Springfield by three o'clock, orders food; a docile elderly waitress in nurse's shoes brings him a steak sandwich, cut on the bias and served on the clubhouse china. He eats and showers, runs a comb through his short black hair, and changes into his best dark suit. During the drive he tries to get himself into the appropriate mood but, still high from his triumph, finds it difficult. The way the guy died doesn't help, either; somehow Beaman, whose face Josh can no longer with any certainty recall, accidentally rode his bicycle off a highway overpass. Who's ever heard of such a thing? Guns, asthma, car wrecks, some genetic deficiency in the heart's stitching: these are deaths one understands. Even if Beaman had been hit by a car while biking it would seem more familiar. More tragic. Perhaps what happened really *is* tragic—Josh doesn't know the whole story, and were he to think about it he would suppose it is tragic when anyone dies in their twenties, whatever the reason—but accidentally pedaling off the side of a lonesome country road seems not so much tragic as, well, moronic.

At any rate that's what he and Whisker decided. On the phone Whisker said that most of the Sigma Taus still living in Boston were planning on coming, even though in the seven years since graduation no one had heard anything from or about Kevin Beaman—not Fat Andy, not Zeke the Freak. Not B-Dog, D-Dog, and P-Dog, not Miklos with the dangling ten-incher. Still, Beaman was a brother, so they come. Josh himself has a date that evening with a paralegal, and the golf and sun and beer have left him drowsy, but he comes. It is the right thing to do.

Those who think of fraternities as elitist suck holes, bogus organizations whose thin sheen of charity and community service only serves to make the more essential pursuits of dipsomania and various forms of date rape all the more repugnant—they should see how they come. They should think about all the brothers who are coming and then consider how many people would do the same for them, and then compare.

Pratt Funeral Home is a single-level structure with a shingle roof of alternating gray, rust, and tan. Latticework hides the sight but not the smell of a garbage Dumpster; on the ground there is a pizza box filled with fluttering napkins. Before going inside Josh has a cigarette, and thinks about after—two or three drinks max, he makes this promise now. Inside it is dim and smells like candles and the petroleous reek of cheap carpeting. Josh clears his throat and enters the tiny, crowded viewing room, and about twenty heads turn, none of them familiar. It's just like Whisker to be even later than he is. Josh forces a grim smile and, with nothing else to do, gets in line to see the body. Immediately a woman with her hand over her mouth leaves the side of the casket and the line moves forward, then moves again, until before he is ready for such a thing to happen, it is his turn. Unsure of what to do with his hands, he settles on clasping them behind his back, which gives him the look of an arrogant cruise ship

captain assessing the midnight buffet. Beaman's face—
overly rouged, way dead—immediately snaps into a space
in Josh's mind. It fills out a forgotten picture. They are
playing basketball in front of the house, and Beaman
keeps calling fouls. He calls a foul even when it's all ball.
Real ticky-tack shit. Four times Beaman has his shot
stuffed, and four times Beaman calls a foul.

Josh spikes the house's old tricolored ball so it pings
high off the driveway. "This is pussy basketball!" he
screams. "Pussy basketball!"

"Play the game," Beaman mutters, walking past.

"That's what I'm saying," Josh says. He fires a chest
pass to the top of the key, and Beaman snags it one-
handed. Something in the catch is like spite. "Play the
game."

There are a couple of perfunctory passes before Beaman
lowers his shoulder and drives in on Josh—he leaps, and
Josh launches him over the hood of Whisker's Honda.
Beaman's body lands on the other side with a brutal
scrape of gravel and completely disappears. A couple of
guys run to him, but Josh stands in the middle of the
court with his hands on his hips, sweat running down his
bare chest. Eventually Beaman pulls himself together and
limps off inside the house. Josh spits.

"Foul," Josh says.

"You're twiddling your thumbs," a woman's voice informs him. She has crossed the sacrosanct space between the side of the casket and the next waiting mourner to stand with him. Josh quickly brings his hands forward. "Don't worry," she says, "no one saw you." She has long pale-blond hair, or maybe it is blond mixed with gray, and she is very tan; her pretty face has wrinkles from a lifetime of sun. Two thin purple straps cross her bare shoulders to hold up her dress. "Wasn't he handsome?" she says. She reaches in and caresses Beaman's cheek and jaw. "I was his favorite, his favorite aunt. His Auntie Amy. And now he's gone. Who could do such a thing?"

"What do you mean, who? I thought it was an accident."

"I don't believe in accidents," Auntie Amy says. "Everything has a reason if you look at it right."

As she moves to leave, she slips her arm through his. Alone as he is, with no sign of Whisker or the others, it feels comforting to have it there. He notices her perfume is more vanilla than flower.

"Is this some dump or what?" Auntie Amy says a bit too loudly, after they've found some space toward the back. "Can you imagine this hole for your only son?"

"I guess the location is good?"

"Location, hell. Cheap cheap cheap. My brother is as cheap as the day is long. I know a beautiful place near Northampton, but would they listen to me? Do they ever?

So this is how we show our love to Kevin—brown carpet and cheesy wood paneling. God, you can barely breathe."

People keep glancing at them, Josh notices, and looking away. Auntie Amy works the edge of a cuticle on a thumbnail the color of port.

"You know, you missed your friends."

"They've already been here?"

She nods, examines the nail. "In their sunglasses and their little suits just like yours. Filed in and filed right on out again."

"I can't believe it."

"You all were planning on having a little fun after?"

"Well, yes, but it's also not right of them to race through. They get like that when they're together."

"Oh, honey," she says, touching his arm, "you don't have to explain anything to me. But if you're wondering, I heard them mention Hurlihue's Pub over in Longmeadow. . . ."

But before he can ask what time they left he catches from across the room a stare so full of naked hate and loathing he forgets about it. The woman wears black and her face is pale and drawn as if she hasn't slept, and she twists a ring around and around her finger.

"It's because you're standing with me," Auntie Amy says. "What's your name?"

"Josh."

"Watch out, Josh. You might not get a thank-you card."

The woman in black comes over. "No one else will say it, so I will," she snaps at Auntie Amy. "You ought to be ashamed of yourself."

Auntie Amy wags her finger with its long purple nail in the woman's face. "Don't you speak for Kevin, Ruth. You've got no right, for two reasons. First you haven't been in this family long enough. And second, I was Kevin's favorite. You, you can slander me all you want. Go ahead, slander away, you've done it all afternoon. But don't pretend like you're speaking for Kevin. Like you know a damn thing about it."

"Haven't you done enough already?" Ruth asks. "Raymond had to go for a walk, he was so upset."

"Maybe he shouldn't have started talking that mess the moment I set foot in here."

"*Slut,*" Ruth hisses.

"Bitch."

"Go to hell!"

"Hey now," Josh says.

Auntie Amy walks away, laughing. People get out of her way. Her high heels thud dully on the worn carpet, and there's a disdainful sass in the swing of her backside. As she goes through the door she waves over her shoulder without looking. Immediately a shout, a curse break out in the hallway, and a man enters. Red-faced, stocky, it is

Raymond, Kevin Beaman's father. He looks familiar to Josh, who thinks they may have once shaken hands on the steps of the house, with music pumping and a tapped keg on ice. He walks past everyone else, goes right up to Josh and embraces him.

"God, he loved you," he says into Josh's shoulder. Josh's arms rise slowly and encircle. "He loved you all so much, his brothers. You meant the world to him. I don't think he was ever as happy as when you were all together."

They stand like that, the shorter man's face growing hot and moist against Josh's chest. Josh has been embraced by other men before, quick popping backslaps from his own father, the one-arm sidesaddle hugs of teammates on the bench, but this is different. Beaman's father's shoulders fill out Josh's embrace so that it feels he will break free any time now, yet the man hangs on long past the understood time for release. They rock imperceptibly on the bones of their feet.

"We loved him too," Josh hears himself say, and the man in his arms sobs wetly, shudders.

"All of you boys," Beaman's father croaks, his chin struggling against Josh's chest like a small animal, "you were so young, you were so young and strong and beautiful . . .

"Oh, my son! My beautiful, beautiful son!"

*   *   *

On his way back to the car he finds Auntie Amy in the lot smoking a cigarette. She says she doesn't know about him but she could use a drink, and if he still wants to go to the Hurlihue's in Longmeadow why doesn't she show him the way?

"I know Longmeadow," he says.

She crushes the cigarette under her strappy purple shoe, tosses her hair.

"Look, don't strand me here. Let me tell them you needed directions."

"Tell them that anyway. Just leave. Next time we're all together I'll be sure to back you up."

He means it to be funny, but she just looks off out over the cars, toward a stand of badly overgrown pines.

"What did you say that got everyone so pissed off?"

"Over drinks?" Vulnerable she is, suddenly. "Please?"

Her white Berlinetta leads him to Hurlihue's, where the waitresses wear red jogging shorts and on the walls hang antique advertisements purchased from a restaurant-supply catalogue. Josh takes a quick tour of the place but no Whisker, no anybody. They climb up into a booth that sits under the approving smile of the Cream of Wheat guy. Everything at Hurlihue's is oversized. Josh can swing his feet without touching the floor, and the frozen mugs are so big and heavy it takes both hands to drink.

"Kevin's father," Josh says after a while. "He seems pretty broken up."

"That's my brother, dramatic to the end."

"I felt bad, you know, because I didn't know Kevin that well. I didn't know what to say."

"Then why did you come?"

"We were in the same fraternity together. It seemed like the right thing to do."

"You know about that sort of thing, do you?" she says. Then, "I'm sorry. It's sad. Very very sad. My nerves are shot." She toys with a postcard-sized menu in a clear plastic holder. "Let's change the subject. No more funeral talk."

"I'm all for that," Josh says.

"Hungry?"

"No food for me, I'm just drinking. In fact, I really can't stay long, I have some plans for dinner back in the city."

"A business thing?"

"A pleasure thing."

"You go on a lot of business things, don't you?" Auntie Amy asks. "I can tell, the way you wear that suit."

"You know, that reminds me of something you said before: 'Little suits.' Like there's something wrong with them."

Auntie Amy smiles. "Some men, like my ex-husband,

a thing like today, he couldn't wait to take his off. He'd be tearing at it as soon as we got home. Sooner. His jacket would be in the backseat of the car, his tie on the floor in the kitchen. But you look so comfortable. You look like you were born wearing one."

"The more expensive ones are actually pretty comfortable."

"Oh, please," she says, pinching his sleeve. "And I suppose this would be a more expensive one?"

"It's not from Sears."

"Oh, you're bad. Bad bad bad. You're one of the bad ones." She lights a cigarette. "Kevin went through that phase the first year or two out of school. Now don't look like that, this isn't about Kevin's funeral. This is about a time in his life when he felt the need to have all the toys the grown-ups have—the suits, the shined shoes, the leather organizer."

"Phase," Josh sniffs. "I can see where this is going."

"It was something he was growing out of."

"Yeah, I get it. Everyone in a suit is yuppie scum. Not that I'm arguing with you. I am. I'm yuppie scum, I admit it." Josh wiggles forward on the padded seat, takes a cigarette from her pack. "I bust my ass, and I make money. I don't like what I do all the time, or even most of the time, but I do it well, and I like what it gets me, and anyway it's like my father said: 'That's why they call it work.' I'm not afraid to work or to buy nice things with the money I make, and if that makes me yuppie scum, well then the world can——"

"Kiss your ass?"

"You got it."

She gives him matches. "Well, you disgust me, but you're honest. You know what you want, you'll be happy. But Kevin, see, he never knew *what* in the hell he wanted, only what he didn't. It used to kill him, that he could have a job with good prospects and be making money, could have all that going for him with so many young people who can't find any job at all, and still be completely miserable. He used to call me at night—oh, Sunday nights were the worst—and say that when he really thought about it, all he wanted to do was ride that damn bicycle of his." She stops, takes a sip of beer. Hides for a moment beneath her pale-blond hair. "And I just kept saying, 'What if you quit? What if you quit *today*? What's stopping you from quitting, except being afraid of what other people will think of you?' "

"Doesn't seem like you have that problem."

"Never have."

"Me neither."

"I know that. I knew it the moment I saw you up at Kevin's side, twiddling your thumbs. I said, Now there's someone who doesn't give a fuck about anyone but himself, and I knew we just had to meet."

Over the next two hours the bar fills up with fortysomething men and women who arrive alone but seem to know each other. Their fun has the focused quality of a competitive sport. They shout and laugh over a jukebox that plays "Long Cool Woman in a Black Dress" and "Rock the Boat" and "Suzie Q" and "Take It Easy." They sing the choruses to each other. Josh buys shots of a sweet neon-green drink called Lizard Spit, which comes in test tubes strapped across the waitress's chest in a customized bandolier. Auntie Amy and Josh drink the first tubes to Beaman. Dinner plans fade.

Josh holds the next aloft. "Here's to manganese."

"Here's to *what?*" Auntie Amy says, laughing.

"Fuck, I don't know. What a day. Fuck it."

"Here's to fuck it!" she shouts.

"Fuck it!"

She is completely unlike any woman he has ever flirted with. It is more than just her apparent age. He starts telling her about his job and what an idiot he has for a boss and she bounces a wadded napkin off his forehead. She kids him some more about his suit. She has what he thinks of as ex-hippie eyes, they are a little too wide open and piercing, bright with a creepy hyper-awareness. He figures she is probably into breathing or stretching or those other ways of getting high without dope. She seems to despise who he is and what he does, and yet when she laughs she lays her fingers across his wrist. Her foot nudges his shin.

"Here's to Sydney Pollack!" she says.

"Here's to Sevvy Ballesteros!"

"To the Doppler effect!"

"To bacitracin!"

When Happy Hour ends and the beers triple in price, Auntie Amy is firm. "I won't let you drive all the way back to Boston tonight. We just lost one boy, we're not going to bury another." Josh agrees. Got drunk, can't go home. From his car phone he leaves a message on the paralegal's machine to the effect that the funeral has run on longer than he expected, and could they get together some other time?—then he is once again following Auntie Amy's Berlinetta, through twilight now, locked in on her taillights, expecting either her or himself to sober up enough to speed off and leave the other. Their drive seems a test of will, some game they play; it is only when the bright yellow square of her blinker ignites before a hotel off of Interstate 90 that he is hit by the reality of what is happening. "Holy fuckamoley," he whispers; he giggles as he sets the parking brake. She insists on registering alone, and while she does he runs across the street, his dress shoes loud and slippy on the pavement, to the 7-Eleven for beer and a package of condoms, returning in time to see her come through the lobby's glass door, where she stands, waiting.

The cinder-block walls of their room are painted light green. It is the kind of room he hasn't seen since spring-break trips in college; its staggering lack of taste charges the air with dirty possibilities. She has an overnight bag with her that she takes into the bathroom, and while she runs water he drinks beer at a small round table. He pulls back the curtain so that he can keep an eye on his car, wisely parked under a floodlight. Suddenly a thought rushes in: setup. This is how it happens, isn't it? And she will take his money and his car, and, worse, leave him without pants? But then he remembers Kevin who from his casket had introduced them, who seems to be with them now, for as long as she and Josh are together. Would she really pull anything in his presence?

Auntie Amy emerges wearing cutoff shorts and a white top printed with tiny blue flowers. She has put on more makeup than she had on before, so much that her features seem to exist independently of one another. Josh sees lips, cheekbones, eyes. She shakes her head at the beer he offers.

"I was just remembering how excited Kevin was the day he quit," she says, sitting down on the edge of the bed. "He came to my house to tell me first and we opened a bottle of wine and we drank to life." She raises an imaginary glass. " 'Fuck 'em! Fuck the rat race! Death to all those conniving, materialistic, self-important bastards, smug behind their desks, stabbing each other in the back, dragging down whoever they can.' He went out the very next day and bought that fancy bike. He said a trip across the country was only the beginning. He was going to do a loop around North America, Canada and Mexico, thousands and thousands of lonely miles on that bike of his—but that's the way he was. It wouldn't have seemed lonely to him, if he had ever been allowed to feel like it was okay. To want to do that. To want to be alone." She turns to Josh. "Why couldn't we leave him alone?"

Josh scratches at the label on the bottle. His stomach doesn't feel so good. He doesn't want to go back to this subject. He doesn't want to think about Beaman framed in pleated silk, or his father's teary embrace, the man's moist heat.

"Maybe this wasn't such a good idea," he says.

"We killed him," she says quietly. "You and me. We're the reason. You because you were what he was riding away from, everything he learned in that goddamn fraternity world of yours. Brutality. Insensitivity. He couldn't play that game. The kind of boy he was, he took it to heart, where it tortured him in ways someone like your-self could not possibly imagine."

"Right," Josh says. "And meanwhile, his own father tells me Kevin thought we were the best part of his life. So who should I believe? Or let me put it this way, who would most people believe?"

"The fraternity was the best part of *Raymond's* life, not Kevin's. Kevin never had a chance to feel differently when it mattered the most."

Out on the interstate a flatulent downshift mocks them. Auntie Amy is looking at her hands folded in her lap. "This is wrong," she says. "I didn't mean to put the blame on you. Because it was my fault, too. I was what he was riding toward. I got him to try before he was ready. You should have seen me, boy, I never let up. 'Why don't you quit? Why don't you quit?' I just kept at him. And you know what's really terrible? I think the whole time I *knew* he wasn't ready."

"It was an *accident*!" Josh says. "A dumb, stupid accident. The fucking moron rode his bike off an overpass! How does anyone do that? You can't make sense of it. No one can. It's stupid to try."

She turns her gray eyes on him. "I know you think it was an accident and that I'm crazy, but I'll bet you call everything you don't understand an accident or crazy. No.

We were the reason. And if you could understand the horrible thing we've done you wouldn't call it an accident. If you were capable of understanding how completely un-forgivable we are, you wouldn't *be* who you are, and you would never be in this room with me now. I suppose you'd call that an accident too? Just the way things happened to shake out?"

She stops. Water is dripping in the bathroom, the television is the color of dead ashes. When she speaks again her voice sounds as if she's explaining it to him for the hundredth time.

"Maybe we didn't mean for him to crash, but we set Kevin on that bike together, steadied him until he got his balance, then pushed and stood back clapping."

Josh gets up from the table so suddenly the bottles on it clink and rattle. He stands at the window looking out at the parking lot. "I haven't talked to the guy in seven years," he explains. "I didn't even talk to him when I knew him. . . ." Outside, his shiny car offers escape, or rather return, return to sane, right-thinking, well-educated people, golfers and coworkers, bosses and clients. To elderly waitresses who bring him steak sandwiches on clubhouse china. He sees his car and, lit up across the highway, a billboard for the Basketball Hall of Fame. On it Dr. J soars, trapped in midair, palming in one of his famously huge hands a tricolored ball. Josh recalls the moment of contact when he sent Beaman over the hood of Whisker's Honda, the wet slipperiness of the other's skin, sweat cooler than his own, thinking, *You call a foul five times in a row, you deserve to get put down. Everyone knows that. Beaman knew it. Pussy basketball. You play pussy basketball and you never have a game.*

When he turns she is looking at him, her hair spilling over her shoulders. Her bare thighs are long gold ovals. He wants to do it to her. He wants what they came here to do, and then he will get into his car, and tomorrow he will be back in the office and it will be like it never happened. None of it. He sits down next to her on the edge of the bed, slides his hand around her back. She recoils slightly, but stays.

"No," she says, "not until you say it out loud."

"What's that?"

"What it is you want. You have to say what it is you want."

"C'mon," he says into her hair. "You know..." She pushes him away.

"No. Say it."

His mouth fills with fluid, he must clear his throat. "Sex," he hears himself say; the word comes out thick. She's nodding even as he speaks.

"Good," she says. "Now we know how horrible we are. Imagine, on a day like today doing what we're about to do. Horrible. But haven't you always suspected it, deep down? That you were horrible? That you could be? That you could be black and awful, horrible and rotten?" The look on his face seems to please her. "Of course," she coos. She runs her hand up the thigh of his dark worsted suit pants and works him until he's straining.

"Look at this place," she whispers. "Perfect. Could it be more perfect? This orange-and-brown bedspread, those cheap ugly paintings? That melted trench on top of the television where somebody left a cigar?"

On her cheeks, tiny, tiny crystals glint in rouge redder than the blood it simulates. Josh reaches to touch eyes, cheekbones, lips in a gesture of intimacy, but she catches his wrist, hard.

"Yes, lover, okay," she says, lying back. "I'll be quiet now."

Buying Beer

Erin Garrett-Metz

Lewis sat in the pickup between Toby at the wheel and John and Isaac crushed together at the window. His unlaced muddy workboots were planted on either side of the gear shift. Toby had to reach over his left leg to shift and both were embarrassed by this, but once Lewis had made a joke of it—don't get any ideas, you fag—it was okay.

They were all pressed in there together, every single one of them wearing jeans and jean jackets like uniforms, all with the same hard, grimy, powerful hands that came with farming. Toby had his father's truck for the night, a special dispensation. The blinkers didn't work so Toby had to use his hand to signal, and the ripped red vinyl seat of the cab was on springs that squawked incessantly, but to Lewis it was a beautiful sound.

They were driving into town to try to buy beer. It was fantastic. The guys in the back were standing up and sitting down and wisecracking and pounding on the metal roof and knocking on the little back window of the cab just for comradeship and they were all out there alone and free and it was the best damn thing that Lewis could think of. They were free of their families and free of their tight little houses and free for a while from the unceasing circle of work.

They roared and clattered into town. Clouds of dust pillowed out behind the back wheels and then settled slowly. An old barbed-wire fence sloped and dipped with the contours of the road, sometimes sagging tiredly sideways, the posts unpainted and splintering with age. Over the darkening fields the mountains loomed, their tops already dim blue with snow though the month was still August. Lewis was off the farm, out of the reach of his father, and he thought maybe he'd never go back, maybe he'd just tell Toby to keep on driving, drive on forever.

On the way, they all decided that because Lewis was growing a beard, he should be the one to go in the store.

"It makes you look older," said Toby, over and over. "Seriously, you look like my old granddad." He steered wildly around a corner, in imitation of his old granddad driving, hunched over the wheel with his jaw jutting out, and they all laughed, even the guys hanging on in the back who didn't know what the joke was about. To sit in the cab meant you were one of the favored ones.

John was quiet, like he usually was, but his quietness was friendly and appreciative and everyone always wanted him around, everyone always wanted to impress him. Most of the things they said were for his benefit, and if he smiled, it was like winning something. But if they all were together and he wasn't there, they weren't quite sure what the point was, and somehow their own wit was lost.

Isaac lifted up his narrow hips, reached into his back pocket, and pulled out his fake ID, or someone else's fake ID, a priceless treasure, a legend among them all, which hadn't worked yet but you never knew, which he'd found just laying on the sidewalk in town and which he now handed over to Lewis. "It looks about as unlike you as it does me," Isaac said, and they laughed uproariously again.

They turned onto Route 7, where the driving was smoother, the seat stopped squealing so much. Toby shifted gears, his elbow pressing against Lewis's thigh, and stepped on the gas. When they saw the red Citgo sign rearing above the gas station, they pulled off. The guys in back thrust their arms through the back cab window to pool their money. There was plenty, more than thirty-five bucks, and they were all shouting out what Lewis should get—a six-pack, no, a few six-packs, no, get bottles, definitely bottles—and whacking him on the back. Toby pulled to a stop right by the window of the store, and the engine grumbled in neutral.

"Get wine coolers," someone said, but was drowned out in a roar of disapproval.

"Get candy if you can't get beer," someone else said, and there was some dissent and laughter until they saw that it had been John who said it and then all agreed and called out their candy orders to Lewis.

John and Isaac slid out to let Lewis get by and Isaac said, "Man, whatever you do, don't lose my ID. Don't let them take it, no matter what."

"No sweat," said Lewis, as if he'd done this before.

John pulled the cap off Lewis's head, an old stained John Deere with a frayed brim, and said, "Take this off, you look like a fucking redneck." Everyone laughed again because they were all wearing caps just like it, with the logo of some feed company or something on them. They pushed Lewis forward.

"Go man, you can do it," they said, and everyone climbed back into the truck to watch.

There was only one other car in the lot, a blue foreign thing so small it looked like a toy to Lewis. It must be the guy's who works here, he thought—good, no one else in there to doubt him. Lewis could see the guy's back through the window. He was leaning over the checkout counter as if he were reading. So Lewis slipped the ID into his back pocket and ran his hand through his matted-down hair and with his friends now whispering

behind him, he walked right into the store like he knew
what he was doing.

An electronic bell pinged to announce Lewis's entrance.
The guy at the counter looked up and pushed a magazine
aside. He had dark skin and black eyes and wrapped
around his head was a white turban. Lewis felt a brief
flare of hope—he's a foreigner, he's not going to be able
to tell how old I am, he's not even going to know it's not
me in the picture, he probably thinks we all look the
same. Lewis aimed a smile at the man but kept his hands
in his pockets and his eyes on his boots, and headed
through the aisles of fluorescent-lit food toward the cooler
at the back of the store. His untied laces clicked against
the gleaming floor. He lingered for a few seconds at the
candy section and ran his eyes up and down it, shaking
his head like he couldn't find what he wanted, and kept
on going.

And then he was there. At the cooler. Cans and cans
lined up before him. It was beautiful. He could feel the
guy's eyes on him but he pulled open the cooler door.
Stale-smelling refrigerated air rolled out.

Lewis surveyed the shelves of beer nonchalantly. He
saw the guy watching him, tiny, in a round mirror an-
gling down from the ceiling. Out of sheer brazenness, he
called back, "You got any cases?" and the guy answered,
pleasantly enough, "Over to your right," in a clear casual

unaccented voice. Lewis was momentarily put off, and reached unconsciously to pull down the brim of the hat that wasn't there, but proceeded bravely over to his right and saw the cases, not just the six-packs, not the bottles in their colored boxes, but the cases, sitting right there on the bottom shelf. American beer.

And without even seeming to hesitate, though he did, inside—inside he turned around and ran right back out of the store—he hoisted one up, resting it on his shoulder and then, for the hell of it, another, letting the cooler door swing shut behind him. Thinking he'd look more plausible with more beer. Nobody would expect an underage kid to try to buy so much. No fear, he said to himself, no fear. And he walked toward the counter with the two cases. They were heavy and cold. He noticed that on the shiny linoleum where he'd walked before, he'd left little crumbles of dried mud like a trail.

Through the window behind the guy at the counter, he could see his friends in the truck just about going crazy watching him. The guys in the back were standing up and looking over the cab for a better view, jostling for position. Toby's mouth was open and even John had his eyebrows raised. It gave Lewis courage. He thunked the beer down on the counter. The guy with the turban was looking Lewis up and down like he wasn't going to let him get away with anything.

"What's the damage?" said Lewis, reaching in his pocket. He could see Toby thumping the steering wheel with his fist in pure joy and bouncing up and down on the seat and John just sitting there with his quiet smile and his raised eyebrows. Isaac looked pale with terror for the fate of his ID. And just for extra effect, because he knew they were watching, Lewis pointed to a rack of chewing tobacco behind the counter and said, "And a tin of Copenhagen while you're at it."

"You go to school around here?" the guy said. And to Lewis's amazement, he reached for the tin of tobacco. He was wearing a blue-and-white-striped shirt that looked familiar, and Lewis wondered if he'd gotten it at Benton's department store. A shirt Lewis had seen in the street window and wanted for himself. The cuffs of the guy's shirt were very bright against his dark wrists. Pinned to his shirt pocket was a tag that said *Citgo*, and underneath, *Hi, I'm Fahmy*.

"Yeah," said Lewis. He wondered if the guy's turban was heavy. It looked like it would weigh his head down. He told himself not to look at it and kept his eyes low. Should he pull out the ID now or wait till the guy asked for it?

Fahmy set the tin down on top of the beer but made no move to ring up the sale. "Where at? The university?" he said. He was leaning over the cases with his elbows resting on them and his chin in his hands. A warm scent of soap, sweet and astringent, wafted between them.

"Uh, yeah," Lewis said again. He was suddenly aware of his own smell. Sweat and hay and manure. And he yearned to be back in the pickup truck. Where they all smelled the same.

"Me too, I'm in the film studies department."

There was silence as Lewis tried to think of what to say in return. He stared for a moment at the orange price sticker on the tin of tobacco. He felt strangely naked without his hat. Is this guy trying to trick me? he thought. He stepped from foot to foot nervously. Who the hell goes to college to study movies? But he said, because the guy seemed to be waiting for a response, because he could think of nothing else, "Yeah, well, I wish summer would last a little longer."

"No kidding," Fahmy said, laughing and smacking the counter as if this were the funniest thing he'd ever heard.

Lewis shrugged. Shit, shit, shit, he thought. Is the guy going to sell this to me or not? He brought a hand halfway up to adjust his cap and then remembered and quickly shoved it back in his pocket again.

"So, what are you studying?" Fahmy asked finally, after he had recovered and stood staring right in Lewis's face in a disconcerting way.

"Algebra," Lewis said, focusing hard now on Fahmy's name tag for lack of a better place to look.

"Algebra?" Fahmy seemed confused. "Really? I didn't even know that was an option. Shows how math-illiterate I am."

Lewis let out a nervous yelp of laughter. "Yup," he said. What was all this goddamn conversation for? He pulled out the mess of wadded bills and quarters from his pockets and spread it out on the counter to speed things up. Then he wanted to kick himself, he should have at least pretended to have a wallet, men don't walk around without wallets, asshole.

"I think I've seen you before," Fahmy said all of a sudden, without picking up the money that was lying there on the counter between them, without even looking at it. "Were you ever in that Spanish Authors class?"

"I don't think so," said Lewis. Jesus, he thought, just bust me or let me go. It was obvious that he wasn't getting away with this beer. Any second the guy would pick up the phone and call the police. And Lewis would sprint out the door.

"I know what it is." The guy broke into a wide smile and Lewis noticed for the first time that he was wearing braces on his bottom teeth. They flashed in the fluorescent light. "I've seen you in the gay men's center, right?"

Lewis felt a cold shock shoulder through him.

There was a long silence.

"What?" Lewis said finally, in a voice that sounded small even to him. "No. No way." The walls seemed to reel in and out and he could feel blood beating in his neck. I look gay? he thought wildly. He backed up a step. He thinks I'm a fucking fag?

Fahmy kept insisting. "You really look familiar, I know I've seen you."

"No," said Lewis, "I'm not familiar. You haven't seen me." Shut up, he told himself. Shut the hell up. Now he just wanted to get out.

"Well, what would you think about meeting me for a coffee sometime then?" Fahmy said.

A trickle of sweat escaped Lewis's hair and rolled down his neck. He could think of nothing to say, nothing. He was running over in his mind what he was wearing, his old jeans, his jean jacket, a plain blue T-shirt, his muddy boots, unlaced, nothing that would send out any weird signals. And then he remembered his hat. His hat was off. It wasn't him, it was his bare head, his longish hair.

Lewis took a deep breath. It wasn't him. It wasn't anything in him. It was the fact that he had no goddamn hat on.

Fahmy seemed to notice Lewis's discomfort. "Oh," said Fahmy. He ducked his head and sent another wave of his soapy smell at Lewis. "I get it. I'm sorry. Your friends are out there, right?" He smiled gently and pushed the mess of money back toward him. "Here, take the beer," he said. "It's yours, least I can do for a fellow starving student."

Lewis swept up the money and stuffed it hurriedly back into his pockets. His face was hot. What was he talking about, take the beer? Did he want some kind of trade?

Fahmy continued, "I know you're probably busy, but if you ever get a second you can call me. I'd love to go out or something." He picked up a ballpoint pen attached to the cash register with a greasy string and wrote a phone number and his name, Fahmy, on the top of one of the cases. Then he underlined it. "It gets pretty boring in here," he said.

Lewis stood there, frozen, staring at the phone number. It's because I don't have my hat on, he thought. It's not me. So would taking the beer be an agreement? And then he saw the tin of tobacco resting on top of the beer. And somehow the sight of it convinced him. It was chewing tobacco, for Christ's sake. This guy didn't know what the hell he was talking about. Suddenly his head felt clear. Lewis glanced up at the guys in the truck. Wait till I tell them about this. They are going to fucking *die*. He could see that they were all perfectly still now, except Isaac, who was shaking his head like doomsday.

Already in his mind he was retelling it, and changing it.

It was decided. Lewis seized the beer with both hands, the tobacco balanced on top, went straight for the door and shoved it open with his shoulder. The electronic bell pinged again.

"Bye," Fahmy called after him. The door closed on his voice. Lewis ran for the truck. He lifted the beer up to the guys in the back and went around to the front again, moving as fast as he could, looking back into the neon-lit window and seeing Fahmy staring after him. John opened the door and reached to pull him into the cab, and Toby was wrenched around in his seat staring through the back window at the wealth of beer in amazement.

John and Isaac slid over and Lewis sat by the window and slammed the door shut. Lewis grabbed his hat out of John's hands. "Get the hell out of here," Lewis said. "Drive!"

The truck surged forward. "What the hell were you doing in there so long?" said Toby, pulling out onto the road with a screech. "We were going *fucking crazy*!"

"You're not going to believe it," Lewis said, jamming the hat onto his head. "Jesus H. *Christ*!" Already what had happened was sinking away. He knew how to tell it now.

Isaac was grinning like mad. He reached around John to punch Lewis on the shoulder, on the knee, anywhere he could reach. "You got two fucking cases," he crowed. "How the hell did you do that?"

"It was the beard, man, it was the goddamn beard," shouted Toby.

Even John said, "Nice going," and held up his hand for Lewis to slap.

"What did he say? Did he card you?" Toby demanded.

"He didn't even need the goddamn ID," said Isaac.

"It was the beard, I'm telling you," said Toby again. "Jesus!"

They were jubilant. They were whacking Lewis's back. They were telling each other what they had seen. They were repeating, over and over, "He got two fucking *cases* out of there, man, *two*!"

John was shaking his head. He whistled. "Holy shit," he said.

Lewis felt like a hero. It was over. He'd gotten the beer. For free, no less. He'd snowed that guy, he said to himself, and then to them. That guy didn't know shit from corned beef hash, he said. He told them all the story. That guy was pathetic, he said, that guy was sick.

At first they didn't believe it. "No way," said Toby, "you're shitting me!" And then they believed it and it was the best story they'd ever heard and Isaac howled with laughter and beat on the old cracked red dashboard with his fists and Toby careened around the road, excited.

Lewis felt like a king. They made him tell it again and again, and when they stopped at the lake access where they always went because there was an old metal trash can there that you could build fires in and no one would bother you, they all piled out and he had to tell it again to the guys in the back, to Dan and Troy and Phil and Randy. They passed around the tin of Copenhagen. He showed them the phone number and the name. Now he believed it. Only now. His heroism and his contempt spiraled higher with every telling.

They shouted, they competed with boasts of how far they would go to buy beer again from that guy: Dave would give him his own phone number, but change one of the digits so it would be wrong. Randy would ask the guy out to dinner, and of course not show up. Even John said quietly (and everyone stopped shouting to listen, because whatever John said was important) that he would kiss the guy right on the mouth for a keg. That topped everything, there was no use in going on after that. That was the best. That was the funniest, imagining John making out with the turbaned guy. "You are truly disgusting," they assured each other.

Lewis had a giddy feeling in his stomach. He couldn't

stop smiling. He laughed for no reason. He told the story twenty more times, and each time it was different.

They all drank the beer. It was the best beer Lewis had ever tasted in his life. They wadded the tobacco into their gums and soon afterwards Isaac walked away from the garbage-can fire and puked quietly in the dark woods and came back pulling up his fly like nothing happened, like he'd just gone out there to piss against a tree. And no one challenged him, they let him be. Now they were almost men and you had to protect your dignity any way you could.

The lake lapped against the pebbly shore and the sky wheeled with stars and Lewis thought, they all were thinking, that life was so goddamn good. His hat was safely and securely settled on his head.

They stayed out drinking and throwing rocks into the lake and building pyramids of empty beer cans which they knocked over with other rocks. By this time they were all in trouble for staying out so late but nobody cared, everyone talked about how great it felt to be out here with just them and how great it would be when their lives were always like this. They all had to get up for the cows or the fields in only a few hours but no one made a move to go. They stood around the trash-can bonfire, and as the night got colder, each boy alternated which hand held the beer can and which hand got warm pressed against his thigh in the pocket of his jeans. Their fronts flickered orange and their jean-jacketed backs were cold and dark. Soon, they thought, their lives would always be like this.

Near two o'clock, Toby drove everyone home. Lewis would be the first to be dropped off, that was unquestionable. He even had the window seat. Their shoulders and arms and legs were pressed against each other. They rode in silence, the four of them sitting there in the front again, the other guys now quiet and solemn in the back, thinking, with their hard palms cupped over their knees.

Lewis was as perfectly content as he'd ever been. He was staring out the window. There was the tall hulking silhouette of a silo. A dead tree with a million delicate fingers reaching up and out. A dog streaking for a few yards behind the truck, barking thinly above the engine's thunder, all furious chase, and then slowing, stopping in the middle of the road.

Toby drove up the long driveway to Lewis's farm and idled the truck at the house. "That was great, man," he said. He shook his head, as if disbelieving what had occurred that night.

John nodded gravely.

"Truly awesome," said Isaac.

"Yeah," said Lewis. "Thanks." Regretfully, he pulled the handle and the truck door creaked open. He stepped down, out of the warm rumbling enclosure of the cab. The night air swooped down around him. The house was dark, the animals quiet in the barns. He looked at the three of them still there in the cab together and felt a gigantic loss seeping into his heart.

John slid over to his accustomed place at the window and leaned to get hold of the door, to pull it shut. Lewis let go.

Toby was already looking ahead down the driveway.

"Later," said Lewis, trying to keep them there.

"See ya," replied Isaac.

John hefted the door closed. The pickup pulled forward.

The guys in the back of the truck had their hands stretched out to him and he clasped each hand once. As the truck rolled back down the driveway, they called out to him softly, and Lewis raised a hand in the air to them. He watched them go. He knew that it had been the best night of his life.

Later, not now, not tonight, he would think about what it meant.

Wes Looks Like Paul Newman and I Don't

Courtney Saunders

My brother came back last week wearing I kid you not a three-piece suit with this canary-yellow vest and a tie with big Hawaiian-looking flowers all over it. I had just come back from work sweaty and stinking from printing T-shirts nine hours straight at four dollars an hour. When I pulled into the drive I saw Mom out back in her garden in that big pink sun hat she wears, holding her little planting shovel and staring with this kind of amazed look on her face. She was staring at my brother Wes and he was standing there with his hands stuffed in his pockets in this huge ray of sunshine that made him look like he was glowing. He was smiling at her with his big shit-eating grin and I could see right then and there that the bastard had come to do it all over again.

They turned to look at me over the fence when I got out of my van. Mom smiled kind of weak and said, "Oh hello!" and Wes smiled that "I'm your friendly corner Ford dealer" smile that also says, "but of course we all know you're my brother the loser" and nodded and winked at me. I nodded back at him and went inside the house and dropped my stuff in the kitchen and went to take a pee. We hadn't seen Wes in two years and he's a certifiable bastard and bad news. In the bathroom mirror I looked terrible and had a zit on my chin wouldn't you know and I could hear them coming in through the back door and Mom ooohing and chirping like she does at him and Wes the bastard haw-haw-hawing.

Mom can't help but fill every surface in the house with these little glass dogs she collects. She has three hundred or so. I knocked one off the back of the john by accident while I was flushing the toilet and it broke all over the tile. When it broke Mom said, "Mark?" through the bathroom door all concerned and I picked up the pieces and piled them on a washcloth. When I opened the door they were both standing there looking at me with their eyebrows raised and Mom said, "Oh, no! I bought that one in England!" and Wes shook his head and smiled that smile I can't stand. I wanted to stuff that broken dog into his mouth.

"What are you doing here?" I said to him, not friendly. He stuck out his hand at me to shake and grinned. Mom took the little glass dog over to the kitchen counter and stood there going "Ooh, ooh, I wonder if I can glue it back."

"Friendly as always," he says. "Still working at the T-shirt factory?"

"Yep." I went to the fridge to get a beer. I didn't offer him one.

"You ever going back to school? How old are you now? Thirty-one?" Wes smirked. I eyed the bastard and leveled this at him.

"When'd you get out of jail?"

Mom looked up at me. She was still wearing that floppy pink gardening hat and was frowning in a worried way. She looked like one of the ex–Miss Americas who do orange juice commercials in pastel outfits. But this is her look. Mom was first runner-up for Miss Illinois way back when and I never hear the end of it. She thinks she would have done better if she hadn't chosen a dramatic piece for her talent. Miss Peoria sang "God Bless America" and that about cinched it.

"Now, Mark," she said, making her eyes wide and staring at me. "We're happy to see Wes," she said. She likes to speak in this *we* tense. Wes snickers at me then and slides over to the fridge and helps himself to a beer.

"That's my beer," I said. Mom was still fiddling with the glass dog. "Ooooh, this little pup was my only Airedale," she was whining. "I just loved my Airedale." Mom has this big thing for dogs and she thinks it's genetic because her grandmother was from England. Apparently English people love dogs more than they do people and I suppose they consider this some kind of great thing. Mom watches the Westminster Dog Show on TV every year and complains that the judges have it in for the Airedales because they never win.

Wes says, "I'll pick you up another, Mom. I'm in London on business a good deal these days." He took a big swallow of my beer.

Mother said, "Oooh, that would be lovely!" clapping her hands together and cooing.

"Oh yeah," I said, "you're in *London*."

"Yes."

"Doing what in London?" I want to know. Wes just stares at me and he's swigging more of my beer. Mom looks all distressed because we hate each other so much and we're standing and staring hard like two gunslingers.

"You *know*, Mark, I was never in prison," Wes says to me then, tapping his toe like he doesn't care, touching his big gold watch. He's wearing Gucci loafers. I've never seen a shoe that says shithead like a Gucci loafer.

He clears his throat then says, "There was a fine. Which I paid."

"Which Mom paid," I corrected him. He just looked at me.

"Why don't you get cleaned up?" he says. "I'm taking us out to dinner. To Antoine's," he says. Antoine's is the most expensive place in town.

"I can't believe this guy," I say then and Mom says, "Mark, please." Then she smiles this huge toothy smile at my brother and says, "Welcome home."

My brother Wes has always been a pathological liar and a crook. Naturally he went to law school and made a ton of money. Then he lost it all, stole some more. He's three years older than me and when we were kids he stole all the money I raised for Scouts and tried to start a loan-shark thing in our elementary school if you can believe it. He never got caught, and that was just the beginning of his life as a blood-sucking bastard. He had the first-graders quaking in their boots. A few years ago Wes nearly went to jail for trying to make off with this old lady's millions after she kicked. There is always some scam with him and he's drained most of Mom's money in shitty investments, his legal expenses, and who knows what else. Now all Mom's got is the house, the diesel-spewing Mercedes sedan, the country-club membership, a closet full of ratty fur coats, and stock in A&W root beer.

Most of the horrible stuff Wes has ever done is conveniently forgotten by lots of people, especially my mother and females in general, because they all think he looks like Paul Newman. Mom just dies for Paul Newman and I have to tolerate the salad dressing, popcorn, and spaghetti sauce. Mom says Paul Newman's good-hearted because he married Joanne Woodward and stayed with her even though she was, she always tries to get this out without sounding awful, *well, a homely girl.* She puckers her lips up. According to Mom, being so gorgeous himself Paul Newman knew that beauty was only *skin deep* and Mom is absolutely sure that Joanne Woodward has got to have the most beautiful inner soul around even if she is homely. I always say how I think Joanne Woodward was always a good-looking lady but Mom is never listening. It's all incredibly screwed up as you can see since Mom loves my crook of a brother only because he looks like Paul Newman who just might have a beautiful inner soul despite his gorgeousness but Wes has got to have an inner soul that looks like shit. The judge said as much.

For dinner we take Mom's car out to the closest thing to French in town. It's in an upscale strip mall. Wes says he's got a business distributing video games in Europe and he's back to make up with us so that we can be a family again. He tells Mom he's met a great girl and shows us a photo of this smiling gorgeous blonde with big green eyes and says her name is Portia. I'm wondering where he got the picture because I never believe anything Wes says. He is pouring wine for everybody and Mom's had a glass or two and her nose is getting pink.

"Oh, she's absolutely lovely," Mom says.

"Portia," I say. "Like the car?" It was a joke but Mom and Wes don't get it of course and look at me like I am the most miserable idiot on the planet. Wes has this way of ignoring everything I say. Like I'm the one who got disbarred and nearly thrown in jail and spent all Mom's money. These days doing something shitty and saying you're sorry makes everyone love you more than never doing anything shitty in the first place. Especially if you look like Paul Newman.

"Is she an exotic dancer?" I ask Wes and Mom says, "Oh, for heaven's sake, Mark. Try to be civil."

Wes pretends to laugh and says that Portia would think it's *so* amusing that I say that since she's an exotic dancer *of sorts*. A ballet dancer with the Royal Ballet in London. *"Prima ballerina,"* Wes says, and Mom's eyes get wide. Not only that, Wes tells us that Portia is a Lady with a capital L. That Portia's charming mother, Lady What's-it, has her own castle and spends all her time making marmalade.

Mom's eyes open wider and she just squeals with delight. "I *do* love marmalade!" Mom is chirping and Wes is going on, "Strawberry, orange, red currant..." I can't believe this guy. I drink more wine.

During dessert Wes tells us that he's so rich now he

can pay Mom back for all the money he "lost" of hers over the years. He's referring to the money he stole. I say, "Ha!" and drink more wine as long as he's paying.

Then Wes pulls this little black velvet ring box out of his pocket. He opens it and it's this huge hunk of Elizabeth Taylor–size diamond ring and I think, Oh shit, the bastard's going to propose to Mom. I wouldn't be surprised if he did and she'd probably say yes.

He says, all meaningful, "This is for Portia. I'm proposing next week."

I pick it up to inspect the authenticity but I don't know anything about diamonds. It's glittering and I wonder if he stole it from an old lady widow. Mom's cheeks are all pink now and she melts into tears and Wes takes her hand and they stare at each other in a meaningful way while her nose runs. His blue eyes are shining but to me they just look greasy.

Mom says, "We always knew you'd come back to us again. You've made us so happy." I have to interrupt the love fest.

"What's your girlfriend's name again?" I ask him.

"Portia."

"Yeah, I know, what's her last name?"

Wes looks at me and smirks in that way he has. Mom's still blubbering over her crème brûlée. "Such a lovely girl . . ." she's saying.

"Humphries-Owen," he says, fixing me with the blue eyes.

When the check comes Wes says, "Allow me," and slaps down a platinum card. I check to see if his real name is on it but the waitress comes and takes it too fast. He says to her, "Thanks so *very* much," all suave, the blue eyes flashing, and as she's leaving the woman is actually blushing pink.

The next day I have to work and my head is pounding from all the wine. We have to do fifty Little League shirts and my co-worker Ed, this not-so-smart guy from Clever, Missouri (I'm not kidding, that's really the name of the town), is listening to Heart turned up loud and he's got an entire finger up his nose. I have to suffer knowing that Mom and Wes are going to the country club today to play tennis and then to sit on their asses drinking gin fizzes while I sit here watching Ed pick his nose, telling me about how girls in Clever are "haughty." The Wilson sisters are screeching on the radio, "He's a magic man. . . ."

"Man, I'll tell you what," says Ed. "You better not even think twice about one of them haughty Clever girls 'less you are ready to *blow* some *dough*." Ed has this plan for making a bundle and getting a haughty Clever girl that involves catching lots of night crawlers and starting a fish-bait empire. He is tormented because he can never drag himself out of bed before dawn to catch the crawlers. He always says, "I'll tell you, there's gold out there for the taking." He says he's got to get himself an alarm clock that works.

I'm trying not to listen to Ed, find myself thinking about this Portia Humphries-Owen. She has pretty white teeth, just a little crooked the way I like. I wonder if anything Wes said is true, if the picture was one of those you get when you buy a frame, if the diamond is a fake. I think about Mom being alone with him, one gin fizz and she'll be down at the bank in her tennis skirt, signing over whatever he didn't steal from her already. I wish Dad was alive. He wasn't partial to Paul Newman or my brother Wes. When Wes would start up with his shit Dad would just lean way back in his recliner looking up at the ceiling yelling, "Boy, stop that buzzing 'round my head!" But Mom falls for it every time.

I decide to try to call the Royal Ballet to check on Wes's story and spend twenty minutes on the phone with the international operator trying to get the number until my manager gets back from the dentist looking pissed off with his lips all floppy from the Novocain and it's back to T-shirts.

After lunch I tell Ed about my brother Wes and he sits there with his arms crossed looking serious, nodding like he understands. I tell him how Wes convinced Mom to buy a race horse called Miracle Mile. Mom bought two dozen big hats to go to the Kentucky Derby in and then Miracle Mile died of brain fever. What the hell is brain fever? Six hundred thousand dollars down the shitter.

"Jeeezus," says Ed. "Man, that is indeed a *load* of dough. Coulda bought yourself half a dozen bulldozers with that kind of money." Ed's always coming out with this kind of stuff. Bulldozers.

He says to me, "Man, what we are talking about is *war,* plain and simple." I'm running off number twenty-two of the Little League shirts. They're real little, for six-year-olds.

Ed says, "you're gonna have to run the man off. A man like that is just here to make trouble." I tell Ed Wes looks like Paul Newman and Ed just shrugs and says, "Who's that?"

My manager goes home early because his mouth is hurting and Ed finishes the Little League shirts. I finally get through to someone at the Royal Ballet in London. I ask for the rehearsal place and get transferred until some lady with an accent and bad English answers. She knows how to say "What?" and keeps saying it over and over. I ask for Portia Humphries-Owen and she says, "What?"

"I am from Sri Lanka," she says. And I ask her if I called Sri Lanka and she says, "What?"

"Is this London?" I ask.

She says yes and we start all over again.

"Is this the ballet?" I ask and she says, "What?"

I ask again and the lady starts laughing and says, "They dance and dance, yes." She's really cheery and her voice is all melodic and she laughs whenever I say anything. I'm getting frustrated. I can hear my own voice echoing over the phone like it will sometimes with overseas calls. I get suddenly self-conscious because my voice echoing sounds hick and nasal. I try to leave my name and number for Portia Humphries-Owen but I can't tell if the lady ever understood or heard me right.

I say, "Tell her I'm Wes's brother," and she says, "Yes yes. Good-bye and good day," and hangs up.

I get back from work stinky and sweating and Mom and Wes are sitting out back by the pool which is empty and full of leaves. Why they are sitting there by the empty pool I have no idea. Wes is telling Mom some charming story about how Airedale dogs are smart despite their reputation for stupidity because in ancient India they were holy animals and were used to hunt lions.

I say, "Any damned dog hunting a lion can't be too brilliant." Mom ignores me and is going on and on about her *cutest* Airedale Josie. The nervous one that used to piss all over the house and got hit by an ice-cream truck. I can't say I was sorry.

Wes turns to me and says, "Ah, the working man arrives. How was the T-shirt factory?" I tell him to fuck off and he asks me if I feel underemployed or right at home in the silk-screening industry.

Mother says, "Oh, you boys," with a devilish smile like we're just ornery and don't really hate each other. I go in and take a shower and that makes me feel a little better but not much. Wes has dinner planned with his old girl-friend the ex—homecoming queen who is no doubt still hot for him even though he's a convicted crook and she's married to an auto-parts magnate. Wes leaves smelling like perfume and wearing the yellow vest and another flowered tie and I'm plopped on the sofa looking through one of Mom's interior decoration magazines.

Mom squeezes in beside me and puts on her "let's have a warm moment together" look and says, "You've got to learn to forgive him, he's your brother."

I don't say anything and we watch a *Little House on the Prairie* rerun. It's the story of this entire family of deaf-mutes that moves to Walnut Grove and Pa makes the whole town feel ashamed for making fun of them. Michael Landon makes this passionate speech from his wagon bed about humanity and dignity with this cute little blue-eyed mute girl watching him, big fat tears popping out and flowing down her pink cheeks. Mom starts crying into her gimlet and Michael Landon's running his hands through his shaggy pioneer hair.

The next day is Saturday and I'm off from work and we're going to go to Tablerock Lake to take out the boat but we never get there because all hell breaks loose.

I'm eating Grape-Nuts with Mom at the breakfast table, telling her how Wes is full of shit about the Airedales in India hunting lions because *National Geographic* says there are no lions in India, only tigers. Mom says to me, "Well, aren't you smart!" super cheerful, but she's only half listening. She's reading some article in *Parade* magazine about the real-life legal problems of the lady who used to play Wonder Woman on TV when Wes comes in looking serious.

"I'm afraid we've got a problem," he says.

"Oh, we do," I say. I'm chomping my cereal, trying not to look at him. He's got his jaw set to look *grave* and I want to laugh out loud because he looks like William Shatner in a tense moment.

Mom says, "What is it, honey?" sipping her coffee. Wes blows air out his mouth like he's thinking deep. He rubs his hair around and sits down.

"Was the security alarm activated last night?"

Mom says, "No, it wasn't, we left it off because we

didn't know when you'd be in. Why?" I put my cereal bowl down and stare at him, waiting to see what sort of shit he's cooking up. He looks at me then.

"Did you tell anyone about the engagement ring? Mark?" He says my name slow like it should mean something to me. Mother's looking all worried and holding her coffee cup tight. I stare at him saying nothing.

"Did you?" he says, looking huffy.

"No."

"Not a word to any of your *co-workers* at the T-shirt shop?"

"Fuck you," I say.

"What is it, Wes?" Mom's asking like she's going to hyperventilate. He looks at her all serious. I can't believe the guy.

Wes is flashing the blue eyes. "I shouldn't have to tell you that the ring was extremely, *extremely* valuable. Extraordinarily." He turns his head away looking troubled and stares out the window. There's the chiseled profile. He's clenching his teeth so that it ripples in his perfect jawline. I get up to rinse my bowl in the sink and try to ignore him.

He says real slow, "Portia's ... ring ... is *missing*. Mother gasps and says, "Ooooh!" I'm rolling my eyes and I turn around to look at him.

He says, "I've looked everywhere, Mom. I'm afraid

there's . . . been a robbery. A *robbery*." Now I understand why Wes took the trouble to show us the rock. Some people come to see their families because they feel guilty. Some come to do laundry. Wes always comes to cash in.

"Oh, for Chrissake," I say. "Mom, don't you see what he's doing?" But Mom is just staring at him, all dewy-eyed. He nods at her tragically like he's just told her he's dying of a terminal illness and gets up and starts pacing. She's hanging on every word and I'm boiling.

Wes says, "The window in my room was open last night when I came in. I left it locked."

"Oh, my God!" I yell, overdramatic, "Quick! Fetch a detective!" Mom is clutching her pink bathrobe. She keeps gasping.

"Oh heavens," Mother says, near tears, "did I open the window? I don't know. It's all too awful!"

I can't take it any longer. I walk right up to Wes, eyeing him hard and pointing. I poke him hard in the chest. He scoffs and pokes me back so I shove him and he shoves me back. Mom's watching it all saying, "Oh, boys, now stop this nonsense. You're only making this worse."

I back off and I say to him real slow, "Listen, you fucking con artist, I don't know where your ring is but I know one thing, *you do*. If you so much as *mention* Mom's insurance policy I'm going to kill you."

Wes stares at me like I'm a piece of shit and I stare back. Mother says, "Boys, *please*," and gets up from the table like she means it this time.

"Mark, can't you see your brother's in a crisis situation here?" She comes over and stares up at us and whispers, "Why can't you just admit you love one another?" All I can see are the red veins in Wes's eyeballs. Mom's cuckoo clock starts going off on the wall.

Wes clenches his Paul Newman teeth and says, "I don't have *time* for your emotional problems right now, Mark." His voice cracks. "This is serious business," he says. "I'm not talking T-shirts here." Then he stares at me with the cold blue eyes and says with a ha-ha-ha, "You just better calm down, buddy, and take some of your medication. All right?"

Wes goes gliding out of the kitchen in his khakis and into the living room and I'm right behind him and Mom comes tripping after me calling, "Boys!"

Wes picks up the phone and I say, "Who are you calling?"

He says, "I'm calling the police."

"No, you're not."

"Yes, I am."

"Put the phone down," I say.

Mom says, "Mark, why can't he call the police?"

And Wes says, "Yes, why can't I call the police?" putting the phone down with his eyes all slanty.

"Because *you've* got the ring, you asswipe." Wes shakes his head and tries picking up the phone again. Before he can do it I knock the phone out of his hand and he shoves me hard. I push him. Wes goes banging up against one of Mom's display shelves and a hundred little glass dogs go scattering to the floor and Mother starts screaming, "Ooooh, no!"

We end up in the front yard, rolling around in the grass and punching each other in full sight of the neighbors and the lady power walkers in jumpsuits who go passing by looking astonished. Mom is just standing on the front steps in her bathrobe screaming. Wes is generally stronger than me and used to wrestle in high school. He keeps trying to catch me in a hold but I won't let him because I'm just flying. I feel superhuman. It feels good hitting Wes and I bloody his nose and he bleeds all over his pink button-down shirt and he punches me in the eye and I wonder if I'll ever see out of it again but I don't care because I hate him so much. I hit him again and he grabs my old Tom Petty concert T-shirt by the neck and rips it in half. I knock Wes down then and pound his pretty Paul Newman head over and over again into the ground and Mom is yelling, "Stop! Stop! Stop!"

Just then the automatic sprinklers go off and the whole yard erupts with water and we're still rolling around in the grass and when we finally stop we're drenched, covered in mud and blood and breathing hard. The little kids next door are standing in their yard and gaping with their mouths open and one's got a blue Popsicle stuffed in his mouth, his little belly hanging out from under his shirt. They start giggling and Wes yells at them to go away and mind their own business. I tell him to shut up but they've already run off screaming.

That night Wes packed up his stuff and flew away to I don't know where. I didn't care. I took him to the airport saying nothing all the way out. He just shook his head and said that he didn't know where the ring was and that he was *disturbed by the intensity of my hatred.* I just watched him go, limping off to his terminal with his garment bag.

When I got back home Mom was in her room with an ice pack on her forehead all propped up on three satin pillows. She said she didn't know what she did wrong to have such children and said she was going to have to see a therapist. I asked her if she wanted to order a pizza. She wouldn't look at me. I caught sight of myself in her dressing-table mirror and I was covered in bruises, but I felt pretty good. Until I saw Mom's dogs. The pieces of all Mom's little broken dogs were on top of a sheet and laid out on the floor like she was gonna sit in front of the TV one long day and glue them all together. There was a whole mountain of them and seeing them like that made me feel awful. I thought about trying to say something to make her feel better but couldn't think of anything so I just walked out and pulled her door to.

The next morning wouldn't you know I found Portia's diamond ring behind the toilet in Wes's bathroom. Probably fell out of his pant pocket. The bastard was lucky he didn't flush it down the toilet. I sat down on the tub wall looking at the ring, watching it glitter. I felt sort of guilty and decided to try and find Wes to tell him. But then I never did. I just put it in the top drawer of my nightstand. I don't know why.

A couple of days later I get a call at work and my manager hands me the phone and looks at me funny. I say hello and this English voice says, "Hello, this is Portia Humphries-Owen. Is this Wesley's brother? Mark?" Her voice is sweet as anything I've ever heard. A voice like this could call you a shithead and it would sound like heaven. She said she didn't know where Wes was, hadn't heard from him in several days. How was he? I told her he was here but had already gone. That I called just to say hello because he told us all about her.

"Isn't that the nicest..." she says. She invited me to come to visit her in London whenever I liked and I said that I would. She said she was dancing *Coppélia* this season, asked me what people do for entertainment where we live and I said that we go to the lake and wrestle. I don't know why she asked this question, but she laughed.

"Do you look like your brother?" she asks.

And I say, "No, Wes looks like Paul Newman and I don't."

And she chuckles and says, "Ah well."

Today I got fired from the T-shirt shop for making all the long-distance calls to Europe. My manager has been in a piss-poor mood lately because of frequent oral surgery making it impossible to eat enough to maintain his three hundred pounds, so he didn't have much sympathy for me. Ed said good-bye and tough break and offered to take me in as an equal partner in the night-crawler business when he gets it rolling.

I don't care about the job. I packed my stuff up and drove my van out to the lake. It's a weekday and nobody's out here but me and I've got my radio turned up loud to the classical station and the music is pretty and sad, all violins. I watch the birds fly in procession, twenty altogether moving the same and evenly spaced like they're connected at the beaks by strings. I think of Portia Humphries-Owen dancing on stage in the Royal Ballet in London with her yellow hair pulled back tight, standing on tiptoe and flapping her arms like one of these pretty birds. I have her ring in my nightstand.

the end of the beltline

Tony Carbone

one morning at work i become very preoccupied with the
new temp. her name is eunice, and i am convinced that
a name that ugly can only be a curse to her; she is very
homely, with a bad complexion and too much hair along
her cheeks. her teeth are short and yellow and crooked,
and her breath smells. she dresses like somebody's mother.
i like her breasts all right, and while her body seems toned
and fit, her calves are disproportionately large and her
ankles are disgustingly thick. she wears ugly red pumps
that clash with her skirt and make her feet look atrocious.
all i can think about is fucking her.

i spend the majority of the morning devising ways of
seducing her. i decide upon an ostentatious abuse of
power. i drop a columbus, ohio, phone book on her desk.

—i'm going to need this typed up.

—this is a phone book.

—stay here as long as it takes, and hold all my calls.

—with all due respect, i believe that all of this information is online now. names, phone numbers, addresses; it's all there.

—with all due respect, this phone book is from 1976! does our country's bicentennial mean nothing to you?

—well of course it does.

—then i'm sure you understand my urgency.

that nite back at her place we take all our clothes off, smoke hashish, eat budget gourmet from the microwave, and watch every richard simmons workout tape in chronological order. eunice occasionally jumps up off the sofa and works out for thirty minutes or so. her body glistens with perspiration and her aroma overpowers my cheese tortellini in red marinara sauce in a very masculine way.

—richard simmons saved my life. i used to be fat. now just look at these calves! i believe my experience will help me in the future. if i'm married and my husband starts getting tired of me, i can put on a lot of weight and then lose it all again with these tapes. then it'll be like he has a whole new woman, and my marriage will be saved. around sunrise she finally loosens up enough to introduce me to her collection of hardcore pornography magazines.

—look at that, she says, pointing at christy canyon's cavernous cunt.—these women have seen more dick than i've seen blue sky. have you ever seen this? she pulls a copy of *traci, i love you* from her rare video collection.

—oh yeah, that's the only one that's legal in this country.

i try not to sound too disappointed.

in the living room. on the floor. my head between her legs. i peel back one sweaty sticky labium and unearth an external SCSI port.

—good lord!

—it's a PCSI 3 ultrawide RAID array adapter.

—your goddamn right it is.

—they wired me up at the temp agency.

—i'll say.

—you can do my ass, but you'll need a two-prong adapter. radio shack opens in an hour. her clit is an old motorola 486 33 mhz CPU.

bzzzzzzzz. bzzzz. bzzzzzzzzzzzzzzzzzzzzzzzzzzzzz. bzzzzzzzzz. bzzz. bzzz. bzzzzzzzzzzzzzzzzzzzzzzzzzzzzzzzzzzzzzzzzzzzzzzzzzz zzzzzzzzzzzzzzzzzzzzzzzzzzzzzzzzzzzzzzzzzzzzzzzzzzzzzzzzzzzz zzzzzzzzzzzzzzzzzzzzzzzzzzzzzzzzzzzzzzzzzzzzzzzzzzzzzzzzzzzz zzzzzzzz. bzzzzzzzzzzzzzz. bzzzzzzz. bz. bz. bzzzzzzzzzzzzzzz.

i think it will take forever for her to come. i slip out while she's cleaning up in the bathroom, taking the copy of *traci, i love you* with me. all day long my tongue tastes ionized.

this morning at work i attend a meeting regarding the new market positioning strategy for our product line. i show up thirty minutes late.

—thanks for waiting.

—no problem.

—hey, you. smart guy. get up so i can sit down.

—aw geez lou, there's plenty of other chairs.

i take my shirt off.

—come clean with that chair right now, scumbag, or i'll stomp your dick in the dirt and fill everybody in about how when you were twelve you got sent to live with your grandma for boppin your little sister.

—aw geez lou, i didn't want her learnin from some stranger . . .

you'll be on your way to the top in no time flat after reading just a couple of chapters in my international bestseller, *how to manipulate friends and intimidate people*, the self-help book that'll carry you across that bridge to the twenty-first century.

this self-help book is somethin else.
put all yo other ones back on the shelf.

it's got tony robbins flat on his ass,
turnin faggot tricks fo face-lift cash.
—nipsey russell,
The New York Times
Book Review

here are just a few of the topics covered:

borrowing small amounts of money and not paying it back taking off your shirt taking off your pants not giving a damn not giving a shit not giving a fuck not giving at the office butting in interrupting cutting people off covert hypnosis mind control how to hire a divorce attorney how to hire a private investigator how to hire a hit man how to buy jurors lying cheating stealing talking under your breath speed-breathing speed-reading speed-thinking speed-talking taking credit for other people's work sabotaging other people's work when you can't take credit for it slacking off in general physical torture psychological torture prank calls stalking starting fights finishing fights abusing waiters picking up waitresses sex for free sex for money sex in vegas sex in thailand power plays power lunches power naps how to get someone's name on a list of convicted sex offenders inventing rumors spreading rumors backstabbing how to use a knife how to use a gun how to conceal a knife how to conceal a gun herbal remedies penis enlargement how to give a great toast brushing flossing physical fitness personal hygiene the power of positive thinking and more . . . it's all here!

one monday morning i get home at 9 A.M. to find my teenage lover spread out on my bed with her shoes off.

—what did you do all weekend?

—i worked all weekend.

—doing what?

—virus trouble.

—oh no.

—how about you?

—i went partying in glasgow. everybody was there! i met some guy named roman polanski. i tried to give him a blow job, but he was too drunk.

—i'm in a made for hbo movie called *life on the streets: freaked in the ass 2*. i play a down-and-out detective who hits the bottle after his wife leaves him and his daughter dies of leukemia. i have a torrid yet impersonal love affair with my lovely partner, sarah. she's got a tough demeanor, but on the inside the reality of the streets is eating away at her soul, and she just can't seem to stay away from men who treat her like shit.

—that sounds cool. when is it on?

—that's just it. it's not on. sometimes i'm just *in* it; saying my lines, going through the motions.

—cool.

i am maniacally digging through her bags, looking for drugs. i finally find some speed hidden in a sealed tampon.

—hey, don't meth around with that!

—i've been awake since thursday morning and i'm not about to sleep now!

—i think i've finally done too much e. the back of my brain always hurts and my spine aches and i have permanent double vision.

—every time i close my eyes i see worms eating the eyes out of my decomposing face. i can smell the rotting of my own flesh. here watch. ooohhh! that time it was a dachshund eating its own shit. okay. all right. here goes. there. back to worms. told ya. she uses toothpicks to pry my eyelids apart à la alex in *a clockwork orange*. she holds me in her arms and waters my eyes with a dropper. i start to cry.

—there's something else that's bothering me.

—what's that, dear?

—why didn't richie and ralph and potsie just beat the shit out of fonzie. i mean there were three of them and only one of him.

—if they beat up fonzie, it would have destroyed their ideal of what is cool. sure they could have done it, but then they would have simply been trapped, body and soul, in their sterile, white-bread middle american lives, unable to live vicariously through the *alleged* experiences of the more worldly fonz.

—gee, how do you know so much about happy days?

—it's what i wrote my term paper on.

she squeezes big dollops of ky jelly into my eyes.

—what the fuck are you doing?

—i'm getting sleepy, and you've got to keep your eyes from drying up.

—yeah, but you know where that thing's been.

—poor baby. i'm going to get the rest of my stuff out of the car.   i'll be right back.

that was the last time i ever saw her.

does my insurance cover this?

or

yeah, that and something about boxer shorts

this morning i am being chased naked through the mall by the seven dwarves as painted by john wayne gacy. don't you think his characters simply jump right off the canvas? backed into a dressing room at the gap, i turn to make my stand. dopey holds the glass slipper by the heel and smashes it. he comes at me with the broken edge. . . .

—NOT AGAIN YOU EVIL FUCKING COCKSUCK-ING BASTARDS! it's the girl behind the cash register (hi, my name is valerie). she draws her pricing gun and blows his head clean off. my face is covered with dwarf blood and green matter, and this exhilarates me. sleepy makes a move, but he's too slow. i go in through his stomach and up through his chest. i rip out his heart and show it to him before he dies. i repeat this five more times, and valerie gives them each one bullet in the head for good measure. she gives me a pair of jeans and a striped shirt to wear (—you've got the right build. you can get away with horizontal). we celebrate at the orange julius. —it's on the inside of my thigh, you know the real soft sensitive part. it looks like a zit but it itches, she says, but i don't pay attention because i spend the next six hours arguing with my lunch, whose sensible arguments are convincing, but i sense duplicity. —hey man, i'm a hot dog, and let's face it, you really don't need to be putting any more poison into your body right now. you need to just set me down and take your ass to see a doctor. he has the fibrous consistency of a cadaver's penis. he hollers bloody murder in my mouth so i have to close my lips around him to muffle the sound. —now who's got who? he whispers to my tonsils just before rupturing into my mouth like a burst appendix. hot salty pus shoots out of my nose and clogs my ears. —good lord, the doctor says,—i've never seen a case of this so severe in a man your age. —what is it, doc? give it to me straight. —it's your testicles . . . —oh, god. not cancer. —no, i'm afraid it's much worse than that. they now hang lower than the bottom of your flaccid cock. this shouldn't happen for at least another two years. —oh man, doc. i thought it was something serious. —oh it's not too bad, all we need to do is remove a band of skin from your scrotum and just hitch them suckers up a little bit. —that's okay, doc. i don't think my insurance covers that. i just came here about my eyes. the doc pulls a switchblade scalpel from his pocket and holds the rusty blade precariously against my jugular with the precision and intuition that only a surgeon can possess. he puts his face close to mine and whispers malevolently through clenched teeth, —this is not elective surgery.

epilogue

when i came to i cracked the doctor's skull with a bedpan and stole away with the removed skin to the all-nite piercing and tattoo parlor in the hospital lobby gift shop. i had them put the skin back where it belonged, except this time tattooed with the moral of the story—*"it's lonely at the top, but you eat better."*

one morning i get to work early and spend several hours trying to decide how to file bill gates's name in my rolodex. should it go under *bill*, or should it go under *gates*? i send him an email outlining my dilemma. i immediately receive the following message:

> Dear Mister Fetchet.
> Thank you for your interest in Bill Gates. Mr. Gates is very busy right now fixing Tiger Woods, therefore he does not have the time to answer your message personally. However, he did want me to assure you that he would have you assassinated if you ever tried to contact him again.

twelve cups of coffee later, it all becomes very clear to me. microsoft operatives are everywhere, and they are behind everything; waco, oklahoma city, ruby ridge, david hasselhoff, television. i must warn others about this threat to national security. i must stop them before they stop me. i kick in the door to the server room and find the head of pr with one lumpy translucent tit plopped on top of the main engineering box. it hums away and blinks internally.

—i have a photographic mammary.

—you . . . you're one of them.

—shut up and close the door. it has come to our attention that the director of marketing has spawned the son of satan.

—little darryl?

—yes, little darryl. i myself found the number of the beast behind his left ear.

—it's all becoming so clear to me now. third quarter profits in the millions, new venture capitalists signing on every day, and in three years we've never delivered a product.

—i'll need your help.

—you can count on me.

at the park, we spread out a blanket and dine on the boy's roasted flesh. she cracks a femur violently over her knee and sucks out the marrow.

—this thing i saw on the discovery channel says the ceremony won't be done until we pick the bones clean and mail them to the heads of time warner, disney, microsoft, and westinghouse.

i reach into the basket and pull out little darryl's little head. i peel away the layers of charred tinfoil. immediately, i realize that something is amiss. i look her squarely in the eye.

—you never saw any show on the discovery channel, did you?

—no.

—you never found the number of the beast on little darryl, did you?

—no.

—then why'd you do it?

—the thought of that evil bastard procreating was more than i could stand. i owed it to myself. you see, i never wanted to turn into what i am now. i...i used to be a hippie. she bursts into tears and collapses in my arms. i hold her close to me and try to comfort her.

—you did the right thing. you did the right thing....

one morning at work i make a list of suspected drug addicts in the office. i storm into the product manager's office and confront her.

—i've got you figured out sister. your lethargy, your allergies and colds, your mismatched socks and missing bras, not to mention your 'i'll be working at homes' and your 'i need to spend more time with the kids'—it all points to one thing. you're a drug addict!

—is this blackmail?

i look at her long and hard, at her thin yet maternal figure, and i realize that i must have wanted to fuck her for a very long time.

—no, it was just a shot in the dark, but come to think of it...

in her car. on the beltline. on the way back to her house. i smoke cigarettes and go through her purse.

—i've got to stop and pick up something to eat for the kids.

—listen i want to get a couple of things straight. there

are two things in this world that i hate: kids and dogs. i hate them in general, but i hate them specifically when they belong to someone i know.

—tell me about it.

the extent of our intercourse is me shooting heroin into the thick swollen rope of a femoral artery that snakes its way down her inner left thigh. her appetite for the drug is voracious, but her appetite for me is nonexistent. she is willing to indulge me, but i can tell that she hates it. i sense she's just a little uptight, so i score some rohypnol from little chrissy who's in seventh grade, and i knock her mom out with it every night after dinner and fuck her while she's passed out. one morning she wakes up and takes me in her arms.

—i like it like that, the way you drug me and rape me like a plastic fuck doll for hours on end.

—all the kids call it the "date rape drug."

—yeah, i know, it's just like being a teenager again.

for christmas i want to buy little chrissy and billy something special, something entertaining *and* educational. the clerk at the toys r us suggests something from the new line of john dupont home chemistry sets. this season's biggest sellers are *jerry garcia! celebrity autopsy* and *lapd crime lab: you plant the evidence!* i end up buying billy *breaking training: urine samples of the dallas cowboys.* he's a little michael irvin fan. and for chrissy, the little cold war scholar, i get *black market chemicals from the former soviet union.* it comes complete with a lead apron and plastic safety goggles.

—what's wrong with mommy? she's purple and she smells like dookie.

—well, little billy, i'm not a degenerate adulterous smack fiend like your mom, so i'm no expert on these matters, but i think ol' fast eddie tried to give your mom a hot shot cause she's getting sloppy and talking too much and coming up a little short with the cash. plus, i think he's kind of pissed off about me.

—fast eddie's mean.

—correction, little billy. fast eddie *was* mean. word on the street is that crack baby and his boyz shot fast eddie in the face with a sawed-off.

—oooohh, gross.

—that's right, billy. it was gross. even his mommy and daddy didn't know for sure if it was him. they had to take his teeth to the dentist to make sure.

—are you my daddy?

—no, little billy, i'm better than your daddy. do you know little joey carmichael from school?

—yeah.

—well, when your daddy found out about your

mommy and fast eddie, he said that's okay, because he was moving to key west with mr. carmichael as soon as mr. carmichael got divorced from mrs. carmichael anyway.

—but joey's got a new daddy named ray. do you think you'll ever be *my* new daddy?

—no fucking way, little billy. no fucking way. no, go take your mommy's pulse again and hold the mirror in front of her nose just like i showed you.

one morning when she is functional again, she storms into my office and confronts me, demanding the truth.

—we need to talk.

—you're sure you want to get into this?

—i need to know the truth.

—you can't handle the truth.

—but i can't handle another day of not knowing—the uncertainty, the lack of fulfillment. i don't think i can go on like this for one more day. i'm begging you, please . . . what do we *do* here?

—we build hardware, and we make software that runs that hardware.

—yes, i know that, that's what everybody says, but what is it *exactly*?

—*teledildonics,* baby.

—oh god, yes!

INT. SECRET LABORATORY. DAY.

Complete darkness. We hear SANDY enrapt in building sexual ecstasy, moaning slowly and determinedly over the steady purr of chip processing and the whirs and stops of lubricated hydraulics. We can hear the hardware start to work harder and faster and louder, and we can hear SANDY respond accordingly. Steadily, her breathing becomes shorter and her moaning more intense.

The lights begin to fade in slowly, in rhythm with SANDY'S growing excitement. We can see LOU looking on at the scene in disgust——SANDY is naked, strapped into an ultramodern, high-tech sex swing. Long, black, lubricated cyber-cocks are pumping in and out of her ass and her cunt and her mouth with increasing velocity. She masturbates two others with her hands. She is wearing a leather mask that covers all of her face except for her mouth, and her eyes are covered with thick 3D lenses. The walls of the room are covered with 360 degrees of images of masturbating men waiting in line for their turn.

CLOSE UP——SANDY'S face and breasts.

One of the cybercocks suddenly shoots a hot rope of

synthetic semen across SANDY'S chest. This excites her even more.

SANDY

Oh God! Fuck me harder! Harder, goddammit! And when you're done, get out of the goddamn way!

LOU is naked and masturbating. He jerks the dildo out of her mouth and inserts his cock.

LOU'S POV—the men standing in line become irate.

HARD-ON #1

Hey, needle dick. What the fuck do you think you're doin?

HARD-ON #2

Yeah, get in the back of the fuckin' line, you faggot.

LOU

Fuck all you fake-ass dickless motherfuckers. I fuckin' made you.

HARD-ON #1

Well, you sure the fuck didn't make us in your image.

POV HARD-ON #1 AND HARD-ON #2—LOU holding up his middle finger at them.

LOU

Fuck you, motherfuckers!

CLOSE UP: LOU'S face. He closes his eyes and makes impending-orgasm face. As he comes—

FADE TO BLACK

—you bastard! i could have done them all. it would have been the world record.

—your children miss you.

—i can no longer stand the company of human beings.

—you're sick.

—i'm beta testing.

—no, you're really sick. that's what i came to tell you.

—what do you mean?

—those men standing in line, they're infected with a virus.

—oh my god. not aids?

—no, not aids. virtual aids.

—i've never heard of that.

—i was here all weekend working on it. i'm the only one that's ever seen it.

—so, what does all this mean?

—it's very simple. if you're ever removed from that machine, your immune system will eventually shut down and you'll die.

—so you really do love me?

—all of this, i made it for you.

—come here. give me a kiss.

INT. RUNDOWN APARTMENT IN JAMAICA, QUEENS. DAY.

DET. DICK BAGLEY and his partner, SARAH, are in bed together. They have just woken up and they are naked. They are kissing passionately.

CUT TO: SARAH in the shower washing herself.

SARAH

Now don't forget. Wait twenty minutes and then come after me. You got that?

BAGLEY—OS

Yeah, yeah. I got it.

SARAH

I'm serious, Bagley. Don't fuck this up.

BAGLEY—OS

I said, yeah, yeah, i got it.

CUT TO: BAGLEY sitting on the bed smoking and reading *People* magazine.

BAGLEY

It says here that Jamie Lee Curtis was born with a dick. You know that?

SARAH——on her way out the door.

Twenty minutes, Bagley.

BAGLEY

Yeah, yeah.

INSERT: Clock radio next to the bed——10:15

BAGLEY sits in bed and smokes. Reads *Wired* magazine.

INSERT: Clock radio next to the bed——11:22

EXT. STREET IN JAMAICA, QUEENS. DAY

BAGLEY crosses the street and enters another apartment building.

POV BAGLEY—he stands in front of apartment 1013 and knocks. DARRYL answers the door.

> DARRYL
>
> What the fuck do you want?

> BAGLEY
>
> I'm looking for . . . uh . . . Sarah?

> DARRYL
>
> Who the fuck are you?

> BAGLEY
>
> I'm . . . uh . . . Lou Fetchet.

SARAH—her face appears over DARRYL'S shoulder.
What are you doing? Tell him your name and stop fucking around.

> BAGLEY
>
> Oh yeah, I'm Dick Bagley.

DARRYL

Mr. Bagley. Come in, we've been expecting you.

INT. DARRYL'S APARTMENT IN JAMAICA, QUEENS.

DARRYL closes the door and locks it behind BAGLEY as they step inside. Several surly Jewish gangsters dressed like market analysts draw their weapons.

DARRYL

All right, Bagley. Hands in the air. You too, bitch.

Two gangsters pat down SARAH and BAGLEY and remove their weapons, then they handcuff them to some rusty radiator pipes in the corner of the room.

DARRYL (raising his revolver above his head)
Lights out, motherfuckers.

DARRYL cracks SARAH in the back of the head with the butt of the revolver, sending her sprawling unconscious onto the floor. Then he cracks BAGLEY the same way. Upon impact:

FADE TO BLACK

tyra banks is the color of a good cup of coffee. she sits across from me in cafe reggio at a table, reverse-oreoed between kate moss and milla jovovich. they stare at me and giggle behind their hands like seventh-graders. the waitress asks me what i'll have, and i say, —i'll have a cup of her, nodding toward tyra because i'm like brad fucking pitt right now. all three of them blush and swoon and giggle even harder. milla and kate whisper something in tyra's ear and then start pushing her out of the booth toward me. she tries to resist, but she ends up landing on her ass on the floor. she gets up and comes over to where i'm sitting.

—my friends kate and milla want me to tell you that they think you're cute.

—yeah?

—yeah. they were wondering if you wanted to come with us back to our hotel room?

on the bed we are naked and all over each other like a litter of kittens. i close my eyes and lunge at them with my hands and open mouth; so much supermodel flesh, so much to explore. my orgasms come one after another and my cock gushes continuously like a fire hose. we are all covered with it. the ceilings and the walls become transparent with it. kate whispers in my ear, —eat me.

—you taste so good i could eat you whole. i dig my

teeth in and take another bite from her scrawny forearm. i pull the skin and muscle away from her radius and ulna with my teeth. her bones are completely stripped clean from the elbow down, so i start in on the other arm, and all the while she moans and screams out my name. i have never tasted anything like it. i devour her so fast that i don't even take time to chew, i just swallow her whole. she only notices that i'm choking on her when her ecstasy is interrupted. she wraps her skeleton arms around me and tries to give me the heimlich maneuver, but she just isn't strong enough: not enough muscle. i am choking to death. . . .

. . . i wake up screaming and gasping for breath. billy and chrissy are standing next to the bed in their pajamas.

—what's wrong, daddy?

—there's nothing to worry about, kids. daddy just realized that his dreams will never, ever come true. that's all. now, who wants to go for a ride?

—i do. i do.

—then let's go.

—we're even gonna take mommy.

—yay! yay!

—but if you unhook me, i'll die.

—you're going for a ride with your family.

—a ride to where?

—to the end of the beltline.

—but there is no end to the beltline. it just goes all the way around the city. that's why they call it the beltline.

—i'm not buying that for one second. there's so much of it that i haven't seen. so much of it that we don't use. it's all got to end somewhere.

EXT. CAR. DAY.

BAGLEY drives and SARAH sits in the passenger seat. Her hair is a mess and her face is badly beaten. They drive for a long time in silence.

BAGLEY

Mind tellin' me what's wrong, partner?

SARAH

Just shut up and keep driving.

BAGLEY

Then you mind tellin' me where we're going?

SARAH

We're going to find Darryl, and we're going to kill him.

BAGLEY

Why we gonna do that, partner?

SARAH

'Cause of what he did to us back there.

BAGLEY

What exactly did he do to us back there? I was kind of knocked out for a while.

SARAH

Oh, Bagley!

She bursts into tears and cries out to him:

We . . . we . . . we got freaked in the ass back there! That's what happened!

BAGLEY casually loads a fresh clip of ammo into his tech 9 and locks one in the chamber.

BAGLEY

All this time. Freaked in the ass and I didn't even know it. It's payback time.

SARAH

Bagley, look at that! Up in the sky!

Looming in the sky over the horizon of the highway
is a tremendous light. As they approach, the light gets
stronger and brighter until they can finally make out
what it is—a giant movie screen suspended above the
road. spread out for miles and miles are thousands,
maybe millions, of cars, and they are all watching
what's happening on the screen. DARRYL and his thugs
are beating and raping SARAH and BAGLEY. BAGLEY
sees what is happening and does not stop. He drives
over the tops of cars toward the screen. DARRYL sees
them coming and addresses them from the scene.

DARRYL

You want some of this? Huh? You want some of
this?

BAGLEY and SARAH have their arms out the windows
and they are firing at DARRYL.

BAGLEY

See you in hell, motherfucker!

BAGLEY and SARAH race toward the screen, screaming
and firing their weapons. DARRYL is firing back,
beckoning them. When they reach the edge of the
cars, they sail off directly into the center of the
screen. There is an explosion. A mushroom cloud

envelops the cars and disintegrates the audience.
Everybody dies.

THE END

i know i am somewhere different and maybe special. there
is a green field and across the green field is a giant party.
i run to it. my parents and my sister are sitting at a table
there. i have never seen them so beautiful before and they
are happy to see me. my dad starts talking to me.

—you know that recurring dream we all have? you
know, the one where we all get into the car late at night
and go to that swimming pool where we're the only ones
there?

—yeah.

—well, this is the place. except it's not a swimming
pool. it's that lake over there.

i turn to my left and see a small lake filled with beautiful blue water.

—that's all the water in the world, son. that *is* the
world over there. the whole entire universe.

—they're gonna peel back the clouds and show us
heaven, my mom says.

—that's right, son, they're gonna peel back the clouds
and show us *god*.

comfortable drops of soothing rain fall from the sky and land on our heads.

—it's starting, my sister said.

we all look up into the sky despite the rain and watch as the clouds are peeled back to reveal dozens of giant helicopters, and suspended below the hovering helicopters is a simple yet enormous tubing apparatus that sucks the water from the lake with giant pipes and then regurgitates it back onto us through smaller holes in the top. everybody cheers and laughs and claps, except me; i start to cry. i feel the humiliation for them, for all of them.

—what is it, son? why are you crying?

—look at the rain, lou. look at the rain. when you were a little boy, you always wanted to know where the rain came from.

—that's not rain, i choke meekly through my tears. that's just a giant fucking sprinkler.

Comprehension Test

Myla Goldberg

After reading each of the following passages, answer the questions to the best of your ability.

We can truly observe America's great melting pot in action in this urban neighborhood which, over the years, has been home to many of America's newest arrivals. As the tides of immigration have shifted, it too has changed. Yet, like a chalkboard upon which yesterday's lesson has been only partially erased, its streets still bear traces of those who came before. Fifty years ago, this neighborhood was home to scores of Eastern European Jews fleeing persecution. Over time, however, Chinese characters have appeared on buildings beside Hebrew ones. What once could have been described as an urban shtetl has become a part of Chinatown.

Shops sell ginger root, dried mushrooms, and preserved duck eggs. Wheeled carts dispense one-dollar cartons of lo mein and rice noodles. An old man sets up his sidewalk stand, resoling Chinese sandals with used tire rubber. Yet around the corner, a row of electronics stores is still staffed by Orthodox Jews with their sidelocks and skull caps. A pickle store still vends its wares in briny barrels.

Though the words RABBI LOEW SCHOOL FOR BOYS are engraved in stone upon this building's facade, it is now an apartment building filled with Chinese families. Dr. Lin's ground-floor office neighbors the very playground he visited as a child. By the time Dr. Lin's children are grown, this neighborhood will have changed again, but one thing is certain: additions to our great melting pot are what help make America the Beautiful.

1. Dr. Lin was shot to death in his office on Friday afternoon. Had he

   (A) ever felt uneasy in his office?

   (B) known his assailant?

   (C) attempted to defend himself?

   (D) pleaded for his life?

   (E) cried out for help?

2. Dr. Lin's murderer successfully fled. Is it more likely that his shots

   (A) went unheard?

   (B) were assumed to be the sound of a car backfiring?

   (C) were shrugged off as someone else's problem?

   (D) went unreported for fear of criminal reprisal?

   (E) went unreported for fear of the law?

3. Were the shots fired

   (A) in anger?

   (B) in fear?

   (C) in desperation?

   (D) in revenge?

   (E) in confusion?

4. As a policeman cordoned off the crime scene with PO-LICE LINE DO NOT CROSS tape, did he feel

   (A) important?

   (B) sad?

   (C) annoyed?

   (D) angry?

   (E) nothing?

[Two NEIGHBORHOOD RESIDENTS approach a sign that has been posted on the gate fronting Dr. Lin's office.

A police sketch appears below the word WANTED. *Beside the poster, a scrap of yellow police tape remains tied to the fence. The two men talk while facing the poster.]*

RESIDENT 1: Did you know him?

RESIDENT 2: No. I passed by yesterday on my way home, but I did not stop.

RESIDENT 1: I came as soon as I heard the sirens, but I didn't see anything.

RESIDENT 2: Today I was expecting for police to be everywhere, but there is nothing.

[The two examine the police sketch. It portrays the face of a black man with generic features.]

RESIDENT 1: I heard a policeman last night say it was a robbery.

RESIDENT 2: It says that the doctor was shot two times in the back. Do you think he was reaching for his gun?

RESIDENT 1: I wouldn't have put up a fight. If I got
shot, my wife would kill me.

[Both men chuckle.]

RESIDENT 2: My little boy plays every day at the playground. That this happened so close . . .

*[RESIDENT 2 spits and walks away. After he has gone,
RESIDENT 1 removes the police tape and puts it in his
pocket.]*

5. When Resident 1 visited the crime scene on the night
of the murder, did he feel
   (A) intrepid?
   (B) involved?
   (C) impelled?
   (D) excited?
   (E) entitled?

6. On the night of the murder, did Resident 2 continue
past the crime scene without stopping
   (A) for fear of being branded a "rubbernecker"?
   (B) in the belief that bypassing tragedy prevents fu-
   ture misfortune?
   (C) to avoid suspicion, regardless of guilt?

(D) indignant that such a thing had occurred in his neighborhood?

(E) in the hope that what had happened would undo itself if ignored?

7. When the two residents spoke, did they avoid eye contact out of

(A) fear?

(B) suspicion?

(C) respect?

(D) shame?

(E) habit?

8. If the two crossed paths on the street again, would they most likely

(A) wave hospitably?

(B) nod curtly?

(C) speak genially?

(D) pass imperviously?

(E) blush self-consciously?

9. If an innocent man walked by the WANTED poster and recognized his eyes or nose, it is *least* likely that he would feel

(A) indignant

(B) nervous

(C) amused

(D) unconcerned

(E) persecuted

10. If someone who had seen the poster passed by an unknown black man on the street, is it *least* likely that s/he would

(A) stare?

(B) smile?

(C) feel suspicion?

(D) return a greeting?

(E) avoid eye contact?

11. The WANTED poster disappeared within twenty-four hours of its appearance. Taking questions 9 and 10 into account, is this

(A) suspicious?

(B) shocking?

(C) surprising?

(D) understandable?

(E) unconscionable?

Doctor Is Slain

A physician was fatally shot in his office
Friday afternoon during an apparent robbery,
the police said.

The body of the doctor, Xang Ling, 35, was found on the floor of his office at about 8 P.M. by a building resident who was walking past the first story window and saw him sprawled inside.

The doctor was shot twice in the back and his pockets turned out, said a police spokeswoman.

There was no sign of forced entry, detectives said.

Dr. Ling had practiced medicine in the neighborhood for several years, according to a resident of the building.

12. Would a loved one save this article out of
   (A) obligation?
   (B) respect?
   (C) anger?
   (D) grief?
   (E) desperation?

13. Would the fact that the victim's name is misspelled affect that decision?
   (A) Definitely
   (B) Possibly
   (C) Maybe

(D) Perhaps

(E) Not at all

14. Would the victim's story have filled more space if the victim had been

(A) young?

(B) female?

(C) rich?

(D) famous?

(E) mutilated?

Since the legendary days of the American West, the reward poster has made itself a mainstay of American culture. From the infamous Jesse James to the Most Wanted at any local post office, this very special placard has undergone quite a transformation, on its way making its mark in history as well as art. A lot has changed since WANTED DEAD OR ALIVE made its first appearance in saloons both real and imagined.

Originally, posters were topped with monetary appeals or the word *Reward* itself. While this straightforward method was sure to get the message across, it lacked sophistication. Modern times have seen the refinement of this brand of appeal. Contemporary posters now invoke the reader's desire for justice first, only within the text alluding to a reward for one's efforts.

A fine example of this modern approach can be seen in the poster that appeared a week after Dr. Lin was found murdered. Tied with twine to the gate fronting the breezeway, it read HOMICIDE. Though a reward of up to $1,000 was offered for information regarding the murder, this was only revealed within the body of text, in both English and Spanish. The poster was, in fact, a pre-printed form with a blank for the inclusion of a phone number to call and a name to ask for. While its mass production can be seen as evidence that this poster's more subtle approach is effective, society's cynics might point out that its content, in this case, was altered. A week after its appearance at the crime scene, $1,000 was found to have been crossed out in black magic marker on both posters, with $25,000 handwritten above the revision.

15. Is it of greater concern that
   (A) money was offered for what should be a voluntary act?
   (B) only $1,000 was offered?
   (C) it took seven days for the poster to appear?
   (D) no posters appeared anywhere else?
   (E) the poster's languages did not include Chinese?

16. Are these posters put up

    (A) because they work?

    (B) to appease the neighborhood?

    (C) to avoid negligence suits?

    (D) more extensively in better neighborhoods?

    (E) with higher reward amounts in better neighborhoods?

17. Was the $25,000

    (A) an offer?

    (B) a demand?

At first, I found that I could not pass his office without stopping. Day or night, coming or going, I found myself momentarily planted before the metal gate, peering in. I wasn't reassured by the face that the WANTED poster briefly presented before disappearing. Its banality reminded me how impossible it was to determine whether the countless faces I passed each day were vessels for dreams or nightmares.

Each time I stopped, I would gaze intently at the passage leading to the doctor's door, as if staring hard enough would cause the murderer's footprints to appear like a photographic image in a tray of developer. I tried to reason away my newfound fear of the dark; the doctor, after all, had been shot on a sunny afternoon.

Like any bruise, the trauma of Dr. Lin's death faded over time. Children returned to the playground. The HOMICIDE poster outside his office yellowed in the rain and eventually blew away.

Days passed without me thinking of the doctor. I realized I wasn't stopping at his gate anymore. In a fit of guilt, I called the local precinct. If the case had been closed, I would be absolved of having gotten on with my life.

"Has Dr. Lin's murderer been found?" I asked the officer in charge of the case.

His voice sounded tired in a way that I had never heard before. He told me that the case was still open.

I wanted to feel entitled to an account of everything that this tired man had and had not done to bring Dr. Lin's murderer to justice. Instead, I felt grateful to have never experienced his brand of fatigue, a weariness that blanched his every word.

I thanked him and hung up the phone.

18. Does this murder
    (A) make future murders more likely?
    (B) make future murders less likely?
    (C) have no effect on future murders?
    (D) change the future?
    (E) confirm the future?

19. Can safety be

    (A) measured?

    (B) assumed?

    (C) proven?

    (D) granted?

    (E) taken away?

STOP
You have completed this test.
Move on when you feel it is safe to do so.

Given the Scalpel, They Dissect a Kiss

Robert A. Cucinotta

One chilly San Franciscan September, our man Hank Price decided to stop being half-assed about it and quit his job and live-in girlfriend to devote himself fully to calculating his odds of having AIDS and to masturbating. While awake he did one or the other, sometimes both—a morbid combination that doesn't bear description.

Credit cards would fund him until he died of disease, worry, or manual immoderation. He searched for an apartment in the cheapest slum in town, the Tenderloin. The Tenderloinians possessed a certain look, as if they'd been without sleep for fifty hours, or as if they'd *been* asleep for fifty hours and had just been jolted awake, and of course there were those who *were* asleep, often on the sidewalk, and they, except for the occasional violent twitch, looked dead. The neighborhood made Hank feel like he was on a hallucinogenic drug—nobody's body parts were in proportion, no one said anything that made sense (certainly not in English), wet leprosy was making a comeback, there was a significant midget population. Sober and fully limbed young men were rare. Fully drunk and semilimbed old men were common. This was not the strong black ghetto he'd expected. This was an old-fashioned, rainbow-skinned, tubercled skid row. Perfect!

Down the street from the runaway shelter and the Help Center, Hank walked into a fifteen-story apartment building. The manager was a tall muscular man with a head as big as a lion's and the blackest skin Hank had ever seen. There was no difference between the color of his skin and the color of his curly, wet, jet-black mane. "You, uh, guys have a, whatdoyoucallit, room for, uh, rent?" Hank sputtered. While he spoke of one thing, the relentless other pushed into his head in Faulknerian style: You, uh, *is my forehead hot, fever* guys have a *oral thrush has a metallic taste, which I don't have, but I do have a tingle,* whatdoyoucallit, *maybe hairy leukoplakia* a room *is that a swollen gland under my arm?* for *or just sore from suitcases* rent?

The manager's mouth opened, and from between square, marble-veined teeth, his tongue, bright red and pointed, flopped out, and if that sounds cartoonish, it was. He roared a laugh. He pounded his desk. He wiped his mouth with his sleeve and said, "Moving *on up*! You got your reference? Fill this out." Hank took an efficiency on the thirteenth floor (he wasn't superstitious), sandwiched between three generations of Cambodians and four generations of Koreans (he was, he sadly discovered, mildly xenophobic). He began a letter to his ex-girlfriend: "There is nothing like a multitude of foreign babies howling all night to drive home any burgeoning madness you may feel." He ripped it up.

How did Hank catch this fear of virus? Vacationing in Guatemala, where he deeply kissed a woman, who then offered sex in exchange for fifty colones (about ten dollars). Hank said no thank you, and blushed. She dropped the price to ten colones (two dollars), then five (one dollar). He declined and ran out of the bar. The next morning, he had a fever.

Perhaps 50 percent of the prostitutes in Guatemala have it (Hank's estimate). One percent of the infected population will have a very small amount of the virus present in saliva (Johnson & Studehiser, *American Pathology*, v. 12, 1992, pp. 44–48). Hank had a two-millimeter laceration on his gum caused by intoxicated flossing. He felt his chances of having it were between one in five thousand and one in five million—rather unlikely. But there was *one* chance, and if you're *the* one, then it doesn't matter that a million other ones wouldn't get it; if you're the one, you're the one, you're the one.

In his room, under four 120-watt bulbs in an over-heated ceiling socket, hero Hank added his AIDS odds ad nauseam. He had a wobbly thrift-store card table and chair, a text on statistical theory, a medical dictionary, an anatomy book, books on AIDS, photocopies of the latest transmission studies, and an adding machine. He'd pad the chair with his lumpy blue feather pillow and pull himself tight to the table, as snug as a kayaker, and in fact, figuring furiously at this unstable chair and table piled high with calculatory fodder took the same sort of balance as a kayaker. Night after night he darted down a river of statistics and medical terms and death possibilities, pitching and rolling on rickety chair and rickety table, punching numbers on clickety ten-key punch as he, mad unscientist that he was, estimated the area of his mouth, her mouth, volume of his saliva, her saliva, virus *in* saliva, length of tongues, weight of tongues, whose tongue, which width, what suction; he made colorful charts on poster board of frequently referenced information and also made tenth-of-a-second storyboards of the kiss, broke everything down to numbers, tried vainly to squash the likelihood of having it to nothing (the only acceptable likelihood), and if there was a chance then he had to locate it, hunt it, chase it down these rapids of obsession and saliva, but often, while paddling furiously through *The New England Journal of Medicine*, the incessant wail of babies rushing around him, he'd get caught in an Erlenmeyer whirlpool of biochemical reactions, or thrown down a waterfall of incoherent frequency distribution ratios, and he'd flip over—Hank, chair, table, tenkey punch, books, journals, coffee cup. Sitting among the flotsam, he'd catch his breath. Then he'd set the table aright and start again.

In the mornings, after an all-night calculating bender, he'd feel dazed, beaten up, his fear of death eased by exhaustion. He'd walk up to the roof and watch the city awaken. Lines of tiny cars running along 101, store owners sweeping the sidewalk, the graveyard-shift crack dealers retiring and the day shift shuffling to the corner. Directly below, on his block, there was always the slight figure of the toothless prostitute, shivering in halter top and jeans, barefoot, skinny from crack or worms or AIDS. The garbage trucks moaned as they hauled away the bodies. One thousand plague victims a day. The air stank. Hank used to think that if he lost a limb, or was disfigured, he would rather die than live. But he saw how silly that was now, as he faced death—not even death, just the *possibility* of death. To not want to live! That's all that is! How quickly would he trade an arm for his life! Returning to his room, Hank would check his lymph nodes (occipital, partoid superficial, auricular, submandibular, submental, paratracheal, cubital, inguinal superficial), all in order, up then down, twice (all always normal), then brush his teeth and go to bed.

One Sunday, the apartment manager, John, invited him down to the lobby to watch Dallas take on Philadelphia in the playoffs. He was offering a distraction, which Hank had left job and girlfriend to avoid. But after a couple thousand hours of odds computing, Hank needed a distraction. They sat at John's desk in the lobby, drinking beer John kept in the small refrigerator behind his desk and eating potato chips.

Dallas running back Chuck Hunsinger danced through Philly's defense all day. He'd gone to the same university as Hank. "Me and Chuck were in the same class," Hank told John. John looked at him askance. "I mean we started school the same year. We went to the same school." "You went to college?" "Yeah. But we took different paths." "Really." "He left school early for the draft and now's a multimillionaire and I . . ." "You here," the leonine manager said, shaking his head. "Different paths. College boy. Shit." Hank tapped his temple. "I'm an intellectual." John smiled, his marble teeth like headstones packaged in red rubber. "You all right. Little weird, but all right."

The TV was fuzzy. It was Sunday, and quiet, and out the front door they could see the rain fall on the littered street. The beer was cheap and very cold, the chips were salty, the game was good. Hank watched the playoffs with John that gray December and January, as San Francisco took rain every day and the Tenderloinians turned blue-cheeked and waterlogged.

After the Super Bowl, Hank returned with renewed passion to fully focused calculating (which we've discussed) and immodest manipulations (which we've modestly ignored, leaving our hero a loincloth of dignity, which we shall now, unavoidably, pull away). One day Hank woke to find his member as blue and knotty as his old feather pillow. He believed he would die shortly. A pressing need to urinate throbbed in him but he wouldn't have tried for a million dollars. He wept and banged his head against the wall. When the paramedics arrived they had to pull him off the stove.

At Saint Luke's, a nurse led him to a curtain-partitioned room. A legless doctor in a wheelchair zipped around, seeing patients. He popped into Hank's room doing a wheelie, examined him, diagnosed broken blood vessels, prescribed aspirin, proscribed onanism. "You don't think it has anything to do with AIDS?" Hank asked. "No, of course not. Why would you think that?" For the first time since he'd wheeled in, he looked Hank in the eye. With one hand on a wheel he stopped his wheelchair, which was rolling backward out the door.

What Hank said was probably incomprehensible, as he was mortified by his misused member and ridiculous fear (especially in front of a man who had obviously dealt successfully with real problems), and distracted by an itch on his back that could have been the start of shingles, and didn't want to waste the doctor's time, so he condensed everything into a few key words: Guatemala, gum trauma, fever, fear, calculator.

"Settle down, now," the doctor said. "What exactly are you afraid of?" "AIDS, shame, pain, and death." The doctor made Hank repeat his story several times. Then he told him that there was only the slightest theoretical chance that he could have caught the disease. He ordered an HIV test to ease Hank's mind (results back in two weeks) and wheeled out. A fat, frowning, possibly female ogre in a white jumpsuit lumbered in, twisted our hero's arm, and drew blood.

During those two weeks, Hank took to long walks, biting his knuckles, one day giving away his excess clothes, another handing out five-dollar bills to any 'Loinians conscious enough to accept them. He orchestrated group hugs with the toothless prostitute (who now wore his sweater and penny loafers) and her new friend, a homeless black transvestite with a mustache and one golden slipper. Sometimes Hank stumbled out of the 'Loin and ended up in the financial district, with its fifty-story glass mono-liths, and he'd get dizzy epiphanies, sick with fear of death and yet seeing all the beautiful buildings, the wonderful ant piles us wonderful ants have built reaching up toward heaven or the void, all of us busy ants going about our business, and he'd get a hot flush of at-oneness with everything and he'd feel that it didn't matter if he died because everything was nothing and everything was beau-tiful and people died all the goddamn time for Chrissake. What was one man's death among the millions of dead? Just who did he think he was? He wrote WHO DO YOU THINK YOU ARE? on a poster board and hung it up.

On the last of these walks he saw his ex-girlfriend hold-ing hands with a beefy fellow with wide shoulders, a strong chin, and a nice suit (marriage material, no doubt). She was tan and smiling, and the man was tan also, and they stood smiling and radiating health like goddamn Greek gods.

She and Hank had lived together for three years, but after Hank's trip to Guatemala (while she visited relatives in Iowa) and his subsequent unexplained impotence, the end was inevitable. She was concerned with career and marriage, he was concerned with immunity deficiency and the solitary vice. When he left, tears were shed, but not many.

"You don't look so good" was the first thing she'd said to our hero in six months. Yes, he thought, the ravages of the virus! She introduced them, current and ex, and he met the current's handshake with fervor. Virus or no, he wouldn't be outshook. He wanted to insult this smiling, well-dressed, handsome ape. He wanted to laugh loudly at their health in the face of the plague. Instead he rubbed his hands and simpered. She said he looked pale and skinny. "Are you sure you're okay?" she asked. "You sound a little sick." "I think I have that bug that's going around," he said, and smiled at his puny wit. They parted.

Back in the apartment lobby, John, sitting at his desk, stopped Hank with a raised hand. John didn't look up from his newspaper, just pointed at Hank with the index and pinkie of his large black hand, the nails pink and translucent like peeled melons, hexing or casting a spell. They hadn't spoken much since the Super Bowl, and Hank had been avoiding him because of the incident with the paramedics. "Hank," John said, and looked up with a jerk. "Why cancha do right? Did you see that dude just walk out a here?" "No." "It's my fren, Eric. He was drunk, usual. Do you know what he saying to me? He say, 'John, you a big manager of this luchury apartment, can't you give me a job?' Now, he's a good fren a mine, I know his baby sister, and I love him, but you know what I tell him? I tell him, 'Nigger, put some water in that ass, cause you be smelling, and then go get you own damn job.' And I tell him that cause it the truth. Now I'm going to tell you the truth. You can't be acking crazy all the time. You got to straighten up and fly straight." "I know." "Why can't you ack right?" "I don't know." "You graduate from college. You young. What ails you? I know you ain't working. You all messed up, banging you head to the wall to the police come. You need some hep." "Yes," Hank mumbled. "And I know a fren got what you need. A conveyance." "A what?" "A conveyance, college boy. A car. I got fren got a '72 Viking, cheap. Need work, but we could get it right." "I don't know anything about cars. I haven't driven since I moved to this town." "I'll see how much he want," he said.

The next morning, Hank was sleeping when John knocked on the door and called his name. Hank tried to ignore him, hoping he'd leave, but finally he just came in. "I was worried about you! My fren got the car downstairs—two hundred dollar!" He looked around the room slowly, then at Hank's posters. "Seroconversion and antibody *what*? First symptoms . . ." he read and stopped, and then said slowly, "Lord God Almighty." Hank got dressed in a second and rushed him out of his room. In the elevator, John looked at Hank suspiciously.

Hank bought the car, and then bought all the parts John said it needed. His credit cards were almost out, but he did anything he could to avoid discussing, almost to make up for, what John had seen in his room. The car looked like a spinach-green flying saucer—both the front end and the back end almost touched ground. It suffered from a dirty carburetor, bent struts, shot shocks, stopped starter, and roaches. They worked until late in the night, though Hank couldn't help much after he'd planted the Roach Motels. He just pointed the flashlight and brought John the wrong-size wrench or ratchet.

Hank returned upstairs exhausted. Someone had puked outside his door. He stepped over it and entered his room. He tried to see it as John had that morning. He took down all his posters and diagrams except the WHO DO YOU THINK YOU ARE? one. He took out the trash pile that had engulfed the trash can. He vacuumed his sheets.

The next day, they rebuilt the carburetor, installed a used starter, and by six, they were ready for a test drive. Hank's test results were also ready, and he considered driving by Saint Luke's. He got into the leafy-green con-veyance, started the engine, and revved her while John made adjustments to the carburetor. It sounded and smelled like a diesel truck. John slammed the hood down and got in. Hank pulled tentatively onto the street. They drove past the toothless prostitute, waving. The homeless transvestite was gone.

Our hero can now take a right on Leavenworth and head straight to Saint Luke's and his results, which will either condemn him or free him. But he guns it straight on Turk, realizing he will never get the results. There is power behind the pedal, so much that on this street with its constant traffic lights, he cannot put it to the floor. The brakes are good and tight, and John is patting his shoulder, saying, "We done this car up right. Now you can get yourself a woman and get her a job and start acking right."

"Yes, sir," Hank says seriously. They make their way out of the 'Loin, away from the sickness and deformity and disenfranchisement, toward the financial district. The buildings, to match the people, stand up straighter, put on fancy facades and glassy suits, and stand tall, and taller, until they are death-ignoring skyscrapers.

Up and down hills, back and front ends scraping, he puts the pedal all the way down and they are flying through a canyon of glass and setting orange San Franciscan glare. John is still patting his shoulder and Hank's feeling good and loving all the businessmen and -women (God, he loves the businesswomen!) who surround them on the sidewalks and in the stream of traffic that shoots through the man-carved glass and he decides that he will straighten up and do right *Hank, you driving a little fast* and stop acting so crazy and if he can't he can't he can't he'll have to do something else like move to central Africa where death is more common than water and credit-card companies have trouble tracking you or get a job and pay them back or hang out at the runaway shelter and pick up chicks *goddamn, boy, that was a red light* or see a psychiatrist or an acupuncturist or his mother in Georgia or study medicine or run a marathon or try to win back his ex-girlfriend or move to Montana (wherever that is) and grow sheep or mug stupefied Tenderloinians or volunteer at the Help Center, but there is no question that something will have to be done, *that's it, pull over, I'm driving*, something.

The Comfort of Paper Trees

Tamar Love

Jane sits on the front patio of Café Sol with Tad, whose eyes follow her hands as she draws a crayon house on the paper tablecloth. They wait to order. Watch their waiter, mobbed, scuttle by without comment. It is sunny, a Saturday, and they are in love, although if asked, only one of them would admit it.

She colors the house yellow, picks up the blue crayon, adds two lines and a circle to the space next to the house. A blue tree. She draws another, considers an owl. Below the tree she sketches a happy paper family—mother, father, boy, and girl—with round heads and beaked noses. Perhaps they are owls, after all. She leans over her cup to select another crayon and notices Tad speaking to her. He is asking about the trees, what's up with the trees, and she looks around, confused. Trees are seldom found in restaurants.

Tad sighs heavily, taps the paper, looks at her with the patronizing smile to which she has become so accustomed. She is dim, she sees him thinking, deficient in brightness. She wants to rip his face from his head—dig her nails into the flesh at the base of his hairline and peel his face away as though it were an herbal mask. She wants to shout at him, beg him to be nice to her, it is Saturday, a fine day, and they are in love. But she does nothing but smile. Because he is Tad. "What did you say?" she asks. "I'm sorry, I wasn't listening."

"These trees here," he points, "what did you mean by them?" She looks down at the circles she has, for no particular reason, colored blue. "There's a green crayon right here in the cup," he continues, stirring the crayons with his finger, "yet you chose the blue." He smirks. "Is everything okay in your world? Or are you feeling a little *blue*?" His mouth flat and hard, his eyes amused. Her fist in his face, once, quickly, so appealing this fine day. "Why are you looking at me like that?" he asks. "Am I drooling or something?" He wipes his mouth with the back of his hand and examines it.

Jane keeps her mouth shut, a decision she has made with growing frequency in the two years Tad has been her lover. In the beginning, it hurt her feelings when he laughed at her. She sulked, which only made things worse. He invariably laughed harder: her silly emotions, her quirky acts of self-indulgence. She used to argue with him when he got that way, react to him, but she soon learned it was easier just to laugh back, even if it meant she was laughing at herself.

Her friends berate her, constantly. Ask her why she puts up with it, the teasing, the slighting and rudeness, the malicious, infantile jabs at her expense. She's tried to explain, but her friends—who have never seen that sugar-sweet puppy-love look in Tad's eyes, never seen Tad-in-Action, charming everyone from her mom to the Ralph's checkout clerk, never seen Tad zip down Beachwood Canyon Drive in his steel-gray Karmann Ghia, doing well over seventy on a recklessly narrow road—simply don't understand. And although it's true that Tad doesn't always treat her as well as he might, she consoles herself with the irrefutable knowledge that he loves her almost as much as she loves him. Besides, she thinks, it's better than being alone.

Tad asks her again why she has chosen to color the trees blue.

"Because they're sad," she says, for want of a better answer. Looks into his eyes and smiles. How blue they are, she thinks, his eyes, the color of ice melting in the sun.

It is then that he kisses her, leaning over the spill of olive oil in the center of the table, taking her face in both hands and laying his lips on hers, holding them firmly, teasing, for one minute, two. She feels the kiss in her stomach, blooming like spilled blood in a pool of water. She sits, motionless, while he withdraws, raises his hand to brush her hair back at the temple.

"Silly Jane," he says, tracing her lip with his finger, "sometimes I think I love you."

She stops breathing. Today is Saturday, she thinks, June fourteenth.

"Look," he says, "the waiter's coming." He opens his menu. "Are you ready to order?"

Jane would like to start over from the beginning, but she doesn't know where that is any more. Sometimes she feels as though she is standing alone, at the center of time, able to see both forward and back, into and out of a great infinity. Here everything seems clear. Here she can stop and wait and take it all in, turn it over and make sense of it before going out into the world again. But as soon as she takes that first step, she slips and slides, like she's wearing new shoes, and she loses focus of everything. If the world moved a bit slower, she thinks, if she could just slow it all down for one damned minute, she might be able to walk in a straight line without falling. As it is, she has no idea of where she's going, and has long ago lost sight of where she's been. She'd like to examine herself, figure out what went wrong, what and when and why, but when she looks inside, all she can see is Tad.

Their good mood stays with them through lunch. Eggplant parmigiana. Smoked turkey with basil. A light Chianti. Tad picks up the check and Jane fixes her lipstick.

Afterward, they stroll down Melrose, peer into shop windows and laugh at the tourists. Tad buys her a small brass incense burner and a bunch of green glass grapes. When they cross the street to the car, Tad takes her hand and keeps it—even after she steps up the curb on the other side. It is a beautiful day.

Tad opens the passenger door for her and suggests they take a drive. "Not far," he says, "maybe through the hills along Mulholland." She smiles, nods, and climbs into the car. Tilts her head back against the seat, opens her mouth wide to catch the sunshine. Tad flings the car toward Cahuenga, and they are off.

A little later they are parked on a low rise near Lake Hollywood. Jane sits on the hood of the car, legs wrapped around Tad's waist, her skirt fallen back to her hips, peering out from behind him, over his shoulder. Tad leans against her, pointing out houses of the rich and famous.

"See that striped house? It's Madonna's."

"No, it's hideous!"

"It is, it is. She paid millions to have it painted that way and the neighbors are suing her."

"For what? Disturbing the peace?"

"More like public indecency."

"You'd think they'd be used to it by now."

Their conversation is unimportant. All that matters is her bare legs around his waist. The sun shining down on them. Heat. Warming the skin. She leans into him, crosses her ankles tighter around him, runs her hands up the back of his head. Kisses his neck. He turns. Imprisoned. Swallows her.

"I like it when it's like this," he says, some time later. "No one else does this with me."

"Does what?" she asks. "Park?" They lie on the hood of the still-warm car, Jane's skirt in the dirt by the wheel. She laughs.

"Yes," he answers. She hears the gravity in his voice and turns toward him. "I mean," he continues, "I have to be so many people for everyone else, all the time. With you I can be myself. It's nice. Jane, I—"

Today is Saturday, June fourteenth. My God, she thinks, I can't believe he's finally saying it.

Tad leans down and kisses her, gently, with his eyes open, and Jane tastes salt from tears she didn't know she was crying. She pulls away. She cannot trust this moment. It may not be happening. He touches her cheek with the tip of one finger and holds it up to the light. It sparkles. Behind it the sky. A world of blue. The happy paper family.

"What's wrong?" he asks. "Why are you crying?"

His eyes, she thinks, so blue. The sun behind his head. Dazzling. "Because," she says, "I feel safe." And she does.

He frowns. "Is there something wrong with that?"

She nods. "I'm afraid."

"Of what? Of this?" He gestures, expansively, the sky, the hills, himself.

She nods again.

"Why?"

"It will go away." She hears the truth in her voice and hopes he does not. She bites her lip, tries to stop crying. She's being a fool.

Tad laughs at her. "Silly Jane," he says, stroking her back, kissing her. "Don't be afraid. Everything will be fine."

Back in the car, careening down the hill, Tad turns the radio to the disco station she loves. They speed along Hollywood Boulevard, singing as loud as they can, shrieking at the pedestrians who turn to stare at them. The song segues into The Captain & Tennille. They love The Captain & Tennille. Jane shouts and turns the volume knob far to the right, singing her own lyrics, waving her arms in hula parody:

> Love, love will keep us together
> Think of me, *boy,* whenever
> Some sweet-talking *boy* comes along,
> Singing *his* song,
> Blah-blah-blah-blah
> You've just got to hold on
> And STOP, 'cause I really love you.
> STOP, I'll be thinking of you.
> Look in my heart and let love
> Keep us together.

She collapses into a fit of giggles as the song ends. Tad looks at her sideways. "You're demented," he says.

"Am not!"

He doesn't answer, leans over and turns down the radio.

"Do you want to go out tonight?"

"What?"

"Do you want to go out tonight?" she repeats.

"Where?"

"The Green Room ... it's Disco Night ... you like it there, remember? Moe's place, over off Sunset?"

He thinks it over.

"We'll have fun. It's been a while since we've been out. Together I mean."

He looks at her.

"I mean, we can go somewhere else if you want. We don't have to go there." She shuts up. Doesn't want to spoil things.

"Why not?" He turns the car toward her apartment, tires screeching madly. *Love, love will keep us together.* She can smell him on every part of her body.

Back at her place, Jane fixes herself a drink while Tad studies her closet. He likes to dress her when they go out. She's not sure why. It might be a weird part of his bisexuality. Or maybe he just thinks her incapable of making herself fit for public viewing. Whatever. He always does a good job.

She used to mind this ritual when they first started dating. She thought it might be a bad idea to let him shape her into something she wasn't or something she didn't want to be. Her friends agreed. But then, as in so many other things, she gave in and let him have his way. Much easier. Besides, she likes this masquerading business. It's fun, like playing dress-up with Mommy's lingerie. And after all, they're her clothes to begin with. It's not like he tells her what to buy—Tad never tries to change her. He just rearranges things a little. If she were alone, it wouldn't matter what she looked like. She reminds herself.

Tad shouts, triumphant, and Jane puts down the drink. Heads for the bedroom. She can hear Lou Reed crooning on the stereo.

Forty minutes later, Tad steers her into the bathroom to admire his artistry. She is astounded. While he always does an interesting job on her, tonight he has taken her to a place she's always wanted to go but never had the directions. He's dressed her in a tight orange halter top and low-slung, frayed brown jeans. Her Halloween glitter platforms. Giantly teased hair and shiny, shiny makeup. A smear of gold glitter gel on her arms. She can see her nipples through the cloth of her shirt.

She turns to him and squeals, throwing her arms around him, smearing burgundy lip gloss down the side of his face.

"Stop," he says, holding her arms to her sides. "You've already ruined your lips. Do you want to fuck up your hair too?"

In the car, Jane breaks the rules.

"What do you mean, what am I wearing?" Tad throws the car into third. "I'm wearing clothes."

"Yes, but I mean tonight. What are you wearing tonight?"

"Do you have a problem with what I have on?" Tad, clad in oversize jeans held up by a homemade rope belt, an A-Team T-shirt, and a yellow windbreaker, looks at her down the bridge of his nose.

"No," Jane says, "I mean, you look fine."

"Then what's the problem?"

"Nothing, I just thought that since I changed——"

"You expect me to drive all the way back to UCLA to change my clothes? Just because *you* changed? I have news for you, dear. I don't *need* change." He slammed the car into the left lane and downshifted. "Now chipper up, we're almost there."

"Where?" She asks, voice small.

"Tony's," he says. "You don't think I'm going to this thing sober, do you?"

Jane, fingernails breaking the skin on the palms of her hands.

It is nearing midnight when they finally arrive at the club. Jane, who used to go to bed at eleven, feels a proprietary smugness as they walk to the head of the long line. The door guy sees them and beckons them forward.

"Tad, man, howsit goin'? You alone tonight?"

Jane slips her hand into the crook of Tad's arm and smiles.

"No," Tad replies, removing her hand from his arm. "Jane, you've met Danny, right?" He looks sideways at the door guy, lips curved. Coy.

Jane, who watched Danny kiss Tad on her balcony two weeks ago, feels mildly nauseous. She hates it when he flirts with men in front of her. She affects a look of mild confusion. "I met you at Tony's, right?" she says, but no one is listening.

"Tad, man, you spinning tonight?"

"No, I'm just here to listen."

"Good deal. But hey, look, the guest list's pretty full, and I got busted last night for letting in too many comps. Is it cool if I comp just you?" He does not look at Jane.

"No problem," Tad says, "Jane has cash." He smiles over his shoulder at her. "Okay, honey?"

"Sure," she says, fumbling with her purse.

He kisses her cheek. "Don't be too long," he says, walking through the door.

Jane's purse slides out of her hand, spilling change and lipstick. The door guy groans in disgust. "I'm sorry," she whispers, bending down to retrieve her things. Idiot. "I'll just be a minute."

"Whatever."

At least he didn't make her wait in line.

*　　*　　*

Down the hall, she finds Tad schmoozing the bar guy. She can't remember his name, but she's pretty sure Tad hasn't slept with him.

"Mango! Mango!" says the bar guy.

"Guava!" Tad yells.

The bar guy laughs and takes out a colored bottle of Stoli. He looks over Tad's shoulder at Jane. "Hi, pretty lady. Need a drink?"

Jane feels herself blush. "I—"

Tad notices her. "Hey, hon, why don't you grab us some wall while I get these drinks." He turns back to the bar guy, who laughs again, louder.

Jane, leaning against the wall by the bar, is having trouble seeing in increments of one. The passing faces smile too broadly. Begin to blur into groups of six or seven. It's not that she's drunk—she always gets like this when she's alone in clubs. It's as if all the people are interchangeable, part of one master unit with which she is shockingly unfamiliar. Each a tiny sun, together a galaxy. Herself a lump of mud. The same story, why Tad dresses her—this in a moment of clarity one night—she does not play well with others. An unproductive member of her peer group. Needs more socializing.

Tad better come soon with the drinks. In Jane's opinion, clubs and sobriety are incompatible.

*   *   *

She's trying to regain her good mood when Tad approaches with two drinks and a blonde. "This is Lara," he shouts over the music, thrusting a martini in her general direction. "We had Modern Europe together. She's never been here before, so I told her she could join us. That's okay, right?" He smiles and turns to Lara before Jane can respond. Jane, for whom this is not okay, takes her drink and begins to nuzzle it. She has become accustomed to his blondes, and his brunettes and redheads. At least they were women, and therefore unlikely to regard him with anything but amusement. She sips her drink viciously. The fucker.

Meanwhile, Lara, who apparently has no idea that Jane means anything to Tad, giggles and drinks her mai tai too quickly. Jane suspects her interest in Tad is based on the Free Drink Principle—which is fine and dandy provided she leaves when her two-drink quota is met.

Tad leans in and whispers something to Lara. A joke, from her hyena laughter. Staring out at the mad, laughing crowd milling around the bar, Jane suddenly hates them all. They look just like ordinary people, she thinks. What makes them so fucking special? She's getting bitter, she knows. Can't help it. It's all about what you can get, not what you can give. Who you know, not who you are. Like the movies. Sick.

She throws back her drink. "Tad," she yells, poking him in the arm, "get me another one?"

"Yeah," he says, moving away. "Back in a minute." Lara, next to him, gives Jane a little smile as they walk away. Bitch.

They don't come back.

Three martinis later Jane is dancing. Tad is gone. She doesn't know where and she doesn't care. She loves it here. It's bearable and possible.

Although orange and purple strobe lights have made the room into disco hell, cool waves of music wash over her like laughter, like the ocean. She bounces around the floor, all elbows and hair. Silly Jane.

This bald guy in front of her, nice enough looking. Big and rough, maybe a little dim. Tad's type. She laughs and dances closer. He looks her up and down, slow, and grabs her by the hip, his hand reaches behind her to grab her ass, pull her into his hard cock. Too close. She pulls back a little. He smiles, dances up and down the length of her body. She holds him by the shoulders and dips backward, hair touching the floor.

The song ends. During the moment of silence, the bald

guy says hello. Touches her face. She shies away. He will expect flirtation. A phone number. Secret huddling in the dark of the upstairs room. He's nice, but Tad . . .

"Hi," she says, dancing away. She smiles so his feelings won't be hurt. Gives a little wave. The martinis are starting to wear off. "Gotta get a drink," she calls and heads for the side bar. Over her shoulder, the bald guy watching her with snake eyes.

Hours pass.

She's danced off most of her good drunk buzz, and it's time to find Tad, drop hints about leaving. She works her way through the lower room, chin slightly raised, smiling briefly at passers-by, looking away as soon as she identifies them as Not-Tad. Struggling through the crowds choking the hallway, she places her hand on the shoulders of those she wishes to pass, and they move away for her. She has learned some tricks.

Downstairs, patio, bar. All filled with Not-Tads. All that's left is the upstairs room. The mellow-out room, with funky acid jazz washing over the clustered forms of the soon-to-be fucking. She hates it when she finds him here.

She sees him right away, sitting at one of the few small tables, lost in rapt flirtation with the bald guy she was dancing with earlier. She's a little surprised—although she had him pegged right away as Tad's type, from the way he was grinding into her she assumed he was straight. Maybe he goes both ways, she thinks with some irony, wouldn't that be nice for Tad? She grabs a drink at the bar and makes her way over to where they're sitting.

"Hi honey," she whispers, an inch from Tad's ear. "Who's your friend?"

Tad jumps, startled, turns his head. "Oh, hi. This is . . . what did you say your name was?" He giggles. So attractive.

The bald guy leans forward, takes her free hand. "Jake," he says, a slow grin spreading over his beefy face. She notices he's missing a lower front tooth. "Didn't we meet earlier?"

Tad looks at her. "We danced before," she explains, "In the disco room. You were with Lara."

Tad seems confused. "Here," Jake says, pulling a chair over from the next table, "Why don't you sit down?"

She slides in between them, spilling a little manhattan on the table. "Whoops," she says, mopping up the mess with her cocktail napkin. She smiles at Jake.

"Why'd you leave before?" he asks. "Thought we were having fun."

"Oh, yeah, um, I needed to get another drink, like I

said. I came back, but you were gone." To Tad, "What were you guys talking about?"

"Jake Jarmel."

"Who?"

"Never mind. Hey, Jake, you want that drink we were talking about?" Tad rises and cocks his head toward the bar.

"Yeah, man, that'd be great," Jake says, making no move to rise. "Whiskey straight up?"

Tad blinks, then walks away. Jane feels a small thrill in her stomach. How weird, she thinks. This is definitely backwards. She leans toward Jake. "So what are you doing with my boyfriend?"

"He your *boy*friend?" he asks, stressing the first syllable. "Coulda fooled me."

"What do you mean?"

"Looks like maybe he's your *girl*friend."

"What's that supposed to mean?"

Jake shrugged. "I don't know. He's cute."

"Oh." She took a sip of her manhattan, staring at Jake over the rim of her glass. Kind of blue-collar for her tastes, but nice. Very nice. Missing tooth and all. Bet he has a big one. She smirks. She is feeling drunk again.

"So you guys have a thing going?"

"Yeah," she says, "for a while."

"Good thing?"

"The best."

"You know, they say variety is the spice of life." He gives her another long, drooly grin and takes her hand, running his index finger up her forearm. "Maybe we could see—"

"See what?" asks Tad, back with the drinks. He is clearly pissed. Jane sits up straight in her chair, avoiding eye contact. She tries to remove her hand, which is hot and cold at the same time, but Jake holds firm.

"See about a party later." His fingers on the sensitive part of her inner arm. Where Tad never strokes, although she's hinted she loves it. She feels herself getting hot. Wet.

"A party?" Tad sits down and slides Jake's drink across the table. He does not look at Jane.

"Yeah," says Jake. "After this place closes, how 'bout the three of us take off?" Under the table, Jane feels Jake's leg slide past her knee and come to rest, she imagines, on Tad's crotch. Tad slouches down and moves his shoulders. To the right, the left. Getting comfortable. He looks at her and raises his eyebrows. She shrugs. Almost starts laughing. *You wanna? Sure, why not?* As though they do this all the time. As though they've ever done anything like this before. It will make him happy, she thinks, testing the validity of the lie. He will have fun, and we will laugh about this later. Jake's leg, under the table, moving, rotating. A small noise from Tad. She could do this. Them.

"How about your place, sweetie?" Jake's hand on her thigh, squeezing the soft flesh next to her pussy.

"Okay."

Jane in her kitchen, mixing up some drinks. A nice spacious kitchen, she thinks, narrow cabinets and all. She keeps it clean, her mother taught her that much. Two lemons, sliced. A plate of sugar. Three shot glasses. She arranges everything on a serving tray and grabs the bottle of Absolut Citron from the freezer. Tries not to think about what she's doing. Why.

A pile of lemon rinds scattered across the coffee table. The bottle empty. Jake on her left, nibbling her earlobe. Tad in the bathroom. Jane, hot and moist, nearly unconscious. His hand on her breast. "You ready?" he whispers, twisting her nipple.

"Wait for Tad."

"Whatever you say." Kissing the back of her neck.

"Tad."

In her bedroom. The three of them. In a pile on her bed. Jane on her back, naked from the waist up, Jake straddling her, licking her nipples. Tad sitting next to her, hand on her stomach, biting Jake's neck. Little grunts of pleasure.

She hasn't touched anyone but Tad in two years. Not let anyone touch her. He feels strange, Jake, his hands doing different things to her, different from Tad. It's nice, but it's not Tad. She turns to Tad and presses against the length of his thigh. Puts her hand between his legs. Tad pulls Jake to him, kissing him deeply. Jake pulls back a little and looks at her. She smiles weakly and nods a little. Jake, mouth against Tad's, begins to unbutton her jeans. She lifts her hips. His hand slips down into her panties.

Tad breaks away and pulls off his clothes. Naked, he begins to undress Jake, biting his neck and licking his back. Jane's jeans are thrown to the floor. She reaches for Tad. Wants him in her. Jake next to her, stroking her. Tad panting. She feels him enter her. Feels him withdraw. He moves behind Jake. She closes her eyes. Now it will come, she thinks.

Jake grunts, lurches, and Jane opens her eyes. Tad is crouched on the floor, holding his stomach. "None of that, man," Jake says. "I ain't here for that kind of thing." He takes her wrists and raises her arms over her head. Kisses her left armpit.

"Then what?" Tad gasps, panting harder. He must have kicked him pretty hard, Jane thinks, struggling to get free. He must be hurt.

"For her," Jake says, holding her wrists tighter, biting her neck. "What did you think?"

This isn't supposed to happen, she thinks. This is supposed to be for Tad. A nice surprise for Tad. She cries out as Jake enters her. Feels a hand over her mouth. She struggles, opens her eyes.

Tad is standing next to the bed, looking down at her with something close to hatred. She pleads with her eyes, get him away from me, get him off. *Bitch*, he mouths, and walks away. She tries to scream, but Jake pushes his tongue into her mouth, thrusts it in time with his cock in her body. She bites him and bucks beneath him, but he only laughs and slaps her across the face, holding her wrists in one hand, pounding into her, harder and harder.

"You like it like this, don't you, baby? I can tell by the way you move."

And somewhere within her, beneath the horrible strangeness of his body and the screams he will not let her voice, she does.

Years pass and he ejaculates, spilling seed onto her stomach in a large, loose pile. Still holding her hands above her head, he traces the outline of her face with his free hand. "That was good, sweetheart. Real good." He grins, his missing tooth winking at her. "Think you'll be wanting more in a little bit?" He moves one of her hands to his cock, already getting stiff again. She squeezes it hard, and he grunts, releasing her. She twists out from under him and runs for the bathroom, sobbing and screaming. Get him out. Make him leave. Get him the hell away from her. Jake shouting behind her, "What the fuck's your problem, bitch?"

Jane stands naked in the shower, shaking, the spray scalding her. She cannot get clean. Cannot stop crying. What happened? she thinks. What just happened? She will have to burn the sheets. Did he rape me, she wonders, or did Tad? She wraps her arms around her body and collapses to the floor. Who let this happen to me? She tries to speak, cannot.

Somewhere in the distance of the living room, she hears conversation. Jake pissed, not understanding why she got so freaked out. Tad, soothing, explaining Jane was easily upset, not very good with this kind of thing. Tad suggesting that perhaps they should talk later, another time. An offer of his phone number. Hers.

She finds her voice, screams, "No, no, no," again, louder. A slow cycle building. The dirt on her skin, the slime. The semen. She stands and pounds her fists against the tile. Howls. The bastard, the fucker.

When Tad slides open the shower door and steps in, she throws herself at him, sobbing. He takes her in his arms and holds her gently.

"Silly Jane," he says, "don't be afraid. Everything will be fine."

Aubergine

Jeff St. John

Auberge woke up with a headache and no memory of the night before. The sound of his screaming brothers filled the room. Several of them were curled under his bed-frame, where it was warmest. He wanted to die, but he got up anyway and made his way to the bucket of water standing by the tin stove. Splashing the water in his face made him feel a little better. He was nineteen and a half, and had been without drugs for three days.

"That bum friend of yours is down there," his mother told him as he walked into the kitchen and sat down. From the street came a voice shouting insults in a friendly way. Auberge shook his head, stood up, and walked past his mother to the window.

"Fuck off!" he shouted down to his friend Hercule, his voice ringing in his own head. Hercule grinned up at him.

"I'm coming up, okay?" He was in the apartment thirty seconds later.

"Get out of this house," Auberge's mother told Hercule when she saw him walk through the door.

"What have I done?" Hercule threw up his hands. Auberge's brothers loved him, and thought he was a spy for the Resistance, or at least a pimp.

"You don't deserve to be in the same room with my children," she shouted at him. Hercule replied with an obscenity in his native dialect, which Auberge's brothers busily took up repeating, much to their mother's outrage. Amid the confusion, Auberge grabbed Hercule and pulled him out into the narrow hallway.

"You got anything?" Auberge asked.

"What do you think?" Hercule replied. His eyes revealed the sickness within. Auberge felt as if he were looking into a mirror. "Fuck," he replied, and looked down at his shoes.

"Let's go down to the docks," Hercule said. "Maybe we can steal something."

"You know there's nothing there," Auberge said to him. But he went inside to get his shirt and day pass anyway.

"Where are you going?" his mother asked as he came back in.

"I'm going to find work," he said, pulling his shirt on.

The buttons were missing; Ceyle and Alexandr liked to play a game with them.

"Don't lie to me," his mother said. "Your brother never lied to me like that."

"Well, I'm not my brother," Auberge said. He felt a hopelessness descending from the gray sky. "Bye." He slammed the door. Hercule looked at him expectantly. "Let's go," Auberge said.

They walked down the stairs in silence. When they got to the street Auberge turned to Hercule.

"I'm gonna go see Artau," he told him. Hercule looked at him.

"Why don't we just try the docks?" he said. "You don't want to do that just yet." Auberge, who had decided two days ago but secretly wanted to give in, experienced a moment of doubt. A sudden thought of his older brother decided him.

"Okay," he said, "why not? It can't hurt to try." They dodged their way down the street, through the early morning crowds. The people's faces wore a uniform look of hunger. An old man with rags wrapped around his arms searched in a pile of refuse beside a burned out building. A fat woman screamed at a young man dressed in soldier's fatigues with the insignia ripped off the shoulders. Hercule laughed at her. Auberge's buttonless shirt flapped in the wind. The pain in his head was worsening, and he pinched his hand between the thumb and finger to get rid of it.

They cut through an abandoned subway tunnel in order to avoid the snipers who hid in the trees along the former Heroes of the Revolution Avenue, now named Colonel Belial Way. People were packed to the walls, squeezing their way through the narrow entrances at either end. Hercule pointed out some graffiti that the Nationalists had sprayed on the cold cement wall. As the walls had sweated, the words had run into an unrecognizable blur.

"Who's been shitting on the wall?" Hercule said out loud. "Why do people spread their shit on the wall like this?"

Auberge looked over his shoulder to see if anyone was listening to them.

"Why don't you shut up," he told his friend.

"Okay," Hercule said. "Hey baby." He was talking to a girl across the way. Auberge looked her over in the dim light of the crowded tunnelway. Hercule was shouting something over the sound of the crowd.

"How old are you?" he yelled at her.

The girl turned her head and said, "Sixteen."

"Sure," Hercule yelled, "but are you married? That's all I have to know is, are you married?" The momentum of the crowd carried her away before she could answer. Several older men gave Hercule bad looks. They exited the subway in a crush of people and moved out along the street.

"She was a nice girl," Auberge said, overcome with self-pity. There were leaves in the road running entwined with rivers of rainwater. "I could be with a girl like that." Hercule didn't say anything. They walked down the Boulevard of the Martyrs to Holy Trinity/Frontage Road. Soon they were down at the waterfront, walking along the avenue named after Admiral Yearling, the first hero of sufficient rank to be killed, in a boat, for the Nationalist cause. The boat-taxi drivers hustled under the rat-infested palms. It cost three hundred Mafia dollars to ride across the river. For no good reason Auberge pulled a chunk of concrete from a decaying wall. He could not believe that he and his childhood friends had swum in the filthy water of the river when they had been children. He could not believe that his older brother had stood on the shore and encouraged him to swim with his face in the water until Auberge had finally gotten it right.

As they had guessed, there was nothing to steal. Hercule sat down on a piling and watched the warehousemen at work behind fences topped with concertina wire.

"Look at that garbage," he said, pointing down to where the water slapped against the pier. "You could pull a dead dog out every day."

"A dead person even," Auberge said. They contemplated the water together.

"We could get up on the roof of that warehouse over there and..." Hercule began.

"And fly?" Auberge said. "I'm not a bird." From the compound a guard motioned at them to be off. Hercule made an obscene gesture and the guard raised his AR15 rifle. "Fuck yourself," Hercule shouted as they walked away. Still, it was only a small victory and nothing had changed. Auberge kicked a soda can.

"I'm gonna go see Artau," he said.

"There may be something else," Hercule said.

"There's never anything else."

They kept walking. Hercule seemed to be thinking.

"We could join the army," he said.

Auberge laughed. "What army?" he said. "They don't want us."

"If we all joined the army, there'd be nobody for them to fight against," Hercule said reflectively.

"Whatever," Auberge said. His head felt like it was going to explode. They were working their way back into the center of the city. At the corner of the avenues of Peace and Freedom, Hercule mentioned the name of a girl he knew who lived nearby.

"Go see her," Auberge told him. "Maybe she'll have

something for you." He did not want to hear his friend try to make excuses to leave.

"You want to come with me?" Hercule asked. "C'mon, let's go. Don't go to Artau just yet."

"Forget it," Auberge said. "It's easy, and I know. That's all. I know." He turned away. "Anyway, you'll be seeing him soon enough yourself." The moment he said it, Auberge regretted it. Hercule spat on the sidewalk.

"Yeah," he said, "fine. Fuck yourself then," and he walked away. Auberge listened to his footsteps recede. Suddenly he was seized by the sudden urge to sprint after Hercule and beg his forgiveness, to go with him to this woman's apartment, to postpone all plans indefinitely. With an effort of will he forced it down, and started walking.

He followed Freedom Avenue to Victory Square, at the center of the city's downtown district. Auberge remembered what it had been like before the war. Now the streets were nearly deserted. The fountain in the middle of the square had been replaced with a statue of Field Marshal Nibelung, the architect of Nationalism. An American-made tank stood guard at the entrance of City Hall.

Auberge stopped at a pay phone, turning his head away from the soldier walking by. His fingers dialed the number from memory. At the second ring a voice answered;

"National Artistic Consulting Corporation."

"This is Aubergine," Auberge said into the phone. There was silence for a few moments. Auberge closed his eyes.

"Hello?" a different voice said. "Aubergine?"

"Yes," Auberge said. He felt so tired.

"Artau says to come over," the voice said. "Use the back door. He has a job for you."

Auberge hung up the phone. He was not at all surprised. His feet knew where to take him. Artau's flat was a five-minute walk from here. A billboard of a television model caught his eye, and he considered her shapely legs with visceral detachment. A limousine rolled by, the radio playing, a tinny voice singing American English. Auberge realized that he was drawing looks from the Nationalist soldiers lounging by the steps of the RaboBanc building. He sped up, ducking his head. At the first alleyway he turned out of sight.

He was standing in the alley that ran behind the bank. As he leaned against the wall, he was jolted by an explosion, a deep thump in the soles of his feet and a metallic vibration that he could almost taste. Chemical dumps were exploding in the industrial quarter. Auberge looked for the telltale plume of smoke, but the skies were too overcast.

From here he could see all of Victory Square: the tank guarding City Hall, the limp flag of the Nationalist government hanging from the flagpole, the lead-gray sky pierced now and then with the screams of attack jets, the soldiers tracking the pigeons with their rifles and slapping each other across the helmets. The statue of Field Marshal Nibelung was silent. Auberge realized, with a start, that his headache had disappeared. At the same moment, he realized that he was staring at the exact spot where his brother had died.

His brother had died in a bus that had been cut apart by a Vulcan cannon that had misfired while being transported by a Nationalist Army truck across Victory Square. Auberge remembered how the top half of the bus had been severed as if by a jagged knife and blown across the street and into the windows of a department store, scattering glass and blood and metal and flesh everywhere in a profusion of color and sound. He and his mother had been seeing his brother off; his brother had been going to find work in the coal mines in the mountains. Auberge remembered his mother's screams, and the screaming of the crowd, and the soldier in the back of the Army truck peeking out from the canopy with a look of amazement on his young face, as if he were peeking into a circus tent. The Army had cordoned off the area quickly and Auberge had tried to calm his mother, who could not stop screaming even though, as one censorious neighbor had told her, people die every day.

Of course the Nationalist government was terribly sorry about the accident and, a week after it happened, they rounded up all the relatives of the victims and, by way of reparation, issued to each head of household a security bond that was worth twenty thousand bank notes, legally invested in government bonds and securities, which would be redeemable in three to five years dependent upon the solvency of the issuing authority at the time of redemption, etc. etc. Auberge had hidden the slip of paper from his mother, who would have burned it. To Auberge the check stood for everything real that had disappeared from his life. It was proof that his brother had existed.

Shortly after his brother's death, Auberge had started using the disposable morphine styrettes widely available on the black market. He had been fifteen at the time, and it was simple to become hopelessly addicted. He would get high and go up on the roof and stare at the sky, holding the check in his hand, and let it flutter in the wind like a flag. While high, he could almost feel the money in his hands. It was only a fantasy, because the check could not be cashed. Under the blank line at the bottom right-hand corner of the check was a title, Chairman of Financial Affairs. Without the signature, the check was worthless. Oh, the signatures that Auberge imagined, etched in the sky! But soon he forgot about the check; the drugs took care of that. There was only so much of his limited future he could sell. Auberge's credit had run out long before he turned, in a moment of desperation, to Artau. Since then, Auberge had learned the true meaning of the check, and all the other symbols of desire.

So it was that Auberge found the terminus of his memory converging upon the doorstep of Artau. As he knocked he felt the cold familiarity settling upon his shoulders like a shroud. The warm fragrant air that struck him when the door opened was like the breath from a dead man's mouth.

"What do you want?" the bodyguard demanded.

"Tell him Auberge is here." The bodyguard didn't even have to; he invited him right in. The two of them proceeded up the stairs, along the second-story balcony, through the green paneled door, and into the study where Artau rose from his chair and greeted Auberge with a smile.

"My dear Auberge," he said, and then paused. "Or are you using your other name today?"

Auberge's hands sweated with the expensiveness of the apartment's furnishings.

"I'm fine, thanks," he said. Artau wore a silk robe embroidered with generic scenes of Oriental splendor. He had the air of a pampered socialite who enjoyed a penchant for senseless acts of violence. His fat fingers were covered in rings. He was a profiteer in a resurgence of opulent bad taste that enjoyed the full monetary support of the Nationalist government elite. He knew a colonel in the Occupational Army and enjoyed the confidences of the Chairman of the Information Bureau, among others.

"Well, Auberge," Artau was saying, "have you been dieting recently?" He smiled his all-knowing smile. They exchanged meaningless pleasantries. The bodyguard was dismissed, and Artau turned immediately to business.

"I could tell, you know," he called out over his shoulder from the closet in which he kept the tools of his trade. "There's some that only do it once." He emerged from the closet with a frilly white blouse. "But you, you I knew would come back, one of these days," he said, as Auberge removed his shirt. The white fabric of the blouse felt scratchy on his skin, tender with strung-out sensitivity. Artau looked him over.

"You never have to shave, do you?" he said, with envious pity. "Lucky boy." A tight knee-length skirt and tights completed the initial outfit.

"You were always small for your age, Auberge," Artau said. "So lithe, like a dancer." He clicked his tongue. "How I wish I was young again," he lied. "There must be some reason I look the way I do now. Something I did in another life."

"There's no reason," Auberge replied. "I'm not skinny because I want to be."

"It's your body," Artau sighed, and looked Auberge's body up and down longingly. "But, frankly, my dear, I would not treat myself so badly. You reek of cheap liquor. How have the girls been?"

Auberge knew how to respond to this. He invented last night's adventures for the pimp, gauging the excited reaction in his cloudy eyes. Artau spoke vaguely of young flesh recovering so quickly from the degradation it underwent. But youth was gone, he said, just as quickly, like a dream. Auberge couldn't stand the odor of the fat pimp's hands, hands that may or may not have wanted to touch him in a more personal way than they did now, adjusting the blouse that hung from his scarecrow frame like a tent, tucking at the waist. He took a deep ragged breath, and Artau stopped his preening to look closely at his face.

"Why do you pretend you are desperate?" he asked Auberge. "You have a mother. Why don't you let her take care of you?"

"It's the drugs," Auberge said. "I owe money to the Mafia. There's not enough food to go around, anyway." He wanted to end the conversation, but Artau continued with the slow languorous precision of a man who is impervious to self-doubt, at least when addressing employees.

"Why this job, Auberge? Do you like the fringe benefits? There's no future in this, you know." He was like a hunter torturing his prey. "Still, you know, you've got a good friend in me," he continued. "Not anyone can give you the connections I can give you. Why, last week, I brought the vice president of the Reeducation Commission my nun—you know, that little sweet thing with the lisp—and had lunch with him beforehand. He was simply delighted with her, you know." Auberge, who had his eyes open but was not seeing, felt the hands leave his body. Artau stood back, clicked his tongue, and proclaimed Auberge to be a little angel.

"You look," he said, "absolutely *perfect*. Give me a smile, won't you?" Auberge complied, and Artau clapped his hands.

"Oh, Auberge," he said, "you deserve a present for that."

Auberge swallowed the pill the fat man handed him with a drink of water, and felt it start to work almost immediately, a churning sick energy in the pit of his stomach that finally matched resonance with the dead certainty that chilled his heart. He felt, for the first time this day, a different person.

"So, Artau," he said in a moment of recklessness, "who are you sending me to today?"

Artau smiled at him. "Why don't you go do your face?" he said.

Auberge, now in transformation, took care of himself in the bathroom with practiced care. Artau was talking on the telephone in the other room, perhaps arranging the details of the transaction to come. Everything that Auberge needed was right where it had been the last time. A sense of invincibility was quickly overtaking him, despite his experience. He put the finishing touches on his cheeks, noting with satisfaction the evenness of the shading, and then he did a quick something with his hair, fluffing it up and securing it with a barrette from the makeup drawer. The person who looked back at him from the mirror was perfect, indeed. Artau had good drugs; Auberge felt as if his head was floating from his body. As he turned, with a trick he had learned a long time ago, he left his reflection back in the mirror, and it followed him out the door and took his place, just like that, as Artau was hanging up the phone and turned to look. Artau drew in his breath in an only slightly ironic gesture of surprise.

"Aubergine," the pimp breathed. In that name was an entire life wrapped in its purple skin.

"Let's get on with it," Aubergine said.

He was no longer himself, but Aubergine of the seven veils, the ripe plum fruit with the bruised tenderness that his clients found so attractive and for which he had been so named, though not by his mother. His face was no longer that of a starving boy of nineteen, but a doll's face, a doll's face, with white china brow and purple rouged cheeks. His legs were smooth and stockinged, his ass pert and girlish under the swath of skirt, his feet squeezed into black doll's shoes. His nose was a button, his eyes two dark drops of glittering jet. His heart was a stone, his stomach a den of slithering snakes. He was no longer himself. His clothes and pass papers were deposited in a drawer under his bathroom sink; he wouldn't be needing them where he was going. Artau believed in the personal touch, and carefully added a beauty mark on Aubergine's collarbone that showed over the collar of the frilled blouse.

"I think," he said, hand on chin, "that we'll have to change the top, though." He went back to the closet as Aubergine stripped the blouse off.

"I don't think that the chairman would like frills, after all," Artau said.

Aubergine stood with the blouse hanging from his fingers.

"Chairman who, Artau?" he asked.

Artau brought out another blouse, blue velvet with silver buttons and a Dutch collar, and long loose sleeves.

"I never sent you to him before?" he said. "Oh, of course not. He's a new customer. A friend of so and so's, you know." He tugged at Aubergine's hair.

"This chairman," Aubergine said, "how much does he pay?"

"I'll tell you that," Artau said, "later."

"What branch is he?" Aubergine asked. "Is he connected with disbursements?"

Artau moved in front of Aubergine and straightened his blouse. "All the branches are connected with disbursements," he said. "That is what this war, is all, about." He punctuated each pause with a tug on Auberge's skirt. Then he stepped back and rubbed his hands together.

"All finished!" he cried. Aubergine gave him another smile, this one unbidden. He was practicing not being himself.

"The chairman is a generous man," Artau said as they walked down the stairs. The bodyguards looked pointedly away as they reached the back door. "Of course all the arrangements have been made, through me." He looked Aubergine in the eyes.

"You seem very curious about this chairman, my dear," he said. "You know I pay well. Please, don't worry your pretty head." He smiled a smile that made Aubergine think of a crocodile, and motioned at the door. Aubergine felt as if he should say something, but no words would come to his aid. The bodyguards, feeling free of scrutiny, were laughing to themselves; Aubergine heard them as a frieze limning the vast rush of sound the pills made in his ears.

"I'll see you later tonight," he finally said. The pimp nodded.

"Yes, Aubergine," he muttered. "I can count on you, can't I? This is a very important client. Maybe a regular."

"Artau, just tell me..." Aubergine began. But Artau was past that. His mind was already somewhere else.

"Good-bye, Aubergine," he said. "The driver will recognize you. You know where to go." He reached up and patted Aubergine on his painted cheek. "Be good, darling," he said, and the door closed with a bang. Aubergine stood staring at its great green profundity. Then he turned quickly and walked away.

It took him only another five minutes to leave the downtown area and enter the ruined industrial quarter. The factories and warehouses had been almost completely leveled by bombing. Across a torn-out pair of railroad tracks he cut through a wide field, littered with the junk of war, that groped its way up to the highway's edge. On the other side, along the stretch of highway leading out of town, was the famous pussy highway, gang-bang avenue, slot pit stop, etc. etc., where the prostitutes of the town came out to display their wares. It is a short step from the hawking of cheap and useless merchandise to the offering of the cheapest entity this society knows, the human body, of which there is always an endless supply. They stood scattered along the dusty shoulder of road, the thin-hipped little girls in thin cotton dresses, the angular, spiky-haired and spike-heeled professionals, the young and fearless children, the fat old whores with their foul language and filthy hair. The blank-faced stares of these empty hearted angels of desire were translated into the attitudes of lost youth and a sick-hearted hot knife twist of fate that was just right, somehow, for the armies of men that passed by. A bit of the spilled liquids was the wisdom running down their backs, the pieces of forgotten memory left like the trash thrown out onto the road.

Aubergine took position along the unsure line separating the boys from the girls. Eyelashes thick with mascara, wine-red lips closed around a cigarette he had found somewhere, he sat out at the curb and waited. He could count over a dozen familiar faces amid the ranks of waiting prostitutes. That fat whore at the end of the row, with the blackened eyes and lips smeared with blood, was a crazy bitch, an alcohol-sodden imbecile who sometimes forgot to charge her customers. He was surprised to see her here, still living, thought he was not sure that what she did could be called that. "I don't feel sleepy yet," he heard someone complaining. A young couple of indeterminate sex withdrew to the burned-out clearing, to do what Aubergine wasn't sure. Their faces were the drawn gray color of war.

His thoughts wandered to a story he had heard another boy tell once, on this very same stretch of road, about getting picked up by some fag-hating mafioso who had driven around threatening to kill him for two hours before fucking him. It had been a funny story with a lot of embellishments at the time he had heard it, but now he could only remember the general details. Suddenly Aubergine felt himself go faint. He clasped his head between his knees. In his moment of weakness he heard the sound of another explosion, this one very far away, but he did not look up. It faded quickly, and the quiet was filled up again. His eyes scanned the pavement and when he could make out the individual pebbles in sharp detail against the surface of the road he looked up. There was a car pulled up directly in front of him.

"Huh?" he said to himself. He did not know where he was.

"Aubergine?" the driver of the car said. Aubergine grimaced. Now everybody knew his name.

"That's me," he said.

The car was an old and well-kept Mercedes sedan. The driver, a pale-faced man with wiry hair, kept the motor running. Aubergine got into the front seat.

"Nice car!" a voice from the crowd called out. Aubergine stared straight out the windshield.

"Could you put up the window?" he asked as they pulled out into traffic. Once on the road, he felt all alone. The driver took surreptitious glances in his direction. Aubergine scratched at his stomach and ignored him.

They drove north, and then at a military crossing the driver turned around and headed back into the city. The highway skirted downtown and thrust through the burned-out industrial quarter into the slums where the refugees lived. Nearing the river, there were newly erected warehouses and factories. As the driver turned onto the road leading up the river Aubergine realized that they were heading toward the bridge.

"Where are we going?" he asked. The driver did not answer him. Traffic here was light, military vehicles and the sleek cars of powerful people. The river passed by them like a panorama on a painted screen. Soon the bridge appeared, a tenuous structure with a high arch to allow riverboats passage. At the entrance to the bridge, the driver showed a pass. Across the river a vista of green hills awaited them. The white forms of mansions stood along the river, where ancient estates of the aristocracy had stood. The revolutionists had destroyed them all, but the Nationalists had erected new mansions on the old foundations.

At that moment Aubergine remembered a tree that overlooked the river where he and his brother had gone swimming when he had been a child. It was a solitary thorn tree that sat on a low bluff overlooking the widest bend in the river in about thirty miles of the capital. Where the current was least treacherous, along a shallow sandbar, Auberge and his brother would swim out and walk in the ankle-deep water among the rushes, collecting birds' eggs to take home with them. Later they would sit under the tree, which had a very heavy shade, although the ground underneath was littered with thorns and they had to sit on thick blankets. They could watch ships steam past like toy boats borne along in any manner they imagined. The tires of the car thrummed across the metal spans of the bridge. Aubergine could see all up and down the river, but he could not make out the lone tree on the hill. Perhaps it had been cut down.

At the end of the bridge, they banked up from the river and followed a brand-new road into this earthly imitation of paradise. The mansions sat beyond gates and long tree-lined drives.

"Nice places," Aubergine commented. They passed several gates before slowing and turning into the most majestic yet, a wrought-iron monstrosity with security cameras atop the two masonry pillars that flanked the drive. The driver pulled up to a small intercom mounted on a pole, and his window slid down.

"The chairman's groceries are here," he said. A moment passed, then the gates swung slowly open and the car moved forward again. Aubergine observed the perfectly manicured lawn, the well-spaced trees piled around with new earth. In a corner of his mind he recognized the surrounding scene from a movie he had seen as a child, an American import. The details of the story escaped him, only the evocative luxury of the setting remained. The driver's eyes were glued to the road. As they approached the grand house he began to tap the steering wheel. They ground to a halt in front of the wide set of stairs leading up to the front door. The driver looked at Aubergine.

"I guess we're here," Aubergine said.

"Get out and walk through the front door," the driver said.

"I'm going to miss you," Aubergine said, waiting.

"Faggot," the driver said, and turned his head. Aubergine lingered a few moments. Then he got out and walked across the gravel driveway and up the white steps. At the front door he listened to the car drive away without turning around. Then he opened the front door and walked in.

Aubergine did not notice the chairman at first. In an expansion of vision he took in the hall, the richly brocaded windows at either end, the gold-patterned wallpaper, the crystal chandelier, the marble bust standing on the chestnut table set between the two staircases leading to the second-floor landing. Only then, as if by accident, did his eyes come to rest upon the old man in the gray suit. He was balding and his stance was at once imperious and anxious. Aubergine looked him over once and closed the door behind him. As the latch clicked shut, the chairman spoke.

"Are you Aubergine?" The words rang in the spacious hall. Aubergine turned to look at him again, forcing his arms to hang loosely at his sides.

"I am," he said. Taking a deep breath, he stepped forward. The chairman looked at him. Aubergine felt the makeup caking on his face. A draft graced the corridor, from somewhere. Aubergine looked downward, along the column of buttons on the chairman's pants, where he saw a bulge, growing, tumescent in the mahogany light.

"I dismissed the servants for the day," the chairman said softly.

"Did you?" Aubergine said archly. A fading sense of himself struggled against the flood he felt rising in him, a confidence that was the inner envelope of madness. As the chairman looked at him with the same old expression on his face Aubergine knew that the four months since the last time had been nothing but the gestation period for this. "Are we in the house all alone?" he asked.

The chairman nodded.

"Well," Aubergine said, tilting his head and smiling, "why don't you take me where you want me to go?"

The chairman led Aubergine up to the bedroom, with a constant slight pressure on his arm. His face was stern, commanding. The servants had been dismissed for the day. Perhaps the chairman had just recently acquired the mansion and was breaking it in, so to speak, before the family arrived. Aubergine did not think about it. He watched with carefully induced calm the passage of windows, the patterns on the carpet. They entered the bedroom and the chairman dropped his arm suddenly, like an embarrassed schoolboy standing next to a girl in line. The sunlight came in through the two enormous windows at either side of the bed, illuminating the room with a harsh dissonorous glow. Aubergine did not know how it had gotten to be so late in the day.

"Do you like it?" the chairman asked suddenly.

"Sure," Aubergine said. "It's nice." He walked in, enjoying in some horrifying way the warmth of the late-day sun.

"Do you want anything?" the chairman asked. "A drink, perhaps? I have some very good wine." Aubergine heard him moving across the carpet, heard the clink of glasses being drawn, the steady pour of a lucid man. He realized that the old man was talking to him. He was talking about the age of this wine, and the cellar from which it had come, which had been the private cellar of a Count Q whose family had owned the estate on which they now stood, as a matter of fact.

The chairman was offering him a glass. Aubergine turned and looked straight into the old man's eyes.

"Do you really think I want that, Chairman?" he asked. "What is it you want me to want?"

The chairman's face crumpled. He did not know what to ask for, Aubergine thought. "Would you like to touch me?" he said to the chairman.

"Yes." He was breathing faster now; Aubergine had to smile.

"Do you think I'm pretty?" He used his best coy voice.

"Yes." The chairman gulped. "I do."

"Would you like to see me naked, my chairman?" he went on.

"Yes," the chairman groaned. Aubergine looked up into the old man's eyes. As the chairman turned away, a rosy gleam suffused his cheeks; he was blushing, Aubergine realized. He had a military bearing as he faced the sun and blinked rapidly. Even now he could not speak, so tightly did he hold himself. The thought of the old man deriving some pleasure from the drawing out of this stupid foregone conclusion filled Aubergine with disgust. This man, who was responsible for the deaths of thousands, etc. etc., could not act in the face of a boy painted in the colors of a little girl. What's more, he was enjoying his inability, his shame. This was, after all, what he had paid for.

"Do you want me to do anything to you?" Aubergine asked now, automatically. At that moment, as the chairman turned to him with a response, a sound came shattering out of the air, shaking the windowpanes and causing the wineglasses hanging before the mirrored bar to rattle in their holders. A ripple passed across the chairman's face. The explosion had come from this side of the river.

"My god!" the chairman said, "they couldn't have broken through . . ." He moved to the telephone. Aubergine was momentarily forgotten. The chairman dialed the phone; Aubergine watched him. "Hello," the chairman spoke into the telephone. "Hello? Yes. This is the chairman of financial affairs on the line. What the hell just happened?"

As Aubergine heard those words a flower seemed to open in his heart. The chairman was whispering into the phone. Aubergine closed his eyes. In this unreal room, stuffed with its relics and falsehoods, he felt a great new freedom set off in the vibrations of an unthinkable holocaust. He wanted to tell this chairman, who held himself so impeccably and who thought himself a human being, about the girl who had been thrown, with her wrists slashed, on a trash heap after being raped by a platoon in the small outhouse by the edge of what had been a playground; about how he and his boyhood friends had come out and stood around her, not knowing whether it was a human being or some ghost driven mad, and how she had writhed soundlessly with the names of those who would save her dying on her lips; he wanted to discuss with the chairman the unfortunate necessity of such measures in the scheme of total war, and how the girl had lain like a piece of flayed meat across the pile of refuse, and how her tiny black shoes had clung so prettily and desperately to her tiny feet. He looked down at his own shoes. In their shiny black reflection he saw death's certainty, the withering of all beautiful things, and instantly hope was born in his heart with the suddenness of rain in a war-torn field, the scraps of paper no longer tagmarks of destruction but tickets for the future of all people. The world faded away into the glossy black leather and disappeared. Aubergine spoke into the nothingness.

"Is everything all right?"

The chairman hung up the phone. "Quite all right," he said. "An old ammunition dump. It's nothi . . ." His voice caught in his throat as Aubergine moved soundlessly to his side.

"I haven't touched you yet. Do you want me to?" Aubergine's voice was carefully modulated, that of a master actor. The chairman licked his lips and placed one hand on the coverlet. His voice hitched in his throat as he spoke.

"I would like that." His eyes were on the opposite wall. "I think I would like that." Aubergine moved closer and touched the chairman's arm.

"You'll want me to touch you some more," Aubergine said, drawing out the words deliciously, "after I get ready." His hand ran downward along the chairman's arm to his hand, toying with the chairman's soft, manicured fingers.

"Oh, where did you come from?" The chairman's breath was shallow in an imitation of passion. His words resonated with the intentions of poetry. "What did I do? This is not, not..." He stopped speaking as Aubergine moved his hands to the chairman's waist, and thence downward, to the foregone conclusion, standing stiffly at attention. Aubergine wrapped his fingers around the chairman and smiled.

"Oh, Chairman," Aubergine said clearly, comfortably, "do you want to fuck me?" The chairman stiffened as if shot through with a jolt of electricity. Now Aubergine was in command; now he moved to the window, to look out from it for the first time, and saw that it faced out to the river. The bridge was barely visible, winking through the trees. If only his brother had died trying to swim across the river to freedom! That was why he had kept the check, had hidden it with him always even as he had lost all hope: because it was the symbol of freedom from the endlessly strung-out days and the crowning shame of the dusty side of the road. He saw his brother standing down by the river, and, again, a bus caught like a toy in a mousetrap, and the shell of a turtle and the blue of a river bird's egg.

"Get on the bed," he commanded the chairman curtly. "I want you to be ready when I come out." The eagerness with which the chairman moved to the bedside filled Aubergine with the throes of some burgeoning emotion; he could only hope that it was laughter.

In the bathroom, stripped down to his underthings, he bent over his shoe and, pulling the check from under the insole, held it between his fingers. "My chairman, if you please, my mother is very poor," etc. etc., and of course blackmail, and of course, there was no other way. He would be free, he thought; they would all be free. It had to happen, and Aubergine began to think about what he would do with all that money. In his exultation he forgot what he had been going to tell the chairman before, forgot perhaps everything he had learned about bridges, and, by an unhappy coincidence, as he rose he looked straight into the mirror above the sink and felt the terrible shock of a stranger's eyes staring into his own. He looked away, but the damage had already been done. He turned the faucets and sipped water carefully from his cupped hands, wishing he could splash the water onto his face.

"Are you coming?" the chairman called from the bedroom, sounding more possessed of his own voice now that the worst was over and only the good part awaited.

"Sure," Aubergine called out, and, taking care not to reencounter that uncomfortable presence in the mirror, turned to the door. The check was in his hand. He felt a certain liberty, as if he were wearing a uniform that conferred upon him the glory and power that men in their wisdom have given to those who shape and guide their destinies. As he entered the bedroom he smiled and said, "There's no sense in this taking any longer than it has to."

Contributors

Alexander Ralph was born and raised in Cooksville, Maryland. After graduating from Swarthmore College, he worked and wrote in New York for two years. He now lives in Berkeley, California.

Amy Gebler received her MFA from Mills College in 1996. She is the Director of Education at Or Shalom Jewish Community in San Francisco, California, and is working on a collection of stories about Jewish-American families.

Paula R. Whyman is a graduate student in American University's creative writing program and previously spent seven years as an editor of commercial and scholarly publications. She is currently working on a story about an ambitious petty criminal in a fictional South American country. Her nonfiction work, focusing on travel, history, and nature, has appeared in *Worldview* magazine and other publications.

Ed Park was born in Buffalo, New York, in 1970. He drew a comic strip at Yale and received his MFA in Fiction Writing from Columbia. He is presently working on a book of stories, *Dementia Americana*, as well as a novel, *Kingdom of Women*. He has written two books, *The Diet of Worms* and *Three Tenses*, neither of which has been published yet. He lives in a small room in Manhattan and works for *The Village Voice*.

Todd Dorman attended Cal Poly University in San Luis Obispo, California, and earned his MFA in Fiction at Columbia University. Also a singer/songwriter/lifetime-hopeful-applicant for honorary Beatle Status, he performs regularly in and around New York City with his eponymous band. He is currently at work on a novel and a collection of short stories.

Lee Harrington has an MFA from Emerson College. She lives in New York City.

Michael Nigro was born in Cleveland, Ohio, and received an MFA in Creative Writing from American University. He has worked as a jack-of-all genres journalist, writing for various music magazines, cultural journals, and inky newspapers. The stage plays he's penned have been seen in Washington, D.C., and his third screenplay, *How Soon Is Now*, was recently a finalist in the *Scenario* Screenplay Competition. Currently he is writing for the groundbreaking TV show *Pop-Up Video* and finishing a book of short stories. He lives in a boxy Manhattan apartment with his wife, Berni.

Amy Boaz is a graduate of Barnard College. She holds a degree in Comparative Literature from New York University's Graduate School of Arts and Sciences. She has worked as an editor for numerous publications in New York, including *The Village Voice* and *Elle*, and her reviews have appeared in *The New York Times Book Review*. Most recently, she has been a book review editor for *Library Journal* and fiction reviewer for *Publishers Weekly*. She is currently writing a novel: a fresh look at *Madame Bovary*.

Rebekah Rutkoff grew up in Gambier, Ohio, and graduated from Oberlin College. She currently lives in Brooklyn.

Kathleen Holt left her tropical childhood home in Hawaii twelve years ago to seek fame, fortune, and excitement in Eugene, Oregon. She has since given up on fame, fortune, and excitement, and has instead settled comfortably into suburban life—complete with house, spouse, and the requisite 2.5 kids (two weimaraners and a cat). By day, she works as the mild-mannered assistant editor of *Oregon Quarterly* magazine, and by night she dutifully checks in with her muse, who on occasion actually answers when called.

David Rowell lives with his wife and son in Durham, North Carolina, where he works as an editor at *DoubleTake* magazine.

Shamira Gratch is twenty-four years old and lives in San Francisco, California. She received her B.A. in Literature and Women's Studies from the University of California at Santa Cruz and is currently working toward her M.A. in Literature at Mills College.

Timothy Hazen was born in Pittsburgh in 1968. He was awarded a B.A. in English from Yale and an MFA in Fiction from the Iowa Writers' Workshop. He lives and works in Iowa City.

Erin Garrett-Metz grew up in Vermont and attended Vassar College. She received an MFA from American University and currently lives in Brooklyn with her husband, Andrew. She is working on a novel.

Courtney Saunders grew up in the Ozarks region of Missouri. She is currently pursuing an MFA in Screenwriting from the University of Texas, Austin. She is a Michener Fellow with the Texas Center for Writers and resides in Austin.

Tony Carbone graduated from high school in Durham, North Carolina, in 1987. He was voted Best Looking by his senior class. He currently lives in Carrboro, North Carolina.

Myla Goldberg was born to parents. After an upbringing, she came of age and received an education. Currently, Myla is working and lives.

Robert A. Cucinotta was born in Philadelphia, raised in Florida, and educated at the University of Florida. He now lives in San Francisco and is working on a novel about two rival college football coaches.

Tamar Love writes poetry, fiction, and nasty letters to rude customer service representatives. She is currently pursuing her M.A. in Poetry at San Francisco State University's Creative Writing Department. She does not wish to discuss her day job.

Jeff St. John grew up in West Virginia, New Jersey, and Japan before moving to Southern California at age ten. He attended UC Berkeley, where he took courses with Leonard Michaels and Bharati Mukherjee. He has since lived and worked around the Bay Area, as office temp, substitute teacher, and bicycle messenger. He currently lives in San Francisco.

Virgin Fiction is an annual contest. Every selected winner receives a $500 contributor's fee. For the 1999 anthology, the following regulations apply:

—The final deadline for all entries is October 1, 1998.

—Entries will be accepted only from writers who will be under thirty-five by June 1, 1999.

—Contestants must not have been published in a book or national periodical.

—Winners will be chosen by the editorial staff of Rob Weisbach Books.

—We are only accepting short fiction (no novels, non-fiction, or poetry). All stories must be under 7,500 words and double-spaced.

—Winners will be notified by January 4, 1999. Only the twenty winning writers will be contacted. All other entries will not be returned.

—For a copy of the complete rules and information on how to enter, please send a self-addressed stamped envelope to:

Virgin Fiction Rules
Rob Weisbach Books
1350 Avenue of the Americas
New York, N.Y. 10019

About the Type

This book was set in Waldbaum, a typeface designed in 1810 by German punchcutter J. E. Waldbaum. Waldbaum's type is more French than German in appearance. Like Bodoni, it is a classical typeface, yet its openness and slight irregularities give it a human, romantic quality.